Blood Secrets

Rivecyber

Published by Rivecyber, 2024.

This is a work of fiction. Similarities to real people, places, or events are entirely coincidental.

BLOOD SECRETS

First edition. November 12, 2024.

Copyright © 2024 Rivecyber.

ISBN: 979-8227188144

Written by Rivecyber.

Chapter 1 The chosen couple

DIMITRI

"Have you thought about taking a chosen mate, Dimitri?" my mother asked, making me roll my eyes. "

You're twenty-two. It's time for you to choose a strong wolf to become your Luna."

I continued to cut into the meat without looking at my mother.

Skol growled. He hated the idea of having a chosen mate.

We would wait for our fated mate.

"Leave him alone, Janet," Mike, my mother's new mate, said. "He's already told you that he wants to wait for his fated mate."

I looked at Mike and gave him a small nod.

I didn't like him very much. I didn't have anything against him, but there was something I didn't like.

My mother married him two years ago. He wasn't a werewolf like my mother and I. I never understood why my mother wanted to marry him, but that was definitely none of my business, so I never got involved. I tolerated Mike because I had to.

Some members of our pack frowned at the fact that Mike was just a werewolf and not a lycanthrope like my mother and I. Technically, that was true. What my pack members didn't know was that Mike actually had lycanthrope genes, but his lycanthrope never woke up.

I didn't care anyway. He wouldn't be able to become the Alpha of my pack even if he was a lycanthrope.

Something was off with Mike today. He seemed absent-minded and a little worried.

"Mike, honey, stop worrying," my mother murmured as she took his hand in hers. "Everything's going to be okay."

Mike looked at her and frowned.

"How can you say that?" he said with a hint of anger in his voice.

What the fuck happened?

" "What the fuck is going on?" I asked before my mother could say anything else.

My mother and Mike looked at each other. Mike sighed, ran his fingers through his hair, and looked down at his plate. My

mother looked at me and I raised an eyebrow.

"Mike's fated mate is dying," my mother said, making my eyes go wide.

I looked at Mike. I was fucking confused.

"I thought you hadn't found your mate," I said, holding back a growl.

I hated wolves who betrayed their mates. A mate was a gift from the Goddess. A mate was meant to be loved and cherished.

What the fuck was he doing here with my mother if his mate was

out there?

Mike looked at me and took a deep breath.

"I found her," Mike muttered. "I just never marked her."

My confusion turned to shock.

How the fuck had he managed to not mark his mate? He was so fucking sure I'd sink my canines into his neck the moment I met her.

"I was young and stupid. I waited for it to happen." I was the only one with werewolf genes in my pack, and I figured that once I had my werewolf, I would be able to do a lot more than just be a Beta in my pack.

Mike stopped talking and sighed.

"I met my mate," Mike continued. "I promised her I'd mark her as soon as my werewolf showed up. Except it never happened. I grew increasingly frustrated. I grew extremely angry.

I spent my days drunk on whiskey and wolfsbane.

I was constantly pissed off. She kept asking me to mark her, but I never did."

Mike stopped talking and looked at my mother.

"So you don't have a mate bond with her?" I asked.

"No," Mike said as he looked at me. "If I did, I wouldn't be able to mark your mother."

Chosen mates and second mates could mark each other, too. The mark wasn't as powerful as when given by a fated mate, but it still held power.

"But you're bound to her, right, Mike?" my mother said with a hint of resentment in her voice.

I raised my eyebrows. What the hell was she talking about? How could I be bound to a woman I'd never marked?

"I am," Mike muttered.

"How?" —I asked, squinting.

"I have a child with her," Mike said, looking at me.

My eyes widened.

He had a child?

"I got her pregnant when I still thought I'd mark her," Mike said. "I left her when my son was two."

My eyes widened even further. What little respect I had for Mike plummeted.

"I feel so fucking guilty," Mike said as he ran his fingers through his hair. "I haven't seen my daughter in 15 years, and now…" He stopped talking and took a deep breath.

"You have a daughter?" I asked, trying to hide my growing anger.

"Yeah," Mike nodded. "She's 17. Her name is Madeline."

" "Is her mother dying?" I asked, clenching my fists.

"Yeah," Mike said. "She has cancer. She called me a few days ago, begging me to take in Madeline when she dies.

" "You're going to," I said.

It wasn't a question. It was a fucking order. I would do it. I wouldn't leave a 17-year-old alone. I'd already done enough damage.

"I'm not sure that's a good idea, Dimitri," my mother said, making me growl.

"Why the fuck not?" I asked, glaring at my mother.

"Mike and I aren't that young anymore," my mother sighed. " I'm not sure we could handle a 17-year-old."

I growled and looked at Mike.

"You're not leaving your daughter alone again," I said. "What pack is she in?

" "My old pack, Red Moon," Mike said.

I knew that pack. I visited it five years ago with my father.

It was a few months before he died, and that trip was one of my favorite memories with him.

"Don't make that mistake again, Mike," I said as I stood up. "You already abandoned your son once. Don't do it again."

I walked away from the table.

I needed to get away from them.

I was so fucking pissed at Mike. How could he do that to his mate and his child?! I would love my fated mate more than anything in the world. She would be so fucking loved and protected.

I would never do what Mike did.

Ever.

CAP 2 Sick

Madeline

, "Mom, please, you have to take your pills," I sighed, trying to get her to open her mouth.

We'd been like this for almost an hour. I'd try to convince her that I needed the pills, and she'd push them away and yell at me that she didn't want them.

She slapped my hand away, and a handful of pills scattered across the floor.

I sighed and knelt down to pick them up.

"Don't bother, Madeline," my mother said. "I'm not taking them."

I looked at her. I wanted to scream. She didn't have to suffer.

She was lying on the bed, clutching her stomach and sobbing silently. She was covered in sweat. Her white nightgown was wet and clinging to her body. She was pale and fucking thin. I could barely get her to eat anything.

She'd lost all her hair months ago. It was so hard to see her without hair, without eyebrows, without eyelashes. It was the first time I realized that my mother was really sick.

I knew she had cancer. I knew she was very sick. But it wasn't until she lost all her hair that I realized she was sick. Her cancer was invisible to me before. It was invisible to the naked eye. Her bald head wasn't.

When the pack doctor told us she had cancer, I couldn't believe it. She was a wolf! She was stronger than a mere human.

She couldn't have cancer. It turned out he was wrong. It was rare for a werewolf to get cancer, but my mom got it.

It progressed quickly, and it was killing her. It had only been six months since she learned of her diagnosis, and she was already lying in bed, waiting to die.

I knew my mother was going to die. But just as I didn't realize she was sick until she lost all her hair, I wouldn't realize she was gone until I woke up one day to an empty house.

I picked up all the pills from the floor. I didn't want her to slip on one of them in case she managed to get up somehow.

I stood back up and threw the pills into the trash can next to my mother's bed.

"Mom, please," I said as I sat down on the bed next to her. "I have to go to work. I won't be able to concentrate if I know you're in pain."

My mother looked at me.

Because of the constant vomiting, the veins in her eyes burst. I couldn't even see the whites of her eyes anymore. Everything was red.

"Don't worry about me, Madeline," my mother said, taking my hand in hers. "Go to work."

She tried to squeeze my hand, but it was useless. She didn't have the strength to do so.

"Of course I'm going to worry, Mom," I sighed as I reached into the bowl on her nightstand.

I grabbed the towel, wringing out the excess water, and gently wiped her forehead with it.

"I love you so much, Maddie," my mother said as tears fell down the side of her face. "I'm sorry I yelled at you."

I stopped wiping her forehead and looked into her bloodshot eyes.

I had to swallow the lump in my throat. I always tried hard not to cry in front of my mother. I had to be strong for her. I couldn't let her see my pain. It would make it harder for her to leave in peace.

"It's okay, Mom," I said softly. "I understand. You don't have to apologize."

My mother sniffled.

"Yes, I do," she said as she tried to lift her head. "You don't deserve this."

She was too weak to lift her hand on her own, so I took it and placed it against my face. She rubbed my cheek with her thumb.

"I love you, Maddie," she said softly.

I put my hand over hers and gave her a small smile.

It was hard to speak. There was a huge lump in my throat.

"I love you, too, Mom," I managed to say.

She gave me a small smile and removed her hand from my cheek. Keeping her hand up was exhausting for her.

"Do you want to take your pills now, Mom?" I asked, grabbing the bottle from the nightstand.

She looked at me with a frown. "I don't want them."

I took a deep breath and placed the bottle on my lap.

"Why, Mom?" I asked. "It won't hurt so much."

She turned her head and sobbed. My heart broke. I put my hand on her head and gently stroked it.

"They're making me numb, Maddie," she murmured. "I don't feel anything. I don't know where I am. I don't feel my wolf. I don't know where you are. I don't want them, Maddie."

A tear fell down my cheek and I quickly wiped it away.

"It's okay, Mom," I said as I leaned down and kissed her temple. "You don't have to take them."

I didn't want her to suffer. I really didn't. But I wasn't going to force her to take something that would make her feel so helpless.

My mother looked at me and gave me a small smile.

"Thank you, my Flower," she said, making my heart clench.

It had been months since she called me Flower.

I smiled and stroked her cheek.

"I have to go, Mom," I said. "I'll see you later, okay?"

"Okay, Maddie," he said, turning to the side.

"Call me if you need anything," I said as I covered her up.

I wished we could connect mentally. It would be a lot easier for her to reach me. But I didn't have my wolf yet, so we had to rely on phones.

She gave me a small nod.

I stood up, walked to the door, and opened it. I glanced at her one more time before closing her bedroom door behind me and quietly walking away.

I headed into the kitchen, hoping to find something to eat before my shift at the cafeteria.

Ever since my mother got sick, I've had to work multiple jobs to pay for her medicine. Our family doctor helped us as much as he could, but treatment was expensive and he couldn't do much. Still, I appreciated any help we could get.

I opened the fridge and sighed. The only food I had left had to be saved for my mother. She definitely needed it more than I did. I grabbed a bottle of water, closed the fridge, and headed into the living room.

I looked towards my mother's room once more. I wanted to go see her one more time before I left, but I didn't have time.

I sighed, put on my jacket and left the house.

CAP 3 I'm leaving

MADELINE

"Fuck," I muttered as I bent down to pick up a piece of broken plate from the floor.

It was the second thing I'd broken today. Mrs. Rose is going to kill me.

"What's wrong with you, Mads?" my best friend Alison asked me.

"You're being really clumsy today."

I ignored her question and headed to the closet to grab a broom and dustpan.

"Madeline?" Alison called my name.

I looked at her as she began to sweep.

"My mom's not feeling well today," I muttered as I looked at the mess she'd made.

"Is she still refusing to take her pills?" Alison asked worriedly.

I nodded, bending down and picking up the broken pieces in a dustpan.

"Has she told you why?" Alison asked.

I stood up and walked over to the trash can. I emptied the dustpan and looked at Alison.

"She said the pills made her numb."

I picked up the broom again and shoved it into the closet along with the dustpan.

"Isn't it better to be numb than to suffer?" I heard Alison ask as she came back.

"It doesn't seem like it," I sighed, leaning against the counter. "She said she doesn't know where she is after taking the pills. She said she can't sense her wolf."

Alison bit her bottom lip and furrowed her eyebrows. She looked me up and down and took a deep breath.

"You need to go out one night," she said, crossing her arms over her chest.

I immediately shook my head.

"That's the last thing I need, Ali," I said. "I can't leave my mother. It's bad enough that I have to leave her to go to work. I can't leave her to go to a party.

I worked at the coffee shop and the library. I took every shift I could. I needed money. We were in debt and I had to find a way to pay it off or we'd lose the house.

" "It's not a party, Mads," Alison said. "It's just you and me hanging out. You need to relax a little."

I sighed and grabbed a dish towel. I started wiping down the glasses.

"Besides, we need to get out as much as we can before I turn eighteen," Alison added. "I'm sure I won't be able to see you after you find your partner."

I snorted and looked at her.

"I don't have time to look for a partner," I said.

Alison let out a dramatic shriek. "You don't want a partner?!"

I looked at her and frowned. Could I have spoken louder? Luckily, we were alone in the cafeteria. It was almost closing time.

"Shut up," I whispered. "I want a partner, but I'm not sure I want to find one right after I turn eighteen. I have to take care of my mother. I have bills to pay. What if my partner doesn't understand?"

"A partner loves you unconditionally, Mads,"

Alison said softly. "He'd understand.

My father didn't love my mother unconditionally. He abandoned her. He left me."

"I can't be sure of that, Ali," I muttered as I began wiping down the counters. "It's best if I don't find him right away."

I kept my eyes lowered, but I could feel Alison's burning gaze on me.

"Have you ever liked anyone?" she asked. "I've known you all your life and I've never seen you interested in a boy."

I felt heat rise to my cheeks.

The only boy I'd ever liked was my savior.

Being a fatherless puppy wasn't a good thing. I was bullied a lot at school. Boys laughed at me, called me a bastard, pulled my hair, and sometimes even hit me.

One day, I was walking out of school when one of my classmates tripped me. He pulled my hair and started calling me names. The other kids laughed and pointed at me. I was embarrassed because I started to cry. I had always tried so hard not to cry.

I didn't want to give them the pleasure of seeing me cry. But that day there was something so overwhelming that I couldn't control my tears. Alison was nowhere to be seen, but someone else came to save me.

She pushed the bullies aside, knelt beside me, and wiped my cheeks. She told me I was safe and they wouldn't hurt me anymore. She

said other things too, but I didn't hear her. I couldn't look away from her beautiful blue eyes. I got lost in them. She had slightly curly black hair and was very tall.

She left after saving me, and I never saw her again. I didn't even know her name.

But every time someone mentioned being in love, he came to mind.

"Maybe when I was a kid," I shrugged.

"Who?" Alison gasped.

I stopped wiping the counter and looked at her.

"I don't remember," I said. "I was just a kid."

Well, that wasn't the truth. He wasn't just a boy. He was my savior.

"I can't believe you've never told me about him," Alison said.

"It wasn't that bad, Ali," I sighed, dropping the dish towel on the floor. "I was twelve."

"I don't care," Alison said. "I'm your best friend. I should have known."

I wanted to repeat that it was just a silly crush on a boy, but my phone started ringing. I pulled it out of my pocket and looked at the caller ID. It was my mother.

"Is everything okay, Mom?" I asked as soon as she answered.

"Flor?" she called me by my nickname.

Her voice was quiet and raspy. She sounded like she was gasping for air.

Did she try to get up on her own again?

"Yes, Mom?" I said as I grabbed the edge of the counter.

"I love you, my girl," she said quietly. "Always remember that. "

My heart stopped beating. Why did she tell me that?

"I love you too, Mom," I said, looking at Alison. "What's wrong, Mom?"

"I'm leaving, Flor," my mom said quietly. "I love you."

I froze. I was completely frozen. I couldn't move. I wanted to run home, but I couldn't move. I couldn't feel my legs. I couldn't feel my body.

No.

Please, Goddess, no.

Don't take my mother away from me! Not yet!

Chapter 4 The funeral

MIKE

I held onto Janet's hand tightly,

I needed her support, I was going to see my daughter for the first time in 15 years, I was going to see my true mate's body being burned, I was going to have to talk to my daughter and ask her to come with me,

To say I was nervous would be an understatement. I was going crazy,

"Mike?" I heard my name being called,

I turned around and saw my old best friend.

"Jack," I muttered his name,

He sighed and walked over to me and Janet. He continued walking towards the funeral grounds with us,

"It's Alpha Jack to you, but I'm letting it slide this time," he said, glancing at me,

He was still mad at me, He didn't usually insist on me calling him Alpha.

"This is my mate, Janet," I said, looking over at her and giving her a small smile.

"Nice to meet you, Alpha Jack," Janet said politely.

Jack looked at her and gave her a small nod. He looked back at me and narrowed his eyes.

"Why are you here?" he asked.

I swallowed and took a deep breath.

"Leah called me," I said. "She asked me to look after Madeline. I'm here to take her home."

Jack set his jaw and looked away from me.

"Maddie won't be happy," he muttered. "She'll refuse to go with you."

I could tell he wanted to say something else. He started fiddling with his fingers. I knew he did that when he was nervous. He was my best friend for years. I knew him.

"But?" I asked, making him look at me again.

"But she'll have to go," he muttered. "Her financial situation isn't good and there's not much I can do to help.

Shit. The cancer treatment probably cost a fortune.

" "Is she poor?" Janet asked, making Jack look at her with wide eyes.

"That wasn't very nice, Janet. I've mentally linked her.

I just want to know what we're up against." She replied. "

We need to know how much it's going to cost us to take care of her.

" "She's in a bit of a pickle," Jack muttered, narrowing his eyes at my partner.

I could tell Jack was mad at my partner for asking that.

I sighed and looked around.

There were a lot of people at the funeral. Most of them were crying and comforting each other. It was obvious that Leah was very loved.

I could see the burial site up ahead. I could already see Leah's body. It was completely wrapped in a white sheet. It was the tradition. Her body was on a wooden frame. It would soon be burned. The tradition was for the funeral to be held at night. The bodies were burned because it was believed that the fire at night would show the deceased the way to the Moon Goddess.

My heart tightened. I loved Leah. I cared for her so much. I just wished my love for her had been enough to keep me here.

My wolf retreated completely. He wasn't able to witness the funeral of his fated mate. He never forgave me for leaving. He understood why I left, but he always missed his pup. I knew he would return when I got close to Madeline. He would want to see her.

I could feel people's eyes on me. I could hear them whisper. I didn't even need to hear what they were saying. I knew exactly what they thought of me. The warriors on the border almost didn't let me in. One of them recognized me and I was sure he was going to attack me. Thankfully, the other warrior mentally linked to Jack, who allowed me into the pack.

His opinions of me didn't matter. I was here for my daughter. I was here to take her home with me.

Everything around me disappeared when my eyes fell on her.

Goddess, she was beautiful.

She looked like Leah, but she had my eyes. Her hair was long and wavy, and the same color as mine. She was a perfect mix of Leah and me, and she was beautiful.

She stared at her mother's body without blinking. But she didn't cry.

Her face was expressionless.

"Is that her?" Janet asked.

I nodded, still not taking my eyes off my daughter. I wanted her to look at me.

I wanted her to smile at me like she did when she was a baby.

Jack walked over to her and held her close. He whispered something to her, and she nodded. She

still didn't look at me.

"Thank you all for coming," Jack said as he released Madeline.

He put his arm around her shoulders and looked at Leah's body.

Luna Maria walked over to Madeline and Jack. She caressed Madeline's cheeks and kissed her forehead. I saw a tear fall down

Madeline's cheek. Maria took Madeline's hand in hers and looked at Leah.

"Leah was an amazing woman," Jack said. —She was a wonderful mother and a great friend to all of us. Everyone who knew Leah knows how much she loved her daughter. Everyone who knew Leah knows how dedicated she was to our pack.

We've lost a great she-wolf, but we're all better people for having known her.

Jack turned to Madeline and asked her something quietly.

She shook her head. Jack nodded and kissed her head.

She looked at someone in the crowd and nodded.

A man walked up to the wooden structure and set it on fire.

I looked at my daughter. She closes her eyes and bows her head. A girl her age walked up to her and hugged her.

"Let the fire lead her," Jack said.

"Let the fire lead her," I murmured under my breath.

I heard the people around me murmuring the traditional proverb.

Janet remained silent. I sighed. It was disrespectful not to say it at a funeral.

Janet. I related it in my mind. Say it.

She looked at me but remained silent.

I clenched my jaw. I knew I would have to talk to her later. I knew Janet wasn't too thrilled about my daughter coming home to us, but she could have at least said the damn proverb.

I looked at Leah's body. She was almost completely gone.

My heart tightened. I wished I could have seen her one more time before she died.

I sighed and looked back at my daughter.

Her eyes were wide and fixed on me. She knew who I was.

She had to know who she was. She recognized me. My pup recognized me.

I gave her a small smile.

Anger flashed in her eyes and she looked away from me.

Fear filled me. Would my daughter want to talk to me?

CAP 5 Moving?

MADELINE

"What is my father doing here?" I asked Alpha Jackson.

There was a sharp pain in my chest that was slowly being replaced by anger. I wanted this man gone. I didn't want him here. He made his choice when he abandoned my mother and me fifteen years ago. I didn't want him here. I didn't need him.

"Did you recognize him?" Alpha Jackson asked, surprised.

Of course I recognized him.

"I have his eyes," I murmured, wiping the tear from my cheek. "And my mother always showed me pictures of him. She wanted me to remember him.

She loved him so much. She loved him even after everything he'd done to her. He was her fated mate, who lied to her. He

promised to mark her, but he never did. He hurt her so much, and she'd never forgive him for that.

I looked back at the fire.

"I'll miss you, Mom," I murmured softly. "I hope you're not hurting anymore."

My voice cracked, and I stopped to take a deep breath.

"I love you," I continued softly. "Please take care of me."

I still couldn't believe my mother was gone. She was the most important person in my life. She loved me the most. She always looked out for me. I didn't know what I would do without her. I didn't know how to move on.

"I'm so sorry, Mads," Ali said softly as she hugged me tightly. "I'll always be here for you. I'll always be your friend. You know that, right?"

I nodded, never taking my eyes off the dying flame.

My mother's body was completely gone.

My mother was gone. She was gone, and she was never coming back.

My heart broke into a thousand little pieces. I wanted to scream and cry.

I wanted my mother to come and hug me. I wanted my mother to call me her little Flower and tell me everything would be okay.

I sobbed and laid my head on Ali's shoulder.

"Maddie," I heard a man's voice.

I looked up and saw my father standing a few feet away. A woman with an ugly expression on her face stood beside him.

Anger took over me and I felt the urge to punch him.

"My name is Madeline," I said as I looked away from him.

"Alison, could you give us some privacy please?"

Luna Maria asked my friend quietly.

"Of course," Ali replied before I could say that I wanted her to stay here.

She kissed my cheek and let go of me. I watched her walk over to her parents.

Her mother hugged her and I felt like crying. I wanted my mother to hold me.

But that wasn't possible anymore. She was gone.

"I'm so sorry for your loss, Madeline," my father said, making me look back at him.

The anger returned. I wanted to wipe that fake sadness off his face.

"Why are you here?" I asked, clenching my fists. "

You made your choice fifteen years ago. My mother wouldn't want you here." I don't want you here.

My father sighed and looked at the woman next to him. He took her hand and squeezed it.

Who was it?

"Your mother called me before she died, honey," my father said.

She wanted me to take care of you after she died."

My eyes widened and my heart raced.

What the hell was he talking about?

"I don't need you to take care of me," I said, trying to keep my voice from shaking. "You haven't taken care of me for the last fifteen years. Why start now?

What did that mean? How was he going to take care of me? Would he send me money? I didn't want it. I was working two jobs. I would make do somehow. I would sell my house, pay off the debt, and find a smaller place to live. I already had a plan. I didn't need one.

"I know you're upset, Maddie, but—" my father said, but I cut him off.

"It's Madeline," I said sternly. "It's not Maddie, and it's not honey."

It's Madeline.

"Your father is trying to be nice," the woman standing next to her spoke up. "She could be a little more polite."

My eyes widened. I swore I heard Luna Maria growl under her breath.

She wasn't rude. I just didn't want this man to call me by any nicknames.

"It's okay, Janet," my father said, still looking at me. "Madeline has every right to be angry."

I took a deep breath and let it out slowly.

I realized that I wasn't even angry at him. He didn't deserve my anger. I was just really sad. Everything hurt and all I wanted was to go home and curl up in my mother's bed. I wanted to breathe in her soothing scent while she was still there. I wanted to pretend she was holding me. I wanted to cry my eyes out and let the pain wash over me.

I had had to keep it together for the past few days and I was so tired of it. I wanted to let go. I wanted to break down.

"You're 17, Madeline," my father said. "You're having some financial problems. Janet and I are here to help you."

I looked at the woman. I seriously doubted she wanted to help me.

The look on her face told me she'd rather watch me burn next to my mother than help me.

"Who is she?" I asked, looking at my father.

He took a deep breath and looked at the woman next to him.

"She's my chosen mate," he said, making my heart stop.

Was she his chosen mate? He left my mother and me and took this woman as his chosen mate?!

"I know it's all a shock right now, Madeline, but you'll have time to get used to it," my father said, looking at me again. "When you move into our pack, you'll-"

"What?!" I interrupted.

"You're moving into his pack?!" Was he serious? I wasn't leaving my pack! I wasn't moving anywhere! I wasn't going anywhere with him!

My father took a deep breath and looked at Alpha Jackson.

"We're taking you home with us, Madeline," my father said.

"You can't stay here anymore. I know I screwed up fifteen years ago, but I'm here now and I'll take care of you."

My heart wasn't beating anymore.

Did he want me to go with him?

No.

No way.

I wasn't going with him. I was going to find a way to stay with my pack.

I didn't need him. I didn't need anyone.
I was going to be fine on my own.

CAP 6 I'm not going to go

MADELINE

"I'm not leaving," I said as I started to walk away from my father.

I had no reason to stay there anymore. My mother's body was gone. I wasn't going to go with my father, and I didn't want to talk to him anymore.

I had no reason to stay at the burial site any longer. I was going to go home, lie on my mother's bed, and cry my eyes out.

I was definitely not going with my father anywhere. There was no way I was leaving my backpack. There was no way I was going anywhere with this man.

"Madeline!" he called out to me.

I didn't answer. I didn't even turn around.

The man left me. He left my mother. I didn't need him or his money out of pity.

"Madeline!" he called out to me again, but this time I heard him following me.

I started walking faster.

"Madeline, stop!" my father yelled.

I ignored him.

My heart was racing. I wasn't leaving. I wasn't leaving my backpack. I wasn't leaving my house. My mom's things were there.

I wasn't leaving the place that reminded me of my mom. Her smell was still there. I couldn't leave. I didn't want to leave.

I felt tears falling down my cheeks.

Someone grabbed my arm, stopping me.

I felt the anger building.

"Maddie, please," my father said.

I tried to pull away from his arm, but his grip tightened.

"I know I screwed up, Maddie," he sighed as he turned me around. "Please let me fix it."

I narrowed my eyes.

"I don't need you to fix it," I said. "I don't need your help.

My mom and I were fine on our own. I'm going to be fine on my own."

"You do need her help, Maddie," Alpha Jackson sighed. "You don't have any money. You're going to lose your home. You need your father's help."

A sharp pain shot through my chest. I felt tears well up in the corners of my eyes, but they weren't tears of sadness. They were tears of rage. I always cried when I was angry, and I hated it.

"I can work harder," I said, my voice hoarse. "I can work more shifts. You can give me work in the warehouse. I can—"

"Maddie," Alpha Jackson interrupted me.

He sighed and pushed my father's hand away. He pulled me into a hug, tears finally falling down my cheeks.

"You have to go with your father, Maddie," Alpha Jackson said softly.

"Why?" I asked, trying to keep my voice from breaking. "I don't need him. I don't want to go with him. I can stay here.

I can stay in the warehouse. I can work as much as you need."

Alpha Jackson sighed as he let go of me. He put his hands on my shoulders and leaned in.

"You know the rules of the pack, Maddie," he said. "You can't live in the pack until you get your wolf."

I clenched my jaw.

"Can't you make an exception?" I asked. "I'm seventeen. I'll be eighteen in nine months."

Alpha Jackson took a deep breath and let it out slowly.

"I can't do that, Maddie," he said, breaking my heart again. "You're not the first wolf to lose a parent. Normally, underage wolves go to live with their relatives. Your father is the only living relative you have."

I tried to swallow the lump in my throat.

"So you're exiling me?" I asked quietly.

"God, Maddie, no!" Alpha Jackson exclaimed. "As soon as you turn eighteen and get your wolf, you can come back and live in the pack house."

I looked down and took a deep breath.

"I'm so sorry, Maddie," Alpha Jackson sighed. "Your mother wanted you to go live with your father."

I looked at my father and his new mate.

"My mother forgave him for what he did," I said. "I will never."

My father closed his eyes and took a deep breath.

"You don't have to forgive me, Madeline," he said as he opened his eyes and looked at me. "You just have to let me take care of you."

I wanted to run away. I wanted to disappear. I wanted to find another pack and start over.

But I knew what would happen as soon as I left my pack. I didn't have my wolf yet, and I was helpless. The rogues would eat me alive, and if they didn't and I somehow managed to get to another pack, they would send the message that there was a 17-year-old wolf on the run. I would end up back here or with my father.

I couldn't run away and start my life in another pack until I turned 18.

"You won't take care of me," I said coldly. "I will find a job in your pack. I will feed myself. I will take care of myself. I will only go with you because I know what would happen to me if I didn't. As soon as I turn eighteen, I will be out of your pack and out of your life."

My father's eyes widened.

"We're fine with it," his chosen mate said.

I hadn't realized I was standing next to my father.

Of course they were. My father never wanted me. If my mother hadn't called him, he wouldn't even know she was sick and dying.

"Madeline..." my father spoke, but I cut him off.

"I've said everything I wanted to say," I said, clenching my fists. "When do we leave?"

My father looked at Alpha Jackson.

"Tomorrow morning," Alpha Jackson said. "Your father and his mate will be staying at the stable."

I nodded and turned around. I ran toward my house.

I couldn't believe I had to leave my home. I couldn't believe I couldn't stay here. I didn't want to leave. I really didn't want to leave.

But

I had to.

It would only be for nine months. Nine months and I would be free. Nine months and I would never have to see my father again.

Chapter 7 The center of my world

DIMITRI

A knock on my office door made me look up from the papers in front of me.

The smell told me it was my mother. When did she get back?

"Come in," I said, looking back down at the papers.

The door opened and my mother walked in.

"When did you get back?" I asked, not looking up.

"About an hour ago," she said as she sat down in the chair in front of my desk. "I was impatient to get out of there."

I looked at her.

"Why?" I asked, furrowing my brows. "Did something happen?"

Mike and my mother were nervous before they left. Everyone in Mike's pack knew he had left his fated mate and they didn't like him very much. They feared some harsh reactions.

"No," my mother shrugged. "I just didn't like it there."

I sighed and looked down again.

"Madeline's there?" I asked as I signed another document.

"Unfortunately," my mother muttered, making me look back at her.

She had an angry look on her face.

"She's an ungrateful brat," my mother said. "She refused to come with us."

I resisted the urge to roll my eyes. She lacked compassion at times.

"Her mother just died," I said, leaning back in my chair. "She's sad and scared. Be a little understanding with the girl."

"Oh, she's not scared," my mother said, shaking her head. "She was rude and disrespectful to Mike. She agreed to come here only on his terms."

I raised an eyebrow at my mother.

"She said she would find a job and take care of herself," my mother scoffed. "She said she would leave as soon as she turned eighteen."

I furrowed my eyebrows.

"Isn't that a good thing?" I asked. "You didn't even want her to come here."

" "Of course that's a good thing," my mother sighed, rolling her eyes. "But the way she said it was rude and disrespectful. I can already see this is going to be the longest nine months of my life."

I sighed and shook my head.

"Suck it up, Mom," I said. "She's Mike's daughter. You love him, right?"

She nodded.

"Do it for him then," I said as I looked back at the papers on my desk. "From the looks of it, the girl is pretty clingy. You probably won't be seeing much of her."

"I hope so," my mother muttered.

I resisted the urge to sigh again. My mother was a nice person, but she sometimes lacked understanding towards others.

"I've come to ask you to come meet her," my mother said. "Maybe her attitude will improve when she sees an Alpha Werewolf.

" "Do you want me to scare the girl?" I asked, raising an eyebrow at her.

I was an Alpha Werewolf and was naturally bigger and stronger than other wolves and other Alphas. I was 6'3" and my muscles were huge. I wasn't even trying to be intimidating.

"I want you to show her that we're werewolves," my mother said. "I want you to show her that she's in the werewolf kingdom now and that she can't be disrespectful to us."

I sighed and rolled my eyes.

"I want her to feel welcome here," I said. "She's family."

My mother narrowed her eyes a little.

"She'll be leaving here in nine months," she said. "She's not my family."

I ran my fingers through my hair and stood up.

"Where are you going?" my mother asked, looking at me. "I'm going to meet the girl," I said. "I want her to know that she's welcome here as long as she wants to stay."

My mother muttered something under her breath. I ignored her and walked out of my office.

My mother followed me. I could tell she wasn't happy, but I didn't care. I wasn't going to intimidate a 17-year-old girl just because my mother wanted me to. If the girl was disrespectful, I would talk to her. If she broke pack rules, I would talk to her and punish her accordingly. But I wouldn't be rude just because my mother told me to.

Luckily, the pack wasn't far from my mother's house, and I walked through the door shortly after leaving my office.

As soon as I opened the front door, I was greeted by an incredible smell.

Something smelled amazing. It made my heart skip a beat and relaxed my entire body. The smell was a combination of ocean and coconut. It smelled like summer.

What the hell was that?

I could hear Mike's voice coming from the kitchen.

I took a deep breath, filling my lungs with that incredible scent. I couldn't get enough of it.

"You don't have to work, Maddie," I heard Mike sigh. "I can take care of you. I want to take care of you."

"It's Madeline, not Maddie," an angelic voice said. "And I already told you that I can take care of myself, Mike." Thank you for taking me in, but that's all I'll accept from you and your wife.

The voice made me shudder. It made Skol stir. It made him tense.

Who is it? he asked. I

didn't answer. I knew who it was, but why did his voice affect me so much? I

finally pushed open the kitchen door and walked in.

It hit me like a fucking train.

The smell and the voice belonged to the perfect little thing sitting on a stool at the kitchen island. It belonged to my mate.

It was my mate.

"Mine!" Skol exclaimed, trying to break free.

She spun around, and it took all my strength not to pick her up.

She was so fucking beautiful.

My heart was pounding in my chest. I could hear it in my ears. I could hear my blood pumping through my veins. My mouth was dry and I couldn't even swallow. My palms were sweating.

My muscles ached from holding back.

Her green eyes locked with mine and I nearly melted into a puddle of useless mucus.

Was she mine? Was she really mine? Had the Goddess sent me a gift? Was she my gift?

"Maddie, this is Alpha Dimitri," I heard Mike's voice. "He's Janet's son."

"Hello, Alpha," she said, bowing her head slightly.

She wasn't the one who was supposed to bow to me.

I was supposed to bow to her. She became my queen.

She became the center of my world.

CAP 8 Done

DIMITRI

My heart was racing.

What the hell is wrong with you? My mother mentally linked me.

I couldn't respond.

I was too shocked and too focused on my perfect little friend to even think of a response.

My heart nearly broke when I realized she didn't recognize me as her mate. I couldn't. I didn't have a wolf yet.

Skol groaned loudly. I had to stop a growl from escaping my lips.

I'd have to wait nine fucking months until she knew who I was. Fuck!

I clenched my fists, trying to keep from hitting anything.

I couldn't let my mother know. I couldn't tell anyone. They would tell her, and I wanted her to find out for herself. I didn't want to rob her of the moment of finding her mate.

The timing was perfect. Everything was perfect. The smell, the sensations, everything. I wanted her to experience it. I couldn't let her know before she turned 18.

Dimitri? My mother mentally linked me again.

I'm fine. I forced myself to respond.

I noticed my princess's eyes narrowing slightly as she studied me with a confused look on her face.

I didn't know how long I stared into her beautiful green eyes.

"Hello, Madeline," I forced myself to speak.

I walked over to her, trying to stop my body from shaking. The closer I got to her, the harder it was to not grab her and pull her against me.

"Welcome to my pack," I said as I held out my hand for her to shake.

My entire body tensed up waiting for the moment our hands would touch. I was dying to feel her skin on mine. I

almost purred when it happened.

Her small hand fit perfectly in mine. It was warm and soft and it sent sparks flying through my body. I had to stop myself from purring, and it was only her hand. I wondered how she would react when I finally kissed her.

"Thank you," she said softly as she pulled her hand away from mine.

I wanted to whine and protest.

"I'm so sorry for your loss, Madeline," I said as I sat down on the bar stool next to her. Her eyes filled with tears and my heart broke. I wanted to comfort her. I wanted to hold her. I wanted to tell her I was by her side.

Skol whined.

"I want to hold her," he murmured.

"I know," I sighed. "We can't do this, Skol. Not yet."

Another moan escaped him. My heart broke for him too. I couldn't feel his wolf yet: This was harder for him than it was for me.

"Thank you," my princess murmured as she ducked her head and took a deep breath.

I balled my fists and tightened my arms against my body. I was going to pull her towards me if I didn't find a way to control myself.

"I was telling Maddie that she doesn't have to work," Mike said as he took a sip of his coffee.

Of course she wouldn't work. She was mine to take care of.

"It's Madeline," he sighed quietly.

"There's no need for you to work, Madeline," I said softly. "Your father and I will take care of you. I need you to focus on finishing high school and that's it."

He looked at me and I nearly melted.

Would I feel like this every time he looked at me?

"I've already finished high school," he told me. "I finished early so I could work and take care of my mother.

I was so fucking proud of her.

" "Thank you for taking me into your pack, Alpha Dimitri continued. "I have to work to support myself. I have to work so I can leave when I turn 18. I won't be staying in your pack for long."

My heart stopped. It wasn't working anymore.

Was he going to leave? Did he really want to leave?

I remembered my mother's words and my stomach turned.

She said she'd leave as soon as she turned 18.

Fuck no.

Over my fucking dead body.

No!

She doesn't know you're her mate, Skol whined. She won't leave when she finds out.

Her words calmed me down a little.

She was right. She had to be right.

"I hope you change your mind, Madeline," I said, trying to keep my voice from shaking. "This is your pack now. You're welcome to stay.

What the hell are you doing?!" My mother mind-linked me, angry. I don't want her here.

I had to stop myself from growling and attacking my mother.

This is her pack now. I mind-linked her back. She's Mike's daughter and she can stay whether you like it or not.

I blocked my mother from linking me again. I could feel her anger, but I didn't give a shit. Maddie was her

Luna now and I had to respect her.

"Thank you, Alpha," Maddie said, looking back at her father.

"Is it okay if I go to my room now?"

I clenched my jaw. I didn't want her to leave.

"Of course, Madeline," Mike said. "Dinner will be ready in an hour."

Maddie nodded and slid off the bar stool.

"Nice to meet you, Alpha," she said.

"Please, Madeline, call me Dimitri," I said. "We're family now."

"Yes, Mads," Mike added, "He's your stepbrother."

I had to stop myself from frowning. Stepbrother sounded so fucking wrong. I wasn't her stepbrother, I was her partner.

Maddie looked at Mike and sighed silently.

"Go unpack," Mike told her. "Do you need help?"

I wanted her to say yes so I could offer her help. I didn't want her to leave. I didn't want to take my eyes off her beautiful face.

"No, thank you," she said, making me sigh internally.

She looked at my mother and me. She bowed her head slightly and walked out of the kitchen.

I felt like whining and following her.

"I know she's your daughter, Mike, but I don't like her attitude," my mother said as soon as Maddie left the kitchen.

I glared at her.

"There's nothing wrong with her attitude," I defended my partner.

"She's respectful and kind."

My mother rolled her eyes and headed to the fridge. "She's cold," my mother said. "And before that, she disrespected Mike and me. She showed you respect because you're an Alpha werewolf."

I clenched my fists, trying to keep from growling at my mother.

"She just lost her mother, Janet," Mike sighed. "Have some compassion."

My mother needed to start having compassion and understanding for Maddie sooner rather than later, dammit. I wasn't going to let anyone mistreat my mate. Not even my mother.

Chapter 9 I want us to be friends

MADELINE

The bedroom was cozy and comfortable. The space was decorated in a simple yet elegant style, with a calming color palette of light beige and soft blue. The walls were painted in a light shade of beige, creating a soothing backdrop for the room. The colors reminded me of summer. I felt like I was at the beach.

The bed was the centerpiece of the room, with a plush duvet and a multitude of pillows inviting you to sink in and relax. The headboard had a sleek, modern design, upholstered in a textured blue fabric that added a touch of sophistication to the room.

In front of the bed was a large window, flooding the room with natural light during the day. The window was framed with light-colored curtains, and in front of it was a small desk.

The bedroom was flooded with natural light, creating a warm and inviting atmosphere. The sun's rays streamed in through the large window, illuminating every corner of the space. The light was dim and soft, casting a warm glow on the walls and floor. The sunlight brought out the natural colors and textures in the room. The natural light made the space feel more spacious and airy.

On the opposite wall was a white dresser and matching nightstand, both with simple yet elegant lines. A lamp on the nightstand provided a soft light.

I liked the room. It was small and cozy and that was the only thing I really liked about this package. I already knew that this room would be my refuge for the next nine months.

I sighed and walked over to my small suitcase. I opened it and the first thing I saw was my mother's necklace.

It was a small, gold, heart-shaped locket. Inside was a picture of the two of them when I was little.

I picked it up and held it to my chest. I couldn't stop the tears from falling down my face.

I hung the locket around my neck and knelt down beside the suitcase to begin unpacking it.

I pulled out each item of clothing, feeling overwhelmed by the weight of sadness and grief I felt. I wondered if the pain would ever subside. I wondered if I would ever be able to numb the sadness I felt. I folded each item of clothing with shaking hands as my mind raced with worries and fears.

Would I find a job? Would I make enough to leave after nine months? Would I be able to survive living under the same roof as my father and his partner?

As I walked to the closet, my tears fell faster and harder. I tried to hang up the clothes, but my hands shook too much to handle the hangers.

Suddenly, a large, warm hand covered mine and stopped me.

"Let me help you, Madeline," a calm voice said.

I didn't need to turn around to know who it was. His voice calmed me. The warmth of his body relaxed me. I wanted to lean against him again. I wanted him to put his arms around me. I raised my eyebrows .

What the hell was wrong with me? He was an alpha werewolf and my stepbrother. He was driving me crazy.

I turned around and saw Alpha Dimitri staring at me. His eyes were filled with sadness and pain. Why? He had just met me. Why would he care? Why did he come here? "It's okay, Alpha," I muttered. "I can handle it."

He sighed, wrapped his large hand around my arm, and pulled me away from the closet. The moment he took his hand off my arm, I felt cold and empty.

What the hell was wrong with me?

It was probably because I was feeling so sad and he was the only person who was nice to me in this pack.

"Please don't call me Alpha, Madeline," he said as he began putting my clothes away in the closet. "I'm Dimitri to you."

I furrowed my eyebrows.

"Why?" I asked quietly. "You just met me."

Alpha Dimitri looked at me and smiled. "I wish we were friends, Madeline."

I sighed and looked down at my feet. I'm not making any friends in this pack. I'm getting out of here as soon as possible.

"I'll be out of your pack soon, Alpha," I muttered under my breath. "I just need a job, that's all."

I could have sworn I heard him growl.

I looked up at him just as he placed his large hands on my shoulders. He leaned down until he was face to face with me.

"This is your pack, Madeline," he said softly. "You don't have to go. You don't have to work. Let your father and I take care of you."

I studied his handsome face for a second.

The defining feature of his face was his sharp, chiseled jaw, which seemed to cut through the air like a knife. His jaw was perfectly defined, with every angle and contour masterfully crafted to create a look of rugged, masculine strength.

Adding to the ruggedness of his face was a short, well-trimmed beard. The beard was expertly groomed, just the right length to add texture and depth to his face without overwhelming his features. The beard perfectly complemented his chiseled jaw, adding a touch of ruggedness to his polished, refined appearance.

He was drop-dead gorgeous, and I nearly drooled.

I had to hold back my gaze.

"My father abandoned me when I was just a baby," I said, trying to keep the pain out of my voice. "He never took care of me, and I don't need him to start now."

Alpha Dimitri's perfect, chiseled jaw tightened.

He shrugged slightly.

"I'll take care of you, Madeline," he said as he squeezed my hand. "I didn't need him to take care of me. I could do it myself."

I felt another tear fall down my cheek.

Dimitri swallowed and wiped it away.

"I'm so sorry for your loss," he said softly. "I wish I could take away the pain you feel.

Why would he do that? He didn't know me. Why would he care?"

I took a deep breath and stepped away from him. I needed distance. His presence was clouding my judgment.

He sighed and ran his fingers through his hair.

"Do you need my help finishing unpacking?" he asked softly. I shook my head.

"Okay," he murmured. "I'm here if you need me." I nodded and he gave me a small smile. I watched him leave the room.

As soon as the door closed behind him, I hung my head and sobbed silently.

I missed my mother a lot.

CAP 10 So fucking hard

DIMITRI

I leaned against the door to her room and took a deep breath.

This was going to be so fucking hard. I just wanted to hold her and comfort her. I wanted to tell her she was mine. I wanted to make her mine.

My mate was hurting and I couldn't tell her she was mine.

I couldn't, fuck.

Her tears were like knives in my heart. Her pain burned my soul like fire.

I wanted to take it all away from her. I wanted to stop it. If I could, I would take her sadness and her pain and bear it for her.

It had only been half an hour since I knew she was mine and I was already in excruciating pain that I couldn't make her mine. Every moment felt like an eternity as I counted down the seconds and minutes until I could tell her. My mind was racing with a million thoughts and scenarios, each one more hopeful and more painful than the last. I hoped she would know sooner.

I feared she would leave before she knew who I was to her.

The pain of waiting was palpable, a physical pain that seemed to grip my entire body and soul. My heart was beating faster
, my palms were sweating, and my stomach was churning with anxiety and fear. All because I would have to wait nine fucking months to have her.

I took another deep breath and forced myself to walk away. If I didn't, he would come back inside and grab her.

I ran downstairs, needing to get out of the house. Her scent was overwhelming. It reminded me that I could fully enjoy her for nine more months.

Nine fucking months.

"Dimitri?" I heard my mother's voice as I opened the front door. "Where are you going?
" "I have to get back to work!" I yelled as I slammed the door and walked away.

My entire body was tense. I couldn't stop clenching my muscles. I couldn't stop gritting my teeth.

How the fuck was I going to survive without her for this long?

The most annoying sound in the world made my mood even worse than it already was.

"Dimitri, sweetheart," I heard Savannah's voice as soon as I entered the pack.

Savannah was one of my pack members. She was the daughter of my father's Omega and it was the biggest mistake I ever made in my life.

I promised myself I would wait for my mate. I promised myself I would save myself for her.

But a year ago, I got drunk on wolfsbane and beer and had sex with Savannah. She's been acting like I was going to make her my Luna ever since that night.

"What?" I sighed as I turned around to face her.

She smiled and walked over to me. She was about to put her hands on my chest when I grabbed them and pressed them against her body.

No one was going to touch me. I belonged to Maddie. Every part of my body and soul belonged to her, even if she didn't know it yet.

"What's wrong, Dimitri?" Savannah asked, pouting. "You don't want me to touch you?"

I sighed and ran my fingers through my hair.

"What do you want, Savannah?" I asked, annoyed.

She frowned at me and crossed her arms over her chest. "I was going to invite you to dinner tonight, but your attitude is throwing me off." "Fine," I said as I turned around and started up the stairs.

"Dimitri," Savannah yelled. "Don't turn your back on me!"

I heard the annoying clicking of her heels as she followed me. I gritted

my teeth.

"I'm not in the mood, Savannah," I said, clenching my fists. "Go away."

"Don't talk to me like that, Dimitri," she said angrily. "I'm your future—"

"Don't finish that sentence," I growled as I turned around abruptly. "I told you, you would never be my mate or my

Luna.

That title belonged to Maddie. No one was going to take it from her."

Savannah's eyes widened. He studied my face for a moment.

"What's wrong with you today?" he asked, making me roll my eyes.

"Leave him alone, Savannah," I heard my Beta's voice and felt relief.

I turned around to see my best friend and Beta standing in the doorway of his office. "We have work to do, Dimitri, come on," William said, looking at Savannah.

Thanks. I mentally linked it.

You're welcome. Will sighed. I wouldn't have to do this if you knew how to drink.

I rolled my eyes as I walked over to him.

"I'll stop by later, Dimitri," Savannah said.

Will closed his office door before I could respond.

"Can we exile her?" Will muttered under his breath, making me giggle.

"Oh, how I wish we could," I said as I sat down on the couch in his office.

I watched as he walked over to his desk and sat down.

"I've found my mate," I said, making Will jerk his head in my direction.

"What?!" he exclaimed as he stood up abruptly.

I sighed and ran my fingers through my hair. Pain flared inside me.

"She's Mike's daughter, Madeline," I said, making Will's eyes widen even further.

"Your stepsister is your mate?" he exclaimed.

"She's not my stepsister," I sighed and rolled my eyes.

"She's my mate."

Stepsister sounded fucking wrong. She was my mate. She was the love of my life. She was my Luna.

Will gasped silently. "Isn't she only seventeen?"

I clenched my jaw and nodded.

"Fuck," Will muttered as he walked over to me and sat down next to me. "How are you holding up?
" "Not great, dude," I muttered. "I want to grab her and tell her she's mine, but I can't do that."

Will sighed and shook his head. "This is so fucked up."

"I have no fucking idea how I'm going to survive the next nine months," I muttered.

I really had no idea. I would go crazy. I had to find a way to be close to her. I had to become her friend. I would go crazy if I tried to keep my distance.

I needed to have her at least as a friend for now. I needed her to calm my heart and soul. I needed her to survive.

Chapter 11 Dinner

MADELINE

Getting in and out of Mike's house wouldn't be a problem.

There was a giant oak tree right outside my window. The branches were huge and thick and one of them was close enough for me to grab onto. It was perfect. I wouldn't have to tell Mike where I was going if he didn't even know I was gone.

I didn't pay much attention to my surroundings as I walked to the coffee shop I saw on the way to Mike's. I didn't care about this pack. I didn't care about anything other than finding a job and getting out of there.

I needed to get a job so I could think about something other than losing my mother. I needed a distraction and a job would be the best distraction possible.

I walked up to the coffee shop without taking my eyes off the door. I set my stance and opened the door.

I didn't care about the layout. I could tell the coffee shop was very modern, but I focused on the guy at the counter and nothing else.

He was about my age, maybe a year or two older. He was wiping down the counter and humming under his breath. He was tall with a well-proportioned body and good posture. He had light golden blonde hair. I noticed he had symmetrical facial features, a straight nose, and a strong jaw. He was very handsome and seemed very kind.

"We're closed," he said without looking up.

"I'm looking for a job," I said, making him look at me.

"Can you help me please?"

He had very lively green eyes that seemed to look into my soul. I suddenly got very nervous.

"Who are you?" he asked as he looked me up and down.

"My name is Madeline," I said, trying not to show him how nervous I suddenly was. "I just moved here."

He raised his eyebrows slightly.

"Are you Mike's daughter?" he asked.

I nodded, making him sigh.

"Mike told me not to give you a job if you asked for one," he said, making my eyes go wide.

He looked down and continued wiping down the counter.

Was he serious?

"What?" I asked, my voice thick with anger.

The guy looked back at me and raised an eyebrow.

"You heard me," he said. "Mike told us not to give you a job if you asked for one."

I gritted my teeth. Mike really had guts.

"Why?" I asked, clenching my fists.

"Shouldn't you know the answer to that question better than I do?" the guy asked as he picked up a glass and began wiping it down with a dish towel.

I did know the answer to that question. Mike wanted to take care of me. Well, it was too late for that now.

"I don't care what Mike says," I said, taking a deep breath. "I need a job."

The guy looked me up and down. "Why?" I raised my eyebrows.

"Why do you need a job?" he asked. "Your father doesn't want you to work. Our Alpha is your stepbrother. You'll be taken good care of here. You don't have to work."

My anger grew. This guy didn't know anything about me. He just assumed I wanted my dad to take care of me. He assumed I wanted his money.

Plus, hearing him call Alpha Dimitri my stepbrother was so fucking weird. I didn't like him. He wasn't my stepbrother. He was an Alpha who took me in and nothing more.

"I don't want my dad to take care of me," I told him. "I want to take care of myself." The guy raised his eyebrows at me. "Can he hire me or not?" I asked, trying to hide how upset I was.

"Shouldn't you ask me first if I own the coffee shop?" he asked, chuckling.

My eyes widened slightly. Shit. He was right. I was probably just an employee. I felt heat rise to my cheeks.

"You're lucky my parents own this place," he said, smirking at me. "Which means I can hire you."

I resisted the urge to roll my eyes.

"Will you hire me?" I asked, making him sigh.

He leaned against the counter and crossed his arms over his chest.

"Why would I?" he asked.

I took a deep breath and let it out slowly.

"I have experience working at a coffee shop," I said. "I can cook and I make great coffee."

The guy bit his bottom lip and narrowed his eyes a little.

"Why don't you want Mike to take care of you?" he asked, making the anger inside me rise.

Goddess, he was really annoying. Why did he care so much?

"I want to make my own money so I can leave when I turn eighteen," I said, forcing myself not to roll my eyes.

His eyes widened. "Do you want to leave when you turn 18? Why?"

I sighed and clenched my fists.

"That's none of your business," I said. "Are you hiring me or not?"

The guy looked me up and down again. He sighed and ran his fingers through his hair.

"Okay," he muttered. "You're on probation, Madeline."

I breathed a sigh of relief. I was going to do really well on the test. I had to do well.

"Thanks," I said, smiling brightly at him.

"Don't thank me yet," he muttered as he turned around and grabbed something from the counter behind him.

He turned around and handed me an apron.

"I'd love to try some of your amazing coffee," he said

as I walked over to him.

"Deal," I said as I grabbed the apron and tied it around my waist.

"My name's Seth, by the way," he said, holding out his hand for me to shake.

"Nice to meet you, Seth," I said as I took his hand in mine.

"You're just saying that because I gave you a job," he chuckled. I definitely did.

"Look, we just met and you already know me so well," I said, smiling at him.

He snorted and pointed at the coffee pot.

"Your amazing coffee doesn't make itself," he said, smiling at me.

I allowed myself to roll my eyes.

"For the record, I didn't say it's amazing, I said it's great," I muttered, making him raise an eyebrow.

I walked over to the coffee pot and started making him a cup. I took a deep breath and closed my eyes for a second. Nine months. Just nine months and I'd be out of here.

Chapter 12 Annoyed

DIMITRI

I barely slept last night.

I kept tossing and turning. I kept imagining Maddie next to me. I kept thinking about her beautiful face and soft skin.

I wanted her so badly and I had no idea how I would survive the next nine months. I would go crazy without her.

I realized I had to find a way to get close to her. I had to become her friend. I had to find a way to be close to her because I would go crazy if I didn't. I wouldn't be able to make it through nine months without her.

"Why are you frowning?" Will asked as

we walked to the coffee shop.

I needed a cup of coffee and a good breakfast. Macy's had it all. I hoped Seth was working this morning. He made the best pancakes.

"I've barely slept," I muttered.

Will sighed. I could feel his eyes on me.

"Is that Maddie?" he asked, making me clench my jaw.

I missed her already. I wanted to go see her this morning, but I didn't want to seem weird. I had to be careful. I had to go slow. I didn't want to scare her. I didn't want to give her one more reason to leave the pack.

Skol growled. She's not going anywhere.

I took a deep breath and looked at Will,

"Yes," I answered his question. "I don't know how I'll survive the next nine months. I miss her so much already."

Will looked at me worriedly. He bit his bottom lip and took a deep breath.

"Why don't you tell her?" he asked. "I'm sure it would be easier for you to wait if she knew."

I sighed and ran my fingers through my hair.

"I can't do that to her, Will," I muttered. "I can't steal that feeling from her when you see your mate for the first time. I want her to experience it." I want to see the smile on her face when she realizes who I am to her. I can't take it away from her.

Will gave me a small smile. You're a very good man, Dimitri.

I took a deep breath and let it out slowly.

Will opened the door to the coffee shop and we walked in.

His scent hit me like a train. It was unexpected. He wasn't supposed to be here. He should be home, sleeping. It was only 6:30 a.m.

What the hell was he doing here?!

I looked around the room and my heart skipped a beat.

I saw her at the counter. She was wearing an apron. She was pouring coffee into a cup. Seth the fuck was standing next to her. He was saying something to her and had a stupid grin on his face. He didn't even notice us coming in.

He wants her, Skol growled.

He wants her, I agreed.

She's ours, he said, and I could see his anger rising.

She is, I said again, trying to contain the jealousy I felt.

I was too close to her. Why did she have that stupid grin on her face? I wanted to wipe it off.

"Seth!" I growled, causing him to flinch and look at me.

My princess looked up with a confused expression on his beautiful face.

"Alpha!" Seth exclaimed as his eyes widened. "I'm so sorry. I didn't hear you come in. Do you want the usual?"

I ignored him completely. My eyes were fixed on my mate.

"What are you doing here, Madeline?" I asked. "Your father and I told you that you don't need to work."

I was so fucking upset. I was so fucking pissed off.

I wasn't going to let her work here. I wasn't going to let her be alone with Seth.

"I want to work, Alpha," he said softly. "Thanks for offering to help me, but I can take care of myself. I've been doing it for a while.

I like it." Will mentally linked me. "It's going to be an amazing Luna."

I couldn't focus on him right now. I was focused on how close Seth was to her. He was too close. She needed to move before I ripped her head off her shoulders.

"You can work in the package warehouse with me," I told her. "You can help me in the office.

I needed her out of Seth's way. I needed her closer to me."

My princess raised her eyebrows. She put down the coffee pot.

"I don't have my wolf yet," she said. "I can't work in the packing house.

She's right, Dimitri," Will said. "That's the rule.

Fuck the rule." I growled at him. "I'll change it for her. I need to get her out of here.

" You mean you have to get her away from Seth? Will asked mockingly.

I looked at him disapprovingly.

"You're family, Madeline," I told her. "I can change the rule for you."

She looked at Seth, making the anger inside me explode.

Why was she looking at him?

Skol was on edge.

I wasn't going to put up with nine months of jealousy.

"It's okay, Alpha," my princess said. "I have experience working in a coffee shop and Seth was kind enough to hire me. I appreciate your offer, but I'd like to work here."

My chest started to ache. Skol whimpered, and I wanted to do the same.

Leave it, Dimitri, Will said. Nothing will happen between Seth and her.

You better not. I'd kill him if he touched her.

"The usual, Seth, please," Will said as he grabbed me by the upper arm and pulled me toward our table.

I was stiff as a statue. I had to control my muscles. If I made one wrong move, he'd grab Maddie and take her away.

I sat down, trying to stay calm. I tried to take a deep breath, but my insides were shaking and it was impossible.

"Goddess, Dimitri, calm down," Will said quietly. "Seth won't do anything."

I clenched my jaw and gritted my teeth.

I wanted to tell her that Seth wanted her, but she moved closer to the table, her scent overwhelming my senses.

"Here's your coffee," she said politely. "Seth told me how you like it. I hope that's okay."

I looked at her and my heart skipped a beat. She could pour me some mud water and it would be the best thing I'd ever drink.

"I'm sure it'd be great," Will said quietly. "My name is Will. I'm Dimitri's Beta. Nice to meet you, Madeline."

"Nice to meet you too, Beta," she said, tilting her head slightly. "Please call me if you need anything else." She

looked at me and gave me a small smile. My knees shook. If I hadn't sat down, I would have fallen to the floor.

I watched her walk away.

I wanted to grab her and pull her back.

How the hell was I going to survive the next nine months?

Chapter 13 His true face

MADELINE

I walked into Mike's house and took a deep breath. I was tired. There were way more customers at Seth's coffee shop than the coffee shop I worked at. I worked my ass off today.

"Where the fuck were you?" I heard Janet's voice.

I raised my eyebrows at her. Why the hell did she sound so angry?

"Answer the question, Madeline," she said through gritted teeth.

Anger was written all over her face. Her brows were furrowed and her jaw was set. Her mouth was tight. The muscles in her face were tense and rigid and her eyes were narrowed. She was glaring at me with so much hatred that I almost turned around and walked out of the house.

I saw a variety of emotions on her face. Annoyance, irritation, and rage were just a few of them. Her posture was rigid and her fists were clenched tightly.

What the hell had I done?

"I was at work," I muttered under my breath.

I didn't know what to do. Why was she so mad at me?

"Job?" she scoffed. "Did you actually get a job?"

I raised my eyebrows slightly. Why was she talking to me like that?

Of course I got a job. I had two jobs in my pack.

"I did," I replied as politely as I could. "

I got a job at the cafeteria.

" Janet slowly approached. I had the urge to back away, but I didn't. I raised my head slightly and set my stance. I wasn't going to let her intimidate me.

"I know you think you can fool your father, but I'm not going to fall for this act of yours," Janet muttered, her eyes narrowing even more.

What act? What the hell was she talking about?

I kept my face neutral. I didn't want her to see that her words had any impact on me. I wasn't a weak girl, and I wasn't going to let her think she could hurt me. "I don't know what you're talking about, Janet," I said calmly. "

What act?"

Janet scoffed and took a step closer to me. She was so close to me now that I had to lift my head and look at her. She was a little taller than me.

"This weak, pathetic little girl you pretend to be," Janet said.

Anger began to rise inside me. I wasn't weak and I wasn't pathetic.

"Oh, I lost my mother. Oh, I don't want your money. Oh, I'll earn my own money," Janet continued mockingly. "I see right through her, Madeline, and I'm not going to let you use your father or my son."

Was I crazy?

I had to be. There was no other explanation for that behavior. I was crazy.

I clenched my fists and gritted my teeth. I was losing any unwillingness to be polite.

"I'm not going to use my father for anything," I said, trying to remain calm. "I didn't even want to come here to begin with."

Janet laughed, throwing her head back.

I furrowed my brows again. I didn't understand why he was doing this. He didn't even know me. I just got here yesterday. I didn't understand what I'd done to make him think I was going to use my father.

"I don't buy that shit, Madeline," he said coldly. "You saw the opportunity to come here, to a pack of werewolves, and take what you could from us."

My eyes widened. Was he serious?

Yes, right? He was serious, and I was crazy.

I shook my head and tried to walk around him. I didn't have to stand here and listen to this.

He grabbed my arm, digging his nails into my skin.

"Don't leave while I'm talking to you," he muttered under his breath.

I tried to remain calm.

"I don't have to stand here listening to your false accusations," I told him, causing him to squeeze my arm tighter.

"Yes, you have to, Madeline," he said coldly. "Don't forget that you live under my roof."

I studied her face for a second. I was trying to find

something, but I wasn't even sure what. All I saw was anger and hatred.

What had I done to this woman?

"I won't be here long, Janet," I said, making her smile.

"Oh, I'm counting on it," she said. "If you're not gone by the time you turn 18, I'll kick you out myself. "

I set my jaw and narrowed my eyes a little.

"You won't have to do that," I muttered under my breath. "

I can't wait to leave."

Janet gave a dark little laugh.

"You're not just leaving home, Madeline," she said. "You're leaving the pack, too. I don't want you around my husband and son."

I didn't want to be around his family anyway.

His son seemed like a nice guy, but I didn't want to be around him or my father. I didn't need them. I didn't need anyone.

She let go of my hand, and I felt the blood rush to my forearm, pricking my skin with a thousand tiny needles. I didn't even realize how tightly she was holding my arm.

"I'm warning you, Madeline," Janet said, pointing at me. "Stay away from my husband and son."

I swallowed, a lump forming in my throat.

"Don't worry, Janet," I said coldly. "Being close to you and your family is the last thing I want.

All I really wanted was to get away from this pack.

Maybe I could leave home sooner. Maybe I could find somewhere else to stay. No one said I had to live under the same roof as my father."

I didn't wait for Janet's response. I turned and ran up the stairs.

I was still having a hard time understanding Janet's reaction. She'd seemed a little cold and distant when I first met her, but I'd never expected anything like that from her.

I was glad she showed her true colors from the start. At least I knew what to expect.

I walked into my bedroom and closed the door behind me. I dropped my bag on the floor and headed straight for the bathroom. I needed a hot shower.

I closed the bathroom door and took a deep breath.

I had to find somewhere else to live. I couldn't stay here for another nine months. I'd only been here a day and Janet had already gone crazy.

I turned on the shower and started to undress.

I couldn't wait to get in the shower and let the hot water relax my muscles.

Cap 14 He's not a werewolf

DIMITRI

I took a deep breath as soon as I entered my mother's house. A huge smile spread across my face. Her scent was so strong in here and it made me so fucking happy.

I missed her and I wanted to see her.

"Dimitri?" I heard my mother call my name.

I could hear the confusion in her voice. She walked into the living room and raised her eyebrows.

"What are you doing here?" she asked.

"I thought I was joining you for dinner," I said as I looked up at the stairs. "Is Madeline here?"

My mother clenched her jaw. I ignored her. I would have to learn to love Madeline.

"She's upstairs," my mother muttered. "She never comes to dinner.

Why now?"

Her eyes narrowed slightly.

"I was here a few days ago, mother," I sighed, looking back up at the stairs.

I wished she would come down soon.

"After spending days begging you to come," my mother said angrily. "And here you are now, coming to dinner of your own free will."

I looked at her and raised my eyebrows. Why the hell did she seem so angry?

"Is it because of that girl upstairs?" my mother continued. "I don't want her anywhere near you, Dimitri. When I told you to find a chosen mate, I didn't mean someone like her."

I had to hold back a growl. "

I know she's our mother, but she can't talk about Maddie like that," Skol said angrily.

She was right. I couldn't allow her to disrespect my mate.

"Don't disrespect her like that, mother," I said, trying hard to keep the anger out of my voice. "She's Mike's daughter. Don't forget that.

Madeline was his Luna too, but I couldn't tell my mother that yet. I had to keep it to myself.

" "I'm not disrespecting her," my mother argued. "

I just don't want you to fall in love with a regular wolf. You're the Werewolf King, Dimitri." You can't mate with someone who isn't a werewolf. We're going to lose the throne and impure our bloodline.

My eyes went wide. My heart raced.

That thought didn't even occur to me.

I wanted her so badly I didn't even think about it.

But she had to be a werewolf. The Goddess wouldn't have mated her to me if she was a normal wolf. Her father had werewolf genes and they must have awakened in Maddie.

Yes. That has to be it. She couldn't be a normal werewolf.

"She could be a werewolf, mother," I sighed as I forced my body to move. "Mike has werewolf genes."

I walked to the kitchen. I had to get out of there before I ran up to find her.

"Mike's grandfather was the last werewolf in his family," my mother reminded me of something I knew all too well. "He impure his bloodline by mating with a normal wolf. If the genes didn't activate in Mike, why do you think they would activate in his daughter?" Her mother was a normal wolf.

I turned to look at my mother. She was pissed off. What was her problem?

"I don't know, mother," I said, narrowing my eyes at her. "

Why does it bother you so much? I never said I liked her.

I didn't. I fucking adored her.

But there was no way I was telling my mother. Not yet. Not until Maddie turned 18 and found out who I was to her.

My mother wanted to say something but was interrupted when Mike

walked into the kitchen.

"What smells so good?" he asked as he walked over to my mother and wrapped his arms around her waist.

He kissed her cheek and looked at me.

"Did you know Maddie got a job?" I asked, still staring at my pissed off mother.

Mike sighed and walked away from my mother. I heard him open the fridge.

My mother and I were still staring at each other. I was trying to figure out what her problem was. She was staring at me with her eyes half closed. Her breathing was ragged and her jaw was shaking.

"Your mother told me," Mike sighed, causing me to look away from my mother and turn to him. "I kind of knew she wasn't going to listen to us. She was always stubborn like that."

Mike shook his head and laughed a little.

"She got that from her mother," he said as he rummaged through the fridge. "Leah was a very stubborn woman.

" "Why didn't you stop her?" I asked.

Mike turned his head to look at me. "I didn't want to make her even more upset. I want her to like me.

" "So you're just going to let her do whatever she wants?" my mother asked angrily.

She walked over to Mike and snatched a cup of pudding from his arms. "Dinner's almost ready," my mother muttered as she put the cup of pudding back in the fridge and closed it.

"I'm not going to let her do whatever she wants," Mike muttered. "She has a job. That's not hurting anyone."

Oh, it would be detrimental to Seth if he kept smiling like that around her.

My mother walked over to the kitchen island and continued chopping the carrots a little too aggressively.

What the fuck was wrong with her? Why was Maddie bothering her so much?

What the fuck is wrong with you? I mentally linked it.

He looked at me but ignored my question.

- What's wrong, honey? - Mike asked my mother.

"Nothing, Mike," my mother replied coldly. "I

You worry that you'll spoil the child if you keep letting her do whatever she wants.

Mike looked at me with a confused expression on his face.

I clenched my jaw and looked at my mother.

"He's got a job, Mother," I said. "Shouldn't you be glad that he's independent and wants to work?"

My mother didn't answer. She continued cutting the carrot with more force than before.

Mike sighed and walked over to her. He stopped what he was doing and pulled her into a hug.

"I know it's hard, sweetheart," Mike said. "We didn't count on having a child when we got together and I know this isn't easy for you.

But Maddie's a good girl. Please stop worrying."

My mother swallowed and kept her gaze down.

Mike kissed her temple and let go.

"I'm going to go get Maddie," Mike said as he walked away from us.

My heart raced and heat coursed through my body.

I was finally going to get to see her.

My mother looked at me. She took a deep breath and continued cutting the carrot.

"She's really nice, Mom," I said. "Give her a chance."

"Don't go near her, Dimitri," my mother said coldly.

"I don't want her to stay in our pack."

I held back another growl.

Well, that wasn't going to happen. Maddie was Luna and this was her pack. She would stay and rule the kingdom with me.

My mother would have to find a way to deal with her.

Chapter 15 Three Kingdoms Part 1

MADELINE

I felt soft fingers caress my cheek.

A shiver ran down my spine. The fingers were warm and soft. I liked the way they felt on my skin.

Who was it?

I frowned slightly and turned my head away. I didn't want to wake up.

Someone giggled.

"Come on, Madeline," someone said. "Dinner will be ready soon."

I wasn't hungry. I ate in the cafeteria.

Someone caressed my cheek again. I furrowed my eyebrows.

"What were you reading?" the same voice asked and I felt the book being taken off my chest.

I turned my head back and slowly opened my eyes.

Alpha Dimitri was sitting on my bed, flipping through the book I was reading. He had a small smile on his face. He looked at me and his smile widened.

"Do you like history?" he asked excitedly.

I looked at him with a confused expression.

Why was he in my room?

"What are you doing here, Alpha?" I asked as I sat up.

I tried to smooth out my wrinkled clothes a bit. I hadn't expected him in my room. Why was he here?

"Your father came to wake you up, but he decided to let you sleep," he explained. "I didn't agree with his decision, so I came to wake you up. You need to eat."

He looked back at the book in his hand.

"I have another book on werewolf history, if you want to read it," he said as he flipped through the pages.

I ignored him.

"I'm not hungry," I said, causing her to look back at me.

"Can I have my book back?"

That book was everything to me. It was nothing more than a werewolf history textbook, but it was my favorite book. My mother gave it to me when I was little. She used to read me the history of the Three Kingdoms, and it was one of my favorite memories of our time together.

"You need to eat, Maddie," Alpha Dimitri said as she handed the book back to me.

"I ate in the cafeteria," I said, clutching the book to my chest.

Alpha Dimitri looked at it and smiled.

"This book means a lot to you, doesn't it?"

His soothing voice made my heart skip a beat.

"Yes," I said, nodding. "My mother gave it to me."

I felt tears well up in the corners of my eyes again. I thought I wouldn't be able to cry anymore, but I was wrong. Just thinking about my mother made me want to sob. I missed her so much.

I looked down at the book and swallowed the lump in my throat.

"Oh, Maddie," Alpha Dimitri murmured as he hugged me. " I'm so sorry you lost your mother. "

I tensed up a little. Why was he holding me?

But I liked the feeling. I felt safe in his arms.

His scent calmed me, and his arms around me made my body relax a little.

"Do you have a favorite part?" Alpha Dimitri asked as he gently rubbed my back.

I raised my eyebrows and looked up at him.

"From the book," he explained, smiling at me.

I pulled away and he let go. I looked down at the book and smiled.

"Yeah, I like it," I murmured. "I love the part about the Three Kingdoms."

Alpha Dimitri caressed my cheek again. I looked at him with a confused expression. Why was he so nice to me? Was it because I had lost my mother? I didn't want his pity.

- Do you know that your great-great-grandfather ruled one of those kingdoms? - Dimitri Alfa asked me.

I nodded, still staring at him.

That was probably the reason my mother gave me the book and read me that story. My father was a descendant of one of the werewolf kings. She wanted me to have some sort of connection to him.

"You could be a werewolf too," Alpha Dimitri said, giving me a small smile.

I frowned and looked at the book.

I had nothing against being a werewolf, but those genes were the reason my father abandoned my mother and me.

Besides, I was sure it wasn't possible. If my father didn't become one, then why would I?

"I doubt it," I muttered. "My father didn't become one."

I looked at Alpha Dimitri. He still had a small smile on his face.

I couldn't help but notice how handsome he was. His dark eyes bored into my soul, making me shiver. I wanted to run my fingers through his short beard and feel his skin on my fingertips. Her lips looked so soft and I wanted to know what...

No.

What the hell was I thinking?

He was older. He was an Alpha. He was a Lycan, for fuck's sake. What the hell was wrong with me?!

I saw his jaw twitch. He looked at my lips and gulped.

I had to look away before another

stupid thought came to me.

I looked away from him and took a deep breath. I wanted to get up and go open a window. I needed fresh air.

"You know some people still believe the Three Kingdoms will rise again," Alpha Dimitri said, making me look back at him.

I raised my eyebrows.

"The Three Kingdoms fell," I said. "The Great War destroyed everything. The descendants of the lycanthrope kings impure their bloodlines. How is that possible?"

Alpha Dimitri smiled at me. He took the book from my hand and placed it on the nightstand next to my bed.

"Do you want to hear something that's not written in the textbooks?

" he asked, making my eyes widen.

I loved hearing stories about our history. I loved hearing stories about the Three Kingdoms. I loved hearing old legends.

He smiled, leaning back against my headboard and putting his legs up. He made himself comfortable and patted the spot next to him.

My eyes widened a little more and I bit my bottom lip.

Did he want me to lay down next to him?

That would be too weird and inappropriate. What if someone walked into the room and saw us lying next to each other? He was an Alpha and probably had a mate. What would she say?

"Come on, Maddie," he chuckled. "You'll love the story, I promise."

My curiosity got the better of me and I lay down next to him. I looked up at him and saw him smiling brightly.

"What do you know about the Great War, Maddie?" he asked as he tucked a strand of hair behind my ear.

My pulse quickened. I knew everything about her, but it was hard to concentrate and answer her questions when all I could think about was her fingers gently touching the back of my neck.

Chapter 16 Part 2

DIMITRI

My heart skipped a beat as she lay down beside me. All I wanted to do was wrap my arms around her and hold her against my chest.

I was in heaven. Her scent in the room was so intense I felt like I was high. My entire body was coated in her and it felt fucking amazing. All I needed was to feel her skin on mine.

But soon I would have it. Just nine months and I would be lying in bed with her pressed against me.

"I know all about the Great War," Maddie said. "My mother told me many stories about it.

The war between the three Lycan Kingdoms was a brutal affair, with the clash of steel and the roar of battle for months on end. It was a war of tooth and claw, of strength and sometimes dirty tactics as each Kingdom fought tooth and nail for dominance over the others.

The three werewolf kingdoms had lived in an uneasy truce for many years, but tensions began to rise when the second kingdom, the Kingdom of the

Golden Fangs, discovered a rich vein of gold in their territory. The first kingdom, the Kingdom of the Blood Moon, eager to get their hands on the precious metal, launched a surprise attack on the second kingdom in an attempt to seize the gold mines.

The third kingdom, the Shadowclaws, long resentful of the other two for their arrogance and aggression, saw this as an opportunity to assert their dominance over the region. They swooped in and attacked both the first and second kingdoms, hoping to weaken them enough to make them vulnerable to a total takeover.

As the war raged on, the gold mines became less of an issue and more of a matter of power and control. The third kingdom, with its superior tactics and secretive nature, began to gain the upper hand and looked set to win.

The First Kingdom, known for their quick reflexes and keen senses, launched a surprise attack on the Second Kingdom, catching them off guard and driving them back to their borders. However, the Second Kingdom rallied and shattered the First Kingdom's army, leaving their once great city in ruins.

As the war raged on, the Third Kingdom watched from the shadows, waiting for the right moment to strike. And when that moment came, they emerged from the darkness like a pack of vengeful wolves, unleashing a devastating assault on the First and Second Kingdoms, crushing their armies and winning the Great War.

However, the surviving werewolves of the First and Second Kingdoms refused to submit to the Third Kingdom's rule.

The war left the Third Kingdom in ruins and in dire economic straits, leaving its people scattered and broken. The Third Kingdom won, but the cost of victory was too great. The entrance to the gold mines was lost, and hope of ever finding it slowly faded away. No one knew where it was and the existence of the gold mine beneath the lands of the second kingdom slowly became a legend.

The surviving wolves united under a new leader who promised to unite the werewolves and put an end to the senseless bloodshed. And so, the new king rose to power, bringing a new era of peace and prosperity to the United Kingdoms.

That new king was my great-great-grandfather.

"Did you know that the Kingdom of the Golden Fangs had a legend about the Goddess of Gold?" I asked as I smiled at her.

Her eyes widened slightly. I saw a small golden freckle in her iris and fell in love with her even more. I was dying to hug her gorgeous face and stare into her eyes until I memorized every hue and every freckle.

"I didn't know," she murmured. "What did the legend say?"

I wasn't surprised. The legend of the Goddess of Gold was kept secret. There was only one book that mentioned her. It was the book only kings had access to.

"The Goddess of Gold is a mortal deity who takes the form of a wolf," I began my tale. "According to legend, anything she touches with the claw of her right paw turns to gold."

I raised my hand and caressed Maddie's cheek. I couldn't help myself. I needed to feel her skin under my fingertips.

"The people of the Kingdom of the Golden Fangs believed that she would be the one to unite the Kingdoms," I continued, focusing on that beautiful freckle on her iris. "They believed that she would be the one to fix the differences that separated the Kingdoms for years."

My princess's eyebrows furrowed.

"But your great-great-grandfather already did that," she murmured. "He united the kingdoms."

I sighed and ran my fingers through her hair absentmindedly.

"Not really," I sighed. "There are many factions in the Kingdom. There are descendants of the third Kingdom who still believe that they should be the ones to rule."

I sighed and gave her a small smile.

"Legend said that the Goddess of Gold would bring peace," I said, "which we don't have in our Kingdom. I have to deal with attacks on the throne constantly."

That was probably the biggest reason I didn't want anyone to know who Maddie was to me. They could use her against me. Someone could take her away from me and blackmail me into giving up the throne. My princess didn't have her wolf yet and would be defenseless. I couldn't allow that.

"I'm sorry to hear that," she murmured quietly.

I smiled at her.

"It's okay, Maddie," I said. "I've learned how to deal with them. I want our people to live in peace and I try my best to keep it. I want to be a good King."

Maddie studied my face for a second.

"You already are," she said, making my heart skip a beat.

I smiled at her. "Thank you."

She smiled back, making my knees buckle. I was desperate to kiss her.

"Do you believe in it?" Maddie asked, making me furrow my eyebrows.

I was so focused on the beautiful smile on her face

that I completely forgot what we were talking about.

"The legend," she explained after seeing the confusion on my face.

"Oh," I muttered, opening my eyes slightly. "That's right. I think the Goddess is real. Maybe we're not worthy of her yet. Maybe she's waiting somewhere and will appear when we least expect it."

Maddie nodded and looked up at the ceiling.

"Do you believe she exists?" I asked, resisting the urge to kiss her cheek.

"Maybe," Maddie muttered.

I smiled and took a deep breath.

I didn't need any Goddess in my life as long as I had Madeline. She was my Goddess. She was my princess. He was everything to me.

Chapter 17 We have to do something

JANET

"Come in," I said quietly.

The door opened and Savannah walked in.

"We need to do something, Savannah," I said as soon as she closed the door behind her.

She raised her eyebrows and walked over to me. She sat down in the chair next to my bed and crossed her arms over her chest.

"What the hell are you talking about, Janet?" she asked, making me sigh.

"Dimitri," I explained. "You need to get him to accept you as a mate."

Her eyes widened slightly. She studied my face with a confused expression.

"I tried," she said. "He's stubborn and wants to wait for his fated mate."

I rolled my eyes and stood up. I began pacing around my room, clenching my fists repeatedly.

"She'll be a spoiled brat, I'm sure," I said, gritting my teeth. "But that's not a problem now."

I looked at Savannah, who looked even more confused than before.

"So what is it?" she asked.

I clenched my jaw and tried to control my anger.

I hated Madeline. She was a spoiled brat who looked too much like her late mother. I hated her attitude and her broken-child behavior. I wanted her gone and I couldn't wait for her to turn eighteen. I would kick her out of the pack immediately.

But what bothered me the most was that Dimitri liked her. I could tell by the way he looked at her. Would he fall in love with her?

Would he take her as his chosen mate?

No. I couldn't allow that. I had to do something about it and stop it before it happened.

"Mike's daughter," I murmured, making Savannah's eyes widen.

"Why?" she asked with a hint of jealousy in her voice.

Good. That was all I wanted.

I knew how much Savannah wanted my child. I knew she wanted to become Luna. She wanted the money and power that came with being married to the King. That was fine by me. She would make my plan work and I knew I would get along much better with Savannah than Madeline or any other pathetic girl like her.

"Dimitri is too affectionate with her," I said, making Savannah's eyes narrow. "I'm afraid he might ask her to be his chosen mate when she turns eighteen."

Savannah clenched her fists and a growl escaped her.

"Over my dead body," she said quietly. "Can't we just get rid of her?"

I sighed and ran my fingers through my hair.

"No," I said as I stopped pacing my room.

"If word got out that we did anything to that girl, Mike would freak out. I don't want to deal with that."

Savannah furrowed her eyebrows and bit her bottom lip. She looked like she was thinking about something.

A few moments later she looked at me worriedly.

"What if she's his fated mate?" she muttered, making me gasp.

"God forbid!" I exclaimed. "That's not even possible. She's a normal werewolf, not a werewolf."

Savannah exhaled in relief. "Oh thank god."

"That would be my worst nightmare." I was so fucking happy that Madeline wasn't a werewolf and it wasn't possible for her to be my son's fated mate.

Although he could take her as his chosen one, just like I took Mike.

I couldn't let that happen.

"You have to make him take you as his mate, Savannah," I told her. "We have to stop that brat from even thinking she has a chance with my son."

I saw the fury in Savannah's eyes. "That little bitch will never."

I smirked and nodded. I knew Savannah was the right choice for this plan.

"How old is she?" Savannah asked.

"17," I replied. "She'll be 18 in nine months.

" "That's perfect," Savannah said as a huge :smirk spread across her face. "Dimitri can't do anything until she's of age."

I nodded and continued pacing my room.

"Which is why we have to work fast," I said. "I want you marked by the time that brat turns eighteen.

" "Do you have a plan?" Savannah asked. "Dimitri's been kind of cold to me lately."

I looked at her and smiled.

"You could fake a pregnancy," I said, making Savannah raise her eyebrows at me.

"Are you serious?" She sighed. "Werewolves notice a change in a female's scent when she's pregnant. She'd pick up on my lie immediately."

I sighed and rolled my eyes. She was wrong.

"No," I said, trying not to sound annoyed. "Male werewolves notice the change in their mate's scent immediately. They only notice the change in other females' scent after two or three weeks. How long has it been since you two had sex?"

"About three weeks," Savannah said, making me furrow my eyebrows.

It could work. We just needed him to believe her for a second. He knew my son. He would take responsibility and take Savannah as his chosen mate.

"That could work," I said, smirking. "You need to tell him you're pregnant. He'll take you as a mate immediately."

Savannah raised her eyebrows.

"He'll know I'm not," she said. "There won't be any change in my scent."

I sighed and tried to hold back my anger. I needed so much guidance.

"He just needs to believe it for a second, Savannah," I said. "He'll mark you and you'll have sex again. Females get pregnant easier when they're marked. You'll get pregnant after I mark you and he won't know a thing.

" "What if I don't?" she asked.

"It won't matter," I said, gritting my teeth. "You'll be marked and that brat will be out of the picture for good."

Chapter 18 Next to him

MADELINE

I snuggled closer to something warm in my bed.

What was it? Was I hugging a pillow? Sometimes I did.

It smelled so good. Like cocoa and cinnamon. It was my favorite drink.

A small smile spread across my face and I took a deep breath of the wonderful scent. I was still half asleep and nothing made sense but I didn't care. I was warm. I was comfortable. I was enjoying the scent of my favorite drink surrounding me. I didn't want to wake up.

But then I felt someone's arms tighten around me.

I was awake within a second.

I opened my eyes and gasped.

Oh no.

No, no, no, no.

I wasn't cuddling a pillow. I was cuddling...

Oh Goddess.

I tried to push away from him but he only succeeded in holding on tighter.

"Shh, Maddie," he murmured softly as he reached up and gently stroked my head. "Sleep."

My eyes flew open.

"You need to wake up, Alpha," I said quietly, afraid Mike or Janet could hear me.

"Five more minutes, Maddie," he murmured as he snuggled closer to me.

My heart skipped a beat. What the hell was going on?

This was out of character. I couldn't believe I had fallen asleep with him in my bed. I couldn't believe I had woken up next to him.

What would happen when he woke up and realized he was sleeping next to me? Would he punish me?

Exile me? Oh

my God.

I stared at his face. He had high cheekbones and a jaw that could cut through steel. Well, at least he looked it.

His beard made him look a little older and more serious, but the relaxed expression on his face as he snuggled closer to me made him seem carefree.

When a small smile crept across his face, I felt my heart racing. Suddenly, I felt so warm.

I needed to get out of his arms and out of this bed.

"Alpha," I called out again, my voice shaking. "You need to wake up."

I was a little harder this time. I even shook his shoulder a little. My hands were shaking and my palms were sweaty, and I hoped he wouldn't notice.

He groaned a little and opened his eyes. He looked at me, making the nervousness inside me grow.

"What do you have against sleep, Maddie?" he asked, a small smile forming on his face.

His deep, husky, morning voice sent shivers down my spine.

Wasn't he angry? Why wasn't he angry? Why wasn't he angry? We fell asleep in the same bed.

We held each other. It was inappropriate.

He stared at my face for a few moments before laughing.

"What's wrong?" he asked softly.

I swallowed

, my throat completely dry. "We fell asleep together," I muttered quietly, never taking my eyes off his dark eyes.

He laughed and nodded. "Yeah, we fell asleep. Why do you look like you saw a ghost?"

I furrowed my eyebrows. I still didn't understand why he wasn't angry.

"It's inappropriate, Alpha," I forced myself to murmur.

His eyes widened and he let go of me. I immediately felt cold.

"Oh god, Maddie," he murmured worriedly. "Did I make you uncomfortable? I'm so sorry. I didn't mean to. I fell asleep by accident."

He sat up, making sure he wasn't touching me anymore.

Was he really apologizing? I should be the one apologizing, not him.

"I wasn't uncomfortable, Alpha," I said as I felt the blood rush to my cheeks. "I was just worried because you're the

Alpha and I'm just a wolf."

He studied my face for a few moments. He looked deep in thought.

"I'm sorry I fell asleep next to you," I continued. "I shouldn't have. I was just—"

"Goddess, Maddie, don't apologize," he interrupted as a small smile crept across his face. "There's nothing to apologize for. We're friends, right? These things happen sometimes."

I raised my eyebrows. He didn't really seem angry.

"I was just afraid I made you uncomfortable," he sighed as he ran his fingers through my hair. "I never want to do that, Maddie.

I want you to be comfortable with me."

Well, thinking back to the moment I woke up, I was more than comfortable. I was at peace and I never wanted to leave the warmth that surrounded me.

"It's okay, Alpha," I murmured as I felt the blood rush to my cheeks once again. "I wasn't uncomfortable."

He smiled brightly and my heart skipped a beat. It was beautiful when he smiled like that.

I forced myself to take a deep breath and looked away. If I kept looking at him, my cheeks would burst. I was sure I was already bright red.

"I'm glad to hear that, Maddie," he said, making me look back at him. "But please stop calling me Alpha. I'm Dimitri to you."

I looked away again as I felt the blood rush to my cheeks again. I swore the temperature in the room was getting hotter by the minute. Why was it so hot in here?

My eyes fell on the clock and I gasped.

"Maddie?" Alpha Dimitri called out to me worriedly as he jumped out of bed.

"I'm going to be late for work!" I exclaimed as I ran to my bathroom.

Shit. It was only my second day. What would Seth and his parents think of me?

"You don't have to work, Maddie," Alpha Dimitri sighed.

I heard him stand up and walk over to me. He leaned against the door frame and watched me brush my teeth. I couldn't answer and tell him I wanted to work.

"Your father can take care of you," he continued, making me frown.

I spat out the toothpaste and looked at him.

"I want to work," I told him. "I'll need the money to move out when I turn eighteen."

Some unknown flashed in his eyes. Was it rage? Was it pain?

"You don't have to move, Maddie," he said quietly. "This is your home. This is your pack."

I was wrong. This wasn't my home. This wasn't my pack. I had yet to find that. My home and my pack would feel like waking up in his arms. My home would be warm and safe. It would smell like cocoa and cinnamon and I would feel loved and accepted.

I wasn't wanted here. Alpha Dimitri's mother wanted me gone and I would make her wish come true.

Chapter 19 The news

DIMITRI

I was grinning like an idiot ever since I woke up next to my roommate. I had a smile on my face that nothing could erase.

I was so fucking happy.

I fell asleep in her room by accident. We were talking about the legend and she fell asleep while I was talking about the details of the war. Her head fell on my shoulder and I almost melted into a useless puddle. I promised myself I would only stay for a few minutes. I ran my fingers through her silky hair and gave her a soft kiss on the forehead. The taste of her skin made me see stars. I breathed in her wonderful scent deeply and without realizing it, I fell asleep next to her. At some point in the night, I wrapped her in my arms.

It was an accident, but I was so glad it happened. It soothed my soul and I knew it would help me cope with the fact that I would have to wait for her for nine fucking months. Maybe there would be more happy accidents like that. I had so many stories to tell her. Maybe she'd fall asleep in my arms again, and I'd be able to calm the raging storm in my soul.

Skol had never been so happy and calm. He looked like he was drugged. He kept mumbling about her scent and the feel of her skin against us. I wondered how she'd act once we'd marked and mated her.

I'd explode with happiness, he murmured, and I had to stifle a giggle.

It was hard for me to imagine a huge werewolf that everyone feared exploding with happiness, but I knew exactly what he meant. I'd explode with happiness, too.

"Why the huge grin?" Will asked as I walked into my office.

I was sitting on the couch, looking through some papers.

"I accidentally fell asleep in

Maddie's room," I said. "I woke up next to my partner, and I don't think I've ever been happier."

Will looked at me and raised an eyebrow.

"Did you accidentally fall asleep in her room?

" he asked, and I could tell he was trying hard not to smile.

I rolled my eyes as I sat back in my chair.

"Yeah," I said. "We were just talking about the legend of the Three Kingdoms and fell asleep."

Will snorted. "You got bored out of your mind, didn't you?"

I rolled my eyes again. "No. She loves history as much as I do."

"Yeah, right," Will muttered as he looked back down at the papers in his hand.

He had a satisfied smirk on his face.

"I'm serious," I said, causing him to look back at me. "

She has a history book on the subject. She knows a lot about the Great War.

" "So she is your mate," Will laughed. "I've never met a person as fascinated by history as you are."

He was right. I was a bit of a history nerd and the history of the Three Kingdoms was one of my favorites.

"She is my mate," I said proudly as a heat

ran through my body.

She was mine and I was damn proud of it. I couldn't wait for her to turn eighteen so I could shout it from the rooftops and let everyone know that this beautiful woman was mine.

"Oh, Goddess," Will sighed and I could hear the annoyance in his voice.

"What?" I asked, furrowing my eyebrows.

"Savannah's coming," he muttered just as I heard a knock on my office door.

I was so wrapped up in thinking about Maddie that I didn't even hear her approach.

I took a deep breath and resisted the urge to roll my eyes.

The door opened and Savannah walked in. She had a huge smile on her face and looked excited.

"What's that about?" Will said to me. "

I have no idea and I don't care." I replied.

"Can we talk?" Savannah asked as she walked over to my desk.

I didn't want to talk to her but I had to be polite. I motioned to the chair across from me and she sat down.

She looked at Will. "Can you please leave us alone?"

"Don't move." "I told her through the mind link.

"We can talk in front of him," I said, causing her to look back at me. "Anything you need to tell me, you can say in front of him."

She sighed, but nodded.

"You're right," she said. "He'll know soon enough, anyway."

I raised my eyebrows and looked at Will. He was staring at Savannah with a murderous glare.

"I have wonderful news, Dimitri," Savannah said, smiling brightly.

I clenched my jaw. Something told me I wouldn't find the news wonderful.

"I know this is unexpected and we hadn't planned on it, but I'm so glad, Dimitri," she said, making my stomach twist painfully.

What hadn't we planned on?

Skol was growling under his breath. I could sense his nervousness.

He walked over to the table and took my hand.

I could feel the tension in the room building.

"I'm pregnant, Dimitri," she said. "I'm pregnant with your pup." My vision blurred. My heart stopped beating. My world stopped spinning.

No.

It wasn't possible. I was careful. We were careful.

She's lying! Skol screamed. *I can't sense it, Dimitri! She's lying! Don't listen to her.*

I narrowed my eyes and pulled my hand away from hers.

"That's impossible, Savannah," I said angrily. "Skol can't sense the pup. We were careful. You're lying."

Savannah's eyes filled with tears.

"I'm not your mate, and it'll take a little longer for Skol to sense her pup," she said quietly.

"She's a fucking liar!" Will mentally linked me. *Don't believe her. She's out to get you.*

I looked at Will and gave him a small nod.

Savannah wiped her tears away and smiled again.

"I can't wait for us to be a family," she said. "I can't wait for you to mark me and make me your Luna."

My eyes widened. Was I crazy?! I

would never do this. I wasn't pregnant and even if I was, the pup wouldn't be mine.

The only one I would mark was Maddie. The only one I wanted to mark was Maddie.

Maddie was my mate. Maddie was my Luna. Maddie was my princess and my queen.

Savannah wasn't pregnant with me and I would never fall for her lies.

Chapter 20 Two weeks

MADELINE

It had been two weeks since I last saw Dimitri Alpha.

He hadn't been home and he hadn't come to the cafeteria. I didn't know why I thought he was weird. Maybe it was because he spent so much time around me when I first came to the pack. I could tell I was hoping to see him again. I could tell I was hoping to talk to him again.

"No, Madeline," I said quietly. "You don't want to see him or talk to him."

I started cleaning the glasses more aggressively.

"What?" Seth asked, making me look up at him.

He stood beside me. He leaned against the counter and watched me

as I cleaned the glasses.

"What are you doing tonight?" he asked, making me look up at him.

I furrowed my eyebrows.

"There's a party in the woods," he said, giving me a small smile. "Would you like to go?"

I didn't know what to say. On one hand, I didn't want to go. I wanted to curl up in bed and read. On the other hand, maybe it wasn't such a bad idea to hang out with Seth and meet

new people.

"Come on, Mads," Seth said, smiling at me. "You only leave the house to go to work. You need to relax and enjoy yourself once in a while."

I bit my bottom lip and took a deep breath.

"Are you afraid your dad won't let you go?"

Seth asked, making me shake my head.

"No, that's not it," I muttered. "He'll let me go."

Well, he wouldn't even know I was gone. I wouldn't even tell him. I'd sneak out my bedroom window.

"It's settled then," Seth said, grinning from ear to ear. "You're leaving."

He took the glass and dish towel from my hands, making me furrow my eyebrows.

"I'm going to finish closing up," he said. "Go home and get ready.

Meet me in front of the coffee shop in an hour."

I was still unsure.

Seth sighed and rolled his eyes.

"Come on, Mads," he said as he pushed me a little. "Go home and get ready. We'll have a lot of fun."

I took off my apron and he took it from my hands.

"Hurry up, come on," he said pointing to the door. "You have 58 minutes to get ready and come back."

I glanced at the clock on the wall. It was 9:02 p.m.

"Hurry up," Seth repeated, making me roll my eyes.

"Okay," I muttered as I walked away. "I'll see you in an hour."

" "57 minutes!" she called out as she closed the door to the coffee shop.

I chuckled and started walking towards Mike's house. The house wasn't far from the coffee shop so it didn't take me long to get there.

"Where were you?" I heard the most annoying voice in the world as soon as I entered the house.

I sighed and resisted the urge to roll my eyes.

We'd been through this every night.

"I was at work," I said as calmly as I could.

Janet narrowed her eyes and took a step closer. I wanted to back away from her, but I wanted to show her that I wasn't scared of her.

"Where's Mike?" I asked, looking towards the kitchen.

"That's none of your business," Janet said coldly.

I really didn't understand why she hated me so much. I'd never done anything to her. I didn't even talk to her most of the time. She kept to herself. I worked, helped around the house, and spent most of my time in my room.

"Did you hear the wonderful news?" she asked, smiling at me.

I raised my eyebrows and shook my head.

"I'm going to be a grandmother," she said, making my heart skip a beat. "My son's mate is pregnant with her first pup."

I didn't know why, but it felt like a hot rod was going through my chest. I tried to take a deep breath, but I couldn't.

Dimitri was going to be a father? His mate was pregnant?

I didn't know why, but my stomach was twisting painfully.

"Aren't you going to congratulate me?" Janet asked. "Hasn't your disgusting mother taught you any manners?"

I gasped, forgetting about Dimitri's pup in a second.

"What did she just say?!

" "What did she say?" I muttered, trying to remain calm.

Janet took a step closer to me.

"I asked about your disgusting mother," she said, repeating the word that made me want to rip her apart. "Didn't she teach you any manners?"

I set my jaw and clenched my fists.

"Don't you ever talk about my mother like that again," I said through gritted teeth. "Take it back."

Janet laughed, throwing her head back.

I really wanted to punch her.

"I'll never take it back, you little bitch," Janet said, looking at me again. "You and your mother deserved to be abandoned. Your mother deserved to die. It would be better for everyone if you had died with her."

My heart broke inside my chest and all the rage I felt turned to pain. I wanted to scream. My mother didn't deserve to die. My mother didn't deserve to be abandoned by my father. She was an amazing woman and she deserved only the best.

I couldn't think of anything to say to the monster in front of me, so I walked past her and started up the stairs.

"I can't wait for you to be 18 and out of my house," she said. "If I'm lucky, maybe you'll be out of my life even sooner."

I would be the lucky one if that happened.

I walked into my bedroom and closed the door behind me. Only then did I let the tears fall. I would never give her the satisfaction of seeing me cry.

My mother didn't deserve to be abandoned. My mother deserved the world.

"You didn't deserve it, Mom," I murmured as I looked up. "You deserved to be loved and cared for."

I sobbed silently. I missed her. I missed my mother so much.

My eyes fell on the clock on the wall. It was 9:32 p.m. I had fifteen minutes to get ready.

I wiped the tears from my cheeks and headed for the closet.

I needed to get out of this house. I needed to get away from Janet if only for a little while.

Chapter 21 In his bed

DIMITRI

I spent every night for the past two weeks sleeping in my princess's bed.

I couldn't get away from her. I couldn't even sleep without her anymore.

I needed her scent and the feel of her body against mine. I needed to know she was in my arms and no one was going to take her away from me.

She never knew because she didn't have her wolf senses yet.

I would wait for her to fall asleep and quietly go up to her room.

I thought my mother or Mike would hear me, but that never happened.

I didn't know how or why, but I never complained. I needed her and I would be so pissed off if I couldn't get to her because of them.

I stayed away from her during the day. I didn't want her to see me angry. I didn't want her to see me distressed. I needed to deal with damn Savannah before I would let my princess see me.

Savannah wasn't pregnant with my pup. I knew that and she knew that. Skol never sensed the pup. She knew that I was careful and that there was no way she was pregnant.

Except she never wanted to admit it. It got my mother involved and they were both pressuring me to mark Savannah. They wanted me to take her as my chosen mate and make her my Luna.

Will and I suspected that they both had the pack doctor involved. I'd been trying to schedule an ultrasound to prove there wasn't a fucking pup in her but the pack doctor kept telling me the ultrasound was broken and he couldn't fix it. It was a fucking excuse and I'd fire the fucker the first chance I got. I sent warriors out to other packs to find me a sonographer and a doctor.

I'd do the fucking test and prove to them that this whole fucking pregnancy was fake.

If I wasn't an Alpha and a King, I'd tell Savannah to fuck off. But I couldn't do that. My position and throne could be in jeopardy if word got out that I'd kicked out a wolf who was possibly pregnant with my pup. I needed proof.

I needed that damn ultrasound picture.

All this bullshit made me incredibly angry. I couldn't control my temper or Skol. He would come out at random times and it was so fucking hard to calm him down. The only way to calm him down was to go with Maddie. We were both happy and calm only at night, when we would hold her in our arms and sleep next to her.

Tonight was the night I needed her more than ever.

Savannah came into my office and tried to sleep with me. She said the pregnancy hormones made her horny. I almost started screaming at her. There were no hormones and there was no fucking pregnancy!

I was disgusted by her touch and I was dying to erase it with the feel of my princess's skin on mine. I was dying to bury my nose in her hair and let her scent fill my lungs. I couldn't wait to kiss her soft cheek and taste her skin on my lips.

So when I walked into her room and saw an empty bed, my heart stopped beating. I blinked trying to make sense of what I was seeing.

It was almost midnight and she wasn't in her bed. She wasn't home either. I would have heard her if she was anywhere else in the house.

Where was I?! Where was my mate?!

Skol growled so loud I was sure my mother and Mike would wake up. I pushed him back and refused to let him out.

Let me find her, Skol, I said. You don't want to scare her.

He looked scary when he was angry and I didn't want her to be afraid of him.

Run, you bastard! Skol yelled at me. Find her.

I turned around and walked out of there as quietly as I could.

Surprisingly, neither my mother nor Mike woke up from my growling.

As soon as I stepped out of the house, I took a deep breath and tried to locate his scent.

"On your left!" Skol yelled at me.

I tried to control my anger. I turned left and ran. His scent led me to the coffee shop. Did he go back to work? Why? The coffee shop closed at nine. Why would he go back there?

As soon as I got closer, I recognized another scent.

I saw the damn red!

Skol moaned loudly. I could feel his anger and pain pulsing inside me.

She was with Seth?! Why? What were they doing?

Were they on a date? Did he take my partner on a date?! Did he touch her? Did he kiss her? Did he...?

Oh, Goddess.

No, no, no, no, no. I would kill him. She was mine!

MINE!

I didn't even realize I was running through the woods.

I was following her scent and running faster and faster by the second.

I had to find her and take her from her. She was my mate. She was mine, not his.

I realized I was running towards the lake. As I got closer, I heard voices and loud music that made me slow down a little.

What the fuck was that? Was I at a party?

As I got closer, I realized he was right. It was a fucking party and my mate was here with that fucker.

My eyes found her immediately and I exhaled in relief. There she was, perfect as ever. I wanted to go to her and pull her into my arms.

"Go away, Dimitri!" Skol yelled at me.

I can't, Skol, I muttered. I can't tell him how I know he wasn't in his room.

I don't care, Skol growled. Tell him you went for a run and saw her.

Get her away from him and walk her back home.

I couldn't do that. I didn't want to be an overbearing mate that kept her from spending time with her friends. I would stay here and make sure she was okay. I would make sure she got home safely and I would get into bed with her as soon as she fell asleep.

If she touches her..., Skol said, but he couldn't finish the sentence.

She won't, I told him. No one will touch her. I promise you, Skol.

She was mine and my hands would be the only ones touching her.

Chapter 22 The party

MADELINE

I swore someone was watching me.

I kept looking toward the row of trees to my right, but I couldn't see anything. It would be easier to see if I had my wolf, but I'd have to wait a little longer.

I was being paranoid. No one was watching me. No one knew who I was.

Why would anyone want to watch me? I was nothing and no one.

"What pack are you in?" a guy whose name I couldn't remember asked me.

I looked away from the row of trees and saw him smiling at me.

He was a little drunk and kept looking me up and down.

"Red Moon," I replied.

"Do you have a boyfriend?" the guy asked.

I swore I heard a growl coming from the same row of trees I was looking at a few moments ago. I was seriously going crazy.

"Stop it, Jasper," Seth said angrily. "She's underage."

Jasper's eyes widened slightly.

"You still don't have your wolf?" he asked, surprised.

Was he so drunk that even his wolf senses were dulled? I should have known I didn't have my wolf yet. I should
have sensed it.

"How drunk are you?" Seth sighed as he handed me a
plastic cup.

I took a sip and frowned a little. I would never get used to the taste of wolfsbane and beer. It was bitter and I never figured out why wolves liked that.

"At least I'm not the one who gets her drunk," Jasper said, rolling his eyes. "I was just asking if she had a boyfriend."

I thought I heard another growl coming from the tree line.

I looked to my right, but I couldn't see anything. I was really losing my mind. I hadn't even had that much to drink. It was only my second drink.

"I'm not going to get her drunk," Seth said. —I didn't even put that much aconite in it.

I looked at Seth and saw him take a big sip of his drink.

"And you weren't asking her if she had a boyfriend out of curiosity," Seth added.

"You were asking her because you want to be her boyfriend. "

Jasper wanted to argue, but I cut him off.

"Aren't you two waiting for your mates?" I asked, looking from Seth to Jasper. "Are you okay with dating before

mate bonding?

" Both Seth and Jasper shrugged a little.

"I'm excited to meet my mate," Seth said, giving me a warm smile. "But I don't see anything wrong with dating someone before we do. As long as my girlfriend is aware that our relationship will end once I find my mate, I wouldn't have a problem dating her.

" "Yeah," Jasper muttered as he poured more beer into his glass. "As long as it's nothing serious, I'm okay with it."

I laughed a little. "So, simplifying what you just said, just sex?"

Jasper laughed, and Seth sighed.

"You're funny," Jasper said when he stopped laughing. "I like you.

Maybe you'll be my mate."

He winked at me and this time I definitely heard a growl.

We all heard it. Both Jasper and Seth looked over at the line of trees. Maybe they'd see something I didn't.

"Probably just two idiots fighting,"

Jasper muttered.

Seth raised his eyebrows but remained silent. He'd had a bit to drink, so his senses probably weren't as sharp as usual.

Seth and I both looked back at Jasper.

"I wish I was a werewolf so I could tell if you're my mate or not," Jasper smirked at me.

Seth sighed and took another big sip of his drink.

"You jealous, man?" Jasper asked, laughing at Seth.

I raised my eyebrows. Why would Seth be jealous?

"I'm not answering that," Seth muttered as he took the glass from my hand and placed it on the table next to us.

I looked at him. Why had he taken the glass from me?

"What are you doing?" Jasper asked. "I wasn't done with that."

"I'm driving her home," Seth said. "It's two in the morning."

Jasper grunted in discontent.

"I'm fine with staying longer, Seth," I said. "You don't have to leave the party because of me."

Seth shook his head and gave me a small smile.

"It's okay, Maddie," he said. "I'm tired and I want to go."

"Let the girl stay, Seth," Jasper said. "I'll walk her home."

I shook my head. Seth grunted a little.

"That's not happening, Jasper," Seth said angrily.

Jasper sighed and rolled his eyes. He looked at me and smiled.

"I look forward to seeing you around here, cutie," he said. "I'll be coming to the coffee shop more often now.

" "See you around," I said, trying to hold back a giggle.

Seth grabbed my hand and started to pull me away.

"I'm sorry if that made you uncomfortable, Mads," Seth said once we were alone. "He's a good kid. He's just a little goofy and doesn't think before he speaks."

I looked at him and smiled.

"It's okay, Seth," I said, making him look at me. "He didn't make me uncomfortable. He's nice."

Seth sighed and ran his fingers through his hair.

"Sometimes I can't believe that asshole is my best friend," he muttered, making me giggle.

He looked at me and smiled.

"Did you have a good time?" he asked.

"Yeah," I replied. "Thanks for taking me.

I did have a good time. I met some of Seth's friends. Jasper made me laugh a few times. I managed to forget about Janet for a while.

Seth smiled and put his arm around my shoulders.

"I'm glad, Mads," he said, "I'll take you with me whenever you want."

I looked at him and smiled. If Janet kept being such a bitch, I was definitely going to have to spend more time away from home.

"Deal," I said, making Seth smile brightly.

"I'm glad you came to my pack, Mads," he said. "
I'm lucky to have a friend like you."

I smiled at him.

"Thanks for giving me work," I chuckled. "I'm lucky to have a friend like you too." I

stopped walking as we reached the tree line behind Mike's house.

Seth surprised me by pulling me into a tight hug. He didn't say anything. He just held me tightly. I furrowed my eyebrows and patted his back gently.

"See you tomorrow, Mads," he murmured as he let go of me.

I gave him a small smile and walked towards Mike's house.

I was dying to shower and get into bed. I hoped to sleep as well as I had the past few weeks.

Chapter 23 Hug her

DIMITRI

My whole body was shaking.

Skol was right. I should have taken her away right away.

I told you so," he growled, his voice shaking.

We were both angry. We both hated Jasper for flirting with her. We both wanted to rip Seth's arms off for hugging her.

I can't wait for her to turn eighteen," Skol said.

I'll kill someone first.

I took a deep breath and tried to calm myself down a bit. I couldn't freak out.

I was just out with some friends. Nothing had happened. Jasper flirted with her because she was fucking gorgeous. Seth hugged her because he's happy to have her as a friend. No one touched what only I was supposed to touch. No one kissed her. No one did anything inappropriate.

I don't agree and I want to claw Jasper's eyes out, Skol growled.

We need to calm down, okay? I muttered as I watched my princess walk towards the house.

But she wasn't walking forward.

What the hell was I doing?

How the fuck do you expect me to calm down if I can't take what's mine? Skol growled loudly. Not only that, I have to watch them flirt with her and...

Will you just shut up? I interrupted him.

I was trying to figure out what the hell Maddie was doing.

She wasn't walking towards the back entrance either. She was walking towards the tree in the backyard.

What is she doing? Skol muttered.

I ignored him and focused on her. She started to climb the tree and I had to hold back a growl.

Is that how she left? Didn't she tell Mike or my mother she was leaving?!

Goddess, Madelinel, Skol yelled.

Something could have happened to her and they wouldn't even know where she was. She would, Skol said. She knows we're her mate. She always snuggles closer to us when we sleep with her.

I smiled. Skol was right. She always felt comfortable in my arms.

She always smiled a little when I held her. Her body knew who I was even before she did.

But it didn't matter. I couldn't tell her. I had to wait a little longer.

It doesn't matter, Skol, I told him. I can't tell her. I can't take that discovery away from her.

Not to mention how scared I was that someone was going to hurt her if word got out that she was my mate. I couldn't let that happen. She didn't have her wolf yet. If someone tried to hurt her, she wouldn't be able to defend herself.

We could teach her, Dimitri, Skol whined. We could teach her to defend herself.

A human against a wolf? I muttered.

Skol groaned quietly.

I took a deep breath and ran my fingers through my hair. I had to be patient. Soon she would have her wolf and discover who I was. That very day I would kiss her and mark her. Make her mine forever. I think she fell asleep, Dimitri, Skol said. Go see her.

I walked over to the back entrance and pulled the key out of my pocket. I'd been doing this for two weeks

now

and I didn't even need to think about my next steps.

A few moments later, I pushed open her bedroom door and stepped inside. Her scent washed over me and I had to suppress a groan. I would never get used to her power over me. Her scent was like a drug I could never get enough of.

She was sleeping in her bed, curled up in a ball. I smiled. This sight was so much better than a few hours ago when I walked in and saw her

empty bed.

I closed the door and kicked off my shoes. I knelt down beside her bed and gently caressed her cheek. She sighed contently and leaned closer into my touch. She always did the same, but she never woke up. My presence helped her sleep better.

"Hello, my love," I murmured softly. "I've missed you so much."

I lay down beside her, making sure she was covered up.

It was cold outside. I never got under the covers with her. I was already crossing enough boundaries just being in her room while she slept. I couldn't stay away. I had to hold her. I had to make sure she was safe. She was the only one who had the ability to calm me down and I needed that after I thought she fell asleep, Dimitri, Skol said. Go check on her.

•

I walked over to the back entrance and pulled the key out of my pocket.

I'd been doing this for two weeks now and I didn't even need to think about my next steps.

A few moments later, I opened the door to her room and walked in. Her scent washed over me and I had to suppress a groan. I would never get used to her power over me. Her scent was like a drug I could never get enough of.

She was sleeping in her bed, curled up in a ball. I smiled. This sight was much better than the one a few hours ago when I'd walked in and seen her

empty bed.

I closed the door and kicked off my shoes. I knelt down beside her bed and gently caressed her cheek. She sighed contently and leaned closer into my touch. She always did the same thing, but she never woke up. My presence helped her sleep better.

"Hello, my love," I murmured softly. "I've missed you so much."

I lay down beside her, making sure she was covered up.

It was cold outside. I never got under the covers with her. I was already crossing enough boundaries just by being in her room while she slept. I couldn't stay away. I had to hold her. I had to make sure she was safe. She was the only one who had the ability to calm me down and I needed that later.

Chapter 24 Don't be rude

MADELINE

I stretched and looked out the window.

A small smile spread across my face. It was snowing outside.

I sat up and glanced at the clock on the wall. It was 7:35. I had woken up way too early, but I had slept really well and felt rested and ready to take on the day.

I was about to get up and go to the bathroom when a quiet knock on the door stopped me.

I knew who it was even before the door opened.

"Come in," I said, prompting Mike to open the door.

"Morning, honey," Mike said as he peeked inside.

"I made breakfast. Are you hungry?"

I shook my head, making him frown a little.

"You need to eat, Maddie," he said as he walked in. "You work all day. You can't go without breakfast again." "I

always eat at the diner," I said, seeing sadness in

Mike's eyes.

It didn't bother me. If he cared about me and my well-being, he wouldn't have left me fifteen years ago.

"Come on, sweetie," he said, giving me a small smile. "Dimitri's here too. We could have a family meal."

My heart skipped a beat when Mike said Dimitri Alpha was here. But I didn't know why. I shouldn't care about him. I shouldn't care if he was here or not.

But I did. I was glad he was here. He was the only one in this house who was nice to me.

Mike took my silence as a yes. He smiled brightly and left my room.

"I made pancakes," he said as he closed my bedroom door and winked at me.

I let out a loud sigh, stood up, and headed to the bathroom. I was hesitant, but a small part of me was curious to see Dimitri Alpha. Maybe his presence would mean Janet wouldn't be as obnoxious as usual and my morning could be quiet. Maybe he wouldn't even look at me like usual.

I took my time getting ready since I wasn't in a hurry.

After a while, I walked into my room to get dressed. I put on jeans, fluffy socks, boots, and the thickest hoodie I owned. I grabbed my coat and walked out of my room.

As I approached the kitchen, I heard Alpha Dimitri's voice and my heart skipped a beat.

"Leave it, Mother," he said angrily. "We're going to end that lie today. The doctor's here and—"

Alpha Dimitri stopped talking as soon as I walked into the kitchen. He looked at me, a huge smile spreading across his face. Janet was glaring at me, but I ignored her and focused on Alpha Dimitri.

"Good morning, Maddie," Alpha Dimitri said. "How did you sleep?"

"Very good," I said, giving him a small smile. "Good morning to you too, Alpha."

I had slept really well the last two weeks. But I didn't know why. Maybe it was the mattress or maybe I was just too tired after work. Whatever it was, I wasn't going to complain. I was going to enjoy it while it lasted.

"It's Dimitri, Maddie," he said softly. "I already told you." I gave him a small, apologetic smile and looked at Janet. She set her jaw and narrowed her eyes at me. I gulped and slowly walked over to the table. Dimitri pulled up a chair next to him and I sat down. Mike was sitting across from me. He had a huge grin on his face.

"How are you, Maddie?" Dimitri asked. "I haven't seen you in a while. Do you like it here?"

I was about to answer him, but Janet interrupted me.

"Don't you remember what I told you yesterday, Madeline?" she asked, causing me to look up at her. "Your Alpha is about to be a father. You should congratulate him. Don't be rude, Madeline."

My heart started pounding in my chest.

Alpha Dimitri growled loudly. I looked at him and my eyes went wide. He looked so angry. He looked like he was about to change.

"Did you tell her?" he yelled angrily. "I told you not to tell her! I told you not to tell anyone."

I froze. I didn't know what to do. I couldn't even breathe.

Alpha Dimitri looked at me and my heart stopped beating.

"It's not true, Maddie," he said and I could swear I heard a hint of panic in his voice. "A wolf that I had a physical relationship with is trying to force me to take her as my chosen mate. She's not pregnant. My wolf can't sense the pup, because there's no pup. A doctor will examine her today and I will prove to everyone that she's not pregnant."

My heart raced. Why would that woman do that to him? Why would anyone lie about something like that?

"I'm so sorry," I muttered under my breath. "She doesn't deserve that.

Why would she? Why would she lie about something so important?"

"He's not lying," Janet sighed angrily. "She's pregnant and my son refuses to take responsibility. That's your pup, Dimitri."

Alpha Dimitri looked at his mother. If looks could kill, she'd be buried six feet away.

"I can't wait to see that fucking ultrasound and not see any pups in it," Alpha Dimitri growled.

Mike sighed and ran his fingers through his hair.

"Leave him alone, Janet," Mike said. "He's right. He needs to prove that he's really pregnant before he does anything. I can't believe you're forcing him into that bond. He's the King. Do you know how many wolves would tell a lie like that just to become their

Moon and Queen? Maybe Savannah is doing just that."

Alpha Dimitri clenched his fists and growled under his breath, Janet glared at me.

"Savannah is a very nice woman," Janet said, staring at me with an angry face. "That's the reason my son chose her in the first place. She's not like other women who would sleep with my son just to get something. Savannah loves him."

I shifted nervously in my seat. Why was he looking at me when he said that? Did he think I would sleep with his son? Was I crazy?

I raised my eyebrows.

"Stop looking at Maddie like that," Alpha Dimitri growled at his mother. "I don't fucking want Savannah. I never loved her. I just fucked her and that's it."

I felt the blood rush to my cheeks.

"Okay, that's enough," Mike said angrily, ending the fight between Janet and Alpha Dimitri. "My daughter doesn't have to hear that."

Alpha Dimitri took a deep breath and closed his eyes. He took my hand in his, making me shudder.

"I'm sorry, Maddie," he said as he opened his eyes and looked at me. "Mike's right." You shouldn't have to listen to us fight.

I gave him a small smile. "It's okay."

"Come on, sweetie," Mike said, pointing at the plate full of pancakes. "Eat up. You've got a long day ahead of you."

Alpha Dimitri let go of my hand so I could eat my breakfast.

I looked at Janet and a chill ran down my spine. She looked like she was about to move and jump on me.

Why did she hate me so much?

Chapter 25 I need her

DIMITRI

I was so pissed off.

Maddie knew?! My mom told her?!

I thought my heart was going to jump out of my chest when my mom told Maddie to congratulate me. I thought Skol was going to come out and rip my mom's head off.

I didn't want Maddie to know because it was a lie. I didn't want Maddie to find out I slept with someone else. I didn't want her to find out from anyone other than me. I was going to tell her. I would never lie to her. But I wanted to be me. I wanted to sit her down and tell her I slept with Savannah. I wanted to tell her I didn't think about my partner at the time and that I knew how wrong that was. I wanted to tell her how sorry I was. I wanted to tell her she was the only one I wanted and that I would never touch or look at another woman again.

My mom stole that chance from me. Maddie knew and her opinion of me changed. I was sure of it.

"What the hell is going on?" Will asked as he walked into my office. "I could feel your aura the moment I walked into the packing house."

I was leaning on the windowsill, staring out at the woods behind the warehouse. I didn't move. I was afraid Skol would come out if I moved a muscle. I was pissed, but he was furious.

He'd tear the whole place apart.

" "Maddie knows," I muttered under my breath.

Will gasped. "How?!"

"My mother told her," I said. "She had the nerve to tell him to congratulate me."

"Jesus Christ," Will muttered.

He was silent for a few moments. I clenched my jaw and narrowed my eyes.

"What did Maddie say?" Will asked, and I heard him sit back in the chair.

"Nothing," I muttered. "My mother and I started arguing, and she didn't get a chance to say anything. I told her it wasn't true. I explained. I—"

My voice cracked, and fear washed over me. I lowered my head and tried to take a deep breath.

What if he didn't believe me? What if he didn't want me when he found out I was his mate? What if...?

"Everything's going to be okay, Dimitri," Will said softly. "She knows you're telling the truth."

I couldn't wait for the night to come. I couldn't wait to have her in my arms. I couldn't wait to fill my lungs with her scent and see her beautiful face.

"She doesn't even know me, Will," I muttered as I forced my body to move.

I turned around and walked to my desk. I sat down in my chair and ran a hand over my face.

"You look like shit," Will muttered under his breath.

I looked at him and frowned. "You'd look like shit too if you had some psycho trying to say she's pregnant with your pup. Don't even get me started on the fact that my mate is within my grasp and I can't do shit about it and she might not even want me after..."

I trailed off abruptly. I heard footsteps approaching and clenched my fists. I knew who it was even before she came in.

Will sighed and ran his fingers through his hair.

"Can we exile her?" he asked quietly just as the door opened and Savannah walked in. "

I'll find a reason." I mentally linked to it.

"Hey, Dimitri," he said, smiling at me.

He kept rubbing his lower stomach and I had to work hard not to roll my eyes.

"The doctor will be here in an hour," I told him.

Savannah sighed and walked over to my desk. Skol was going crazy inside me. I had to use all my strength to keep him in.

"Is it really necessary, Dimitri?" Savannah asked, pouting. "I'm carrying your pup. Why would I lie

about something like that?

Maybe because you want to force your way into becoming Luna. "

Will mentally linked to me angrily.

I glanced over at him and saw him staring at her with a murderous glare.

"I'm wondering the same thing, Savannah," I said coldly. —I don't even know where you got the idea to lie about something that could be so easily proven.

Savannah sighed and looked down at her stomach.

"I can prove it," she said quietly before looking up at me. "And I'm going to prove it to you, Dimitri. We're going to be parents. I'm going to be your mate and your Luna. You're going to have to choose me, Dimitri."

It felt like someone was knocking the air out of my lungs.

I wanted Maddie. I needed Maddie.

I glanced at the clock on the wall. It was only eleven in the morning. I had to wait hours until I had my princess in my arms. I didn't know if I could hold on that long. My body needed her. My soul needed her.

"Well, since you're not Luna yet, I'm going to have to ask you to leave," Will said as he stood up. "Dimitri and I have work to do.

Thank you." I connected it mentally.

He understood that I couldn't even answer him. I was too angry and in too much pain.

I needed Maddie.

Savannah sighed and looked me up and down.

"I'll see you in an hour, Dimitri," she said before turning around and walking away.

Will sat back down as soon as she was out the door and closed the door.

"Do you want to go to the cafeteria?" Will asked, looking at me worriedly. "Maybe you'll feel better if you see her.

" I wasn't sure about that. I could see her, but I couldn't hold her.

And I needed to hold her.

"Okay," I murmured. "We can go after the ultrasound.

I'll feel better afterward. I don't want her to see me like this. "

Will nodded and took a deep breath.

"Dimitri?" he called softly.

I looked up at him and saw a worried look on his face. His eyebrows were furrowed and he kept biting the inside of his cheek.

I waited for him to continue.

"What if Savannah really is pregnant?" Will asked, anger erupting inside me.

I clenched my fists and gritted my teeth.

"If she really is pregnant, that puppy isn't mine," I said coldly. —I was careful and didn't get her pregnant.

I wasn't going to let her ruin my life. I wasn't going to let her take me away from Maddie. I belonged to Maddie and I was going to make sure no one messed with that.

Chapter 26 Pregnant?

DIMITRI

"Alpha Dimitri," the doctor said, bowing his head slightly.

"Hello, Dr. Jackson," I said, giving him a small nod. "I hope your trip here was pleasant."

"It was, Alpha," Dr. Jackson said, giving me a small smile. "Thank you for choosing me and trusting me to do this exam."

"I have a question, Doctor," I said as I sat down in the chair next to the bed.

"Please ask me anything, Alpha," the doctor said, giving me a small smile.

I swallowed and looked at Will. His face was expressionless.

"In case Savannah is pregnant, will you be able to tell how far along she is?" I asked, even though I already knew the answer.

I needed to be sure.

"Yes, Alpha," the doctor nodded. "If you're pregnant, I'll be able to tell you the age of the fetus."

I nodded and looked back at Will. His expression didn't change.

"And paternity?" I asked. "Can you do that on an unborn pup?"

The doctor nodded again. "Yes, Alpha. You won't be able to until six weeks gestation, though."

I nodded and took a deep breath.

"Thank you, doctor," I said just as I heard Savannah and my mother approach the room.

Will's jaw twitched. My heart raced.

I knew I wasn't pregnant. Even if I was, this pup wasn't mine. I just needed proof. I needed to be able to tell Maddie that I wasn't the father. I needed to assure my mate that I was completely hers, even if she didn't know it yet.

The door opened and Savannah walked in. My mother followed her in and closed the door.

I wondered why Savannah's parents weren't there. Why did she trust my mother and not her own family?

But I would never ask. I didn't give a shit. I was dying to get rid of her once and for all.

"Hello, miss," the doctor said kindly. "Please lie down and lift your shirt up a little."

I liked Dr. Jackson. He didn't waste my time.

Savannah looked at me, feigning pain. "Do we really have to do this, Dimitri? I'm carrying your puppy."

I resisted the urge to roll my eyes at her. I remained silent and pointed at the bed.

"You're going to regret this, Dimitri," my mother said, making me clench my jaw. "You'll apologize to Savannah in a minute."

I remained silent. I didn't even look at my mother. I kept my eyes fixed on Savannah and watched her lying on the bed.

My heart hammered in my chest. It felt like it was going to break my ribcage.

The doctor approached Savannah and put some clear gel on her lower abdomen. She flinched a little.

"I'm sorry, miss," the doctor apologized.

"It's okay," Savannah said, giving him a small smile.

The doctor started the exam, and I held my breath.

I could feel the nervousness in the room rising. Skol was on edge. I could feel his anger pulsing through me.

I looked at Savannah and saw her staring at the ultrasound screen. I looked back at her, but I couldn't see anything. I didn't even know what to look for.

"Well, miss, it looks like you are indeed pregnant," the doctor said, making my heart skip a beat.

No.

No, no, no, no!

It wasn't mine! It wasn't fucking mine!

Skol would know.

I could hear my blood pumping through my veins.

My mother and Savannah laughed excitedly.

"How far along are you?" I forced myself to speak.

Savannah looked at me and opened her eyes. "What does it matter, Dimitri? I already told you I'm pregnant. We're going to be parents in six months."

I didn't even look at her. I couldn't. Skol would rip her head off if I looked at her. She thrashed around and tried to get out.

"How far along are you, Doctor?" I asked, gritting my teeth and trying to keep Skol from getting out.

"Dimitri..." my mother spoke, but I interrupted her.

"I need to know how far along she is," I growled, looking at my mother. "

I haven't touched her in over a month. Skol can't sense the pup. If she's less than a month old, I'm not the father."

My mother looked at Savannah. She opened her mouth to speak, but I interrupted her again.

"How far along are you, Doctor?" I asked, looking from my mother to him.

"About two weeks, Alpha," the doctor said, and a huge rock fell from my chest.

A smile spread across my face and I looked at Will.

"That's not possible!" Savannah yelled as she tried to sit up. "Look again!"

I sighed and rolled my eyes. "Don't be ashamed, Savannah.

You tried to trap me, but it didn't work. Maybe you should talk to your pup's real father. Maybe he wants to take you as his chosen mate."

Savannah's eyes widened. My mother growled.

"Don't be rude, Dimitri," my mother said, making me look at her in disbelief. "Ultrasounds can be wrong. Savannah is telling the truth. He's your son.

Is she serious?" Will mentally linked to me.

I didn't respond. I didn't know what to say. He looked like he meant it.

What the fuck was wrong with him? Shouldn't I be mad at Savannah for lying and trying to trap me?

"What the hell are you talking about, mother?" I forced myself to speak.

"You should be mad at her for lying to me. This pup is not your grandson, mother."

Savannah sniffled, but it didn't bother me. Not even a little. If she wasn't actually pregnant, I would have exiled her. But I wasn't going to hurt an innocent puppy just because its mother was a lying bitch. I'd find another way to punish her.

"Could the ultrasound be wrong, doctor?" Will asked angrily. The doctor shook his head as he wiped the gel off Savannah's lower belly.

"No," he said. "The fetus is about two weeks old. The ultrasound wasn't wrong.

" "Then you are!" Savannah yelled at him before looking at me. "I want another doctor! "

I clenched my fists. I saw fucking red.

"You can have a million fucking doctors, Savannah, and this puppy still wouldn't be mine," I growled. "I'll order a paternity test as soon as I can and prove this puppy isn't mine."

I stood up and stormed out of the room. I couldn't stand to be around her anymore.

I couldn't wait to see Maddie. I needed her scent to calm me down. I needed to feel her against me to remind me that everything was going to be okay.

Chapter 27 Celebration

MADELINE

"We have guests, Mads," Seth said as he opened the kitchen door.

I nodded and gave him a small smile.

"I'll be right out," I said. "Give me a second to finish washing this."

Seth nodded and closed the door. I only had one dish left to wash, so I was out the kitchen door in a few minutes.

My stomach twisted painfully when I saw Janet sitting in one of the booths. Across from her sat a gorgeous woman and they both had huge smiles on their faces.

"Can you go serve them, Mads?" Seth asked. "I'm swamped. I really was. There were a lot of people tonight."

I gave him a small nod and walked over to the counter.

I sat in the booth where Janet and her friend were.

"Hi," I said, giving them a small smile. "Welcome to Macy's Diner. Can I take your order please?"

Janet looked at me and the smile disappeared from her face. It was replaced by anger. She looked me up and down and then a small smile appeared on her face.

"You should congratulate us before you take our order, Madeline," she said, making me furrow my eyebrows.

I looked at the woman sitting across from her. She was looking me up and down with disgust written all over her face.

"I'd love to, Janet, but I don't know why to congratulate you," I said calmly as I looked back at Janet.

She smiled and looked at the woman in front of her.

"We just got back from the exam," Janet said, walking over to the table and taking the woman's hand in hers. "Savannah is pregnant with my son's puppy."

I felt like a knife was being stabbed into my chest.

Why? Why did I care?

Was she pregnant? Was she really pregnant?

I looked at the woman and smiled.

"Congratulations, Miss," I said, forcing a small smile.

She looked up at me and narrowed her eyes. "I'm not a Miss. I'm your

Luna and you should get used to calling me that."

I swallowed the lump in my throat and bowed my head slightly.

"My apologies, Luna," I said quietly. "May I take your order, please?"

Calling her Luna sounded wrong. It burned my tongue and left an uncomfortable feeling in my stomach. She didn't belong with Alpha

Dimitri. He was such a kind man and I could already tell that this woman in front of me was a bitch. She was going to destroy this pack.

I clenched my jaw and forced a small smile.

I didn't care. This wasn't my pack and I was leaving the day I turned 18. Alpha Dimitri was just a nice man trying to make me feel welcome. I shouldn't care about his pregnant mate or his pack. They wouldn't even remember my name once I was gone.

"I'll just have a salad and a glass of water," Janet said and I could feel her eyes shooting daggers at me.

What had I done to make him hate me so much? Was it just because I was Mike's daughter? Did I remind him of the fact that Mike had a predestined mate?

"I'll have the same," said Alpha Dimitri's companion.

- Anything else? - I asked, forcing another small smile on my face.

Janet looked me up and down and narrowed her eyes.

"Make sure someone else brings us our order," Janet said coldly. "I don't want my grandson to contract some kind of disease because of you."

I felt anger boiling in my blood.

Janet looked at Alpha Dimitri's mate and sighed. You never know what kind of diseases these stray wolves carry.

The woman looked me up and down and frowned in disgust.

I wanted to wipe that ugly expression off her face.

"Go away, orphan," the woman said. "And make sure we don't bring the food."

I clenched my fists, gave them a small nod, and ran into the kitchen.

I was holding back angry tears. I hated that about myself. I often cried when I was angry and it only made me look weak. I wasn't weak.

I went back to the kitchen and took a deep breath.

"What's wrong?" Seth asked, causing me to look at him.

I gave him a small smile and shook my head.

"Nothing," I said. "Can you serve Janet and the woman with her? They both want a salad and a glass of water. I'll take a few of their tables."

Seth was silent for a few moments. He raised his eyebrows and gave me a small nod.

"Of course, Mads," he said, pointing at the plates on one of the counters. "Table three ordered burgers."

I nodded, walked over to the counter, grabbed the plates, and walked out to take them to our guests at table three.

"Enjoy your meal," I said as I set down the plates.

These guests were much nicer than Janet and Alpha Dimitri's mate. They smiled at me and engaged in small talk. I could feel Janet's eyes on my back the whole time.

I was so ready to leave this pack. I wished I didn't have to wait eight more months to do so.

I needed to spend as much time away from that house as possible.

I walked back into the kitchen and saw Seth preparing his salads.

—Is there going to be another party soon? —I asked, causing him to look up at me.

He smiled and raised an eyebrow at me.

"I don't get along very well with Janet," I sighed as I leaned against the counter. "I need to get out of that house."

Seth chuckled and looked back down at the salads he was preparing.

"There's another party next weekend," she said. "But if you want to get out of there, you and I could take a trip together. There's a wonderful lake not far from here. The walk is a bit long, but the lake is worth it."

—Yes! — I answered as soon as he stopped talking.

He looked at me and smiled.

"Deal," he said. "I'll tell my mother we won't be working tomorrow."

Guilt washed over me. I should have known better than to agree.

"Will that be okay with you?" I asked, biting my bottom lip. "We can go another time."

"Don't worry, Mads," Seth said, giving me a small smile. "My mom will be glad we decided to do something other than work."

I gave him a small nod and smiled.

He finished making the salads and walked out of the kitchen.

I took a deep breath and let it out slowly, trying to get rid of the sharp pain in my chest.

I couldn't wait to leave the pack.

Chapter 28 Consequences

DIMITRI

I had to stop myself from slamming into my office.

I couldn't believe the bitch was pregnant. She must have talked some poor bastard into sleeping with her and thought I wouldn't notice the time was off.

She must have thought I wouldn't care.

But I did. Of course I did. I had a beautiful mate who I loved with every part of my body and soul. I cared if someone tried to take her away from me. I cared if someone tried to destroy my future with her.

I needed Maddie. I needed her so bad.

I braced my hands on the windowsill, leaned forward, and took a deep breath.

"We need to think this through, Dimitri," Will said angrily. "We need to make the best decision possible for you and our pack."

I pictured Maddie's beautiful face in front of me. I pictured myself in her bed, holding her close to me. I remembered her scent and let it soothe my soul. It wasn't even close to the real thing, but it helped a little. It helped me take a deep breath and focus on Will.

He was right. I had a decision to make.

I turned around and walked over to my desk. I sat down and ran my fingers through my hair. Will was already sitting in his usual spot.

He had an angry look on his face.

"You should have been more selective about where you put your dick in," he muttered angrily.

I glared at him. "I know. You told me that."

He rolled his eyes and clenched his jaw. I knew how much he hated Savannah. I should have listened to him, but I never thought she was capable of something like that. She and I were friends for a long time before we slept together. She thought she was a nice person, but I was a naive fool.

"I'm sorry," Will muttered as he looked down at his lap. "It's like my anger has doubled since I met Maddie. She's my Luna and I need to protect her. I'm having a hard time controlling my anger now that there's a bitch trying to take

Maddie's rightful place.

" I understood him. He was a Beta and protecting his Luna was an instinct for him. It was his duty and his privilege to protect her.

"I know," I muttered. "I'm not even sure how I've managed to keep Skol inside all this time. He wants to tear Savannah apart."

Will nodded and set his jaw. He looked at me and I saw determination in his eyes.

"We're not letting Savannah take what belongs to Maddie

," he said. "Maddie is your mate and my Luna and I'll be damned if I'm letting Savannah take her place."

I smiled. I was so proud of my friend. Of course we weren't letting that bitch take Maddie's place. I was so fucking glad that Will was as protective of Maddie as I was. She knew she could count on him to keep her safe.

"We have to consider the potential consequences," I said, getting straight to the point. "If Savannah tells anyone she's pregnant with my pup, my wolves will expect me to mark her and make her my Luna."

Will nodded. "That's my main concern."

I swallowed and tried to take a deep breath.

"I have to wait four weeks so I can do the paternity test," I said. "I already ordered her not to tell anyone, but that was after she told my mother and her parents. I don't know if she's told anyone else."

"We have to talk to her and get her to tell us who knows," Will said.

I nodded. I have to order everyone not to spread the lie. My mother and Savannah's parents were already under my order. I didn't even think it would be necessary to put my mother under the alpha order, but I was so fucking wrong. I ordered her not to tell anyone after I told Maddie. I wish I'd done it sooner.

I wished Maddie didn't know. I wished I'd had the chance to tell her and explain.

"You should probably order them not to talk about it among themselves either," Will added. "I have a feeling Savannah's going to gloat about it around Maddie.

I saw the damn red." Will was right.

I ordered them not to tell anyone who didn't already know, but my order didn't stop them from talking about it to people who already knew.

"You're right," I muttered. "I should have thought of that sooner.

Why the fuck didn't I?"

"You have a lot on your mind, Dimitri," Will sighed. "You can't think about everything. That's what you have me for."

I gave him a small nod and took a deep breath.

He was right. My mind was in black and white. I was trying to figure out a way to get rid of Savannah as soon as possible. I was trying to keep up with my work in the pack. But most of all, I was trying to figure out a way to survive these long days without Maddie in my arms. I couldn't wait for the day when I could go see her whenever the fuck I wanted. I was dying to be able to kiss her and touch her whenever I wanted and needed to.

I glanced at the clock on the wall. Waiting until tonight would be torture.

"Are you still sleeping in Maddie's room every night?" Will asked, making me look back at him.

"Yes," I nodded. "I can't sleep without her."

Will shook his head, but a small smile crept across his face.

"What if she wakes up and sees you there?" he asked.

"I don't think that will happen," I said. "She sleeps better when I'm there." Will laughed and shook his head again.

"I hope you're right, man," he said. "If she wakes up and sees you there, she'll go crazy."

I frowned at him.

"She won't," I muttered. "She'd think of an excuse to be there."

I wasn't going to stop sleeping in her room. I wouldn't be able to fall asleep without her. There was no way I was going to stop. She was the only one who could keep me calm while I had to deal with Savannah. She was the only one keeping me from transforming and destroying everything around me.

I needed her, and I was dying to have her in my arms again.

Chapter 29 Behave, Madeline

MADELINE

I walked into the house and closed the door softly.

I didn't want Janet to know I was home. If Mike wasn't here, she would make sure to insult and threaten me.

"Honey!" I heard Mike's voice calling out to me from the kitchen.

Part of me was relieved that he was home. Another part of me was dreading going in there and seeing Janet. My stomach turned every time she looked at me. I could feel the hatred radiating off of her and it made me sick.

"Maddie?" Mike called out to me when I didn't answer.

I took a deep breath and headed into the kitchen. Mike was making dinner. He looked at me and smiled.

"Hey, honey," he said softly. "Are you hungry? I'm making lasagna."

I looked at Janet, who was sitting at the table. She was staring at me with such hatred that I winced.

"No, thanks, Mike," I muttered as I stared back at her. "

I ate in the cafeteria."

Mike frowned a little.

"Are you sure, honey?" he asked with a hint of concern in his voice. "Did you eat enough? Maybe just a small piece."

His fake concern was really annoying. Did he care if I ate enough when he was leaving my mother and me?

"I'm not hungry," I said politely.

Mike gave me a small nod and smiled.

"Okay, honey," he said. "Would you like to sit with us and talk for a while? I'd love to hear how your day was."

I swallowed the lump in my throat. Since when had he wanted to know how my day was?

I was so angry at him and I couldn't let it go. I felt the anger eating away at me, but no matter what he did or said to me, I couldn't stop it. I was mad at him. He left me.

He left my mother. He didn't care about me. He didn't try to contact me or ask about me. If my mother were still alive, he wouldn't even be in my life.

"I'm actually really tired, Mike," I said, my voice hoarse. "I'm going to take a shower and go to bed."

I saw the disappointment in his eyes. But I didn't care. It only made me angrier. What gave him the right to be disappointed?

"Okay, honey," Mike said, giving me another small smile. "I'll see you in the morning."

I nodded and looked at Janet. She was still looking at me angrily.

"Good night, Janet," I said politely.

"Good night, Madeline," she muttered coldly.

I looked back at Mike and gave him a small nod.

I turned and walked out of the kitchen. I wasn't lying to Mike. I was tired and just wanted to take a shower and go to bed. I hadn't eaten at the cafeteria, but I wasn't hungry. Even if I was, Janet's cold stare would kill my appetite.

As soon as I entered my room, I dropped my bag on the floor. I was about to open the bathroom door and walk in when someone burst into my room.

I turned around and froze to see a furious Janet standing by my bedroom door.

She looked furious and I felt fear wash over me.

"Is that any way to talk to your father, Madeline?" she asked as she took a step closer to me.

I raised my eyebrows slightly. I wasn't rude to Mike.

Janet walked over to me. I tried to take a step back but froze.

"You're rude and ungrateful, Madeline," Janet saddened as a silent growl escaped her. "

I won't tolerate that in my house."

I swallowed the lump in my throat.

"I'm sorry, Janet," I muttered under my breath. "I just wasn't hungry. I—"

She cut me off with a slap so hard I nearly fell over. I held my burning cheek and stared at her with wide eyes.

"Don't talk back, Madeline," she growled. "Mike may tolerate your rudeness, but I won't."

I swallowed and forced my legs to move. I took a small step back.

But it was a mistake. It only made her angrier. She took a step closer and grabbed me by the neck.

My eyes widened and I tried to move her hand, but it was no use. She was a werewolf. Even if I already had my wolf, she would be stronger than me.

"Don't you even think you can escape me, Madeline," she growled. "I'll do whatever the fuck I want to keep you at bay."

I tried to swallow, but her hand on my neck barely left me room to breathe. It was impossible to swallow or speak.

She smiled and loosened her hand a little.

"Don't even try to complain about this," she said coldly. "No one wants you here, Madeline, not even your father. He took you in out of guilt. He agrees with me that you need discipline."

My eyes widened again. I wanted to ask him why he wasn't here then. If he thought I needed discipline, why wasn't he here then? I didn't ask because I was afraid. I didn't want him to hit me again.

Janet smiled at me again. She let go of me and stepped back.

"Behave, Madeline," he said, making me clench my jaw.

"Don't make me hit you again because I will. Make things easier for all of us and make yourself invisible until you're gone."

I wished that would happen immediately. I wished I could leave the pack today.

But I couldn't. Not until I had my wolf. Not until I made enough money to start somewhere else.

Janet turned and walked out of my room, slamming the door shut.

I swallowed and took a deep breath. I wanted to cry, but I refused to. She didn't deserve my tears. I wasn't going to break her. I wasn't going to let her turn me into someone weak. I wasn't weak.

I clenched my jaw and walked into the bathroom. I needed that shower more than ever. I needed to wash the memory of her hands off my face and neck.

Chapter 30 Where is it?!

DIMITRI

Today was a little calmer. Skol wasn't as angry and my need to destroy everything around me wasn't as strong as it was yesterday.

Sleeping next to my princess helped me like I knew it would. I couldn't even remember what I was worried about while I was lying next to her. Everything seemed so irrelevant while she was in my arms. She was the only thing that mattered.

"You look better today," Will said as he walked into my office.

I smiled and gave him a small nod.

"Maddie is my cure for everything," I said, making him shake his head.

"I'm just waiting for the day you tell me she woke up and saw you there," Will said, chuckling. I

rolled my eyes. That wasn't going to happen. Skol was watching her and would let me know if he noticed her waking up.

"Not gonna happen, Will," I said. "Skol watches her while we sleep."

Will laughed again and gave me a small nod.

"Are you hungry?" he asked. "I was thinking you might want to go to the cafeteria and get something to eat."

My heart raced. I'd see Maddie again.

"I could eat," I said as I stood up.

Will smirked and followed me out of my office.

"Are you really hungry or do you just want to see Maddie?" Will asked teasingly as we walked out of the package room.

"Both," I muttered, looking up at him.

He had a huge grin on his face.

"I'm so happy for you, man," he said. "Maddie seems like a great girl."

A small smile spread across my face.

"That's amazing," I said, remembering how she clung to me the night before.

I felt like she needed me as much as I needed her. She held onto me tighter than ever before. Her body knew who I was to her, and I was dying for her to know that, too.

Luckily, the coffee shop wasn't far from the warehouse. Will and I arrived within minutes.

I saw Seth's mom, Macy, behind the counter. That was rare. Normally it was Seth who worked during the week.

Will and I sat down at our usual spot, and I glanced toward the kitchen door. Maddie wasn't out, so she had to be in the kitchen.

"Morning, Alpha," Macy said as she approached our table. "Morning, Beta. Can I take your order?"

I raised my eyebrows slightly.

"Morning, Macy," I muttered, glancing behind her.

Macy serving us wasn't usual. Even when she worked, she spent most of her time in the kitchen. Seth, and now Maddie, served everything.

Why was Macy serving us? Where were Seth and Maddie?

Did Maddie have the day off?

No.

I knew her schedule. She was supposed to be here today.

I stared at the kitchen door, waiting for Maddie to come out. I missed her already and I needed to see her.

"Where's Seth?" Will asked, making me look back at Macy.

She smiled and looked at Will.

"He and Maddie took the day off," she said happily. "They went on a hike together."

My heart stopped beating.

Skol stirred, and I could feel his anger pulsing. I had to bite back a growl.

"Hiking?" I forced myself to speak.

I couldn't breathe. I didn't know where I was, and I couldn't breathe.

Relax, Dimitri. Will mentally linked to me.

"Yes," Macy nodded. "Seth took her to Whispering Willow Lake."

Fear washed over me. This hike was dangerous. The trail was difficult even when the weather was perfect. It was steep and narrow, with jagged rocks and loose gravel underfoot. The trail wound along the edge of a cliff, with a sheer drop off to one side. It was even more dangerous now that it was snowing. What the fuck was Seth thinking? Not to mention that Maddie didn't have her wolf yet. Someone could attack them. Something could happen to her. She could fall and hurt herself. She could get hypothermia. She could—

I had to stop thinking about all the bad things that could happen to her. I couldn't let anything happen to her.

I had to go find her.

"It's a dangerous trail, Macy," Will said, his voice worried. "Why did Seth take her there?"

I tried to swallow the lump in my throat.

"Oh, don't worry, Beta," Macy said. "Seth knows that trail well. Nothing bad will happen.

I couldn't count on that. I had to go find her. If something happened to her...

Ask him how long ago they left." I mentally connected to Will.

"When did they leave?" Will asked.

"About an hour ago," Macy said, smiling.

Thank goodness. They didn't get far.

I stood up, making Macy look at me in confusion.

"I'm sorry, Macy," I muttered. "I remembered I have something important to do at the office."

I didn't wait for her response. I ran toward the trail.

Dimitri, maybe you shouldn't—" Will sent me a mental message, but I cut him off. "

I'm going to her," I growled. "Something could happen to her. I'll kill Seth if she's hurt.

Do you need help?" Will sighed.

No. Go back to the office and wait for me.

Will didn't mentally link me back. I forced my legs to run faster. If they'd been gone an hour, they surely hadn't made it to the most dangerous part of the trail. I didn't want them to get any closer. If something happened to her—"

Stop! Skol yelled at me. Stop thinking about it and run. We have to get her back.

She was at the beginning of the trail, and I caught a whiff of her sweet scent. I breathed it in deeply, letting it calm me down a bit. My whole body was shaking. I wasn't sure if I was shaking because I was scared or because I was angry. I wanted to tear Seth apart. Not only was he alone with my mate, but he put her in danger. I couldn't even think about him without wanting to tear him apart with my claws.

I took a deep breath, trying to calm my racing heart. I had to focus and find her before something happened to her. It would kill me. I had no reason to be in this world without her.

She was my heart and soul and I couldn't let anything happen to her.

Chapter 31 The walk

MADELINE

"Let me help you, Maddie," Seth said as he put his arm around my waist and lifted me up.

There was a huge boulder in our path. It was covered in snow and I couldn't see where I was going. Seth managed to get over it, but I couldn't. I was too short and didn't have the coordination to do it.

Seth put his arm around me and pulled me against his chest. He smiled at me as I walked over to him.

"I forgot you don't have your wolf yet," he laughed as he set me down.

"I don't think it'll get any better after I have my wolf," I muttered. "

I've always been a little clumsy."

Seth laughed as he fixed my hat and scarf.

"Are you cold?" he asked, making me shake my head.

"I'm okay," I said, giving him a small smile.

I was cold, but there was no way I was going back to that house any sooner than I had to. I wasn't going to let Janet hurt me again.

Seth smiled and took my hand in his.

"Watch where you step, okay?" he said as he continued walking. "

There are a lot of rocks here. "

I nodded and looked down at my feet. Seth wasn't wrong. I could see the sharp edges of the rocks beneath my feet. I couldn't see the size of the rocks or how many there were. The ground was covered in snow and was very slippery. I suddenly felt nervous. I could already imagine falling and breaking a few bones. I gripped Seth's hand tighter and gulped.

"I'm not going to let you fall, Mads," he said softly, causing me to look up at him.

He stopped walking and looked at me. He gave me a warm smile and I was so grateful for it. It helped me relax a little.

"I know," I said as I smiled back.

He smiled and turned around.

"I'm so excited to show you the lake," he said as he began walking again. "It's one of my favorite places in our territory."

A wave of excitement washed over me and for a moment I forgot about the slippery path I would have to cross to get there.

"It's beautiful in the spring, but I think I like it even more in the winter," Seth continued. "There's something magical about a frozen lake."

"I agree," I said as I looked around.

A small smile spread across my face. The branches of the trees were frozen and the ice made them look like they were glowing. The green branches of the pine trees around us created a beautiful contrast with the whiteness of the snow. The sun made it look like the snow on the pine branches were glowing.

The view was beautiful and I couldn't wait to get to the lake. I loved winter and the scenery that the snow created.

"Wait, Mads," Seth muttered as he pulled me back up.

There was another huge boulder in our path. I was just setting myself down when I heard someone yell my name.

"Madeline!" the voice shouted.

Seth and I both turned sharply. Seth's arm around my waist tightened. My eyes widened as I saw alpha Dimitri running toward us.

He looked terrified and panicked. He was running so fast and wasn't even looking where he was going. I was afraid he would slip and fall.

1◇

My heart raced. Had something happened? Had something happened to Mike?

Alpha Dimitri growled loudly when he saw Seth hugging me.

His eyes burned with fury, making my brows furrow.

"Alpha Dimitri," I muttered. "Did something happen?"

He didn't respond. He continued to approach us at a fast pace and ripped me out of Seth's arms as soon as he was close enough.

I gasped and grabbed onto his shoulders to keep from falling backwards.

Alpha Dimitri growled loudly. My entire body vibrated with the force of his growl.

"What the fuck were you thinking, Seth?!" Alpha Dimitri shouted.

"This trail is dangerous even without snow! He doesn't have his wolf yet! He could have fallen." Something could have happened to him! Are you crazy?!

My eyes widened as I looked at Seth. I could see a mix of fear and rage on his face. Alpha Dimitri held me tight. I couldn't move. I was so close to him that I could feel his heartbeat. His heart was pounding, hard.

"It's okay, Alpha," I forced myself to speak. "Seth's taking good care of me. Nothing will happen. I'll be okay."

He looked at me, a shiver running down my spine. I had no idea why his eyes on me were making weird things happen inside my body.

"You'll be okay because I'm taking you home," he said, growling under his breath.

He looked at Seth and set his jaw.

"I'm taking you both home," he continued. "That's an order, Seth."

I looked back at Seth and saw him nod. He set his jaw and looked at me.

"You can put her down, Alpha," Seth said. "I can take care of her."

Alpha Dimitri growled loudly again.

"I'm not putting her down," he said, causing the nervousness inside me to rise. "I'm not going to risk her getting

hurt."

I gulped and opened my mouth to tell him that she wouldn't be hurt, but he looked at me before I could say a word.

"Don't start, Maddie," he muttered under his breath. "I'm just making sure you're safe.

But why? Why did he care so much?"

Alpha Dimitri turned around and started walking back. I looked at Seth, who was following us. His fists were clenched and he had an angry look on his face.

"Don't you ever do something like that again, Madeline," Alpha Dimitri said sternly, causing me to look back at him. "You can't put yourself in danger like that."

I wanted to ask him why he cared, but the look on his face told me not to.

It was probably because of Mike. I was Mike's daughter, and he didn't want anything to happen to me.

I sighed and looked back at Seth. I saw him looking at me with a mix of emotions on his face. I gave him a small smile, but he didn't smile back.

I felt guilty. I ruined our trip. I would have to find a way to make it up to Seth.

Chapter 32 Tell him

DIMITRI

My heart was racing and it took a lot of my strength to stop Skol from taking over me and killing Seth.

Will you stop? I growled at him. I need to focus on her and get her home safely. You're distracting me.

Skol growled but let up on his pressure to get me to let go.

Did you see his arms around her? Skol growled. He's touched her. He's touched what's ours.

I clenched my jaw and forced myself to breathe as deeply as I could.

I saw that and wanted to rip her arms out. I shouldn't have touched her. I couldn't touch her. No one could touch her.

I held her tight and focused on her scent. I knew it would calm me down. And I needed to calm down before I turned around and snapped Seth's neck.

"Mine," Skol growled softly.

I focused on my mate in my arms and noticed she was shaking. A growl escaped me, making Maddie look at me in confusion.

"You're cold," I said as I stopped walking and set her down.

I started to take off my jacket, but she stopped me.

"I'm okay, Alpha," she said, looking up at me.

Her big green eyes made my knees go weak. Her skin was pale, but her lips, cheeks, and the tip of her nose were red from the cold. She looked adorable, and I wished I could capture her lips with mine.

"You're cold," I repeated, my voice quiet and raspy.

I took off my jacket, wrapped it around her, and picked her up again. I could tell she didn't want me to carry her, but I didn't give a shit. She'd put herself in danger. As I ran and tried to find her, I kept imagining her getting hurt.

I needed to hug her to remind myself that she was okay.

A small smile appeared on my face as I picked her up.

She had my jacket on and could smell my scent on it. Other men could do the same. Other males could smell me on her and they'd know to back off. But it wouldn't last long. Not until I marked her. After I did, my scent would be on her for the rest of our lives. Everyone would know she was mine.

No one would dare touch her or take her away from me.

I heard Seth behind us and rage hit me like a train.

I forgot he was there for a moment.

"What the fuck were you thinking, Seth?" I asked again. "What if something happened? She's cold. She could have fallen. She could have hurt herself."

"I would never let that happen, Alpha," Seth muttered. "He was taking good care of her.

I saw red. He touched her more than once, didn't he? He helped her more than once, didn't he? What exactly did he do? What exactly did he touch?

" "He's right," my princess added, making me look down at him.

"I wasn't in danger, Alpha. Mike shouldn't have sent you after me.

Oh, my princess.

He didn't send me after her. I went after her because she was my whole life.

I went after her because she was the most important person in my life. I went after her because just the thought of losing her made me sick. It made me want to scream and claw at my chest. I couldn't lose her. I couldn't let anything happen to her.

◈ ◈

But I couldn't let her know. I had to let her think Mike had sent me after her.

"Of course he did," I muttered. "He was worried something might happen, Maddie."

He looked at Seth and sighed.

"We can go on another hike, Seth," he said, making jealousy and anger flare up inside me. "Maybe there's another trail that isn't as dangerous and Mike won't care about me."

I gulped and forced Skol back.

No! he screamed. Mine! I

gritted my teeth and focused on breathing. He couldn't let out even a grunt.

"Sure, Mads," Seth said quietly. "We can go for the weekend."

No.

No, no, no, no.

Fear and jealousy would kill me.

"It's winter, Maddie," I said, trying to keep my voice from shaking. "It's not the time for hiking."

I clenched my jaw and kept my eyes on the trail ahead of us. I had to keep my anger in check. I couldn't let her see how fucking pissed I was. I didn't want her alone with him. He liked her and I was terrified that she would start to like him too. He probably hoped she would be his mate. He wasn't a werewolf and even if she was his mate, he wouldn't be able to tell until she got her wolf.

But she wasn't his. She was mine.

Maddie didn't say anything else.

"We need to tell Seth she's our mate and order him to stay away from her," Skol growled. "I'll go crazy if she runs off with him again."

I believed her. I'd go crazy too.

We can't do that, Skol, I muttered. I could still tell him.

You could go against Alpha's orders, but it was very painful to do so. Some wolves even died from the consequences of going against them. I couldn't risk it though. I couldn't risk Seth telling him.

She won't, Skol growled. Tell her and order her not to tell him.

I resisted the urge to roll my eyes.

We should tell everyone, Skol continued. Everyone should know that she belongs to us.

I swallowed. There was nothing I wanted more, but I had to think about her. She was my priority, not the jealousy or fear I felt.

How would she feel if she found out that everyone knew before her? She would be devastated, Skol. Finding your mate is something very special and beautiful. I'm not taking it away from her. I won't tell anyone. I'm not risking it.

Seth wouldn't go against your orders, Skol said stubbornly.

I ignored him. I wasn't going to risk it. I didn't even know Seth that well and I couldn't be sure he wouldn't try to tell her.

I looked at my princess and took a deep breath, letting her scent wash over me. I couldn't wait to lay down next to her again. I couldn't wait to hug her and kiss her soft cheek.

I was sure that my fear and anger would disappear as soon as I lay down beside her. Nothing else would help me. She was my cure for everything.

Chapter 33 The sample

DIMITRI

"How long until we get the results?" I asked the doctor as I watched him write something down.

I was dying for six weeks to come and I thought I was going to go crazy waiting for it. The only thing keeping me sane was Maddie and sleeping next to her every night.

I wanted the results as soon as possible. I wanted to send Savannah to hell as soon as possible.

"Why are you so eager to get rid of me and your daughter?" Savannah asked as she wiped her cheeks. "This is your pup, Dimitri. I am your Luna. We should be together, Dimitri."

I turned bright red. She wasn't my Luna and her pup wasn't mine.

"How long, doctor?" I asked, keeping my eyes on Savannah.

"A couple of weeks, Alpha," the doctor said, making the anger inside me explode.

I wanted it done today. I wanted it done now.

Savannah sobbed and hung her head.

"I wish you'd believe me," she said, sobbing loudly. "You're going to regret this. He's your pup, Dimitri."

I swallowed and clenched my jaw. I really wanted to punch him, but I wasn't going to hurt his pup. I wasn't that cruel.

I walked over to her and put my finger under her jaw. I lifted her head and studied her face for a few moments. She took this as a sign that I'd changed my mind.

She smiled and wrapped her arms around my waist. I pulled them back immediately. I was Maddie's. She had no right to touch me.

Her eyes widened and another fake tear fell down

her cheek.

"I'll give them some privacy," the doctor said as he gathered his things and walked out of the room.

I kept my gaze on Savannah the entire time. She looked angry, but I didn't give a shit. I was the only one who had the right to be angry. She lied to me and tried to take me away from my mate. She deserved to be punished and would be as soon as she gave birth to her pup.

Are you here? I mentally connected with Will as soon as the doctor closed the door.

I'm here. he replied. I'll walk him out. Don't worry.

I needed to secure the sample. I was afraid that Savannah or my mother would try to tamper with it. I was afraid that they would falsify the results to force me to take Savannah as my mate. I wasn't going to let that happen. The doctor and the sample he took had better security measures than I did when I traveled to other packs. Nothing was going to happen to the doctor or the sample. No one was going to tamper with the results.

Keep me posted. I told him and turned my focus back to the woman in front of me.

"I know what your plan was, Savannah," I said, causing his eyes to go wide. "You always wanted to be Luna, didn't you?

You thought you could do that by faking a pregnancy."

She gulped and shook her head. She wanted to speak, but I didn't let her.

"Your first plan backfired when I didn't believe you," I continued. "My reaction wasn't what you expected. You probably thought I'd be happy and accept you as my mate immediately.

I'd mark you, sleep with you, and you'd get pregnant.

I'd never know when exactly it happened and you'd get what you'd always wanted. "

She shook her head again.

"I didn't..." she spoke, but I cut her off.

"So you had to find another way to trick me." I sighed. "You found some poor man, fucked him, and got pregnant, thinking I wouldn't question anything. Do you think I'm stupid and naive?"

Anger filled me and I had to push Skol back. I was ready to go out and tear her apart.

"I haven't fucked anyone," she yelled. "This is your pup."

I laughed and shook my head.

"We both know that's not true, Savannah," I said. "In a couple of weeks, we'll have official confirmation and I wouldn't have to put up with you or your lies anymore."

She sniffled and hung her head.

"I can't wait to see the look on my mother's face when she realizes you've been lying," I said, causing her to look back at me.

Will suggested that my mother was somehow involved in Savannah's plan, but I didn't want to believe it. My mother could be unreasonable sometimes, but she was my mother. She would never hurt me like that. She just got excited at the idea of having a grandchild. I knew how hurt she would be when we got the test results back, but I also knew that I would have a real grandchild soon. Well, as soon as Maddie agreed to have a puppy with me. I was still a little young and I wouldn't be upset if she wanted to wait a little longer.

However, I couldn't wait to have puppies with Maddie. I imagined her being pregnant and my heart was bursting with happiness. Maddie and our child would have me wrapped around her little fingers. Maddie already did, but she just didn't know it yet.

"Your mother believes me," Savannah yelled. "She knows he's your pup."

I sighed and shook my head. "I wish she didn't. It'll hurt her more when the results come back."

Savannah's eyes widened again. I leaned down to look into her eyes.

"For the record," I said quietly. "The only pups I'll ever have will be with my fated mate. She'll be the only one to bear me a child and the only one I'll name Luna and Queen."

Anger flashed in Savannah's eyes and I smiled.

"You're nothing compared to my mate," I continued. "She's everything to me and I won't let you take her from me."

I didn't wait for his response.

I turned abruptly and walked out of the room, slamming the door behind me.

I had to get out of there before I lost control. I had to find Maddie. She was the only one who could calm me down. I needed her scent to enter my lungs and remind me that she was real and mine.

Chapter 34 Your partner

JANET

"He's found his mate!" Savannah yelled as she walked into my house.

I looked at her and raised my eyebrows. What the fuck was she talking about?

"Who?" I asked as I set my cup down on the table.

"Dimitri!" Savannah yelled, slamming the door shut.

My eyes went wide and I let out a loud gasp.

I studied her face closely, trying to see if she was lying to me.

"What the hell are you talking about?" I asked, my eyes narrowing. "He didn't find her. He would have told me."

Savannah clenched her jaw and slammed her hand on the kitchen island.

"He found her, for fuck's sake!" she yelled, her face growing redder. "He would never accept me or this fucking puppy!"

My eyes widened even further.

Savannah was crazy. Not only was she rambling on about something that never happened, she even looked like she was going to explode.

My son never found his mate. I would have known. He would have told me.

"Savannah..." I spoke, but she cut me off.

"Stop, Janet," she growled. "You got me into this damn mess and now he'll never make me Queen!"

I stood up and walked over to her. The madness in her eyes scared me a little.

I clenched my jaw and kept my cool.

"Calm down and tell me what happened," I said sternly. "There's no way Dimitri has found his mate. I would have known. He would have told me. He would have made her his Luna by now.

You misunderstood."

She chuckled darkly and clenched her fists. I watched her nails dig into her skin.

"Not if she's underage," she said angrily. "He didn't make her his Luna because he can't yet."

I furrowed my eyebrows again. But who? Who could it be? Who could it be?

And then it hit me.

"Madeline," Savannah said at the same time I realized.

No!

Fuck no!

I would never let that bitch become the Luna of this pack! She would never become queen! She would never become my son's mate.

I growled loudly.

"That's impossible!" I exclaimed, clenching my fists tightly.

"She's not his mate!"

Savannah rolled her eyes and walked over to the table. I turned to face her. She sat down, closing her eyes and taking a deep breath.

"Maybe it's not her, but he found her," she said quietly, "I'm sure of it." Anger made my blood boil and my heart race.

This wasn't Madeline. This couldn't be Madeline. That poor little bitch couldn't become the new queen. She wasn't good enough to be my son's mate. She wasn't good enough to be Luna. She was a desperate little girl who looked too much like her stupid mother.

She'd become Luna over my dead body.

"You'll be Luna," I said, making Savannah look at me. "If he really found her, we'll find out who she is and get rid of her.

If it was Madeline, I'd kill her. I'd find a way to get rid of her for good."

"He'll never let us near her," Savannah said, rolling her eyes. "If he found her, she's protected. We won't be able to do anything.

It would be so easy if it was Madeline. She was already terrified of me.

I've already punished her a few times. It would be so fucking easy to control that little bitch."

"But it has to be Madeline," Savannah sighed. "He changed after she came here. You were the one who said he liked her from the beginning. Who else could it be?"

I clenched my jaw and narrowed my eyes.

I didn't want it to be her, but Savannah was right. Dimitri had been very fond of her from the moment he saw her.

My stomach turned.

"You're right," I muttered angrily. "If he found her, it has to be Madeline."

My vision reddened and I suddenly felt the urge to move and destroy the house.

I didn't want it to be true. I had to find proof that it wasn't true.

Where had Savannah gotten the idea that she'd found her mate? Maybe it was her jealousy talking.

"Why do you think she found her?" I asked, gritting my teeth. "Did she tell you?"

She looked at me and shook her head.

"No," she told me. "But the way she talked to me told me that she'd found her. The things she said..."

She stopped talking and raised her eyebrows.

"What did she say?" I asked as I sat back down.

"He said the only kits he'll ever have will be with his mate," he sighed. "He said his mate will be the only one who will be his Moon and his Queen."

My vision went black. She was an idiot. That didn't mean she'd found her mate.

"What the fuck is wrong with you?" I growled at her. "That doesn't mean I've found her!"

She looked at me and rolled her eyes. "No, but what she said next does."

My heart skipped a beat.

"What did she say next?" I asked.

She clenched her fists and growled under her breath.

"He said I'm nothing compared to her mate," she said quietly. "He said she's everything to him and he won't let her take him from her."

I gulped.

"That still doesn't mean I've found her," I muttered, doubting my own words.

Savannah looked at me and shook her head.

"It doesn't mean," he said. "But it looks like he found her."

It looked like it. It really sounded like he did.

If it was Madeline...

" "We need to find out if it's that little bitch," Savannah said, gritting her teeth. "Dimitri's going to find out soon enough that he's not the father. I'll lose him. We need to find a way to keep him tied to me. We need to eliminate any threat."

I let out a dark chuckle.

"Don't worry," I said, smirking. If it really is Madeline, I'll make sure she never becomes his mate.

I'll take care of her before she gets her wolf.

Savannah smiled at me.

"What are we going to do to her?" she asked excitedly.

I kept the smile on my face and clenched my fists.

"We'll tear her apart," I said. "She'll leave the pack before she even gets her wolf. She'll die out there, and we'll be rid of that little bitch."

Chapter 35 Fleeing

MADELINE

I wasn't going to put up with this for another five months.

I closed my bedroom door and wiped the blood from the corner of my mouth. There was a huge lump in my throat and I couldn't swallow it no matter how hard I tried.

But I wasn't going to cry. I hadn't cried once in the past four months and I wasn't going to cry now either.

I'm going to leave and find a way to survive until I turn 18 and get my wolf. I'm going to hide somewhere. I'll be okay.

And even if something happened to me, they wouldn't miss me. I had no one to miss me. I had no family left. No one would even know I wasn't living or breathing anymore.

I walked over to my closet and opened it and pulled out my backpack. I couldn't take my overnight bag with me. It was too big and I couldn't run with it. I needed something small and practical. I wasn't going to take much anyway. I wouldn't need much to hide in the woods for a few months.

I grabbed two pairs of sweatpants, two shirts, a hoodie, and a few pairs of underwear. I had some energy bars in the closet, so I packed those in my suitcase, too. That was all I could fit in my backpack. I reached behind the folded shirts until I felt a small box at the tip of my fingers. I pulled it out and opened it. The tears I had been trying so hard to hold back were now falling rapidly down my cheeks. It was a locket with a picture of me and my mom in it. I carefully pulled it out and hung it around my neck. I didn't want to open it and look at the picture because I would never be able to stop crying if I did.

I missed my mom so much.

I pressed the locket to my lips and closed my eyes.

"I miss you, Mom," I murmured under my breath. "I miss you so much."

I took a deep breath and opened my eyes. I didn't have time for this. I had to go.

I grabbed some clean clothes and ran to the bathroom. I had to shower and change before I left.

I sighed contentedly as the warm water relaxed my muscles a little. I hissed when it grazed my split lip.

Janet had screwed up. She had never hit me hard enough to leave a mark or draw blood. She was always so careful not to let anyone know.

Not that anyone would believe it if they found out. She was a former

Luna and I was nothing and no one. I didn't even have my wolf yet. I wasn't even a member of the pack. No one would believe that their Luna was abusing me.

Well, it wasn't just her anymore. A few weeks ago, Alpha Dimitri's mate joined in as well. She was surprisingly strong for being pregnant. They both hated me for some unknown reason and they both enjoyed torturing me. They wanted me gone, and I would make their wish come true.

Mike had no idea and was never home. He made me breakfast every morning and then disappeared late into the night. He kept smiling at me, calling me sweetheart and telling me how happy he was that I was here. Well, we were one now. I wasn't glad to be here and I was going to run away never to come back.

I finished showering, dried my body with a towel and put on clean clothes. I tied my hair into a ponytail and looked at myself in the mirror. My lip didn't look too bad.

I took a deep breath and walked out of the bathroom. I couldn't waste any more time. I had to leave before Mike came home.

I grabbed my jacket and backpack and walked over to the window I used to sneak out of the house.

I looked into the bedroom and gulped. This room was my only safe space in this house. No matter what happened to me, I could always sleep peacefully here. That had changed in the last two days and it was another sign that it was time for me to leave.

I sighed, opened the window and threw my backpack and jacket on the floor.

I grabbed the nearest tree branch and walked out of my room.

I put my jacket on as soon as I stepped on the ground. I threw my backpack on my back and started walking into the woods. I didn't look back. I didn't need to. I didn't want to see that house again. Apart from my room, nothing in that house held a special place in my heart.

I had barely set foot inside the woods when I heard my name being called.

"Maddie?" Seth's voice chilled me.

What the hell?

I looked to my left and saw him approaching me in nothing but short sweats. He was sweaty and his hair was a mess.

"What are you doing?" he asked, his eyebrows furrowing.

Holy shit.

I couldn't believe I'd been caught so soon. I'd expected trouble at the border, but not just a few feet from

Mike's house.

"I'm going for a walk," I muttered as I felt the nervousness building inside me.

It was a lame excuse, but it was the only thing I could come up with.

Seth narrowed his eyes and crossed his arms over his chest. I gulped, trying to think of something to say. My mind was completely blank.

"With a backpack?" he asked as he walked over to me and pulled the backpack off my shoulder.

I tried to stop him, but he was stronger. He opened the backpack and growled.

"What the hell, Maddie?!" he exclaimed as he looked back at me.

I gulped again and tried to take a deep breath.

"You're not leaving, Madeline," Seth said as he grabbed my arm and started pulling me deeper into the woods. "

Why the hell are you leaving?! Are you crazy?!" They'll kill you!

Where the hell was he taking me?

"I'll be okay, Seth," I sighed as I tried to wriggle out of his grip.

He growled and looked back at me.

"I'm not letting you go, Madeline," he said angrily. "You're my best friend and I'm not losing you."

I gulped and let him drag me into the woods. I couldn't escape his hold no matter how hard I tried.

Chapter 36 The results

DIMITRI

I had a huge smile on my face.

I was holding the envelope that proved Savannah's pup wasn't mine and I felt like I was going to explode with happiness.

I had been right all along. The pup wasn't mine.

"I can't believe you had to wait almost three months for the results to come back," Will sighed, shaking his head.

"I don't give a shit, Will," I said, placing the envelope on the desk. "The results are here and that's all that matters. The pup isn't mine. I can finally tell her to fuck off."

Will laughed and shook his head.

"You've told her that several times already," he said, making me roll my eyes.

"Yeah, but now she can't hurt me no matter what she does," I said, smiling again. "Even if she goes against my orders and tells someone, her lie can't hurt me. I have proof that the pup isn't mine."

I opened the envelope and looked at the results again. I smiled brightly.

"Are you sleeping with Maddie again tonight?" Will asked me.

I looked up at him and nodded.

"I need to," I said. "I miss her too much."

I hadn't slept in her room the past few nights because we had a problem with the borders. I barely left my office. I hadn't seen Maddie in a few days and it was driving me a little crazy. My heart wouldn't be able to make it through another night without her.

I swallowed and clenched my fists. I imagined lying next to her.

I imagined her turning to me and resting her head on my shoulder. I imagined giving her a small kiss on the forehead. I imagined breathing in her intoxicating scent.

I missed all of that so much and I was dying to go

see her tonight.

"It's a quiet night at the border," Will said, making me look back at him. "You definitely have to go see her. You almost ripped Peter's head off today."

I sighed and gave him a small nod.

Peter was the leader of my patrol and I was furious with him because none of my wolves were able to capture the rogues that were causing trouble on my border. They kept attacking my wolves and backing away. They never tried to cross the border, but they were always present there. I wanted to capture one of them and torture the answers out of them.

But most of my frustration came from not having seen my mate for a few days. I missed her like crazy and needed to spend some time with her before I ripped someone's head off for real.

"Is Savannah coming?" Will asked, smiling a little.

"Yes," I nodded. "My mother is coming too. I wanted to tell her as soon as possible.

I was dying to see Savannah's face when I showed her the paper. I was a little sad because I knew my mother would be disappointed, but she would give her a grandchild as soon as Maddie

wanted to have children.

I could hear them approaching my office and couldn't help but smile widely.

"I can't wait to see Savannah's face," Will murmured quietly.

I looked at him and smiled in satisfaction.

"It'll be priceless," I said just as the door opened and my mother and Savannah walked in.

Savannah's belly was huge. She was only a month away from giving birth.

"I have wonderful news!" I exclaimed as soon as they walked in.

Savannah smiled happily. My mother looked at me with half-lidded eyes.

"Have the test results come back?" Savannah asked excitedly. "Have you finally seen that I'm telling the truth?"

I smiled, my heart skipping a beat. I was so fucking happy.

"The results came back," I confirmed. "And they proved that I was telling the truth all along. The puppy isn't mine."

Savannah's eyes widened. My mother groaned quietly.

I opened the desk drawer and handed the copy of the results to Savannah.

"I'm sorry your pup is left without a father," I said, "But maybe you could talk to the real father and ask if he'd like to be involved."

I hated Savannah, but her pup was innocent. He deserved at least one decent father. I didn't know who the father was, but I hoped it would be someone who would take good care of his son.

Savannah sniffled and looked down at the paper I'd given her.

I looked at my mother and expected to see sadness on her face. The anger I saw surprised me. What surprised me more was that she wasn't mad at Savannah. She was mad at me.

"You faked test results for your mate?" my mother asked angrily. "Why did you do this to

Savannah, Dimitri? I raised you better than that."

My eyes widened and anger flared inside me. What the fuck was he talking about?

Does he know about Maddie? Will mentally linked me and I could hear concern in his voice.

I didn't answer him. I couldn't.

"What the fuck are you talking about, Mother?" I growled. "What mate?"

"You found your fated mate, didn't you?" Savannah sobbed. "I knew when that doctor took your sample a few months ago and you talked about her like you already knew who she was. You found her and faked the results.

My heart stopped beating. I screwed up.

" "I didn't find her," I said, trying to remain calm. "I talked about her like that because I was pissed off that you tried to take her away from me. I never even got a chance to find my mate and you thought you could trick me into making you my

Luna.

" Will growled under his breath. I clenched my fists. I really wanted to punch him.

"Get the fuck out of my office," I growled. "The moment you give birth, you will be exiled from the pack. I will not tolerate this kind of behavior."

Savannah's eyes widened.

"Dimitri!" my mother scolded me. "You can do that! This is the mother of your-"

"Don't finish that sentence!" I yelled as I pounded my fists on the desk. "Get the fuck out of here, both of you!"

I was furious. It took so much fucking effort for me to keep Skol from surfacing and ripping them both to shreds.

My mother took Savannah's hand in hers and began to lead her out of my office. Savannah was sobbing uncontrollably.

"You really need to go see Maddie," Will said softly as soon as my mother closed the door. "You're going crazy."

She was right. I needed my princess and I needed her right now.

Chapter 37 Who did that to you?!

MADELINE

Seth dragged me to one of the patrol cabins in the middle of the woods.

I could feel the anger coming off of me in waves.

"Seth, I..." I spoke, but he cut me off.

"Don't even start, Madeline," he growled as he slammed the door shut.

He crossed his arms over his chest and looked at me with narrowed eyes.

"Do you have any idea what couldn't have happened?" he asked through gritted teeth. "You don't have your wolf yet. You couldn't defend yourself. You'd be dead the moment you set foot over the border. Why would you try to leave, Madeline? Why?"

His voice was shaking as he finished speaking. His face was a mix of anger and fear.

I gulped, guilt washing over me.

"Why, Madeline?" Seth asked again after I didn't respond.

I tried to take a deep breath, but the lump in my throat prevented me from doing so. I

couldn't think of an answer. I didn't know what to say to her. I couldn't tell her the truth.

"Madeline..." Seth spoke but stopped abruptly.

His eyes widened and his breath caught in his throat. I furrowed my eyebrows in confusion. What the hell had happened?

He walked over to me so abruptly that I didn't even see him move. He gently grabbed my chin and tilted my head up slightly.

Shit. He saw it.

"What the hell happened?!" he yelled as he bent down to get a better look at my split lip. "Who did that to you?"

I gulped and tried to work my brain. But it was completely useless. No matter how hard I tried, I couldn't come up with an answer.

"I fell," I muttered, knowing immediately that it was the most pathetic excuse possible.

Seth looked up and growled.

"Don't lie to me, Madeline," he said sternly. "Someone did it. Who did it? Was it Mike?"

My eyes went wide and I shook my head as best I could because he was still holding my chin in his fingers.

"No," I said, my heart racing. "It wasn't Mike. No one hurt me. I fell."

Seth growled again. He let go of me and stood up straighter.

"Is that why you tried to leave?" he asked sternly. "Is someone hurting you? You tried to get away from them, didn't you, Madeline?

Shit.

He was right about everything and I hated it. I couldn't tell him the truth. I couldn't tell him that his Luna and his future Luna had been hurting me for months.

So I just shook my head.

Seth groaned in annoyance. He ran his fingers through his hair and began to pace around, still staring at me.

"Goddess, Madeline, you didn't want to leave because everything is great," he said angrily. "You wanted to leave because something happened."

He looked at my lip and gulped.

"Someone hurt you, Madeline, and I want you to tell me who it was

," he continued. "I want you to tell me who it was to rip his head off his body."

A shiver ran down my spine. He would be punished if Alpha Dimitri heard him talk about his mother and his mate like that. I couldn't let him do that. I couldn't let him get hurt because of me.

"No one..." I spoke, but Seth interrupted me again.

"Don't do it, Madeline!" he exclaimed, pointing a finger at me. "Don't lie to me!"

I took a deep breath and let it out slowly.

"I fell and bit my lip, Seth," I muttered.

His eyes widened and he stopped pacing. He clenched his fists and furrowed his eyebrows.

"Why are you lying to me?" he asked. "I can protect you, Maddie. I want to protect you. I need to protect you."

My heart skipped a beat. The softness of his voice made me shiver. No one in this pack cared about me as much as he did, and I couldn't let him get hurt. I couldn't let anything happen to him. I had to protect him, too.

I looked down at my feet and closed my eyes.

"I fell," I repeated softly. "I fell and bit my lip. No one hurt me. I want to leave this pack because I don't belong here. I want to go back to my old pack."

He didn't respond, but I heard him slowly approach me. He put his arms around me and kissed the top of my head.

"I can't let you do that, Mads," he murmured. "I can't let you go. I'd die if anything happened to you, Madeline."

He placed a finger under my chin and slowly lifted my head. I opened my eyes to see him looking at me with so much love in his that I almost burst into tears.

"I'll protect you, Maddie," he whispered. "I'll always protect you."

He looked at my lips and a rush of heat washed over me. His arm around my waist tightened. He clenched his jaw and swallowed.

"You don't have to tell me who did it," Seth said softly, making my brows furrow. "But you have to let me protect you, Maddie. You have to stay with me and let me protect you."

I took a deep breath and let it out slowly. Seth reached up and caressed my cheek softly. He looked at the cut on my lip and frowned.

He let go of me and walked over to one of the cabinets in the small living room.

"What are you doing?" I asked.

"I'm taking care of your lip," he murmured and turned around. I saw a small first aid kit in his hands.

"You don't have to do that, Seth," I protested. "I'm fine."

Seth rolled his eyes, grabbed my hand, and pulled me over to the couch. He sat down and forced me to sit next to him. I watched as he opened the medicine cabinet and pulled out some clean gauze and some rubbing alcohol. He put some rubbing alcohol on the gauze and turned to me.

"You can stay with me, Maddie," he said as he began to wipe the gauze across my lip, making me flinch a little.

I raised my eyebrows.

"You can come live with me," he explained. "It'll be easier for me to protect you if I can keep an eye on you at all times." I was about to tell him that he didn't need to when the cabin door slammed open and a very pissed off Alpha Dimitri burst inside.

Chapter 38 Don't do that again!

DIMITRI

I thought I was going to lose my mind when I saw her empty room.

I thought I was going to lose my temper and fly into a rage. I was already on edge and walking into her empty room made me boil with rage.

But that was nothing compared to storming into the patrol booth and seeing her there with Seth. That was nothing compared to watching her tend to her split lip.

My heart stopped beating and I nearly passed out.

She was hurt. My princess was hurt.

I stared at her with wide eyes, unable to move. I couldn't look away from the wound on her lip. It wasn't big, but it felt huge to me. It was a symbol of my failure as a partner. I didn't protect her. She was hurt and I wasn't there to stop it.

"What the fuck happened?!" I forced myself to speak.

I looked at Seth and saw red. One of his hands was on her knee. He was touching her. He was touching what belonged to me! I could feel my heart beating in my eyes. Anger was coursing through my veins, making it impossible for me to feel anything else.

Skol was screaming and thrashing around inside of me. I tried to ignore it, but it was so fucking hard.

"She..." Seth spoke up, but Maddie cut him off.

"She fell," she said, making me flinch. "I went for a walk and I fell. Seth is helping me."

I gritted my teeth and tried to take a deep breath. But it was impossible. Panic had taken over me. I forced my body to move and slammed the door shut. I walked over to her and grabbed the gauze from Seth's hand.

They were both staring at me with wide eyes.

"Move," I growled at Seth, making him narrow his eyes slightly.

"It's okay, Alpha," he said. "I can take care of her. You don't have to—"

"Move," I growled again, interrupting whatever he was going to say next.

I was furious and jealous as hell. I wanted to rip her head off, but I couldn't do that to Maddie.

Seth looked back at her and did as he was told. I sat down next to my princess and lifted her head so I could look at her lip.

"How the hell did you manage to hurt your lip like that?" I asked, trying to hold back a growl.

I lifted the gauze and gently patted her lip. She flinched a little, causing me to grab her tightly around the waist. She relaxed under my touch and a wave of relief washed over me. Her body knew who I was.

"I fell and bit it," Maddie muttered, looking at Seth.

I frowned and remembered what he'd said earlier. I didn't realize it before because I was so fucking angry and scared that I didn't

hear properly.

She went for a walk.

We had a problem and she went for a walk in the woods.

Fear exploded inside me and I nearly threw up. If something had happened to her... If they had somehow trespassed on my territory and hurt her...

My vision blurred and I growled loudly. She flinched and I gripped her tighter.

"You said you were out for a walk?" I asked, blinking hard to regain my vision.

She nodded and I nearly screamed in terror. I tossed the gauze onto the small table and cupped her cheeks. She was breathing heavily and I was sure my heart was going to jump out of my chest. She stared at me with wide eyes.

"Don't you ever do that again!" I exclaimed, trying to control the fear I felt.

I took a deep breath and clenched my jaw.

"Listen to me, Madeline," I said sternly. "I forbid you to go out for walks without me present. I forbid you to leave the house unless it's to go to work. If you want to go somewhere, I'll go with you.

Is that clear?"

My heart was beating so fast that my ribs were starting to ache. Skol's panic wasn't helping matters one bit. He was even more scared than I was.

Maddie's eyes widened even more. Her eyebrows furrowed.

"That's not fair, Alpha," Seth spoke up, causing the anger inside me to rise. "She's not a prisoner. She can go wherever she wants."

I growled loudly and looked at Seth. I'd just started my patrol, so I didn't know about the rogues yet. But that didn't give him the right to question my decisions. I was his Alpha and Maddie was my mate. Mine!

"We have a rogue problem," I said, keeping my eyes on Seth. "They could have overstepped our boundaries. They could have attacked her. They could have hurt her. I'm not forbidding her from leaving the house because I want to take her prisoner, I'm forbidding her because I want to keep her alive."

Seth's eyes widened. He looked at Maddie, and I saw pure terror on his face.

I ignored him and looked back at my princess. I still had her face in my arms. I caressed her cheeks with my thumbs and looked at her lip. My heart clenched painfully. I wanted to heal it. I wanted to kiss it and make it go away.

"I'm sorry I scared you, Maddie," I said, looking back into her gorgeous green eyes. "I can't let anything happen to you. Please do what I say, okay? I can't let them hurt you."

"She will, Alpha," Seth spoke instead of her. "I'll make sure she follows the rules."

He looked at her with a stern expression. His arms were crossed over his chest and his jaw was set.

"I was thinking she could come live with me," Seth said, causing me to freeze. "I'd keep an eye on her and make sure something like that never happened again.

Fuck no. Over my fucking dead body.

" "No," I growled at him. "I can keep her safe.

I was moving in with my mom. Enough was enough. I couldn't let her get hurt and I couldn't let Seth take her away from me.

I looked back at my princess and gave her a small smile.

"Come on, Maddie," I said softly as I pulled my hands away from her beautiful face and took her hand in mine. "

I'll take you home. "

I stood up and pulled Maddie behind me.

"Thanks for helping her," I told Seth. "I'll take it from here."

He wasn't happy, but there was nothing I could have done.

I was her alpha and my word was final. Seth gave me a small nod and looked at Maddie.

"I'll see you at work tomorrow, okay?" he said, and Maddie gave him a small nod.

Seth walked over to the door and bent down to grab a backpack off the floor. He turned around and handed it to Maddie.

"Are you staying here?" Maddie asked, making him nod.

"I'm on patrol tonight," Seth confirmed.

"Be careful," Maddie said with a hint of concern in his voice.

Seth gave her a small smile and hugged her. I held onto her hand tighter, wishing I could pull her away from him.

"I will, Mads," Seth said quietly.

He finally let go of her and I pulled her out of the cabin. I had to get her as far away from the woods as possible. I had to get her as far away from Seth as possible.

Just five more months and she wouldn't have to go through something like this again.

Chapter 39 She is not my partner

MADELINE

I let Alpha Dimitri drag me out of the cabin. I couldn't escape his hold even if I wanted to.

"You can't put yourself in danger like that again, Madeline," he told me sternly. "Do you know what I'd do to—"

He stopped talking and took a deep breath. He looked at me and clenched his jaw.

"Do you know what that would do to Mike?" he finished his question, but I got the feeling that wasn't what he really meant.

His jaw twitched.

"I'd kill him, Maddie," he said. "It would hurt him so much if something happened to you."

I looked away and swallowed. Mike had never cared about my safety, so why start now? He didn't even realize that his own mate had been abusing me for months. Every room in the house was soundproofed, but that was no excuse. If he cared, he would have noticed that I flinched every time he came near me. He just didn't care.

I wondered what Alpha Dimitri would say if he knew I wasn't going on a walk. I was leaving his pack for good.

"Promise me you'll never leave the house without me, Maddie," he said, making me look back at him.

I furrowed my eyebrows. How was that going to work? Would I have to call him to tell him I wanted to leave the house? Would I have to wait for him to come get me? He had work. He couldn't be my
    personal bodyguard.

"I can't promise you that," I said, making him sharply turn his head toward me. "You have work to do. You don't even live there.

Are you going to abandon everything and everyone just because I want to go on a walk?

His mate wouldn't like that and it would give him another reason to hurt me.

"Oh, I'm moving out until the threat is over," he said, making me gasp loudly. "I'm not going to let this happen again." I'll be there most of the time, and you won't be allowed to go anywhere if I'm not there to take you.

Was I crazy? I was, wasn't I?

"You can't do that, Alfal," I exclaimed and stopped walking. "What about your mate? She's about to have a child. You can't..."

He growled loudly, interrupting whatever I was going to say next.

"She's not my mate and her child isn't mine," he said, making me gasp in shock.

How?

Alpha Dimitri sighed and ran his fingers through his hair. He gripped my hand tighter and looked at me with a sad expression.

"She lied and tried to trap me," he said. "She wanted to become Luna and Queen by trying to convince me that she was pregnant with me. I knew she was lying the moment she came to tell me that she was pregnant.

My heart clenched painfully. He must have been in a lot of pain.

"How did you know she was lying?" I asked quietly.

"I'm a werewolf and my wolf would have known if she was carrying his pup," Alpha Dimitri explained. "Plus, the timing didn't match up." She got pregnant after we had—"

He stopped talking and took a deep breath. I furrowed my eyebrows. He looked a little embarrassed. Why?

"I only slept with her a couple of times," he muttered, looking down at his feet. "It meant nothing and now I regret it."

He looked at me and swallowed.

"I regret everything about her," he said. "She tried to separate me from my mate and I—"

He stopped talking and my heart skipped a beat. Her mate? So she found her?

" "You found your mate?" I asked quietly and an unfamiliar feeling stirred inside me.

I didn't recognize it, but it was uncomfortable. I chose to ignore it. It didn't matter.

The fact that she had found her mate shouldn't have made me uncomfortable.

He clenched his jaw and swallowed.

"No," he muttered. "But I already love her with all my soul and heart.

I fought for her, Maddie." I did everything I could to prove to everyone that that pup isn't mine and I did it all for my princess. I can't lose her before I even have her so I fought as hard as I could.

My heart skipped a beat. The intensity of his gaze sent shivers down my spine.

"I fought and I won," he continued quietly. "I will never let anything or anyone come between me and her. She is the most important thing in my universe and I am going to prove it to her until my dying breath."

His voice was shaking as he finished speaking. I froze completely. My heart was racing and it was all I could feel. I was glad we had stopped walking a while ago because I couldn't feel my legs anymore.

The way he talked about her made me want to...

No.

I couldn't even let myself finish that thought. I wasn't her. I never would be. I didn't want to be her. I wanted to leave this pack and never come back.

I cleared my throat and forced myself to speak because the silence was getting awkward.

"She's a lucky girl," I murmured under my breath.

Alpha Dimitri smiled, making my knees buckle.

"I'm glad you think so," he said as he reached up and caressed my cheek. "And I hope she'll forgive me for the mistakes I made."

I smiled back at him and nodded.

"I'm sure he will," I said softly.

His smile grew and I felt something weird in my stomach. It was a tickling feeling I'd never felt before.

"I'm so glad you came to my pack, Maddie," Alpha Dimitri said. "I'm so glad I met you."

I didn't know what to say to him. I was glad I met him too, but I wasn't glad to be here. I wanted to leave and I would leave the first chance I got.

I forced a small smile on my face and decided to tell him just a small part of the whole truth.

"I'm glad I met you too," I said, forcing a small smile. "Thank you for taking care of me."

Alpha Dimitri smiled and pulled me into an unexpected hug.

"Always, Maddie," he said as he placed a small kiss on the top of my head. "I'll always take care of you."

I shuddered and swallowed the lump in my throat.

Five more months and that would no longer be possible.

Chapter 40 Time flies

DIMITRI

I paced around my office, trying to figure out what the fuck to do.

"The packs are reporting multiple attacks, Alpha Dimitri," Peter said quietly. "Something serious is going on."

"Maybe we should call a meeting," Will suggested. "

We need to figure out what the fuck they want.

" I clenched my fists and continued pacing. I was pissed off and wanted to take these bastards on alone. I wanted to capture them all and torture the answers out of them. Why were they attacking the packs? Why were they attacking my kingdom? What the

fuck did they want?

Every rogue we've captured so far let us torture them to death. None of them talked. None of them told us the truth. None of them told us who was behind it and what their ultimate goal was. I could only guess, and my only idea was that they were after my throne.

"Hazio," I said, trying to hold back a growl. "Call every Alpha in here. We have to fight back. I can't let them kill our people. I can't let them hurt anyone else. "

Will nodded and walked out of my office.

"Do you need anything else, Alpha?" Peter asked, forcing me to look at him.

I stopped pacing and shook my head.

"No," I said. "Keep the borders safe and capture as many as you can. Hopefully at least one of them will talk."

Peter gave me a small nod and walked out of my office.

I ran my fingers through my hair and closed my eyes. I was so fucking angry lately. I wanted to wreak havoc on the scoundrels who were attacking my packs and my Kingdom. I wanted to show them what happened when you messed with one of the strongest werewolves in existence.

I clenched my fists and opened my eyes.

I wasn't going to let them win. I wasn't going to let them destroy what my father fought so hard to build. I was going to protect my Kingdom. I was going to protect my people. I was going to protect my father's legacy.

I took a deep breath and pictured my princess's face in front of me. Knowing that her birthday was only two weeks away was the only thing keeping me sane. Just two more weeks and she would be mine. Just two more weeks and I would sink my fangs into her perfect neck.

I could finally kiss her and I could finally run my fingers over her body.

Living with her for the past 4 and a half months was torture. She was so fucking close, yet so fucking far away. I saw her every day, but I could never touch her. Well, except at night.

I slept with her as often as I could. I couldn't pass up the chance to hold my princess in my arms.

My mother wasn't too happy about me moving away. She suspected it was because of Maddie and she didn't like it. I ignored her and never confirmed or denied it. Mike was thrilled that I was living with them. He kept saying how wonderful it was that Maddie and I got along. She kept repeating that we were step-siblings and I wanted to rip my ears off every time she said it. She wasn't my step-sister. She was my partner.

My beautiful, kind, perfect little partner that I hadn't seen all day and that I missed so much.

Two weeks.

Just two more weeks and she would be mine. Just two more weeks and I wouldn't have to spend a second without her. She would be by my side at all times. I would make sure she was always around and that I could always see her. I had 9 months of frustration to heal and I knew it would take a lot.

I needed to go home and see her. I was so fucking angry about everything that was happening and she was the only one who could calm me down.

I also needed to go home to make sure she was safe. Ever since the scoundrel attacks started, I was constantly terrified of them breaking into my territory and hurting her. I knew I would know as soon as they crossed the border and they would never be able to get to her, but my fear wasn't rational. I was completely paranoid and guided by nothing but my overprotectiveness and over possessiveness. She was mine and just the thought of someone hurting her made me ready to kill.

Let's go home, Skol said. You make me nervous when you think about these things, Dimitri.

I knew that already. I could feel his nervousness growing. He shifted and quiet growls escaped him.

But he was right. It was time to go home to my princess.

I'm going home. I mentally linked to my Beta. Keep me informed of the meeting.

Say hi to Maddie. Will said. I've already started texting. 'I'll let you know when I hear from anyone.'

Thanks. I said and cut our mental link.

Luckily, my mother's house wasn't far from the pack house and I was walking through the front door only 5 minutes later.

"Dimitri?" I heard Mike's voice coming from the kitchen.

I looked up and groaned. I knew my princess was upstairs. She never spent time with my mom and Mike. I wanted to go see her, but I knew my mom would tell me off for not saying hello.

I clenched my fists and walked into the kitchen.

My mom and Mike were sitting at the table, eating dinner. I raised my eyebrows. Where was Maddie? Why wasn't she eating with them?

"Where's Maddie?" I asked before either of us could speak.

"She said she's not hungry," Mike said, pointing to the chair at the head of the table. "Come eat with us."

She wasn't hungry? Oh, she was in a sermon. She had to... eat.

"I'll eat a little later," I said. "I'm going to go get Maddie."

She needs to eat.

Mike smiled and gave me a small nod. "I couldn't convince her. Maybe she'll listen to you."

Of course she would. She had to listen to me. I wasn't going to let her get sick. She wasn't eating enough anyway. I wasn't going to let her skip meals.

I turned around and ran to her bedroom.

"Maddie?" I called out as I pounded on her bedroom door. "Dinner's ready. You need to eat."

My heart raced when she didn't answer. Was she asleep?

"Maddie?" I called out as I opened the door.

My eyes fell on the open window that I knew she used to get out of the house without Mike or my mother seeing her. She wasn't here. She was gone. Gone without me.

My heart stopped beating.

Chapter 41 Drunk

MADELINE

Two more weeks and I could leave this pack. Two more weeks and I'd never have to see Janet's face again. Two more weeks and I'd never have to hear her call me a little orphan again.

Things got a little better after Alpha Dimitri moved in. Janet has only hit me twice since then and it wasn't hard enough to leave marks. Her insults never stopped though. She took every opportunity to insult me and tell me she'd get rid of me the first chance she got. Savannah had been gone since she had her pup. She was in some kind of jail and Alpha Dimitri was trying to find the pup's father. Janet visited her all the time and always came back with a message from Savannah. It was always something about me taking the father from her pup and her getting revenge. I had a hard time

understanding what the hell she meant by that but I didn't really care. Just two more weeks and none of it would matter.

I would leave and never see any of those people again.

My heart sank at the thought of not seeing Alpha Dimitri and Seth. They were the only ones who cared about me. They were the only ones I cared about. Seth was my best friend and Alpha Dimitri was...

I didn't know what it was. He was my stepbrother, but calling him that just felt wrong for some reason. It felt more like a...

I took a big gulp of my drink, stopping that thought from forming in my mind.

"Goddess, Mads, slow down," Seth laughed as he sat down next to me.

He ran his fingers through my hair and I smiled at him.

"Everything okay?" he asked, looking at the empty cup in my hand.

I shrugged and rested my head on his shoulder. I would miss him so much. He had become one of my best friends.

"Seth!" Jasper yelled, beckoning Seth to come over. "Come on, buddy!"

I lifted my head off of Seth's shoulder and turned around to pour myself another drink.

"I'm fine, Jasper," Seth yelled, making Jasper groan.

I chuckled and looked at Jasper, who was pouting at Seth.

"Go over there," I said to Seth as I poured some wolfsbane into my beer. "What are you guys doing?"

"Beer pong," Seth said, shaking his head at Jasper.

"I'm not in the mood."

I glanced over at Jasper who ran back to his friends. The party was packed tonight. Everyone was screaming and I was sure the whole pack knew there was a party in the woods again tonight.

I knew Alpha Dimitri would be mad at me for leaving and not telling him where I went. He always insisted I tell him where I was going. Most of the time he would tag along. I wasn't sure why he was so protective, but I wasn't going to lie and say I didn't enjoy his company. I liked spending time with him.

Except tonight. I needed to get out of that house and forget he lived there. As much as I liked Alpha Dimitri, he reminded me of Janet and I fucking hated Janet.

I took a long sip of my beer, trying to erase everything she'd said and done over the past few months.

"God, Maddie, slow down," Seth said as he took the glass from my hand.

He glanced at the bottles beside him and groaned.

I looked at him and frowned. "I'm fine, Seth."

Seth rolled his eyes and poured the rest of my beer onto the floor.

"Hey!" I exclaimed as I tried to stop him.

He threw the glass down and grabbed my arm. He pulled me over and started dragging me. I swayed a little, causing him to growl at me.

"How much have you had?" he asked as he stopped walking. "I left you alone for ten minutes, Madeline. How much have you had?"

I shrugged as I leaned against the tree behind me. I didn't even realize how drunk I was until I stood up and started walking.

"God, Madeline, what the hell is going on?" he asked. "You've been weird lately. No, you've been weird ever since that night you tried to run away."

I looked at him and saw his jaw clench.

"You didn't fall that night, did you?" he asked as he caged me in his arms and leaned down to look me in the eyes.

—I let it go because I didn't see you hurt again, but you didn't fall...

Someone hurt you, didn't they?

I gulped and pressed myself closer to the tree.

"Who hurt you, Madeline?" Seth growled, his eyes narrowing.

I spoke before I thought things through.

"It doesn't matter," I muttered. "I'm leaving here in two weeks anyway."

Seth's eyes widened. He let out a loud gasp.

"What the fuck are you talking about, Madeline?" he yelled as he grabbed my shoulders tightly. "You're not leaving the pack!"

"Yes, I am," I argued. "I'm not staying here. I didn't even want to come here."

Seth growled and hollowed my cheeks.

"You can't leave," he said, his voice filled with panic. "I can't let you go, Maddie. I think you're my mate and I can't let you go."

My heart skipped a beat and my breath hitched.

What the hell did he say?

Seth's eyes widened as he realized what he'd said. He muttered a curse and closed his eyes.

"What?" I forced myself to ask.

Seth opened his eyes and rested his forehead against mine.

"I can't be sure, Maddie. I'm not a werewolf," he murmured softly. "But I feel connected to you and a big part of me believes you're my mate. I've been waiting for your birthday for months. I've been waiting for the moment when my wolf

feels yours and knows for sure."

My heart was pounding out of my chest. I liked Seth, but I never thought of him as my—"

"Goddess, Maddie, I'd be a fool to let you go,"

Seth murmured as he looked at my lips.

A rush of heat washed over me. Was he going to kiss me?

Seth leaned in, his soft lips brushing mine lightly.

A shiver ran down my spine. Seth growled softly. He wrapped his arm around my waist and pulled me close to him. I gripped his shirt tightly to keep from falling. I couldn't feel my legs.

Seth's lips captured mine just as a loud, feral growl interrupted us.

42 She's not yours!

DIMITRI

I was going crazy.

As soon as I ran into the woods following their scent, I could tell there was a party going on.

Were they crazy?! A lot of those kids were on my patrol and they knew about the rogues. Everyone in the pack knew something was up and they needed to be careful. What the fuck were they thinking?! If the rogues crossed the border, they would be in serious danger. My Maddie would be in danger.

Thinking about that made me run even faster. All I could think about was getting there, finding her, and getting her home where I knew she would be

safe.

I was getting closer to the party and was already trying to see what was going on through the thick branches when my eyes caught something that

completely broke me.

Seth was holding my partner in his arms. Seth was kissing her.

I saw his lips against hers and I couldn't control the growl that escaped me.

My heart shattered inside my chest. I could feel the little pieces tearing me apart inside. I couldn't breathe and a rock full of pain and sadness formed in my throat.

I barely managed to keep Skol inside. He was going crazy inside me. I didn't know if he was moaning or growling.

Probably both.

Seth's head snapped up. His eyes widened at the sight of me. I looked at Maddie and saw her staring at Seth with a mix of surprise and confusion on her face. Why? Maybe she didn't expect me to kiss her. Maybe she didn't want to.

His arm was still around her waist and it was driving me crazy.

"Let go of her and move," I growled, trying hard to stay calm.

Seth looked at Maddie and gulped. Why the fuck wasn't he moving?

"Get him away from her before she kills him." Skol shouted, causing me to move on instinct.

I grabbed Seth by the arm and pulled him away from her. I stood in front of Maddie, never taking my eyes off Seth.

I reached behind me and placed my hand on Maddie's waist, letting the tickling calm me down a bit.

"Alpha, I-" he spoke but I cut him off.

"I don't want to hear it, Seth," I growled. "She's not yours to kiss."

His eyes widened and he tried to look at Maddie. I moved so he couldn't see her.

"What the fuck are you doing here?!" I screamed. "You know about rogues! You know it's dangerous and you brought her here!"

I was so fucking angry that even touching Maddie wasn't helping. I wanted to rip Seth's head off.

Seth opened his mouth to speak but Maddie cut him off.

"It's not her fault," he muttered. "I wanted to cum.

" She sounded weird. Was I-"

I turned around abruptly and grabbed her cheeks. I looked into her eyes and growled.

"Are you drunk?!" I exclaimed. "Who the fuck let you drink?!"

I couldn't believe I hadn't smelled it before. I was so angry and so fucking hurt when I saw Seth kissing her that I didn't pay attention to anything else.

"I'm fine," Maddie muttered. "I'm not drunk."

I could smell the alcohol and wolfsbane on her breath. Her eyelids were half-lidded. Her words were slurred a little.

"Don't lie to me, Madeline," I said, trying to hold back a growl.

I glanced over my shoulder at Seth. He was looking at Maddie with a worried expression. I wished I could tear his eyes out so he wouldn't look at her again. I wished I could kiss her right now to erase the trace of his lips from hers. I wished I'd gotten home a little earlier and stopped her from leaving.

The party was over. I mentally connected to all the wolves in the woods and all the noise suddenly stopped. *I forbid you from organizing another one until the situation with the rogues is resolved.*

Seth took a deep breath and swallowed.

"Go home, Seth," I told him.

I had to get him out of here before I lost my mind.

"Maddie..." Seth spoke up, but I cut him off.

"She's mine to take care of," I said, making his eyebrows furrow. "Go home."

"I'll be fine, Seth," Maddie said quietly. "You can go home."

Seth clenched his fists and looked at me. I could tell he was thinking hard about something. Maybe he suspected she was my mate.

I didn't care at this point. I had to keep it a secret for just two more weeks.

"Fine," Seth finally muttered. "I'll see you tomorrow, Mads."

I watched him walk away. He kept looking at Maddie, a wave of anger hitting me every time his eyes landed on her. She wasn't his!

I waited until I couldn't see him anymore before looking back at my princess. I was still holding her beautiful face in my hands.

"Did it make you uncomfortable when he kissed you?" I asked softly.

It would kill him if I kissed her against her will.

"No," he said shaking his head. "He told me that he thinks I'm his mate."

My heart skipped a beat. Skol moaned loudly.

Had I told her that? Did she want me to be her mate? Did she want him?

Maddie laughed and shook her head.

"It doesn't matter anyway," she muttered and tried to move. " He's not my mate."

My eyes widened. How did he know?

"I want to sleep," Maddie muttered and tried to move again.

She couldn't move much because I was pressing her against the tree and caressing her cheeks.

I nodded and let go. She thought I would let her walk on her own, but I could tell she was a little unsteady, so I picked her up bridal style. I was dying to carry her like that after I married her.

Maddie gasped and wrapped her arms around my neck.

"What are you doing, Alpha?" she asked, looking at me with wide eyes.

I hated that she wouldn't stop calling me Alpha. I told her to call me

Dimitri, but she ignored me. My stubborn little mate.

"I'm not going to let you hurt yourself," I told her.

"But I can..." she said, but I cut her off.

"I don't want to hear it, Maddie," I said sternly. "I'm already mad at you. Don't make it worse."

I didn't want to lecture her now. I couldn't even process everything that had happened. I just needed to get her home and make sure she was okay. I would deal with my overwhelming emotions tomorrow.

Chapter 43 Another punishment

MADELINE

My head was killing me.

I'd never had that much to drink before and I swore I'd never do it again. The throbbing pain in my head was definitely not worth it.

"Morning, sleepyhead," I heard someone say and I froze.

Who the hell...?

And then I remembered.

Alpha Dimitri drove me home last night. He tucked me into my bed. Why was I still here?

I opened my eyes and looked to my left. Alpha Dimitri was sitting at my desk, flipping through a stack of papers. He looked up at me and smiled.

"How's your head?" he asked, making me furrow my brows.

Why was I here?

"Fine," I lied as I sat up in bed.

Alpha Dimitri looked at me and raised an eyebrow. He stood up and walked over to the bed. My

heart was pounding. I had no idea why I was so nervous around him. He sat down and took my hand.

"I know when you're lying, Maddie," he said quietly. "I know you."

A shiver ran down my spine. Why did his words make me feel so good? Why did he want him to know me?

"How's your head?" he asked again.

I decided to be honest this time.

"It hurts," I said quietly, making Dimitri nod.

He reached out and placed his hand on my forehead. The pain immediately subsided.

What? How?

The only one who could take the pain away was my mate. It was Alpha Dimitri...

No.

No, no, no, no. He wasn't. He couldn't be. His touch didn't take away the pain, it only lessened it. His palm was cool and felt good against my warm forehead. That's why the pain lessened.

He wasn't my mate.

I was thankful he couldn't read my mind. I felt ashamed that the thought came to me. I was nothing and he was a King.

I couldn't be his mate.

"Why did you leave without me yesterday, Maddie?" Alpha Dimitri asked, furrowing his eyebrows. "Do you have any idea how scared I was?

Do you have any idea what would happen if the rogues entered our territory?"

I gulped. The fear in his voice made my insides twist.

"Not to mention that you got drunk," he continued, narrowing his eyes at me. "Do you have any idea what could have happened to you? Someone could have used you. Seth could have forced himself on you and—

" "He would never do that!" I interrupted.

Alpha Dimitri removed his hand from my forehead. His jaw tightened.

"He's not that kind of person," I continued to defend Seth.

—He's my friend.

I remembered Seth saying he could be my mate. I wasn't so sure about that. I didn't want him to be my mate. Not because I didn't like him, but because I didn't want to be tied to this pack in any way. I didn't want anyone in this pack to be my mate.

"He kissed you," Alpha Dimitri said with a hint of anger in his voice.

He looked down at my lips and a strange feeling spread through my stomach.

What the hell was wrong with me?

"He didn't force himself on me," I said quietly.

Dimitri swallowed and clenched his fists. He gave me a small nod and looked down at his lap.

"I'm sorry," I said.

I didn't even know what I was apologizing for. I had a feeling I needed to tell him I was sorry.

He looked at me and raised his eyebrows a little.

"For putting me in danger," I said the first thing that came to mind. "

I didn't mean to."

Alpha Dimitri nodded again. "Don't do that again, Maddie. Don't leave the house without me."

I gave him a small nod. I could tell that keeping me safe was important to him. I could tell how stressed and worried he was because of the rascals on his border. I didn't want to add to his stress. I didn't want him to worry about me.

"Thanks, Maddie," he said softly and pulled me into a hug.

I relaxed into his arms and took a deep breath. I couldn't help but enjoy his scent. It was soothing and made the pain in my head more bearable.

There was a knock on my bedroom door and someone opened it before I could answer.

"Morning, Mads..." I heard Mike's voice.

He stopped talking and let out a chuckle. Alpha Dimitri let go of me and I looked at Mike.

He was grinning from ear to ear.

"What the fuck is going on here?" I heard the voice I feared the most.

Shit. Janet was going to kill me.

She walked into my room and gasped loudly.

"What the fuck are you doing in his room, Dimitri?!" Janet screamed, making the pain inside my head worse.

Alpha Dimitri opened his mouth to speak but Mike beat him to it.

"Oh, relax, Janet," Mike said cheerfully. "They're brothers.

We should just be glad they're getting along."

A feeling of unease washed over me every time Mike called Alpha Dimitri my brother. It just seemed wrong to me and from the look on Alpha Dimitri's face, I could tell he felt the same way.

Janet glared at me and my stomach dropped. She would punish me the first chance she got. This was a reason for another punishment and she wouldn't waste the chance.

Shit.

"Stop it, mother," Alpha Dimitri growled. "Maddie wasn't feeling well and I was helping her."

Janet looked me up and down and clenched her jaw.

"Are you okay, sweetie?" Mike asked worriedly as he walked over to me and caressed my cheek. —Should we take you to the pack doctor?

—I'm fine, Mike, —I said. —Thanks.

Mike placed his hand on my forehead and gave me a small smile.

"You don't have a fever," he said. "Maybe you ate something bad?"

I looked at Dimitri Alpha who had a small smile on his face.

"Probably," I nodded, looking back at Mike.

"Okay, sweetie," Mike said as he caressed my cheek again.

"You're not going to work today. You need to rest and let us take care of you."

I shook my head immediately.

"No, I'm fine," I said, making Mike frown. "

I have to go to work.

" "Listen to Mike, Maddie," Dimitri Alpha said sternly. "I'll let Seth know you're staying home today."

I looked at Janet. I didn't want to stay here with her. I knew Mike would be leaving soon and that Alpha Dimitri had to go to work. I'd be stuck in this house with her.

Janet smirked, realizing she'd be at his mercy all day.

"I can stay home with you, sweetheart," Mike said softly. "I'm sure Jack can manage without me for a day."

Mike was one of the best fighters Alpha Dimitri's pack had. He worked as a trainer at the training center. I didn't know until recently. I never asked because I didn't want anything to do with him. I didn't want to get close to him.

This was the first time I was glad he was staying here. At least he wouldn't be alone with Janet.

"No, Mike, we need you there," Alpha Dimitri said, extinguishing the small spark of hope that had awakened inside me. "I'll stay with her."

My eyes widened. Mike smiled brightly. Janet looked like she was about to explode with anger.

I didn't care. I was so happy not to be alone with her.

I hoped she wouldn't get another chance to punish me in the next two weeks.

Chapter 44 His birthday

DIMITRI

Tomorrow was her birthday and I was going to explode with happiness.

I glanced at the watch on my wrist and my smile grew wider. Just four more hours and she would know she was mine. Just four more hours and I would kiss her until we both couldn't breathe. Just four more hours and I could tell her that I loved her more than anything in this world.

"Your cheeks are getting holes," Will murmured, causing me to look up at him.

He was staring at a map on his desk and had a small smile on his face.

"Shut up," I murmured, looking back down at the papers in front of me.

"Where is he going to change?" Will asked, causing me to shrug.

"She hasn't told me," I replied. "I'll pick her up when she's done with work and ask her where she wants to go."

"There's a wonderful clearing near the Wishing Pool," Will said. "Maybe you could take her there.

" I set the papers down on the desk and smiled. It was actually a great idea. This place would be perfect for her first shift. It would be a perfect place for her to realize that every bit of my body and soul belonged to her.

"That's a great idea," I said, grinning widely. "I'll take her there."

I was so fucking excited. I imagined the moment when she realized who I was to her. I imagined her jumping into my arms and smiling widely. I kept imagining our

first kiss.

Everything I imagined was perfect, and I would make sure it happened just the way I imagined it. I would kiss her just as softly and caress her body just as gently. I would make it perfect. A day I would never forget.

Skol was a nervous wreck. He was the happiest he had ever been, but his nervousness made him thrashing around all day long and I wanted to strangle him. I tried to calm him down, but no matter what I said, he just kept getting nervous. I understood, though. Today he would see his mate for the first time. I was just as excited to see his wolf as he was.

"Impossible," Skol said. You have no idea how excited I am to change and have her in my arms. She'll be beautiful, just like Maddie.

I smiled and shook my head.

"Skol?" Will asked, making me look back at him.

"He's excited," I said, giving him a small nod.

"I can imagine," Will chuckled. "I'm surprised he survived nine months without telling her."

I sighed and rolled my eyes.

"I had to stop him a bunch of times," I muttered, making Will chuckle again.

The hardest moment for Skol was when Savannah claimed her pup was mine. Skol was terrified that Maddie would never forgive me for sleeping with Savannah. He was terrified that Savannah would somehow prove that her pup was ours. I was about to explode.

I took a deep breath to try and calm my excitement. I had work to do. The meeting with the Alphas of my Kingdom was scheduled for seven days from now. I had to focus a little more on work. I still had time until Maddie got off work.

I stood up and walked around the table to get a better look at the map.

"So these are the places where most of the attacks occurred," Will muttered, pointing at the red dots on the map.

Most of those places were on my borders. Others were mostly in my most powerful packs.

They were definitely trying to take my throne, but what I couldn't figure out was who was behind it all. Who was so powerful as to unite the rogues and claim they could take me down?

I clenched my jaw and stared at the blue dots. They indicated the possible locations of the next attacks.

"Did you talk to Peter about sending more wolves to these places?" I asked, pointing at the blue dots.

"Yes," Will replied. "I hope we'll have more wolves available after the meeting.

" "The packs will have to cooperate and send their warriors to defend the territory," I said. "This is their kingdom too."

Will nodded and looked at the watch on his wrist.

"There's not much left to do, Dimitri," he said, looking at me. —Go with Maddie.

My heart skipped a beat and I couldn't help but smile. Will laughed and rolled his eyes playfully.

"Go," he said. "It's annoying to see you this happy

." I chuckled and shook my head. "I can't wait to see you this happy, man."

Will looked at me and smiled.

"Just put a mind link on me if anything happens, okay?" I said as I put my jacket on.

"Don't worry," Will said. "Enjoy your time with your partner. I can take care of everything for one night.

" "Thanks," I said as I walked out of my office.

"Be careful!" Will called out after me. "You're too young to be having puppies!"

I rolled my eyes and shook my head. Will was joking, but the thought of having puppies with Maddie made me smile. I imagined her pregnant with my pup and my heart burst with happiness. I knew Maddie wouldn't be ready right away, but I hoped she would want puppies soon.

I didn't even realize I had a huge smile on my face until I ran into Mike at the exit of the warehouse.

"What's that smile about?" Mike asked, smiling at me.

I stopped smiling immediately. I didn't want Mike to suspect anything. I had three and a half hours left and I wasn't going to screw it up.

"Will said something funny," I replied, making him frown a little. "How was training?"

"Good," Mike said. "We have some really talented wolves in our pack."

"Cool," I said as I walked through the front door. "See you at home, Mike."

I didn't wait for his answer. I didn't care. All I cared about was Maddie. I was so fucking happy and I couldn't wait until midnight.

I couldn't wait to tell her how much I loved her. Tomorrow would be the best day of my life and I would never forget it.

Chapter 45 Excitement

MADELINE

"I'm so excited," Seth said, making me look up at him.

He had a huge smile on his face and it made me happy. I liked seeing him happy.

"You're more excited than I am," I chuckled as I looked back at the counter and continued cleaning it.

"Of course I am," Seth said as he walked over to me. "I'll finally know for sure if you're my mate."

I felt nervousness creep up on me. I was planning on leaving tomorrow. I didn't want to meet my mate.

Seth ran his fingers through my hair and I looked at him. He smiled and caressed my cheek.

"Are you nervous?" he asked and I nodded.

"A little," I said. "But I'm excited to meet my wolf."

Seth smiled and leaned against the counter.

"I'm excited to meet her too," he said as he crossed his arms over his chest. "It'll be amazing, just like you."

I felt heat rise to my cheeks. I shook my head and looked back at the counter.

"How are you celebrating your birthday?" Seth asked. " Jasper thinks we should throw you a party."

I gulped and kept my eyes on the counter. I wouldn't be here for that celebration. I was leaving tomorrow night.

I glanced over at him and was about to tell him I didn't want to celebrate when the door to the diner opened and Dimitri Alpha walked in. He had a huge grin on his face. My knees buckled and I had to lean on the counter to keep from falling to the floor.

He was so fucking handsome.

What the hell was wrong with me?

"Hey, Maddie," Dimitri Alpha said cheerfully. "You ready to go home?"

I furrowed my eyebrows a little. I wasn't planning on going home. I was planning on staying here with Seth until it was time for my shift.

Seth said he'd support me and help me get through it. I told him it wasn't necessary, but he insisted. I felt like I was using him, especially since I was leaving tomorrow. I had no idea how to tell him I couldn't stay in this pack. Seth meant the world to me, but I just couldn't stay here.

"I was planning on staying at the diner," I told him. "Seth and I made plans.

I wasn't even sure if Alpha Dimitri knew it was my birthday tomorrow. I wasn't even sure if Mike remembered. It didn't matter anyway. I wasn't planning on celebrating with anyone.

"No way, Maddie," Alpha Dimitri said sternly. "Tomorrow is your birthday. You're coming home so we can have dinner and get you ready for your first shift."

My eyes widened. Did he know? Did Mike remember?

"I promised I'd be there when she changed shifts, Alpha," Seth said. —Maybe I can have dinner with you and your family tomorrow?

Alpha Dimitri's smile faded. He narrowed his eyes and looked at

Seth.

"We'll be there for her when she changes shifts, Seth," Alpha Dimitri said sternly. "First shift is a family event. Maddie can spend the day with you tomorrow."

"Okay," Seth agreed immediately, making me look at him with wide eyes.

What? Why did he agree so quickly? Did Alpha Dimitri order him to?

Why? What the hell was going on?

Alpha Dimitri smiled and looked back at me.

"Come on, Maddie," he said excitedly.

Seth looked at me and clenched his jaw. I furrowed my eyebrows at him.

"Come on, Mads," Seth said as he reached behind me and unbuttoned my apron.

Seth pulled my apron off of me and set it on the counter. I froze. I couldn't understand what had just happened.

"Go, Maddie," Seth said softly. "We'll go out tomorrow."

I nodded and he hugged me. He kissed the top of my head and took a deep breath.

Alpha Dimitri growled softly.

Seth let go of me and I forced my frozen legs to move. I walked over to Alpha Dimitri and he took my hand. He smiled at me and looked over. to Seth.

"Good night, Seth," Alpha Dimitri said. "I'll see you tomorrow."

Alpha Dimitri started pulling me along behind him. I kept my eyes on Seth the whole time. He looked so sad and I just wanted to go back and hug him.

"Did Mike remember my birthday?" I asked Alpha Dimitri as we walked out of the cafeteria.

Chapter 46 My wolf and my partner

MADELINE

"Are you ready, Maddie?" Alpha Dimitri asked as he walked out of the house and closed the front door.

I raised my eyebrows and looked behind him. Where was Mike? They both insisted on being with me during my first shift. Had Mike changed his mind?

"Mike will be joining us later," Alpha Dimitri said, taking my hand in his.

I was even more confused than I had been a few seconds ago. Mike was determined to be with me tonight, and he changed his mind right before we had to leave the house. What was that about?

"There's an amazing place near the Wishing Pond,"

Alpha Dimitri said. "It'll be a perfect spot for your first shift."

I nodded and let him lead me away from the house. There was no point in asking about Mike. It wasn't unexpected. I was surprised that he remembered my birthday. I didn't expect him to spend it with me or do anything. I always thought he'd be with my mom during my

first shift.

I felt tears well up in my eyes and a lump formed in my throat. I never let myself think about my mother. I missed her too much and it still hurt. It always would. The pain of losing her would never go away.

"What's wrong, Maddie?" Alpha Dimitri asked with a hint of panic in his voice.

I looked at him and raised my eyebrows. How did he know something was wrong?

Was I crying? I didn't feel any tears falling down my cheeks though.

"I just miss my mother," I murmured. "I always thought she'd be here for my first shift."

Alpha Dimitri took a deep breath and hugged me. The pain in my soul eased a little.

"I'm sure she's with you, Maddie," Alpha Dimitri said softly. "She wouldn't miss this for the world. She's watching you from somewhere and she's so proud of you."

I hugged him back and smiled. His words and soothing voice made me feel a little better.

"Thank you," I said softly.

"You don't need to thank me." "I'll always be here for you."

I let go of him and took a step back. He smiled and started walking again. He looked at his watch and a huge grin spread across his face.

"What time is it?" I asked, causing him to look at me.

"11:55 p.m." he said excitedly. "We made it just in time."

I stopped walking and looked around. We were in the middle of a small clearing. I looked up and could see the moon clearly. It made me smile. I looked to my right and saw a Wishing Pond. The surface was glistening in the moonlight and the sight was beautiful.

The trees had lost most of their leaves and their branches were swaying slightly in the cold breeze. Alpha Dimitri was right. This place was beautiful and I would surely remember it.

I looked back at Alpha Dimitri. He was smiling and the way he looked at me made me shiver.

I couldn't help but notice how handsome he was. He had grown a little beard, which made him look a little older. It only added to his attractiveness.

He glanced at the watch on his wrist, and the smile on his face grew. He would break his perfect lips and high cheekbones if he kept smiling like that.

"It's one minute to midnight," he said as he looked back at me.

Something started to stir inside me. My body shuddered, and my skin felt a tingle. Dimitri gulped and clenched his fists.

The wind blew a little harder, and a delicious scent of cocoa and cinnamon filled me. I raised my eyebrows. What the hell was that?

Alpha Dimitri glanced at the watch on his wrist, and I swore I saw a small tear fall down his cheek. The pain in my chest surprised me. I hated seeing him cry. It hurt me. It caused me pain.

Why was he crying?

"Happy birthday, Madeline."

"Happy birthday, Madeline."

Two soothing, melodic voices wished me a happy birthday at the same time.

Alpha Dimitri's voice sounded a little different. I tilted my head and raised my eyebrows slightly.

'Hey, Maddie,' my wolf's voice made me focus on her.

'Hi,' I said, trying to contain my excitement. 'I'm so glad you're here. What's your name?

I'm glad to be here too, Maddie,' she said softly. 'My name is Skye.'

I smiled and took a deep breath. The scent of cocoa and cinnamon relaxed me. Where was it coming from?

It's coming from our mate,' Skye said, leaving me frozen.

Mate? I hadn't even transformed yet and I already had a mate. Where was I? Was it really Seth? Had he found me?

I started looking around with a confused expression. Where was my mate? Where was that smell coming from? Where...?

My eyes caught Alpha Dimitri's and I knew.

My heart stopped beating and my breath caught in my throat.

He was looking at me with so much love in his eyes that I almost fell to the floor.

No one had ever looked at me like that. No one had ever loved me like that.

'Hello, my love,' he said softly, his voice shaking. —I've been waiting for this moment for nine months.

I couldn't breathe.

Alpha Dimitri was my mate? Did he know it all along?

"I love you, Maddie," he said as he took a small step towards me. "I've loved you from the moment I saw you."

My heart started to race. I was going to faint.

Alpha Dimitri was my mate? My fated mate?

How was that possible? I wasn't a Lycan. I wasn't worthy of him. I wasn't meant to be a Luna. I was nothing and I was no one.

Skye was telling me something, but I couldn't focus on her.

All I could think about was the fact that my mate was now in front of me. He reached up and caressed my cheek.

My skin erupted in tingles and a rush of heat rose to my cheeks.

Alpha Dimitri leaned into me and rested his forehead on mine.

"I can't believe you finally know," he said as he wrapped an arm around my waist and pulled me towards him. —These last nine months have been the longest of my life. —He

raised his head and smiled at me.

"I'd do it all over again if I had to," he said softly. "I'd do it all over again if you were waiting for me at the end of those nine months. But I'm glad I don't have to."

He laughed, and my knees buckled. I would fall if he didn't hold me tight.

"Mate," I murmured without thinking.

Alpha Dimitri smiled and leaned down to give me a soft kiss on the tip of my nose.

"Yes, princess," he said. "I'm your mate. Every part of my body and soul is yours."

Was he mine?

He was mine, but I couldn't accept it. I wasn't made for him. I wasn't part of his pack. I wanted to leave, and I would have to reject him.

My heart broke inside my chest, and Skye howled loudly.

I ignored both her pain and my own. I couldn't be his mate.

I just couldn't.

Chapter 47 Rejecting my partner

Madeline's POV

"You need to change, my love," Alpha Dimitri said softly. "We have all the time in the world to hold each other."

He smiled and took a small step back.

I couldn't focus on my wolf. I couldn't focus on anything but him.

I was in shock. My heart felt like it was going to jump out of my chest. The pain paralyzed me completely. I made my decision, but I was too weak and scared to tell him.

I couldn't be his mate.

He was my stepbrother. His mother and father were mates. His mother verbally and sometimes physically abused me for months. The woman who almost became his mate helped her. Everything and everyone was against us.

I didn't want to stay in this pack from the moment I arrived. I didn't want to stay with the man who abandoned me and my mother. I didn't want to be around the woman who hated me from the first time she saw me.

I already loved my mate and I would love him until my last breath, but I couldn't stay. I couldn't.

Skye was thrashing and screaming inside me. It hurt too much to hear what she was saying to me.

My heart was breaking inside my chest, but I had to do it.

I had to reject him. I couldn't stay in his pack and I couldn't be his mate. I wasn't worthy of being his mate.

I wanted to leave. I needed to leave.

So I took a deep breath and prepared myself to say the words I knew would break his heart and mine. I knew it would hurt and I knew I would regret it for the rest of my life, but I had to do it. I had no choice.

I looked into his eyes and saw only pure love. I wanted to sob and rip my heart out. My wolf was screaming at me, trying to stop me from saying the words that would set us both free.

But I made a decision. It was better for both of us if I left.

"I, Madeline Clark, refuse—" I started to speak but Alpha Dimitri stopped me by putting his hand over my mouth.

He pulled me closer to him and growled.

"What the hell are you doing?" he yelled. "I'm not going to let you do this, Maddie. I've waited for you for months and I'm not going to lose you."

His eyes held so much pain and his voice was full of panic.

"You're mine, Maddie," he said as he leaned down and placed a kiss on my forehead. "You're mine and I'm not going to let you go."

My heart raced inside my chest. It felt like there were a thousand knives stuck in my heart. Alpha Dimitri was shaking, loud growls escaping his lips and his grip on me getting even tighter.

"Why, Maddie, why?" he yelled and I nearly screamed in pain.

He pulled me closer to him and rested his forehead on mine.

"I can't stay here," I forced myself to murmur. I

didn't even recognize my own voice. It was filled with pain and sadness.

Alpha Dimitri raised his head and raised his eyebrows.

"Yes, you can," he said, digging his fingertips into my hip. "This is your pack, Madeline. You are the Luna of this pack. You are the Queen of our kingdom. You can stay. You have to stay."

I shook my head and closed my eyes. I ducked my head and tried to take a deep breath. But it was impossible. The pain was gripping me inside and I couldn't do anything.

"I'm not worthy," I muttered. "I'm just a wolf. I'm not a werewolf. I'm not made to be Luna. I'm not made to be a Queen."

Alpha Dimitri placed his finger under my chin and tried to lift my head. I wouldn't let him.

"I can't stay with my father," I continued, my voice now laced with panic. "He never wanted me and he doesn't want me now. I said I'd leave as soon as I had my wolf and I had to leave. I can't stay here. I can't be your mate. You deserve..."

My voice cracked. I remembered the day Janet told me no one wanted me here, not even my own father. I believed her. I didn't belong here.

Alpha Dimitri lifted my head up using a little more force this time. I saw a mix of hurt and rage in his eyes.

"This isn't about your father, Madeline," he said sternly. "This is about you and me. You're made for me. You're made to be Luna. You're made to be queen."

I gulped. Skye was still talking to me, but I couldn't focus on her no matter how I tried.

"Things have changed, Maddie," Alpha Dimitri continued. "Nothing is the way it was when you got here. You found your mate. You found me, and I won't let you leave me."

Alpha Dimitri looked down at my neck and touched my marking spot with his thumb. My body exploded and I had to hold back a moan. His breathing quickened and his grip on me tightened. His dark eyes bore into mine and I was sure my heart was going to jump out of my chest.

I couldn't help but think of his strong arms that wrapped around me completely. I couldn't help but think of his broad chest that was pressed firmly against mine.

"Alpha, I can't-" I started to speak but he cut me off.

"I will not accept your rejection, Madeline," he growled. "You are my mate. You are the greatest gift the Goddess has ever given me. I will not let you go."

My heart hammered against my ribcage.

His scent flooded my senses. He leaned in close and nuzzled my jaw. My skin burned. Every part of my body ached to be touched by him.

"I can't let you go, my love," he murmured. "I've waited for you all my life."

His lips brushed the scarred spot on my neck and I nearly burst into flames.

Convincing him to accept my rejection would be the hardest thing I would ever have to do.

Chapter 48 I would kill myself

DIMITRI

My heart was pounding. I'd never felt so much pain. I'd never been so scared in my entire life.

Did she want to reject me? Did she want to leave me?

Fuck no.

I would never allow it. She was mine. She belonged here with me. I couldn't let her go. She would kill me.

I kissed her mark and she squirmed. I pulled her even tighter against me.

I continued to kiss her neck softly. My taste buds were going to explode. I'd never tasted anything as delicious as her.

"I love you, Maddie," I said softly as I traced my lips along her jaw. "I love you, my queen."

She grabbed onto the back of my jacket and pressed herself even tighter against me. We were as close to each other as possible now.

I was in fucking heaven.

She buried her head in my chest, a small sob escaping her.

"I can't..." she spoke, her voice muffled. "..."

"You can, princess," I said as I rested my head on hers.

"You were made for this. I'll be with you every step of the way."

I tangled my fingers in her hair and gently pulled her head up. Her cheeks were red and wet from her tears. I leaned into her and brushed the tip of her nose against hers. I wished I could kiss her, but I didn't want to while she was scared and crying. Our first kiss would be special.

"You and I are moving into our own house, Maddie," I said softly as I pressed my cheek against hers.

The physical aspects of the bond washed over me completely.

My whole body tingled. My heart pounded in my chest. It felt like I was being tickled from the inside out and it was the strangest, most pleasurable feeling I had ever experienced.

"You don't have to see Mike again if you don't want to," I continued. "

I'm not going to let you leave me just because of him."

Maddie held me tighter. She sobbed softly.

"It's not just because of Mike," she cried. "I don't belong here. I never did. I—"

I lifted my head and clenched my jaw.

"You belong here, Maddie," I said sternly. "You're my mate. You're a Luna of this pack. You're the Queen of this Kingdom. This is your place. I have no idea why you think I don't, but I'm not going to let you leave me for that. I'm not going to let you go, Madeline. Forget it."

I'd lock her up if I had to. I didn't give a shit. She belonged here with me and I'd be a crazy son of a bitch to let her go.

Not to mention how painful it would be. Not to mention there were rogues everywhere. They'd kill her. If they found out she was my mate, they'd capture her and torture her. Grief and rage flared inside me just thinking about it. I couldn't let her go. I just couldn't.

"We have a huge problem with rogues, princess," I said worriedly. "If you left they might hurt you." "If they found out you were my mate, they could take you away and torture you to get to me. That would kill me, Maddie. I would die if something happened to you. I can't let that happen. I can't let you go."

His eyebrows raised slightly. I saw concern written all over his face.

"What about the rogues?" he asked, making me smile a little.

"And you say you're not cut out to be Luna," I said softly as I pinched the tip of her nose. "Look at how you work already."

Her eyes widened in surprise and I chuckled.

"We don't know much," I answered her question. "They attack our borders daily and we don't know why. We captured a few but they never said a word about why they were attacking us or who was behind it all."

Maddie's eyebrows furrowed again.

"I think they're after my throne," I continued. "That's why it's extremely dangerous for you to leave, love. You're my greatest strength and my greatest weakness. If they caught you and asked for my throne in exchange for you, I would give it to them. I would give every damn thing I own just to get you back. If they hurt you, I would be sorry. If they killed you, I would die. We're bound together even without the mark, Maddie.

You're my heart and soul and I can't lose you."

Maddie gulped and another tear fell down her cheek. I wiped it away with my thumb.

"Promise me you won't leave, Maddie," I told her as another wave of fear washed over me. "I'll make sure you never have to see Mike again if you don't want me to. I'll get rid of everything in this pack that bothers you. You're my number one priority and I'll do whatever I have to to make this a place where you feel comfortable."

Maddie closed her eyes and rested her forehead on my chest. My heart nearly exploded with happiness. I tangled my fingers in her hair and pulled her against my chest. I leaned into her and kissed the top of her head.

"I don't want to hurt you," she said, her voice cracking with fear and pain. "I can't hurt you. I just found out you're my mate and I already feel connected to you in so many ways."

I smiled and gave her another kiss on the head. She looked up at me and swallowed.

"But I'm worried you'll get hurt if I stay," she continued softly. "I don't know what the Goddess was thinking when she gave me to you, but I'm not made for—"

"Stop it," I cut her off. "Stop saying you're not made for this. Stop implying that this was some kind of mistake. Our bond is not a mistake, Madeline. It's the most beautiful thing that's ever happened to me. You're the most precious thing in the world to me, Maddie.

You're not a mistake. This is not a mistake."

I couldn't hold back my tears. Hearing her say that the Goddess shouldn't have brought us together was so fucking painful. It felt like a million knives were being stabbed into my chest at the same time.

Maddie reached up and wiped the tears from my cheeks.

"I'm sorry," she said softly. "I never meant to hurt you, I..."

Her voice cracked and she stopped talking.

"I know, Maddie," I said as I rested my forehead against hers. "Please stop talking about leaving me. Please."

She took a deep breath and held on to me tighter. I understood her fear, but I wouldn't let her leave me because of that. I would never let her go.

She was my heart and soul and I wasn't going to lose her.

Chapter 49 Not tonight

Madeline's POV

Janet was going to kill me.

I was sure of it.

She hated me from the start because she knew I was her son's mate. She didn't think I was good enough for her son so she tried to get rid of me. She tried to get me to take another wolf as a mate. She lied to her own son just because she didn't like him.

Pain spread through my body as I remembered Savannah.

She tried to take my mate from me. She lied to him. She tried to get me to take her as my chosen mate. She lied to him about her pup.

My stomach twisted and I tried to take a deep breath.

I always wondered why Janet hated me so much and now I knew the answer. She believed I wasn't good enough for her son.

And she was right. I wasn't good enough.

But how could I leave him? How could I leave when it hurt just to think of not touching him and not feeling him in my arms? How could I leave the pack and never see him again?

Skye howled loudly. Her pain became my pain and every emotion inside my body doubled.

She lowered her head and buried her nose in my neck. I took a deep breath and let her scent calm me a little.

"I love you, Madeline," she said, making my heart skip a beat. "I love you. Please don't leave me."

I wasn't going to leave him tonight. I couldn't leave him tonight. I would try to talk to him again tomorrow. I would try to make him see that maybe it would be better if I left. Maybe it would be—"

"No!" Skye yelled at me, interrupting my thoughts. "You will never leave. You will never leave our mate. I won't let you, Madeline."

Skye—" I spoke, but she interrupted me.

"No, Madeline," she said angrily. I'm not going to listen to you. I understand why you don't want to stay. I understand that you're angry with Mike.

I understand that you're scared of Janet. I understand that you don't feel good enough to be his mate, but you're wrong.

You're good enough, Maddie. You're more than enough.

You're just what he needs.

I closed my eyes and let the tears fall down my cheeks. "

It wasn't your fault that Mike left your mother, Madeline," Skye continued softly. "You're good enough."

Hearing her talk about one of the biggest secrets she kept made me sob. I'd never said it out loud. I'd never talked about it. I'd never admitted it to myself, but she was right. I knew why Mike had left, but all those years of bullying left a mark on my heart and soul. Other kids called me a homewrecker, among other things. They told me that my father had left because I wasn't a good daughter. I knew it wasn't true, but it hurt and I had a hard time remembering the real reason he left me and my mother.

I couldn't even think about it now. All I could do was hold on to my mate tightly and sob.

"Oh, my love," Alpha Dimitri said softly.

He lifted me up and I wrapped my legs around his waist. He held me tightly against his chest. I didn't want him to let me go. I didn't want to be separated from him. I had never felt safer in my entire life.

"Let's go home, princess," he said softly, making me furrow my eyebrows.

But I still hadn't shifted.

"What's with the shifting?" I asked as I lifted my head from his shoulder and looked at him.

He smiled and wiped my tears away.

"Not tonight, sweetheart," he said. "You're too tired to shift now. I'm sorry. I didn't expect you to realize so soon that I was your mate." *I hoped Skye would take over before you realized.*

"Did she know my wolf's name yet? Was Skye talking to her wolf yet?"

"I did and I'm so in love," she said, sighing contently.

"Besides, I want to go home and have everyone know that I've found the love of my life," she said, smiling widely.

Did she want everyone to know? Did they not know already?

" "They don't?" I asked, furrowing my eyebrows.

"No," she said as she began walking towards Mike's house.

"I didn't want to risk them telling her. I didn't want to take away from you finding your mate." *I wanted you to experience it all without anyone interfering.*

My heart raced. *Why did Janet hate me then?*

"Plus, I was afraid someone would try to hurt you if word got out," he sighed. "I tried to be there for you as much as I could, but I couldn't risk someone trying to hurt you when I couldn't be with you. Especially when you didn't have your wolf yet."

I nodded and swallowed the lump in my throat. *Why did Janet hate me then? Why did she hurt me? Why did she try to get rid of me?*

"Can we not tell anyone tonight?" I asked quietly. "I just want to go to bed."

Alpha Dimitri smiled and gave me a small nod.

"Of course, princess," he said. "Whatever you want. We couldn't tell anyone but our parents tonight anyway."

He chuckled. My stomach turned.

"I'm sleeping with you tonight," he said, making my eyes widen. "I'm not risking anything, Maddie." " I don't want you to get an idea and go out the window.

" "Sleep with me?" "But...

" "It won't be the first time," he said after seeing my confused face. "I know it might sound weird, but I've been sleeping with you for months. I couldn't get away from you no matter how hard I tried. I couldn't hold you like I wanted to while you were awake, so I did it while you were sleeping. "

To say I was surprised would be an understatement.

"Did you sleep with me the whole time?" I murmured under my breath.

He looked at me and nodded. I saw guilt in his eyes.

"I'm sorry," he said softly. "I never did anything. I didn't even get under the blanket. I just held you. I needed to hold you."

"I'm not mad," I said. "I'm just a little confused. Is that why I've been sleeping so well?"

I wasn't really mad at him. I was a little surprised, but not mad. I didn't want him to feel guilty.

"Yeah," she said, laughing.

"I thought the mattress was amazing," I muttered, furrowing my eyebrows.

Alpha Dimitri laughed, making my heart skip a beat.

"Oh, the mattress sucks, love," he said, shaking his head. " But I haven't slept better in my entire life, either."

I gave him a small smile and rested my head on his shoulder. He kissed the top of my head and took a deep breath.

"I love you, princess," he said softly. "You're my whole world."

I closed my eyes and let the warmth of his words seep into my body. I could let myself enjoy it just a little. I could let myself believe that I was really his and that I was made for him.

I could let myself believe that for just a little while.

Chapter 50 Protecting Her

Dimitri's POV

My heart was hammering inside my chest.

I was lying on her bed, waiting for her to finish her shower and come lay down next to me. I couldn't believe that the day I had been waiting for had finally arrived. I finally knew.

I could finally hold her for as long as I wanted. I could finally kiss her. I could finally call her my love, my princess, and my queen. I could finally tell her how much I loved her. I could finally tell everyone that she was mine and mine alone.

The bathroom door opened and she stepped out, making my heart skip a beat.

"Come on, love," I said softly as I lifted the blanket so she could crawl under it.

I laid down on top of the covers. I didn't want her to feel uncomfortable.

She raised her eyebrows and slowly walked over.

"You'll be cold," she muttered under her breath as she sat on the bed and looked at me.

I had to bite my cheeks to keep from smiling. I wouldn't be cold. I was a werewolf. I could sleep outside in the snow, but if my queen said I'd be cold if I didn't get under the covers with her, who the hell was I to argue with her?

"Are you saying I can get under the covers too?" I asked, making her blush.

She nodded and pulled the covers over her. I leaned down to kiss her cheek and smiled. I stood up and pulled the covers off. I thought about taking off my shirts and sweats, but that would probably be too fast. I was lucky she let me get under the covers with her.

I laid down and pulled her closer to me. I buried my nose in her hair and took a deep breath. Her scent relaxed my muscles and made my heart race. She rested her head on my chest and wrapped her arms around my torso. I was in heaven. It was everything I'd ever wanted.

"Dimitri?" Skol called out just as I felt Maddie tense up.

My heart raced. I lifted Maddie's head so I could look at her face. Her eyes were wide and filled with fear.

"What's wrong?" I asked, trying hard not to scream.

"It's Skye," Maddie murmured, making me furrow my brows.

My heart was pounding out of my chest. Was something wrong with Skye?

"What?" I asked, my voice filled with fear. "Is something wrong, Maddie?"

She didn't answer. She just stared at me, confusion and fear written on her face.

"Maddie?" I called out, trying to breathe through the panic consuming my body. "

She said she won't change," Skol said, leaving me frozen.

Maddie was apologizing to her for not giving her a chance to change when Skye said she wouldn't have anyway.

I raised my eyebrows.

Why? Why?

"Skye doesn't want to change," Maddie said in a shaky voice. "She doesn't want to..."

Her voice cracked and she started breathing heavily.

Fuck!

"Breathe, Maddie," I said as I caressed her cheeks. "Breathe, honey, come on. We'll figure it out.

" "Why, Skol?" I asked my wolf. "Talk to her.

I did," Skol said calmly. "She said she can't let anyone see her yet. She said she's protecting Maddie by staying hidden."

But what the fuck? I was even more confused than before. I focused on Maddie, who was still having trouble breathing.

"Breathe, my love," I said softly as I leaned into her and kissed her cheek. "Everything's going to be okay, Maddie." She gulped and shook her head.

"She said she was protecting me," Maddie said, her voice hoarse and filled with pain. "I don't understand. Protecting me from what?"

I took a deep breath and tried to calm my racing heart. I needed to stay calm in order to help Maddie.

I wanted to scream and growl. What did Skye need me to protect her from?

Was my mate in danger? Why didn't Skye tell me then? Could I protect Maddie? I could protect her from everything.

"She can't tell you, Dimitri," Skol said. "You can't know. No one can know."

He sounded oddly calm. Did she know?

Yes, he said. "I know, and I won't say anything. Skye's doing the right thing, Dimitri. No one can see her."

My heart was pounding out of my chest.

"Please don't question us," Skol continued. "Just know that we're doing what's best for her. We're protecting her."

From what? I yelled at him.

Skol was silent for a few moments.

"Focus on Maddie," she said calmly. "She needs you."

I wanted to yell at her, but I knew it was useless. She was right. I had to focus on my mate.

"Listen to me, Maddie," I said softly as I leaned over and caressed her cheek. "I talked to Skol and he agrees with Skye. He hasn't told me why he doesn't want to change, but I trust him.

There's a reason Skye doesn't want to change and he'll tell us when she's ready." Maddie was still panicking.

"But what will I do without my wolf?" she cried. "How will I—" She

stopped talking and swallowed.

"You have me," I said. "You have Skol. We'll never let anything happen to you, okay? You'll have to be by my side at all times from now on, is that clear?"

I wasn't going to let her run around without her wolf when there was a horde of rogues on my borders.

"Is that clear, Maddie?" I repeated my question after she didn't answer.

She nodded and wrapped her arms around my neck. I held her tight.

"We'll figure it out, love," I said softly as I kissed her temple. "I'm here for you, Maddie. I'm here for everything, my love."

"Thank you," she murmured, her voice low and raspy.

"You don't need to thank me," I said as I held her closer to me. "You are the greatest gift the Goddess has ever given me, my love. I will always be here for you and I will never stop loving you." I reached back and turned off the lamp.

"Try to get some sleep, princess," I murmured as I held her tighter. "I'm here and I'm not leaving you."

She snuggled closer to me and placed a small kiss on my chest. My heart nearly exploded with happiness.

I smiled and closed my eyes.

I didn't know what Skye was protecting her from, but I would find out and make sure the threat was gone. I wouldn't let anyone hurt her. I wouldn't let anyone touch her.

She was mine to love and to protect, and I would do both until the day I took my last breath.

Chapter 51 Waking up next to her

Dimitri's POV

I was never happier than the moment I woke up next to her.

This time was different. This time I was under a blanket with her. She had her arms and legs around me and she was practically lying on top of me.

I chuckled and kissed her forehead.

"Good morning, princess," I murmured softly.

She shifted a little and pressed herself closer to me. I held her tight and closed my eyes.

"From now on, we'll wake up like this every day," I murmured, a small smile spreading across my face.

Just thinking about it made my whole body tingle. She was truly mine and I would wake up next to her every damn day for the rest of my life. She

held me tighter and sighed in content. I smiled and opened my eyes. I looked at her and my heart skipped a beat. She really was in my arms. I really had survived nine months without her. I had

survived Savannah's attempt to take me away from her. I survived Seth's attempts to push her away from me. I survived everything and my reward was her.

Dimitri? My mother mentally linked me and I flinched a little. I was so lost in thought it surprised me.

What, mother? I mentally linked her again as I buried my nose in Maddie's hair.

Where are you two? she asked. Breakfast is ready.

I'll be right there. I said as I began to gently rub Maddie's back.

I cut the mental link with my mother and began to plant soft kisses all over her face. She furrowed her eyebrows a little and shifted.

"Wake up, princess," I said as I ran my fingers through her hair. "Breakfast is ready."

"Five more minutes," she murmured sleepily.

I chuckled and gave her another kiss on the cheek. If it were up to me, I would have stayed in bed with her all day.

But we had to get up. We had to go talk to our parents. I had to tell the pack that I had found their Luna. We had to prepare a Luna ceremony. We had work to do and I would have to wait until tonight to lay with her like this.

"We have work to do, my love," I said softly as I lowered my head and placed a soft kiss on her neck. "

We can go back to bed later.

" Maddie moaned quietly and opened her beautiful eyes. She stared at me for a few seconds before her eyes widened and she tried to pull away from me.

"Oh, I'm so sorry!" she exclaimed and I was left fucking confused.

I gripped her tighter and pulled her towards me.

"Why are you sorry, princess?" I asked with my eyebrows furrowed.

She looked down at our entwined bodies and I understood what she meant. I chuckled and she looked back at me.

"We're partners, Maddie," I said as I tucked a strand of hair behind her ear. "Our bodies seek each other out."

It would be weird if we didn't wake up like this. And trust me, I have no problem with it. If I could just find a way to have you even closer to me, I'd be the happiest man on this planet."

She gulped and relaxed a little.

"Did you sleep well?" I asked as I leaned into her and kissed her cheek again.

I couldn't stop myself. If I could just attach my lips to her skin, I would. I couldn't wait for her to let me kiss her lips.

I was so fucking jealous of Seth, who got to do it before me. Those lips were mine to kiss. Her whole body was mine to kiss and worship.

"I did," he said softly. "And you?"

I smiled and rubbed the tip of my nose against hers.

"Best sleep ever, princess," I said.

She bit her bottom lip and I growled softly. I wanted to too. I wanted to bite it softly. I wanted to kiss it.

I wanted to taste it. Fuck,

I gulped and took a deep breath. I smiled at her and pulled her even closer to me.

"We need to get up, princess," I told her. "We need to go tell our parents that we're mates."

Her eyes widened and she suddenly became nervous.

"Don't be nervous, love," I told her softly. "We'll do it together and they'll be thrilled."

I smiled and reluctantly moved my arms so she could sit up.

"You go to the bathroom first," I told her. "I'll get dressed here."

She gave me a small nod and moved away from me. I instantly felt cold and wanted her to come back. I watched her get up and head to the bathroom. I waited for her to close the door so I could get up and straighten out my wrinkled clothes. I was really hot during the night, but I didn't want to take my clothes off. I didn't want Maddie to be uncomfortable.

I sat on the bed and put my shoes on.

"Will?" I thought about my Beta as I waited for Maddie to come out of the bathroom.

"How did it go?" She replied immediately. "

I'll tell you all about it a little later," I told her. Maddie and I are having breakfast. We'll be going to the pack later. Inform the pack that I'm having a meeting today.

"Of course." Will said. "Will you tell them about Maddie?

" "Yes." I said. "She's their Luna and everyone needs to know.

I'm so excited." Will said. "Everything will be ready when you get here.

Thank you." I said just as Maddie came out of the bathroom.

I could tell by the look on her face that she was really nervous. I stood up and walked over to her. I caressed her cheeks and smiled.

"Don't be nervous, princess," I said softly. "Everything will be perfect."

Maddie nodded and I kissed her forehead.

"Come on, love," I said as I took her hand in mine. "

Let's go tell her."

Maddie looked at her hand in mine and took a deep breath. I lifted her hand and kissed it. I couldn't stop. I couldn't stop feeling her skin against my lips. I really wanted to stick close to her and never leave.

I opened the door to her room and we started walking down the stairs together. I had a huge smile on my face and nothing could wipe it away.

I could finally tell everyone that Maddie was mine.

Chapter 52 She is my partner

Madeline's POV

This wasn't going to go well.

I could already picture Janet's face when we told her. I could already feel the hatred radiating off of her. She'd go crazy, and I didn't want to tell her that.

But I couldn't stop Alpha Dimitri from telling her. I would have to tell her why, and I wasn't going to. How was I going to tell her that her mother had made me feel like garbage for the past nine months? I couldn't do that. I couldn't hurt her like this.

I would have to put up with anything she said or did to me. I could handle it. I could handle it for him.

I looked at him, and my heart skipped a beat.

I could handle anything for him.

Alpha Dimitri looked at me and smiled. He grabbed my hand, pulled it up, and placed a soft kiss on my palm. My knees buckled and I nearly fell over. "

Don't look at me like that, princess," he said softly. "Save that look for later, when we're alone."

My eyes widened and I looked away from him immediately. I hadn't even realized I was looking at him in a special way.

Alpha Dimitri chuckled and my heart skipped a beat. Oh my god, what was wrong with me? I wasn't even sure I wanted this and...

Stop it,' Skye sighed. 'Of course you do. He's our mate.

He loves us and we love him. I won't let you leave him, Madeline.

' 'Is that why you don't want to change?' I asked. 'Do you think staying without my wolf will keep me in this pack?'

Skye sighed. 'No, but it's an added bonus.'

I wanted to argue with her, but we had just entered the kitchen and I didn't have time.

'Happy birthday, sweetheart!' Mike exclaimed and started to approach me with a huge smile on his face.

I was only a few steps away when his eyes landed on my hand in Alpha Dimitri's and he abruptly stopped walking. He gasped and looked at us.

"She's my mate," Alpha Dimitri said quietly as he pulled me close and kissed my head.

Fuck. I didn't expect him to say that right away.

Fuck. I should have let go of his hand before we walked into the kitchen.

I looked at Janet and my heart skipped a beat. To say I was pissed would be an understatement. I wasn't pissed. He looked like he was about to turn and tear me apart. He was staring at me and I could feel his hatred seeping into my body.

"Are you kidding me?!" Mike yelled and I forced myself to look at him.

It was so hard to look away from Janet. It was like his hatred was magnetic. I couldn't run away from him no matter how hard I tried. I could still feel his eyes locked on me. I could still feel his anger in the air.

Mike had a huge grin on his face and he looked like he was about to cry.

-Oh, Goddess, I'm so fucking happy!- Mike exclaimed as he took those last steps towards me.

He pulled me away from Alpha Dimitri and hugged me tightly.

"Congratulations, sweetheart," Mike said. "I'm so happy for you.

Dimitri is a wonderful man and I know he'll be an amazing partner."

I gulped and wrapped my free arm around Mike. Alpha Dimitri still held my other hand tightly in his.

"Thank you," I said and gently patted Mike on the back.

Mike let go and looked at Alpha Dimitri. His eyes narrowed slightly and he pointed a finger at him.

"Take care of my girl, Dimitri," Mike said sternly. "Don't make me beat you up."

Alpha Dimitri snorted and pulled me into his arms again.

"Don't worry, Mike," he said. "She's my greatest treasure and I will always keep her safe."

I looked up at him and he leaned down to kiss my forehead.

"Did you hear that, sweetheart?!" Mike exclaimed. "Our kids are mates!" I know it's a little weird that we still call them brothers, but whatever."

I looked at Janet and saw that she was still staring at me with a pissed off face. Mike Dimitri Alpha noticed too. "

Janet

?" Mike called out to her, his voice cracking with confusion. "What's wrong?"

Janet growled under her breath. She clenched her fists and narrowed her eyes at me.

"I don't approve of this," she said coldly. "Reject her, Dimitri. Right now,"

Mike gasped. Dimitri Alpha growled and pushed me behind him.

"I don't give a fuck, mother!" Alpha Dimitri yelled. "I'm not rejecting her! She's mine. Mine.

" "What the hell, Janet?!" Mike exclaimed angrily. "Why do you have a problem with this?!"

Janet glared at Mike angrily.

"She's not a werewolf," Janet said. "She's not strong enough to be a Luna. Savannah should have been Dimitri's mate."

Hearing that name was like a knife being stabbed in my chest.

"You can still fix this, Dimitri," Janet said as she looked at him. "Savannah will take you back. She loves you.

You can still—"

Alpha Dimitri growled so loud I could feel the vibrations in my bones.

"Shut up, mother," Alpha Dimitri said angrily. "Don't mention that bitch's name in front of me and my mate. I'm not leaving Maddie for anyone. She's my mate and your Luna and you will respect her."

Janet glared at me.

"You said you would leave this pack, Madeline," Janet said. "Go away

." Alpha Dimitri growled again. He turned around, putting an arm around my shoulders, and started leading me out of the house.

"Dimitri!" Janet yelled after him.

"I'm so sorry, Princess," Alpha Dimitri said softly. "I had no idea she would react like that." "

I knew it.

" "Please don't listen to her, my love," he continued. "You are my. mate and my Luna. You will not leave, and I will not choose anyone else."

Chapter 53 Angry

Dimitri's POV

I was so fucking mad at my mother!

I wanted to punish her for suggesting I reject Maddie and accept that lying bitch as my mate.

Was I crazy?! How crazy was I?!

"Alpha?" my princess called me and I raised my eyebrows.

Had she really just called me Alpha?

I stopped walking and turned to look at her. She was staring at me with wide eyes and I just wanted to pull her in and kiss her.

"Are you okay?" she asked worriedly.

Of course I wasn't okay. My mother had insulted my mate in front of me. If it was anyone else, I wouldn't be breathing by now. No one insulted Maddie. No one hurt Maddie.

"Did you just call me Alpha?" I asked instead of answering her.

She furrowed her eyebrows slightly and bit her bottom lip.

"I'm sorry," she murmured. "Force of habit."

I pulled her towards me and wrapped one arm around her waist. With my other hand I caressed her cheek and tilted her head up slightly.

"I'm Dimitri to you," I said as I leaned towards her and kissed her cheek. "Or whatever nickname you want to give me. I'm not Alpha to you. I'm your mate. I'm the love of your life."

I placed another kiss on her cheek, this time closer to her lips.

I was having a hard time holding back. I wanted to taste her.

She shuddered and wrapped her arms around my waist. My heart skipped a beat. She turned her head slightly and our lips parted a few inches. I felt her breath on my lips and I almost fainted.

"Are you okay, Dimitri?" she asked in a shaky voice.

I didn't even understand what she was asking me. My mind was completely focused on her. I was surprised that she fit so perfectly in my arms. I was overwhelmed by her scent.

I was overwhelmed by her breath on my lips.

What the fuck had she asked me?

She gulped and looked down at my lips. I had to stop myself from moaning. I was going to kiss her. I couldn't hold back. I had to kiss her.

I was about to press my lips to hers when

Will mentally linked me.

Where are you? He asked me.

I was going to kill him. I was really going to fucking kill him.

I gulped and pressed my lips against Maddie's cheek. I wasn't going to let our first kiss be interrupted by anyone.

Let's go there. I told Will as I looked at my beautiful mate.

I remembered what he had asked me and gave him a small smile.

"I'm okay now that you're in my arms, princess," I told him softly. "I wasn't okay when my mother was calling you names."

He looked down at my chest and I leaned in to give him another kiss on the cheek.

"I'm so sorry, princess," I said. "I don't know what's wrong with her. I'll talk to her. I'll make sure she knows you're my mate and the love of my life."

I caressed her cheek and she looked back at me.

"And that will never change, princess," I added. "You will never stop being the love of my life."

She held me tight and looked down at my lips. I swallowed and felt a wave of heat wash over me. She wanted me to kiss her. I could tell.

I brushed my thumb over her bottom lip. She gasped a little. Her lip was soft and wet and it made the lust inside me explode.

"Tonight, my love," I told her quietly. "Tonight, I will kiss you."

I would love to do so much more than just kiss her, but I had to take it one step at a time.

I reluctantly let go of her and took a step back. I took her hand in mine and started walking again. I had to take a deep breath to try and calm my body a little. My insides felt like they were burning.

Having her in my arms was doing all kinds of weird things to my body.

"Where are we going?" my love asked and I could hear her panting a little.

I smiled in satisfaction. I was glad I wasn't the only one affected by our embrace.

"To our office, Princess," I said. "We have a lot of work to do."

She was silent for a second. "Work?" she asked in a confused voice.

I looked at her and saw that she had a confused look on her face.

"Yes, Princess," I said. "We need to start planning Luna's ceremony. I'll give a speech today and let everyone know that I've found their Luna."

I smiled at the thought. A few more hours and everyone would know she was mine.

"We need to move you out of that house too," I said. "Our house isn't ready yet. I didn't want to pick anything out without you. We'll stay in the packing house until our house is finished, Princess."

She fell silent again.

"Stay in the storage room?" she muttered under her breath.

I looked at her and nodded. "Yes, Princess. I'm not letting you stay with my mother any longer, especially after all the stupid things she said today."

She raised her eyebrows and I saw an emotion I couldn't quite place. Was it concern? Why was she worried?

But I didn't have time to ask her. We walked into the warehouse and I saw Will smiling at us. His smile was the widest I'd ever seen. I chuckled and shook my head at him.

I looked at my partner and saw her looking around in wonder.

I forgot I'd never been here before.

"Welcome to our packhouse, princess," I said softly, causing her to look at me. "Do you like it?"

She looked at the huge chandelier above us and nodded.

"I love it," she murmured and I smiled widely.

Everything was perfect then. If she loved it, I wouldn't change a thing. I would forbid everyone from touching anything without her permission.

I pulled her close and kissed her head. I felt them watching us and I wanted to smile at them and tell them I was their Luna.

But I didn't have time. I had to go to work. I would tell everyone later.

I gripped her hand tighter and pulled her towards Will.

It was time to get to work.

Chapter 54 Beta Will

Madeline's POV

I was nervous.

Well, no. I was more than nervous. I was knackered and didn't know what to do. I kept thinking about Janet and her reaction when Alpha Dimitri told her I was her mate. I wondered what she would do. I wondered how she would punish me for this. I wondered how she would kick me out.

I was completely consumed by her thoughts and I barely noticed Beta Will's presence.

"Luna," she said politely, bowing her head. "Welcome to your pack house. It's wonderful to finally have you here."

I swallowed and forced myself to focus on Beta Will.

"Thank you, Beta," I said quietly. "Call me Maddie, please." She lifted her head and smiled at me.

"Only if you call me Will," he said, making me smile a little.

It would be so hard to call him that. I felt like I didn't belong here.

I felt like I wasn't good enough to be here and call him and Alpha Dimitri by just their first names.

"I'll try," I said and Beta Will winked at me.

Alpha Dimitri pulled me closer to him and kissed the top of my head. I was getting used to having him around. I was getting used to feeling his lips on my body. In fact, I was starting to crave him.

I wanted him to kiss me. I wanted his lips all over me and the thought scared me.

I wasn't even sure I wanted to stay. Janet wouldn't let me stay. "Stop it, Maddie," Skye said sternly. "If you even think about leaving again, I'll tell Skol. I'll tell him about Janet too. Stop thinking about leaving, because you won't."

I ignored her and went back to focusing on Alpha Dimitri and Beta Will.

We were walking now and I could hear them talking about something.

"Is it ready?" Alpha Dimitri asked.

"Yes," Beta Will said, giving him a small nod.

"Everything is ready. Do you want me to send Pete to get his things?"

Whose stuff? Who was Pete?

"No," Alpha Dimitri said. "I'll go. I don't want another man's scent on his stuff. It'll drive me crazy."

Oh, they were talking about me.

"I can go get my stuff," I said, looking at Alpha Dimitri.

I didn't want to bother him. I could go back and get the things I needed.

Alpha Dimitri smiled at me and shook his head.

"No, princess," he said. "I don't want my mother to see you and say anything else that might upset you. I'll go. Don't worry.

" "What did your mother say?" Will asked before I could protest.

"I'll tell you later," Alpha Dimitri sighed, and I could hear annoyance in his voice.

Beta Will opened the door and Alpha Dimitri pulled me into the largest office I'd ever seen. My former Alpha's office was only half the size of this one. There was a huge desk in the center of the room. It was completely covered in papers and folders. Off to the side was another desk, but it looked brand new and there were no papers or folders in sight. I loved the huge windows and natural light in the room. I could see the forest behind the warehouse and it made me smile a little.

"Do you like it, princess?" Alpha Dimitri asked.

I looked at him and nodded. He smiled and leaned down to kiss my forehead.

"I'm glad," he said. "This is your desk."

He pointed to the empty desk in the room and my eyes widened slightly. My desk?

Well, that made sense, didn't it? I was a Luna, right?

"I know it's common for a Luna to have her own office, but I want you here with me at all times," Alpha Dimitri continued. "I can't imagine going through an entire day without you. I need you by my side at all times and I need to see you always."

I couldn't say anything. I stared at the desk, trying hard to calm my racing heart.

It was real. I was Luna. I was his mate. I would have to lead the pack and I would have to make decisions. That desk would be mine.

I would have to sit there, look at papers and be a Luna.

Oh Goddess, I wasn't made to be a Luna! I wasn't made to be her mate! I couldn't do that! I couldn't...

"Maddie?" Alpha Dimitri called out my name with a hint of worry in his voice.

I couldn't answer him. I couldn't even breathe.

"Princess?" Alpha Dimitri called out to me as he spun me around and caressed my cheeks. "What's wrong, my love?"

It hurt to see the worry in his eyes. I didn't want him to worry.

"I'll give you two a minute," Beta Will said softly.

I watched him leave the room as I tried to force my lungs to take in air.

"Madeline?" Alpha Dimitri called out my name and this time I could clearly hear the panic in his voice.

I looked back at him and instinctively buried my nose in his chest.

His scent immediately calmed me down.

"Maddie, love, please tell me what's wrong." Alpha Dimitri shouted as he put his hand on my head and held me close to him.

I felt his lips on the top of my head and I relaxed even more. I had to tell him something. I couldn't let him worry.

"It's all going so fast," I murmured under my breath. "I'm a little overwhelmed."

Alpha Dimitri held me tighter. He gave me another kiss on the head and ran his hand up my back.

"I'm sorry, princess," he said softly. "I should have been a little more considerate. I've been in this relationship nine months longer than you."

He laughed and I looked up at him. Goddess, he was beautiful when he smiled.

"I'm so sorry, Maddie," he said as he caressed my cheek. "I'm a little ahead of myself. I'm so excited to finally be able to share it all with you."

I reached up and caressed his cheek. I couldn't hold back.

I had to touch him. I had to reassure him that everything was okay. He leaned into me and I nearly melted.

"It's okay," I told him. "It's going to take me some time to realize that this is real."

He smiled and placed his hand on mine.

"It's real, my love," he said softly. "You are my mate. You are Queen and the Moon of this Kingdom and this pack."

My heart raced and the fear I felt before returned to my body.

"I'll be here every step of the way, Maddie," Alpha Dimitri continued softly. "You will never be alone. I promise."

He held me close and I let his presence reassure me.

I hoped he was right. I hoped everything was truly okay.

Chapter 55 The plan

Dimitri's POV

I was getting a little bit hasty and had to slow down a bit.

This was all very new to Maddie. She found out about me yesterday and I was already overwhelming her with everything.

I kissed the top of her head again and looked at her. I wanted her so fucking much.

"Let me know if I'm rushing things okay?" I said and she looked at me. "I don't want to burden you with anything. We'll go at your pace princess."

She nodded and gave me a small smile. My heart melted.

"There's one thing I definitely have to do today though," I said as I caressed her cheek.

I had to tell the pack about her. I couldn't wait any longer.

They had to know who she was to me. Seth had to get the fuck out of the way. Every other pack member had to know that she was their Luna and they had to respect her. I would take everything else as slow as she wanted.

"What?" she asked as her eyebrows furrowed a bit.

"I need to tell the pack about you, princess," I said as I leaned down and kissed her forehead. "I want to tell everyone.

I want everyone to know who you are to me."

She gulped nervously but gave me a small nod.

"Don't be nervous," I said softly. "Nothing bad can happen to you while I'm here. You're my world and I'll do whatever I have to to protect you."

She pulled me into a hug and rested her head on my chest. My heart doubled and a small smile spread across my face. I rested my head on hers and ran my fingers through her hair.

"My whole world," I murmured softly.

She was exactly that. My whole world. My whole heart and soul was hers. I was nothing and I didn't even want to be something without her.

Can I go back? Will mentally linked me.

I lifted my head and kissed her temple.

Yes. I mentally linked it again.

The door opened a second later and Will walked back in.

"Is everything okay?" he asked with a hint of concern in his voice.

I looked up at him and smiled.

"Yeah," I said. "Maddie was a little overwhelmed by everything."

Will smiled and shook his head.

"Don't worry, Mads," Will said softly. "I'm here for you. She overwhelms me with her plans all the time, too."

Maddie giggled and I rolled my eyes at her. My heart skipped a beat, though, at the sound of her giggle. I wanted to hear that sound all the time.

"Speaking of my overwhelming plans, when is the speech?" I asked as I let go of Maddie.

She walked over to her desk and ran her hand across the surface. I smiled, a warm feeling washing over me. I'd fantasized about seeing her at that desk for nine months. It belonged there.

I'd also fantasized about leaning her over the desk and... I wanted to do all kinds of things to her, but I knew I'd have to wait a little longer.

"6pm," Will said. "The whole pack's coming."

I nodded, still staring at my mate. I couldn't help but admire her beautiful body. I tried to imagine what she'd look like bent over the table and I could feel my cock getting hard at the thought.

I could picture her moaning my name as she spread her legs and allowed me to enter her beautiful body. I could picture myself grunting as I pulled her head back and kissed her neck. I could picture her clenching around me and screaming my name as she came.

My heart was racing and my cock was hard as a rock.

Fuck, fuck, fuck.

I had to calm down before Will or Maddie noticed.

I ran over to my desk and sat down.

"Should we talk about Luna's ceremony plans today or should we just put it aside for now?" Will asked, but I could barely focus on him.

Maddie looked up at him and I couldn't help but stare at her beautiful lips. I could just imagine them wrapped around my…

No! Fuck!

I needed to calm the fuck down!

"Dimitri?" Will called after me.

I forced myself to swallow and managed to look away from her. Goddess, I was going to go crazy.

"We're doing what Maddie is okay with," I managed to say.

"If she wants to postpone the planning, we'll do it."

Will looked at Maddie and I forced myself to hold his gaze. My cock was painfully hard now and it wouldn't help if I looked at her.

"I'd like to postpone it," Maddie said and her voice sent shivers down my spine. "Maybe we could do it in a few weeks."

I wanted to moan. Even the sound of her voice was turning me on. Fuck!

"That makes sense," Will said, looking at me. "We have that meeting with the Alphas in a week."

I nodded and tried to focus on something other than Maddie.

"A meeting?" he asked and I could hear the confusion in his voice.

"You know about the problem with the rogues we've had for months now, right?" Will asked her.

I didn't want to let myself look at her. My cock wasn't as hard anymore and I needed a few more minutes to calm down completely. If I looked at her again, I knew I'd be back to square one.

She must have nodded because Will started talking again.

"The other packs have the same problems as us," Will said. "We're going to have a meeting with all of them to discuss our next steps."

I allowed myself to look at her and immediately regretted it.

She was frowning and biting her bottom lip. All my effort to calm down disappeared in a second.

Get out of here. I mentally connected with Will.

I felt his eyes boring into me.

"Why?" he asked, confused.

"Now, Will." I said sternly. "Go and make sure everything is ready for my speech."

I kept my eyes on his bottom lip and my heart started racing even faster than before. I wasn't going to be able to wait until tonight. I had to taste those lips immediately.

"See you later, Mads," Will said, causing Maddie to look at him with a confused look on her face. "I have work to do before our Alpha's speech today."

I heard Will leave the room. I heard him close the door behind him.

I kept my eyes on Maddie the whole time. I couldn't look away, no matter how hard I tried. She wasn't biting her lip anymore, but I could see it was still a little red and it was driving me crazy.

"Come here," I said as soon as Will closed the door.

Maddie looked at me and I was sure I was going to pass out from need.

Chapter 56 Our first kiss

Madeline's POV

I wondered why Beta Will had left. We were in the middle of a conversation and he abruptly excused himself.

I wanted to ask him to tell me more about the Rogues. I wanted to ask him if there were any similarities between the attacks. I wanted to ask him if he knew what the Rogues wanted.

"Come here," Dimitri Alpha said as soon as Beta Will left the room.

I looked at him and my whole body shivered. I knew exactly why he had said that to me. He wanted me. He needed me. I could tell by the look in his eyes.

A strange, tickling sensation spread through my gut.

I suddenly felt warm and gasped.

I slowly moved closer, still staring at him. He was still gulping and clenching his jaw.

He took my hand and pulled me onto his lap as soon as I was close enough. I straddled him and he gripped my waist tightly. I felt something hard beneath me and I had to force myself to focus on something else. If it was what I thought it was...

I forced myself to focus on his dark eyes. I put my hands on his shoulders and instinctively leaned closer to him.

I wasn't sure I was breathing.

"I know I told you I was going to kiss you tonight, but I can't wait," he murmured as he stared at my lips.

A shiver of pleasure ran down my spine. I shifted slightly on his lap and he groaned.

"You need to stop doing that," he said, my attention snapping back to the hard thing beneath me.

I wanted to moan but I held back. The bond was calling to me, drawing me to him. The need I felt for him was indescribable. Knowing he wanted me too made it all that much more intense.

"Can I kiss you, Madeline?" he asked as he leaned down and brushed the tip of his nose against mine.

My fingers tangled in his hair, my breathing quickening.

"Please, princess," he moaned.

The need in his voice made my whole body tingle.

He needed me. He wanted to kiss me. I needed to kiss him.

I didn't know if I was doing the right thing but I couldn't help but nod. I wanted his lips on mine. I wanted to kiss him too. I needed to kiss him too.

Alpha Dimitri moaned as he caressed my cheeks and rested his forehead on mine. He kept staring at my lips and breathing heavily.

"I've wanted to do this since the moment I smelled your scent nine months ago," he murmured and I could feel his warm breath on my lips.

I closed my eyes and took a deep breath. His scent penetrated my lungs and my whole body melted against his.

"I've wanted to do this for so long," he murmured as he caressed my cheeks with his thumbs.

I opened my eyes and he lifted his head. He gave me a small smile as he leaned into me. My heart raced to the point I was sure it would jump out of my chest.

His warm lips finally pressed against mine and I disappeared. I didn't know where I was. I didn't know what day it was. I didn't remember my own name.

Everything was him. The air around me was him. The feeling on my skin was him. The tingling inside my body was him. Everything was Dimitri, and nothing else mattered.

He moaned and parted my lips softly. His tongue brushed against mine and I pulled him closer to me.

I never wanted to end the kiss. I didn't want to separate my body from his. I could feel our bond growing stronger with each brush of his lips against mine. I felt his need pulsing through my body.

If just kissing him was this intense, what would it feel like to mark him? How would that affect our bond? How strong would our bond be then?

He tangled his fingers in my hair and held me down as he gently massaged my tongue with his. The quiet grunts and moans escaping him made it that much harder to ignore the throbbing between my legs.

I lowered my head to the back of his neck and pulled him even closer to me.

Our lips moved perfectly together and I relished the taste of him on my mouth and his soft lips sliding against mine.

He tasted incredible and I could already see myself becoming addicted to him. We hadn't broken the kiss yet and I wanted more. I would always want more.

He broke the kiss too soon for my liking. We were both panting hard and clinging to each other as much as we could. My whole body was pressed against his but I wasn't going to complain. Everything was fine.

"I love you, Madeline," he said, resting his forehead against mine again. "I love you so much.

I loved him too. How could I not? He was my mate. My heart and soul were made to love him. My whole body belonged to him.

"The kiss was fucking perfect, princess," he continued softly. "I've never felt anything like this. "

I swallowed and nodded.

"Me neither," I said softly and he smiled.

"I'm glad to know that," he said and let out a small chuckle. "I'm glad I'm the only one who can kiss you and make you feel this good."

He wasn't wrong. He was the only one who could kiss me. I never wanted to feel another man's lips or hands on me. Nothing would make me feel this good. Nothing would make me feel this good.

He was made for me as much as I was made for him. I belonged to him and he wouldn't let anyone else touch me.

Chapter 57 The dress

Dimitri's POV

I kissed my partner! I kissed her and it was fucking perfection. I wanted more. I couldn't wait to do it again and again and again. I was addicted to her now and I would never get enough of her lips. I was so happy and I couldn't stop smiling. "I don't think I've ever seen you so happy," Will said as he helped me fasten my cufflinks. "You haven't stopped smiling since you left your office." My smile grew even wider. "We kissed and it was perfect," I said and Will chuckled. "I figured something like that would have happened," he said as he smiled brightly. "I'm so happy for you. She's a great girl and I can already tell she's going to be an amazing Luna." Heat spread through my extremities. Will was absolutely right. She was amazing in every way. I heard the door to my dressing room open. Maddie peeked through the door and I saw her eyes roam up and down my body.

The blood rushed to her cheeks and I had to hold back a giggle.

I was so flattered. It was obvious that my partner thought I was hot. "Is everything okay with the dress, princess?" I asked. I had laid out a dress for her for today's speech.

It was a simple but gorgeous black dress that matched my suit perfectly. "Yes," she said quietly. "I just need a little help zipping it up." I walked over to her immediately. My breath caught in my throat as she opened the door and let me in. She was fucking beautiful.

The dress hugged her body perfectly. I could see every single curve of her body and it was driving me crazy.

I closed the door and gulped. I froze and could barely move. I could only stare at her. Her ass was fucking perfect in the dress she had chosen. She pulled her hair back into a ponytail and I could perfectly see her bare back. I felt my cock harden and had to hold back a moan. She was so fucking perfect. She turned around and raised her eyebrows. "Is everything okay?" she asked softly. I had to force myself to swallow because I wouldn't be surprised if she started drooling. "Everything is more than okay, princess," I said as I slowly approached her. "You are perfect and I can't stop admiring you." I

finally made it to her and ran my hand up her bare arm.

She was standing in front of the mirror and I had a perfect view of her beautiful face. She blushed and took a deep breath. I

gently moved her ponytail. I moaned softly and my cock grew painfully hard. I put my hand on her back and gently ran my fingers down her spine. She shuddered and leaned into me. I lowered my head and placed soft kisses on her neck.

She moaned quietly as I ran my lips down her jaw. My hand reached her lower back and I wanted to continue but I didn't want to make her uncomfortable. I found her zipper and slowly started to pull it up. I didn't take my lips off her jaw or her neck. She reached up and tangled her fingers in my hair, pulling me even tighter against her. I wrapped my other arm around her waist, holding her tight. I finished zipping her up but didn't stop kissing her neck. I didn't want to

stop. I reached the spot where my mark would soon be and she gasped.

I held her tighter and licked her mark. "Dimitri," she cried out and it sent a jolt of lust through my cock. Fuck. I didn't know putting clothes on a woman could be so arousing. Well, she was the only woman who could get me this fucking horny while putting her clothes on instead of ripping them off her delicious body. No one came close. "Fuck, princess," I murmured against her neck. "You're driving me crazy." She was panting hard and her fingers were completely tangled in my hair. "I'm not the one kissing you like that," she murmured, making me laugh. I lifted my head and looked at her beautiful face. "I'm not the one that's so fucking hot," I said, making her blush again. "I'm not sure I want to show you off to the pack. Maybe we should cover you up a bit." She smiled and shook her head. "On the other hand, I want everyone to get jealous," I added as a small smile spread across my face. "I want them to see how fucking perfect you are and know that you belong to me."

She gulped and looked at my lips. She didn't have to do it twice.

I leaned down and captured her luscious lips with mine. She opened up for me and I slipped my tongue into her warm mouth. My eyes rolled back. She tasted fucking amazing. She tasted like coconut and watermelon. She tasted like summer and I adored her. I would never get tired of her. I didn't want to get enough of her. I wanted to be addicted to her. I turned her around and deepened our kiss. She was completely relaxed in my arms and it made me smile.

She trusted me. She wanted me. She needed me. My hands roamed over her perfect body. Her hands were wrapped around me tightly.

We were as close as we could possibly be. "It's time," I heard Will's voice. "Stop flirting with each other." I moaned and reluctantly stopped kissing her. Her breathing was labored and her lips were swollen and wet. The sight of her triggered another jolt of lust in my cock and I wanted to moan again. "Dimitri?!" Will called out to me. "I'm coming," I said as I leaned into her and gave her a soft kiss on the lips. I let go of her and fixed her dress a little. "Is my hair and makeup okay?" she asked. "I wasn't sure what to do." I smiled and caressed her cheek. "It's perfect, princess," I said softly. She smiled at me and my heart skipped a beat. I still couldn't believe she was mine and I was hers. I was dying to make it official in every way possible.

Chapter 58 The speech

Madeline's point of view

To say I was nervous would be an understatement.

My heart was going to jump out of my body. I was sure of it. I was going to jump up and start bouncing from wall to wall. My legs were going to give out and I was going to pass out.

There were a lot of people around me, but I wasn't paying attention to anyone. I was completely focused on him and the way he spoke to the huge crowd as if it were nothing. He smiled at them and spoke in a calm but stern voice. I could tell they adored him. I could tell by the way they cheered for him when he walked on stage and how they clapped after every little

pause he made.

He looked at me and my knees buckled. He was so fucking handsome and I was so sure it was all a dream. I would wake up and it would be just another day in my life. I would go to work, endure a few insults from his mother and go to bed. There was no way the man on stage belonged to me. There was no way he wanted me and loved me. There was no way she could kiss me and touch me like she did.

I felt Skye stir. She growled a little and tried to talk to me but I ignored her. I couldn't lose my focus. I had to be ready because Dimitri would ask me to join him at any moment.

"Are you ready, Mads?" Beta Will asked me quietly.

I forced myself to look away from Dimitri. Beta Will was looking at me with a small smile on his face.

I wasn't ready but I knew it didn't matter. In a few minutes I would have to go up on stage.

I gave him a small nod and looked at the guards surrounding us. They were all smiling and glancing at me from time to time. They already guessed who I was.

I looked back at my partner and felt a tickle in my lower belly. He had a smile on his face as he spoke about something. I couldn't focus on his words though. I was completely overwhelmed by the way his lips moved. I admired his posture and the way he carried himself. He was a king and it showed. I couldn't see the crowd but I knew every eye in the room was on him. He demanded attention and he got it.

Why did the Goddess think I would be a good fit for him? It was clear that I wasn't good enough. I wasn't cut out to be Queen and everyone would know it right away. Maybe they would even laugh the moment I stepped on stage. If not then, then surely the moment I stepped next to him. Our difference would be so clear then. Everyone would see that I wasn't good enough to be there.

His brows furrowed slightly and he looked at me. His eyes narrowed but he continued speaking in the same tone as before.

What was that about?

'I told Skol,' Skye said, making me want to whimper.

'Why, Skye?' I asked, trying hard not to shake. '

Because I'm not going to let you lie to yourself,' Skye said sternly. I won't let you doubt him or the Goddess. I won't let you abandon him."

I took a deep breath and Dimitri looked back at the crowd.

"I'd like to thank you all for coming today," Dimitri said and I forced myself to listen. "It's always a pleasure to see you all and to be able to talk to you. My pack and my Kingdom hold a special place in my heart and it makes me very happy to share some exciting news with you."

The crowd cheered again and Dimitri smiled.

"Nine months ago, a wonderful young girl joined our pack," Dimitri said and my heart skipped a beat. "Many of you already know who I'm talking about. Those of you who knew her know how wonderful and amazing she is."

He looked at me and smiled.

"From the moment I saw her I knew she was my mate," Dimitri continued and I could hear loud gasps. "

Unfortunately she was underage at the time and I couldn't tell her. She turned eighteen yesterday and I was never happier than the moment she realized who I am to her."

My knees buckled again and Dimitri looked back at the crowd.

"I've found your Luna," he said and the crowd began to cheer and applaud.

Dimitri smiled happily and looked back at me. He held out his hand and my heart stopped beating.

"Breathe, Mads," Beta Will whispered. "They will love you."

I began to walk towards Dimitri. I never took my eyes off him because I knew I would get scared if I looked at anyone or anything else. I could hear the cheers of the crowd, but I focused on him.

My body shook as I finally placed my hand in his.

He kissed it and pulled me close.

I took a deep breath and looked out at the crowd. My eyes landed on Janet and my stomach turned. She looked like she was about to move and pounce on me.

"Meet Madeline Clark, your Moon and Queen," Dimitri said as he gave me a kiss on the top of my head.

The audience cheered and started clapping. Seeing so many smiling faces helped me relax a little. My eyes landed on Seth and my heart tightened a little. He was smiling at me but I could see the pain in his eyes.

I had to talk to him.

"Are you ready, princess?" Dimitri asked quietly.

I looked up at him and gave him a small nod.

Before the speech, Dimitri told me that I would be making him a member of his pack today. He already notified my former Alpha, who gave his permission.

He smiled at me and looked at Beta Will who nodded and walked back into the small room we came out of. My eyes landed on two thrones behind us and doubt began to creep into my heart again. Was I really meant for this? "I will now make Madeline a part of our pack," Dimitri said, causing the crowd to cheer again. "

We will be having a Moon Ceremony very soon.

" I heard Beta Will walking towards us. He was carrying a dagger and a golden goblet. He handed them to Dimitri and gave me a small smile.

Dimitri placed the goblet on the small table behind him. He turned to me and I shook his left hand.

The time had come for me to become a member of his pack. It was something I swore I would never do, but now I stood before him and waited for him to cut off my left palm.

Chapter 59 A part of his pack

Madeline's POV

"I love you," Dimitri whispered as he took my left hand in his.

I kept my gaze fixed on the dagger. He placed it on my palm and made a small cut. My blood began to flow and Dimitri flinched slightly. I raised my eyebrows and looked at him. His jaw twitched.

I watched as he made a cut on his left palm. He didn't even wince. It seemed like my cut hurt him more than his own. He took my left hand in his and I flinched the moment his blood began to flow through my body.

He gulped and gripped my arm tighter.

"Do you, Madeline Clark, accept my invitation to my pack?" Dimitri asked the first of many questions he had for me.

"Yes," I said, my voice shaking a little.

I couldn't look away from him. I was mesmerized by his eyes and the fact that I had a piece of him inside of me. I could feel his blood warming my insides and it was a feeling I never wanted to end.

"Do you promise, Madeline Clark, to always act in the best interest of our pack?" he asked, swallowing.

"I promise," I said and looked at his lips.

I remembered how they felt against my neck and felt a tickle in my lower belly. His jaw twitched and I swore I heard a very low growl escape him.

"Madeline Clark, do you promise to never act against your alpha and your pack?" he asked, his voice shaking slightly.

"I promise," I said again and looked into his eyes.

The lust I saw in them almost made me moan. He wanted me as much as I wanted him. It was hard for me to admit it, but I did. I wanted him so badly.

Dimitri continued to ask me questions. I answered them all. We never took our eyes off each other and I completely forgot that there was an entire pack watching us. I only saw him. All I felt was him. All I wanted was him.

"Do you, Madeline Clark, accept me as your Alpha and King?" Dimitri asked his last question.

I took a deep breath and swallowed. I was about to do what I swore I would never do.

"I accept," I said as I felt his presence inside me.

He was my Alpha now and I was bound to him.

I saw Beta Will approach us with the cup. Dimitri took the cup from Beta Will and let go of my hand. He placed his left hand over the cup and let a drop of blood fall into it. The water inside sizzled as his blood touched it.

He handed me the cup and I took it from him.

"Welcome to the pack, Madeline Clark," he said as I took a sip from the cup.

As soon as my lips touched the liquid, I felt a strong attraction to everyone present. I could feel their emotions. I could hear their voices inside my head. They were all mentally linked to me at the same time.

I was surprised by all the noise in my head, but I focused on the voice that brought peace to my mind and soul.

Welcome, my love. Dimitri mentally linked me. I can't wait to take you to our room and show you that you belong to me.

I gulped down the liquid and handed the cup back to him.

Stop thinking that you don't, he said. You're mine and that will never change.

Dimitri set the cup on the table behind him. He took my left hand in his and looked at the cut. Pain flashed in his eyes and I wanted to tell him it was okay. It was a small cut.

But I didn't get the chance. Dimitri lifted my hand and gently licked the wound. It closed immediately and I gasped silently.

"I'm a werewolf, princess," he said softly. "One of the best things about me is that I can heal my mate."

I had no idea I could do that. I stared at him with wide eyes. He winked at me and turned to the crowd. He smiled brightly and the crowd cheered again.

"Madeline Clark is now a member of our pack,"

Dimitri announced excitedly. "You can congratulate her during the little reception we have planned. Thanks for coming."

The crowd began to clap and cheer. Dimitri waved at them and started to walk away, pulling me behind him.

I looked at the crowd and smiled. They were still mentally linked to me, but I couldn't focus on any of them. It was very difficult.

It would take a while until I got it right. With Dimitri, though, it was easy. Probably because he was my mate.

Dimitri led me back to the room where he was waiting with Beta Will. It was empty now. He closed the door and hugged me. He kissed me hard and growled.

"Feeling your blood inside me has been the hottest thing I've ever experienced," he murmured against my lips and my heart raced. "I can't wait to mark you. I can't wait to experience it."

I nodded and kissed him back. He growled and tangled his fingers in my hair.

He took a few steps forward and pinned me against the door. He lowered his lips to my neck and I moaned. He kissed and sucked on me, making my legs shake and my knees buckle. He reached my marked spot and bit down gently. I saw stars.

"Stop thinking you're not made for me," he growled. "You're mine, Madeline. The Goddess made no mistake. You're made for me and I was made for you."

I gulped and tangled my fingers in his hair. I needed to feel him as close as possible.

He lifted his head and raised an eyebrow.

"Tell me you understand me," he said. "Tell me Skye won't have to say that to Skol again." His

breathing was labored. The pain in his voice nearly made me cry.

"I understand," I said softly. "I'm made for you. I'm yours."

His eyes darkened and he growled.

"Repeat that," he said as he leaned into me and held me tighter.

I was shaking all over now. Everything around me was him. He was in the air I breathed. He was on my skin. I could only hear his voice. He

was everywhere.

"I'm yours," I repeated and he moaned softly.

He kissed me again and I saw stars. I was his. I was completely his.

Chapter 60 The reception

Dimitri's POV

I couldn't stop smiling. I was floating on clouds and I felt like I was high.

I probably was. I was high on her. I was high on her presence, her smell, and her words. She said she was mine. She confirmed it. The only thing missing was my mark on her neck and my ring on her finger.

She would have them soon. I already had a ring for her. I was waiting for the perfect moment to ask her to marry me.

I held her hand as we walked through the crowd. Everyone wanted to congratulate her. Everyone wanted to meet her. They kept coming up to us, smiling, and telling me how lucky I am to have a Luna as beautiful as her.

She kept blushing and I kept grinning like an idiot.

They were absolutely right. I was one lucky bastard. She was beautiful and kind. She was everything I wanted and needed.

I was so fucking happy that now everyone knew who she was to me. I was happy that I could finally rip the head off anyone who looked at her lustfully.

I kept her away from my mother on purpose. I could see my mother's angry face, and I didn't want to burden Maddie with that. I was nervous enough as it was.

"You have beautiful hair, Luna," I heard a little girl say.

Maddie crouched down so she was face to face with the girl who was smiling brightly at my companion. She let go of my hand and I had to hold back a groan. I didn't want her to let me go among so many people.

"It's not as pretty as yours," Maddie said with a small smile on her face. "Who braided your hair?"

The girl looked up. "My mother. She knows how to do them better than my father. He always messes them up."

Maddie giggled and my heart doubled.

"Your mom makes the most beautiful braids," Maddie said softly and the girl smiled widely.

"Thank you, Luna," the little girl said.

Her mother smiled at Maddie and me. She congratulated us and took the little girl away. Maddie didn't stop smiling at her.

I can't wait to have a child with you. I mentally linked with her and she looked at me. You're going to be a wonderful mother.

I was getting hard just thinking about being pregnant. I could just imagine how incredibly beautiful she was going to be and it made my whole body shake with need.

I'm a little young to be a mother. She mentally linked back and I smiled.

I know, princess. I said as I pulled her to me and kissed the top of her head. We have all the time in the world to be parents.

I want to enjoy being with you first.

She smiled at me and my heart skipped a beat. I wanted to pick her up and take her to our room. I wanted to get her away from the crowd and enjoy her.

But first I had one more thing to do. I had to introduce her to the council members.

I smiled at her and took her hand in mine. I looked around the room until my eyes landed on Landon. He was standing by the dessert table, talking to Rayan and Kendrick.

I took a deep breath and started to approach them. I smiled at my pack members as I passed by. They bowed their heads and continued to smile happily at my companion.

Landon looked at me as we approached them. Kendrick, being the youngest and the biggest fucker out of all of them, started looking my mate up and down. I tensed up immediately. I'd rip his fucking head off if he touched her. He might be a member of a thousand fucking councils, but he wasn't going to escape my wrath.

"Alpha Dimitri," Landon said politely as he bowed his head slightly. "Congratulations on finding your mate."

"Thank you, Landon," I said, still staring at Kendrick. "I've never been happier."

Maddie squeezed my hand and took a step closer to me. I could tell she wasn't comfortable with the way Kendrick was looking at her. My anger grew and I was ready to rip her eyes out.

"Kendrick," Landon said calmly and Kendrick finally looked away from my mate.

He looked at me and smirked. It was barely noticeable, but it pissed me off.

"Alpha Dimitri," Kendrick said. "Congratulations." She's beautiful."

I set my jaw and pulled Maddie closer. I forced a smile.

"She is," I said. "She's beautiful, and she's mine."

Rayan laughed and shook his head.

"You don't need to claim anything, Alpha," Rayan said with a small smile on his face. "She's beautiful, but we're a little old for her."

I gritted my teeth but kept a fake smile. I hated them and I hated having to be polite to them.

I looked away from them and focused on my love. I put my hands on her shoulders and had her stand in front of me. I made sure to hold her tight.

"These are the council members, Madeline," I said, trying to sound calm. "Landon is the Lord Chancellor of our Kingdom.

Rayan is the Lord Protector, and Kendrick is the Royal Secretary."

Maddie nodded and shook their hands. I nearly went crazy when Kendrick took her hand. There was a glint of lust in his eyes and I almost flinched on the spot.

"Nice to meet you," Maddie said politely.

"I'm glad to meet you too, Luna," Landon said, taking her hand. "I'm looking forward to working together."

I didn't look forward to it. The three of them were slimy, greedy leeches. The only reason I had to put up with them was because of an agreement between the three fallen Kingdoms. Dimitri? My love mentally linked me.

I leaned down to kiss the top of his head.

"Yes, princess?" I asked.

"Is it okay if we take a break?" he asked. "My head hurts."

My heart raced, and I immediately began to worry.

Did his head hurt? Why? Was something wrong?

I looked at Landon and gave him a forced, but polite smile.

"Will you please excuse us?" I said, bowing my head slightly.

"My mate and I must continue to greet our pack members. After all, some of them traveled a long way to be here."

"Of course, Alpha," Landon said. "We'll have time to talk about everything later."

I gave him a small nod and took Maddie's hand in mine.

"Bye," Maddie said politely as I started to lead her away.

I needed to get her away from there. I needed a pack medic to check her out. I needed to make sure she was okay.

Chapter 61 Mind Link

Dimitri's POV

"What's wrong, love?" I asked as soon as I closed the door behind us.

I led her back to our office. I knew no one would bother us here.

I caressed her cheeks and kissed her forehead. She wasn't hot. She had no temperature.

"It's the mind link," she murmured. "I'm still controlling it ." I raised my eyebrows slightly. Did the mind link make her head hurt?

"What do you mean, princess?" I asked as I caressed her cheek. "The mind link shouldn't hurt." She sighed and shook her head slightly.

"It doesn't really hurt," she said. "It's kind of tiring hearing them talk to me all the time. I can even tell who's who and I can't even respond. I'd like to respond though. I don't want them to think I'm ignoring them."

I was confused. What the hell was she talking about?

"It's easy with you," she added. "I guess it's because you're my partner."

I was really confused.

Maybe she was too. Maybe she was tired. A lot has happened in the past 24 hours. Her whole life turned upside down. She was probably really confused and tired.

I took her hand and walked over to the couch. I sat down and pulled her onto my lap. She straddled me and rested her head on my shoulder. I started playing with her ponytail and gently rubbing her back. She sighed contently.

"Thank you," she murmured softly. "Your touch has silenced her a bit. I had no idea mind links were this intense."

I frowned again. Mind links weren't intense.

They were like talking. You didn't have to keep anything to yourself. If you didn't want to make a mind link with someone, you just blocked them.

I turned my head and kissed her cheek. She smiled a little and my heart skipped a beat. I began to gently rub her temples and she relaxed even more. She took a deep breath and let it out slowly.

"How are you, princess?" I asked softly.

"The best," she murmured. "Thank you so much."

"You don't have to thank me," I said. "You're my mate and I'll always take care of you. You'll never suffer when I'm around."

I hated seeing her hurt. When I cut her palm, a wave of pain washed over me. I was dying to finish the ceremony so I could heal her.

She lifted her head slightly and gave me a small smile.

"How are you holding up?" she asked. "Will you teach me how to distinguish voices and how to respond?"

I furrowed my eyebrows again. I leaned towards her and kissed the tip of her nose. Her words confused and scared me. I didn't understand what she was talking about. I didn't understand how she couldn't make out the links and respond.

"Can you explain to me what exactly you hear, princess?"

I asked quietly.

I needed more information before I spoke to her. I didn't want to scare her.

"Well, the voices," she said, sighing tiredly. "There are a lot of them in my head. I can't figure out who they belong to exactly.

The only one I managed to decipher was yours. That was easy."

She raised her eyebrows and bit her lower lip.

"The rest are a mess," she continued. "I wanted to answer them, but I couldn't figure out who was trying to mentally link me."

She shook her head and sighed again.

"It's a little overwhelming," she added. "I'm not used to mentally linking and feeling so many people's emotions."

I froze.

What the hell was she talking about?

Feeling so many people's emotions?

My heart raced and a wave of fear washed over me. "

She's not talking about mental links, Dimitri," Skol said calmly.

I clenched my jaw and swallowed.

What do you know? I asked, but she ignored me.

Skol—I screamed when she didn't answer.

I felt her pull back, and the rage inside me erupted. She knew something about my mate, but she refused to tell me?

I was going to shove her own claws up her ass.

Maddie's contented sigh brought my focus back to her. She closed her eyes and settled into my arms. I held her tighter and kissed her cheek again.

"Whose emotions can you feel, princess?" I asked, trying to keep my voice from shaking.

Maddie opened her beautiful eyes and looked at me. Her eyebrows raised slightly and she studied my face for a second.

"Well, everyone's," she said, making my heart stop. "Though I've never been told that was part of the mind link, too."

I swallowed and caressed her cheek. I took a deep breath and leaned in to kiss the tip of her nose.

"It's not, Maddie," I said softly. "I can't feel other people's emotions. I can't hear them in my head all the time."

Her eyes widened slightly. She lifted her head and sat on my lap. I kept my hands on her hips, making sure she couldn't get up. I couldn't let go.

"What are you talking about?" she asked quietly.

I took another deep breath and held her tighter.

"I don't know what's going on, Maddie, but what you can hear and feel isn't a mind link," I said. "

This is mind linking." I finished my sentence through our mind link. Do you hear the difference between my voice and everyone else's?"

Her eyes widened even more. I saw the fear in her eyes and pulled her close to my chest immediately.

"Don't be afraid, princess," I said quietly. "We'll figure it out. I promise. We'll fix it. I'll fix it."

Maddie hugged me tightly. She pressed her body against mine and I could feel her shaking. My heart broke. I hated seeing her scared or hurt. I fucking hated it.

"I'm here, honey," I said, wrapping my arms around her. "I'm here, and I'm never leaving. We'll figure this out."

I turned my head to kiss her temple just as I heard Will approach my office. He walked in without knocking.

—Dimitri, the guests are... he said but stopped as soon as he saw us.

His eyebrows furrowed and I saw concern on his face.

—What happened? — he asked worriedly. —Are you okay, Mads?

—

—Go inside and close the door—, I told him and he listened to me.

I had to tell him what had happened. He could help us solve this.

Chapter 62 What is happening to me?

POV Maddie

I was so scared.

I could clearly hear their voices inside my head. I felt their emotions as if they were my own.

What the hell was happening to me?

"Come in and close the door," Dimitri told Beta Will and my heart raced.

No, please. I mentally connected to Dimitri. "He'll think I'm crazy."

"He won't, princess," Dimitri said as he turned his head and kissed my temple again. "He'll take this seriously, I promise."

He gently ran his hand down my back. I felt a wave of calm wash over me. "

We have to figure this out, my love," Dimitri continued. "He's my best friend and your biggest protector. He would never think you're crazy."

I swallowed and felt my heart race. But what if...?"

Beta Will sat down on the couch next to us.

"Is everything okay, Mads?" he asked worriedly. "Are you hurt?"

The genuine concern in his voice made me relax slightly.

He sounded like he really cared about me.

"Will you explain it to me, Princess, or do you want me to?" Dimitri asked.

I took a deep breath and lifted my head. Dimitri let me sit up, but he didn't take his hands off of me. I knew he wouldn't let me get up. I didn't even want to. I felt safe with him. I couldn't hear the voices when I was in his arms. Everything was quiet and peaceful.

"Can you please?" I asked quietly.

I knew I wouldn't be able to explain it properly. I was embarrassed and scared.

My voice would shake and nothing would come out.

"Of course, Princess," Dimitri said as he reached up and caressed my cheek.

He looked at Beta Will who was smiling at us.

"Before we start I just want to thank Maddie," Beta Will said and I furrowed my eyebrows. "I've never seen Dimitri so happy and I have you to thank for that."

My heart clenched painfully. I almost left him.

I wanted to leave him. A small part of me still screamed at me that I shouldn't be with him. I was still sure he'd be better off without me.

"Madeline," Dimitri said sternly and I looked at him.

He raised an eyebrow.

"Skye's telling me everything," he said. "Enough. You promised me."

I tried to swallow the lump in my throat.

I'm sorry. I mentally linked it. *I'm scared. What if something bad happens to me? You don't need a sick Luna. You need...*

I need you, Madeline. He stopped me as his eyes narrowed and he held me tighter. *You're not sick and I wouldn't be better off without you. Stop saying it. Stop thinking about it.*

"Can someone explain to me what's going on?" Beta Will asked, interrupting our conversation.

Dimitri and I looked at him. Dimitri sighed and ran his fingers through his hair.

"Maddie asked me for a little break because she had a headache," Dimitri started to speak and I tensed. "We came here and she said the mind link was a little tiring and she needed a little break."

Beta Will raised his eyebrows. My heart raced.

"I was a little confused so I asked her to explain," Dimitri continued as he pulled me back to him. "She said she couldn't tell the voices in her head apart and respond to them. She also said it was tiring to feel everyone's emotions."

Beta Will's eyes widened. He looked at me and I felt a wave of embarrassment wash over me. Dimitri kissed the top of my head. "

There's nothing to be ashamed of, my princess. He mentally linked me.

I was starting to understand the difference between the mind link and whatever the other thing was. The mind link was like talking face to face. I could clearly hear the voice of the person who was mind linking me. I could block the mind link. I couldn't block the voices I heard. The voices weren't clear. They were a complete mess and I couldn't even understand what they were saying.

"You can't feel emotions through the mind link," Beta Will muttered, still staring at me.

"I already explained that to him," Dimitri sighed. "I told him that what he was feeling and hearing wasn't a mind link. It was something else." Beta Will looked at Dimitri and nodded.

"Do you have any idea what that could be?" he asked and Dimitri tensed a little.

I looked up at him and saw him staring at Beta Will with an unreadable expression on his face.

"Maybe so," he muttered and I froze. "But I'm not sure I'm right. I'm not even sure it's possible

." My stomach started to turn and I felt like I was going to throw up.

"Tell us," Beta Will said nervously.

I wasn't sure I wanted to hear it.

Dimitri looked at me and gave me a small smile. He raised his hand and caressed my cheek.

"I think Maddie reads their minds," Dimitri said and my whole world stopped spinning. "I think she has powers. I think she's special."

"Read their minds?!

What?!

No! That was impossible!"

My eyes widened and I was about to speak but Beta Will cut me off.

"That was the first thing I thought," he said and I looked at him with a shocked expression on my face.

Were they serious?

"We need to find someone who might know a little more about this," Dimitri said, making me look back at him. "We need to find out what exactly it is and what it means."

Dimitri caressed my cheek again. He leaned towards me and gently kissed my lips.

"We need to find out who you really are, Maddie," Dimitri added quietly. "

I'm pretty sure this has something to do with Skye refusing to change," Dimitri added through the mind link. "She knows what's going on, Maddie."

My eyes widened. I think so. Skye knew. She had to know.

"Skye?" I called her. What's happening to me?!

Chapter 63 I've had enough

Dimitri's POV

"I'll be back soon, princess," I said as I kissed her softly.

I didn't want to leave her, but I had to get back to the reception. I could tell she felt better when I was with her. I could tell she didn't want me to leave her.

"I can go with you," she said, but I saw how tired she was.

I wasn't surprised. If I was right and she really could read people's minds, that had to be exhausting.

"No, love," I said, giving her a small smile. "Stay here and rest. I'll be back soon and we'll go to our room."

I didn't get a chance to grab her things, but it would be fine for one night. She could sleep in my shirt and I had everything she could possibly need.

"Keep her safe," I said as I looked at Will. "Put a mind link on me if anything happens."

He nodded and gave me a small smile.

"Don't worry," Will said. "She'll be okay."

I kissed her forehead and reluctantly let go. She looked at me and gave me a small smile. But it didn't reach her eyes.

"I'll be right back, okay?" I said, trying to stop myself from pulling her towards me.

If I did, I'd never leave.

She nodded and I started to walk out of the room. I had to leave before she changed her mind and left me.

I closed the door behind me and felt my heart tugging at me to get back to her. I really hated leaving her alone. Not being able to see or touch her was driving me crazy.

I took a deep breath and hurried down the stairs. The sooner I got this over with, the sooner I could get back to her.

"Dimitri!" I heard Mike's voice as I walked back into the reception area.

I looked at him and he motioned for me to come over to where he and my mother were standing.

"Where's Maddie?" Mike asked as soon as I got close to them. "We wanted to congratulate her.

" "You want to congratulate her," my mother muttered angrily.

I looked at her and clenched my jaw. I had had enough of her behavior.

"Enough, mother," I said angrily. "She's my mate and you're going to have to accept that."

My mother rolled her eyes and anger exploded inside me.

"What do you have against her?" I asked, trying not to growl. " What did she do to you?"

My mother clenched her fists and narrowed her eyes.

"She's not cut out to be Queen," she said angrily. "She's not cut out to be the Moon of my pack. She's just a poor orphan who deserves to be cast aside."

My eyes widened. Skol began to thrash and growl. I wanted to yell at him, but Mike beat me to it.

"Janet!" he exclaimed angrily. "Take that back! You're talking about my daughter." My mother giggled and looked at Mike.

"Your daughter?" she scoffed. "The one you abandoned? You knew all those years ago that she wasn't worth your time. Maybe you could talk some sense into my son."

I blushed.

But I didn't have time to react. Mike growled, his canines elongating. He grabbed my mother's arm and started to pull her away.

"Dimitri!" My mother mentally linked me, but I ignored her.

Deal with her, Mike. I mentally linked him instead of her.

Don't come back to the reception. I don't want to cause a scene.

Mike turned around and gave me a small nod.

I could see how angry he was.

I was angry too, but my pack members were all around us and I really didn't want them to witness me strangling my mother.

"Alpha," I heard Kendrick's voice behind me.

I turned around to see him smiling at me. His smile, like everything he did and said, was fake.

"Kendrick," I said politely. "Are you enjoying the party?"

"Very much so, Alpha," he said, tilting his head slightly. "I would enjoy it even more if your precious Luna were here."

I clenched my jaw and swallowed. I had to fight hard to keep a smile on my face.

"She asked to be excused," I said calmly. "She's had a really rough day and is a little tired."

Kendrick smiled, making my stomach turn. He always gave me the creeps and that feeling was intensified now that he had a partner. He was a man in his forties. He was bald, pale, and always seemed sweaty. He was overweight and looked much older than his age. Every time I saw him, he was wearing royal robes.

I wondered if he had any more clothes in his closet.

It's a shame," Kendrick said, sighing quietly. "She's a real beauty and I think I'll enjoy spending time with her.

Please let her know that I look forward to seeing her again."

The anger intensified and I had a hard time keeping my smile.

I wished I could somehow stop him from seeing her, but I knew that wasn't possible. She was a Queen and she had to work with the council members.

"I'll let him know," I said, trying to sound calm. "Thank you, Kendrick."

He gave me another fake smile, gave a small bow, and walked away.

I clenched my fists and wished I could strangle him. I didn't like any of the Council members, but I hated Kendrick. There was something about him that made my skin crawl.

I took a deep breath and started walking through the crowd. I stopped to talk to a few members of my pack. They were all asking about Maddie and that made me happy. They already liked her and cared about her.

Is everything okay? I made a mental link with Will.

Yes. He replied. We're talking and getting to know each other. Will you be back soon?

Yes. I told him. I just need to say goodbye to everyone.

Good. Will said. I think your presence helps her with the vocals. She's been struggling since you left.

My heart raced and my need to protect Maddie exploded inside me.

I'm coming right now. I said as I hurried towards the stage.

I already missed her anyway. I wanted to get back to her as soon as possible.

Chapter 64 The voices

Madeline's POV

The voices came back in full force as soon as Dimitri left the room.

My heart raced and I tried hard to ignore them. My head felt like it was going to explode and I just wanted Dimitri back. Everything was better when he was here.

But I couldn't keep him from his pack. He was an Alpha. He had a job.

He couldn't be with me all the time.

"Maddie?" Beta Will called to me and I looked at him.

He sat down next to me and gave me a small smile.

"Are you okay?" he asked and I nodded.

"I'm okay," I said. "I'm just a little tired."

But I wasn't lying. I was tired. I was exhausted. And hearing all those voices in my head was making it worse.

I wanted Dimitri. I wanted him to wrap his arms around me. I wanted to close my eyes and sleep.

"Can you hear them again?" Beta Will asked worriedly.

I swallowed the lump in my throat and nodded.

"It's easier when Dimitri's here, isn't it?" she asked as a small smile spread across her face.

I nodded again and her smile grew.

"I can't tell you how happy it makes me that I finally have you," Beta Will said. "It's been so hard watching him have to go through all that shit the past nine months. I wanted him to tell you sooner, but he refused. He wanted you to experience it all."

My heart clenched painfully and I looked down at my lap.

If he had told me I was his mate before I turned eighteen, I probably would have run away. I was embarrassed to admit it, but it was the truth. I'd wanted to leave the pack ever since I got here.

If I'd found out I was going to be tied to this place forever, I would have left before I ever got a chance to experience the bond.

I wasn't sure I could leave him now.

I started to love him. I loved him. I loved him with every part of my heart and soul. I belonged to him. I wanted to feel his body against mine. I wanted to be surrounded by his scent. I wanted to be close to him.

No, I couldn't leave him now.

"I know it's a shock, Maddie, but you're not alone," Beta Will spoke again and I looked up at him. "You have Dimitri. He's an amazing man and he's going to be an amazing partner. He already is." He smiled and I nodded. He really was an amazing partner. He'd already done so much for me.

"You have me too," Beta Will continued. "It's my duty as a Beta to keep you safe. You're my Luna and we have our own bond that I can't and won't break. The need and duty to protect you is written in my blood."

He smiled and took my hand in his.

"But I also want to be here as a friend, Maddie, not just a protector," he added softly. —I know we just met and it'll take you a while to relax around me, but I want to be your real friend. I want to be here for you and help you with everything. I want to do it for you and for Dimitri. — I felt tears welling up in the corners of my eyes.

"Thanks," I said, trying to swallow the lump in my throat. "I'm sure we'll be great friends."

I needed to find a way to relax a little first. I needed to find a way to stop feeling so guilty.

I needed to find a way to allow myself to believe that I really was Dimitri's mate and the Luna of this pack.

But it was surreal. It all felt like a dream. I'd been planning to leave the pack just hours ago, and now I was a part of it.

"I can't help but think you're a little insecure about it all, Maddie," Beta Will said after a few moments of silence.

I sighed and gave him a small nod.

"I find that hard to believe," I said truthfully. "I feel like I'm going to wake up and realize I've been dreaming the whole time."

Beta Will smiled and shook his head.

"It's not a dream," he said. "I know it feels like it, especially with how fast everything is going, but it's not a dream, Mads."

I took a deep breath and let it out slowly.

"I just hope I'm a good Luna," I murmured under my breath. "I hope I'm worthy of Dimitri."

Beta Will squeezed my hand and smiled at me.

"You'll be an amazing Luna," he said. "You're already worthy of Dimitri. He should be worrying about being worthy of you."

Beta Will winked at me and I laughed a little.

"Don't worry so much, Mads," Beta Will continued. "That man is hopelessly in love with you and has been for the past nine months. He fought so hard for you before you even knew who he was to you. It's clear he thinks you're more than worthy of him." My heart skipped a beat and I felt like crying.

I needed to talk to him. I needed to apologize for how I'd behaved after I found out he was my mate. I'd hurt him so much and he'd done nothing but love and care for me.

Suddenly, the voices in my head grew louder. I groaned and put my hand to my forehead.

"Dimitri's on his way," he said worriedly. "He'll be here in a few minutes." I looked at him and raised my eyebrows.

"And the reception?" I asked.

"You're more important than that, Maddie," he said. "Besides, the pack doesn't need him for food and fun. He'll just give a short speech, thank everyone for coming, and then he'll be back." I nodded, feeling a wave of relief wash over me.

"Is it bad?" Willi asked quietly.

I raised my eyebrows and sighed.

"He's louder," I said and he nodded.

"It's okay," he said quietly. "Just a few more minutes and he'll be here."

I looked at the door and gulped. I was dying to see him again. I couldn't wait to be in his arms again.

Chapter 65 Sorry

Dimitri's POV

I was dying to get back to my office.

My arms burned with the need to hold her. It hurt to know she was hurting. I couldn't wait to get there and hold her. I missed her so much. I had been needing her and wanting her to make up for it for me for nine months. Being away from her for even a few minutes was a complete waste of time.

I finally got to my office and opened the door. Her scent filled my lungs and my body completely relaxed.

She looked at me and smiled.

"Princess," I murmured as I closed the door and ran to her.

My heart melted when she held out her hand to me. I moaned softly when I finally touched her. I pulled her close and hugged her tightly. I put a hand on her head and kissed her temple.

"Does it hurt?" I asked and she shook her head.

"Not anymore," she said and smiled.

I looked at Will and saw him smiling at me. I rolled my eyes.

"Can you come down and make sure everything's okay?" I asked as I ran my fingers through Maddie's hair.

"Of course," Will said. "Do you need anything else?"

"No," I said, shaking my head. "See you tomorrow."

Will nodded and looked at Maddie. He smiled a little.

"Bye, Mads," he said and she looked up at him.

"Bye, Will," she said smiling back.

I couldn't help but caress her cheek. She was so fucking beautiful that I needed to touch her to make sure she was real.

I still couldn't believe she was mine.

I heard Will walk away but I didn't take my eyes off Maddie. I couldn't stop staring at her. I just couldn't get enough of her.

I heard the door close and Maddie looked up at me. She reached up and caressed my cheek. My heart raced and I leaned in further into her touch. My whole body was shaking and my heart felt like it was going to jump out of my chest. She studied my face for a few moments before leaning in and kissing me.

My heart skipped a beat.

I moaned and tangled my fingers in her hair. I held her tighter and deepened the kiss.

It was the first time she had initiated it and I was sure I was going to explode with happiness.

She stopped kissing me but didn't pull away. She rested her forehead against mine and took a deep breath.

"I'm sorry, Dimitri," she said softly and my breath caught.

Why was she sorry? Did she kiss me like that because I was going to leave her?

No, no, no, no.

I held her tighter. She reached out and ran her fingers through my hair.

"I'm sorry I tried to reject you when I found out," she said softly. "I'm sorry I acted like that. It's just..."

She stopped talking and took a deep breath.

I relaxed a little. She wasn't going to leave me. Not that I would let her, but it was nice to know that she loved me too.

"I'm mad at Mike," she continued. "I didn't want to stay here. I didn't want to be around him. I wanted to leave this pack from the moment I was told I would be living here."

She lifted her head slightly and caressed my cheek.

"I tried to push you away because I wanted to get away from Mike and I'm so sorry," she added. "You didn't deserve it and I will spend the rest of my life
making up for it."

I sighed in relief and kissed her softly.

"I love you, Madeline," I murmured against her lips. "You have nothing to make up for. You made up for it the moment you stayed and let me love you."

She wrapped her arms around my neck and kissed me hard. I held her tighter and pulled her onto my lap. She straddled me and my heart began to beat faster.

"I love you too," she said softly as she stopped kissing me.

My eyes went wide and I was absolutely, positively certain I would pass out from the excitement. Hearing her say that was like injecting me with the best drug in the fucking world. It was addictive and I wanted more.

"Say it again," I murmured as I rested my forehead against hers. "Please say it again."

"I love you," she repeated and smiled a little.

Something between a moan and a sob escaped my lips. I kissed her again, tangling my fingers in her hair and pulling her as close to me as I could. I felt her smile and I couldn't help but do the same. The happiness I felt was hard to describe.

We stopped kissing and I held her tight. She hugged me back and took a deep breath.

"I'm so sorry about Mike, princess," I said softly. "

He made a huge mistake leaving you. " I got really mad at him when he told me he had a daughter and a partner and that he had abandoned them. Partners and children are a gift from the Goddess and should be cherished."

Maddie pulled her arms away from me. She looked at me and nodded.

"I almost made the same mistake as my father," she murmured softly.

I caressed her cheek and smiled.

"Good thing I'm stubborn," I said, chuckling. "I wasn't going to let you do that. I was never going to let you leave me."

Maddie smiled and gave me another soft kiss on the lips.

"Thank you for being so stubborn," she said, making me giggle.

I kissed her soft lips and cheek. I hugged her again and held her tight.

"Are you tired, princess?" I asked. "Do you want to go to our room?"

She nodded and I smiled. I couldn't stop smiling and I couldn't wait to lay down next to her.

I tried to let go of her so we could get up and leave the office, but she held on tighter and made herself comfortable.

"Five more minutes," she murmured softly, and I laughed.

I held her tighter and kissed her temple.

"Okay, my princess," I said, chuckling. "Five more minutes."

It was like she thought I wouldn't hold her like that when we got to our room. I would always hold her like that. I would never let her go. It was impossible for me to do that. She was a part of my body and soul, and I would never let her go.

Chapter 66 Yes, alpha

Madeline's POV

Waking up in Dimitri's arms was the best thing in the world. I'd never felt safer. I'd never felt more loved.

"Good morning, gorgeous," he said as he placed another kiss on my neck. "How'd you sleep?"

I ran my hand up his muscled back and pressed myself closer to him.

"So good," I said, keeping my eyes closed. "And you?"

Dimitri's hand ran up my body until he reached the back of my knee. He pulled my leg up and draped it over his waist.

I hadn't gotten my stuff from Mike's yet, so I was sleeping in one of Dimitri's t-shirts. My legs were bare, and the feel of his soft fingers on my bare skin did all kinds of weird things to me.

"Sleeping with you will always result in the best sleep of my life," Dimitri said softly.

I smiled and opened my eyes. He was already looking at me and the love I saw in his eyes made me shiver.

He smiled and gave me a soft kiss on the lips.

"I'm going to go get your things today, princess," he said as he stopped kissing me.

I took a deep breath and bit my bottom lip.

"Can I go too?" I asked and he raised his eyebrows slightly.

"Are you sure?" he asked. "I don't want my mother to make you uncomfortable."

I gulped and felt a wave of nervousness and fear wash over me. I was embarrassed to admit it, but Janet scared me.

I was afraid of what she might do or say.

But my love for Dimitri was far greater than my fear of his mother. If I was going to stay with him and be a Luna, I had to start acting like one. I wanted to make peace with my father and Janet.

I wanted to start over.

"I'm sure," I said, trying not to show him how nervous I really was. "I want to talk to Mike and your mother. I want to start over."

Dimitri gave me a small smile. He nodded and caressed my cheek. "

It's okay, princess," he said. "But if he says anything bad, I'll get you out of there. I won't let him hurt you."

I smiled and kissed him softly. He moaned and held me tight.

"There's nothing I'd like more than to stay in this bed with you, but we have work to do," he murmured against my lips.

I nodded and tried to let go. But he didn't let me. He wrapped his arms around me and kissed me hard. I chuckled and he smiled.

"Letting you out of this bed is a little harder than I thought," he murmured against my lips.

I smiled and ran my fingers through his soft hair.

"We'll be back here tonight," I said and he nodded.

"That's the only reason I'm letting you go now," he said as he moved his arms so I could get up.

I snorted and sat up. Dimitri got off the bed and I couldn't help but stare at his muscled arms. The shirt he wore to bed was tight and I could see the contours of his body perfectly. The sight made me drool a little.

I tried to imagine what he looked like without a shirt on and had to hold back a groan.

"Stop it, Madeline, or I'll never let you out of that bed," Dimitri said, his voice low and raspy.

He rolled over and I saw his jaw clench. My eyes went wide and my eyebrows raised. How had he-"

"I can smell your arousal, Madeline," he said, clenching his fists.

"You need to get out of that bed and go get dressed before I come back and check how wet you are."

I breathed heavily and I was sure his words were only making me wetter.

"Maddie," he growled and I jumped out of bed immediately.

I ran to the bathroom, trying hard not to look at him again. "You're going to kill me, woman." He mentally linked me and I couldn't help but laugh.

"I'm sorry," I said. "You're very handsome."

I heard him moan and bit the inside of my cheek to keep from laughing.

"Hurry up, will you?" he said. "The sooner we leave, the sooner we can get back."

"Yes, Alpha," I said, trying to sound a little seductive.

He growled and I heard him walk over to the bathroom. I guess he sounded a little more seductive than he intended. My heart skipped a beat as he opened the door and burst inside.

He closed the distance between us and kissed me hard. I moaned quietly and he picked me up. I wrapped my arms around his waist and he slapped my ass. He pressed me against the wall and started kissing my neck. My whole body shuddered as he reached my sweet spot and started sucking on it. I tangled my fingers in his hair and tightened my legs around him, pulling him tighter against me.

"Fuck, Madeline," he growled as he gently bit down on my sweet spot.

I shuddered and moaned loudly.

"Say it again," he said softly.

I knew exactly what he wanted to hear. I started kissing his neck until I reached his ear. I gave him a soft kiss behind and tightened my legs around him.

"Yes, Alpha," I whispered softly, and his whole body shuddered.

"Fuck, fuck, fuck," he murmured, and I continued to kiss his neck.

He reached under my shirt and squeezed my hip. His touch sent shivers down my spine, and I moaned again.

We were both panting hard. I could feel every muscle in his body tensing. He kept groaning and groaning. I swore the temperature in the room was getting hotter by the second.

I'd never done anything like this before, but somehow I knew what to do.

I knew kissing his jaw would make him moan. I knew biting his bottom lip would drive him crazy.

"Fuck, Maddie, fuck," he moaned softly, and he kissed me hard.

My body felt like it was going to go up in flames. He slowed his pace a little, and I could feel him taking deep breaths.

"We have to stop," he murmured as he stopped kissing me.

He rested his forehead against mine and took a deep breath. I didn't want to stop, but I knew he was right. We had to stop.

"You're going to drive me crazy," he said as he gave me another soft kiss on the lips.

I smiled and kissed him back.

I couldn't believe that just two days ago he wanted to leave the pack. I couldn't believe that I would ever think I could survive without him.

I was completely his and no one could take me away from him.

Not even myself.

Chapter 67 The talk

Madeleine's POV

Dimitri lifted my hand and kissed it.

"Are you sure, princess?" he asked. "Can I go in alone?"

I shook my head and took a deep breath.

"No," I said. "I'm Luna and I have to."

Dimitri groaned and I looked at him, my eyebrows furrowing. Had I said something wrong?

"How does everything you say turn me on so fucking much?" he muttered.

I chuckled and shook my head. Dimitri rolled his eyes playfully and opened the door to Mike's house.

"Mike?" he called as we walked in.

I heard footsteps approaching the living room and a second later Mike walked in with a huge smile on his face.

"Mads!" he exclaimed as he walked over to me. "Congratulations, sweetie! It's so nice to finally have you in our pack."

Mike seemed really excited and I could tell he wanted to hug me. But he didn't push me. He knew I wasn't comfortable.

"Thanks," I said, giving him a small smile.

"Where's my mom?" Dimitri asked, making Mike look at him.

"She's in the kitchen," Mike said, looking back at me. "I've been trying to talk to her but..."

He stopped talking and shook his head a little. Dimitri tightened his hand around mine. I could feel his anger growing.

"It's okay," I said before Dimitri could do or say anything. "I came to talk to you both."

Mike raised his eyebrows a little.

"Can we go to the kitchen?" I asked, giving him another smile.

"Of course, sweetheart," Mike said, letting us walk past him.

Dimitri pulled me closer to him as we entered the kitchen.

Janet looked at me, her thoughts immediately filling me.

I want to kill that little bitch. I'll find a way to get rid of her.

I gasped silently and stopped walking. Her thought was like a punch to the gut. I raised my eyebrows in confusion. I hadn't been able to hear anyone's thoughts all morning. Dimitri's touch kept them at bay. Why could I hear her thoughts then? Dimitri was standing next to me. He was holding my hand. I couldn't hear Mike's thoughts, but I could hear hers.

Why hers?

Are you okay, princess? Dimitri mentally linked me. We can go if you changed your mind.

I didn't change my mind. I had to. I could handle some of her thoughts. I kept my eyes on Janet's and took a deep breath.

I'm okay. I mentally linked him again. I want to do it.

"Do you want coffee?" Mike asked as he walked past us and over to Janet.

"Yes, please," Dimitri said, looking at me. "Maddie?"

I nodded, still looking at Janet.

You'll pay for everything, Madeline. She mentally linked me. Don't get too comfortable with my son. He's not yours. He'll never be yours. You'll never be Luna or Queen. You should have left when you had the chance.

I tried so hard not to react to her words. I tried so hard not to flinch. I tried so hard not to show how hurtful her words were.

'We have to tell Dimitri,' Skye whined. He can't talk to you like that, Maddie.

I swallowed the lump in my throat.

'We can't,' I said. 'She's his mother. I don't want him to fight with her because of me. I don't want him to lose her.'

Losing my mother was the most painful thing I had to go through.

I didn't want Dimitri to go through that.

Skye whined but remained silent.

'Sit down, guys, please,' Mike said and Dimitri pulled me towards the table.

Mike placed two cups of coffee in front of us and sat down. He smiled at me.

I took a deep breath and tried to remember all the things I wanted to say to him. I wanted to talk to him before I talked to Janet. I figured talking to Janet would be a lot harder and I knew I wouldn't be in the right frame of mind to talk to Mike after my conversation with Janet was over.

"I'm mad at you, Mike," I said, being as direct as possible. "I've been mad at you for a long time. I didn't want to come here and I wanted to leave the day I turned 18. I didn't want to be around you and I never wanted to see you again."

Mike's eyes widened and he swallowed.

"You walked out on me and my mother," I continued, trying hard to keep my voice from shaking. "I needed a father and you took that away from me. You chose power over your family and that's something I have a hard time accepting."

I saw tears in Mike's eyes. I could feel my heart clench painfully. Dimitri kissed my temple and put his arm around my shoulders. I could feel Janet's burning gaze on the side of my face.

I didn't let it distract me. I had to stay focused on Mike.

"But I can't leave this pack," I continued after a few moments of silence. "My mate is here. I love him and I don't want to leave him."

I love you, too. Dimitri mentally linked me.

I looked at him and smiled.

"So I need to find a way to forgive you, Mike, and I wanted to start by telling you how I truly feel," I said, looking back at Mike. "I needed to let it all out. I need to start over. I want to be a good Luna and I can't do that with this rage I'm carrying around."

A tear fell on Mike's cheek and he walked over to the table to take my hand in his.

"I'll try to forgive you, Mike," I said before he could speak.

"You did what you thought was best at the time. You found your happiness here. You found a partner and a child and I don't want to blame you for that."

I took a deep breath and squeezed his hand.

"But I need time," I continued. "I'll need time to get over this anger."

"Goddess, I'm so proud of you." Dimitri mentally linked me and pulled me close to his chest. *You're an amazing Luna.*

"I'm so sorry, sweetheart," Mike said. "I completely understand your anger." *You're right to be angry and I'll give you all the time you need."*

Mike squeezed my hand and smiled through his tears.

"You're already an amazing Luna and I'm so proud to be your father," he added.

I smiled back and took a deep breath.

What a pathetic, lying bitch. I can't wait to get rid of her, dammit.

The thoughts of Janet made me shudder.

I looked at her and took a deep breath. It was time I tried to talk to her.

Maybe there was a way to salvage this. Maybe there was a way for us to have a civil relationship.

Chapter 68 Skol

Dimitri's POV

To say I was proud of her would be an understatement.

I was so fucking proud and so fucking turned on by the way she carried herself and talked. I imagined bending her over the table and sliding inside her. I imagined telling her how good she was. I imagined her moaning my name and calling me Alpha, like she did this morning.

Fuck, fuck.

I had to focus. I couldn't do those things to her now.

We were at our parents' house and this wasn't the place for me to be thinking those thoughts.

I watched as my princess took a deep breath and looked at my mother.

"Janet..." she spoke quietly but my mother cut her off.

"It's Luna Janet to you," my mother said, the anger inside her erupting. "And don't you even think you can sell me some pathetic story about wanting to have a relationship with me. It will never happen, Madeline. I want you out of my son's life and out of my pack."

I saw the damn red. I groaned loudly and tried to get up. Maddie stopped me and shook her head.

"Let me do this, please." She mentally linked to me.

I looked at her and clenched my jaw. She looked at my mother and raised her eyebrows.

"Why?" "What have I done, Luna? If you could just tell me, maybe I could fix it. If you could just—"

"You can't change who you are, Madeline," my mother interrupted. "You're an orphan who's not good enough to be Luna and Queen. My son deserves better. My son had better. He had a perfect family and you had to come and ruin it."

By the time my mother finished speaking, she was yelling at Maddie and pacing the room.

I was furious. How dare she speak to my partner like that?!

"Apologize!" I yelled as I stood up. "I won't let you speak to my partner like that. Apologize now."

My mother looked at me and crossed her arms over her chest.

"Don't make me order you, mother," I said, growling. "I will. Apologize to her right now, dammit."

My mother's eyes narrowed and her jaw clenched.

"Apologize, Janet, or I'm leaving," Mike said, making me look at him with wide eyes. "I'm not going to stand by and let you talk to my daughter like that."

He was furious. I saw his eyes change color. His claws and canines lengthened.

My mother let out a loud gasp and looked at Maddie.

"Do you see what you've done?!" my mother screamed, pointing at Mike. "My mate wants to leave me because of you!"

My mother looked at me and continued talking before any of us could protest.

"What the fuck do you see in her, Dimitri?!" my mother screamed. "You have a perfect match. You have a child with her. Savannah still loves you and will accept you right away." Stop messing around and go back to your real partner-.

The growl that escaped me made the windows in the house shake.

I couldn't hold Skol back. He was furious.

He took control in a second and ran at my mother. He grabbed her by the neck and snarled in her face. She opened her eyes and tried to pull his hand away. I watched what he was doing and gave him all the control.

I wanted him to scare my mother.

"Skol!" Maddie screamed and grabbed his arm, trying to pull him away from my mother.

Mike shifted and growled at Skol.

"Let her go, Skol, please!" Maddie pleaded, trying to push him away.

"Apologize," I said, my voice deep and cold enough to chill my blood. "Now."

I could feel my mother gulping. Skol only grabbed her by the neck. He didn't squeeze. She could still breathe and talk.

"It's okay, Skol, she doesn't have to do this," Maddie screamed. "

Let her go, please. Let's go home."

Skol narrowed his eyes at my mother and growled.

"Apologize," I ordered and my mother whimpered softly.

"Skol..." Maddie spoke again, but Skol cut her off with a loud growl.

"Apologize," I repeated the order, and my mother whimpered loudly.

Mike growled, but Skol ignored him completely. Mike was completely harmless. Even if he attacked, Skol could take him down in one move.

"I'm sorry," my mother muttered under her breath, still trying to wriggle out of Skol's grip.

Skol growled in her face and squeezed her a little tighter.

"We will always choose Maddie over you," I told him. "Maddie is our mate. Our priority. Stop insulting her. Stop talking about Savannah like she's our mate. Stop hurting my mate."

My mother's eyes widened. The hatred Skol saw in her eyes made her growl again.

"Come on, Skol, please," Maddie yelled, pulling on her arm again.

Skol released my mother. He looked at Mike and growled. "

Give me back the controller, Skol," I said, but he ignored me.

"No," he said. "I want Maddie."

He turned to our companion and shuddered. It was the first time he had seen her in her own body.

He pulled her to him and picked her up. He had her wrap her arms and legs around him. He buried his muzzle in her fur and took a deep breath.

"Mine," I said softly as Skol ran out of the house.

Maddie ran her fingers through his fur and Skol growled in ecstasy.

"Mine, mine, mine," I repeated over and over as Skol ran back toward the barn.

"I'm yours, Skol," Maddie said softly, causing both Skol and I to shiver in excitement.

Skol ignored everything and everyone we passed on the way to the warehouse. He was completely focused on Maddie. I could feel him sniffing her, licking her, and touching her. She kept giggling softly and Skol felt like he was drugged.

Skol ran into our office and slammed the door shut. He turned around and pinned Maddie against the wall.

She smiled and ran her fingers through his fur again. He purred and licked her face softly.

"Hi, Skol," she said softly. "I'm so glad to see you." Skol purred again and buried his nose in her neck. He licked her gently, and Maddie shivered. "

Let me go back, Skol," I said, feeling the need to hold Maddie growing inside me.

He growled, and I could feel his anger growing. I knew he wanted more time with Maddie, but I didn't give a shit. I wanted to hold her.

Skol reluctantly set Maddie down and took a few steps back.

I backed up and immediately picked her up. He wrapped his arms and legs around me as tightly as he could. I took a deep breath and let his scent calm me.

Chapter 69 Your first time

Madeline's POV

I continued to gently rub Dimitri's back. I could feel the rage pulsing inside him. I wanted to calm him down. I didn't want him to be angry at his mother. No matter what he did or said, I didn't want his relationship with her to be damaged. I didn't want him to lose his mother.

"I'm so sorry, Maddie," he murmured after a few minutes.

"I'll talk to her. I promise. I won't let her say anything bad ever again."

I turned my head and placed a soft kiss on his neck. He moaned quietly and tangled his fingers in my hair, pulling me close to him.

"I love you, princess," he said as he made his way to the couch and sat down.

I lifted my head and smiled at him. I leaned into him and kissed him softly. I couldn't hold back. Feeling his lips on mine was the best thing I'd ever experienced. I never wanted to stop kissing him. If we could live with our lips pressed against each other, I'd love it.

Dimitri chuckled and I stopped kissing him. I looked up at him and raised an eyebrow at the small smile on his face.

"Skye is a great source of information," Dimitri said, confusing me even more.

He cupped my cheek and parted my lips with his thumb.

"I'd be fine with having your lips on mine all the time too," he said and my eyes widened.

Skye! I exclaimed, making her laugh.

Dimitri's smile grew and I rolled my eyes.

He slapped my ass and I gasped.

"Don't roll your eyes at your Alpha," he said and his voice made my whole body shiver.

It was deep and seductive. It made my lower belly flutter and ache. It made my heart race and I suddenly felt like my whole body was on fire.

I stared at him with wide eyes. My breathing quickened as I felt his hand squeeze my ass.

"Be a good girl and kiss me," he said in that same deep, seductive voice, and I had no choice but to obey.

My lips brushed his just as he grabbed the back of my neck and squeezed a little. He wrapped his arm around my waist and pulled me closer to him. I ran my hands up his muscled arms and he shuddered.

"Fuck, Madeline," he murmured as he began to kiss my neck.

I moaned loudly and tangled my fingers in his hair. He pulled me closer to him and sucked on the spot where I was standing.

My eyes rolled back in my head. My body felt like it was about to explode.

"You're driving me crazy," Dimitri growled, pulling my head back.

He was panting hard. He didn't take his eyes off my lips.

"Goddess, I don't want to scare you, but I don't know how long I can hold back from making love to you, Madeline," he said, and I had to bite back a moan. "I need to make you mine in every way possible. I need to be inside you."

He looked down at my breasts and moaned.

"I can't stop imagining it and you being this fucking gorgeous and seductive doesn't help at all," he said as he reached up and placed his hand on the side of my breast. "I need to make love to you, Madeline."

My heart was about to skip a beat. He squeezed the back of my neck gently.

"I love you," he said softly.

Goddess, I loved him too. I loved him so much.

"I love you too," I told him. "And I want you to make love to me too."

His eyes widened and he pulled me in for a kiss. His lips touched mine and the sensation sent a jolt of pleasure through my lower belly.

If someone had told me just two days ago that I would tell Dimitri Alpha that I wanted him to make love to me, I would have told them they were crazy. I was having a hard time keeping up with my emotions. The bond made everything inside me move at an insane pace. I loved this man so much and I had no idea when that feeling had started.

You loved him even before you knew it, Maddie,' Skye said. 'You just didn't allow yourself to love him.'

I raised my eyebrows slightly. "

You didn't know who he was, Maddie," Skye said. "But your heart knew.

Your heart knew from the moment you met him."

Dimitri stopped kissing me, and I felt like moaning. He rested his forehead against mine and took a deep breath.

"We have to stop because your first time won't be on a couch in our office," he murmured.

A funny thought occurred to me.

"How do you know it's going to be my first time?" I asked, biting my cheek to keep from laughing. "Maybe it wouldn't be."

His head snapped up, and I could hear his heartbeat increase.

"What?" he asked, squeezing me tighter.

His breathing quickened, and anger flashed in his eyes. I smiled and caressed his cheek. I leaned toward him and gave him a soft kiss on the lips.

"I'm kidding," I said, trying not to laugh. "You'll be my first."

He visibly relaxed and a growl escaped him.

"That was not funny and you will be punished for it, Madeline," he said seductively, a mix of pain and pleasure swirling in my lower belly.

He smirked at me and leaned into me. My heart felt like it was going to jump out of my chest as he went straight to the spot I was marking. He began to suck hard. His hands ran down my body until he reached my ass. He slapped and squeezed it. He lifted his hips and his hard cock pressed against me, making me shudder and moan. He continued to lift his hips at a steady pace. I couldn't help but move my hips too.

I needed to rub against him. I needed to feel him. I needed to touch him. I needed...

Oh, Goddess.

An unfamiliar sensation began to intensify between my legs. My movements quickened. I was hurtling towards something I'd never felt before. I threw my head back and moaned.

One more caress and I would explode.

Dimitri suddenly stopped moving and I felt like moaning.

He grabbed my hips and looked down at me. He had a big grin on his face as he leaned into me and bit my bottom lip.

"That's for being bad," he murmured. "Only good girls cum, Madeline."

My eyes shot open and he leaned in to kiss me. My heart was pounding against my ribcage. All I could hear was the blood rushing through my veins. The area between my legs was throbbing painfully. Dimitri's kiss only made it worse.

"I love you," he whispered and gave me another soft kiss on the jaw.

I tried to compose myself a little.

"I love you too," I murmured, my voice weird.

It sounded like I had been running for hours.

Dimitri chuckled and held me tight. I closed my eyes and took a deep breath. Being in his arms was amazing and I didn't want him to let go.

Chapter 70 I trust you

Dimitri's POV

Stopping her from cumming was the hardest thing I had to do. I imagined her cumming and moaning my name so many times that I couldn't believe I'd managed to stop myself.

On the other hand, I didn't want to miss her first orgasm. There were too many layers of clothing between us. I wanted to feel and taste her orgasm. I wanted to feel her tighten around my fingers. I wanted to lick her clean and taste every fucking drop.

I took a deep breath and let it out slowly. I needed to calm down a bit. I was so fucking hard. It was painful and my cock wouldn't stop throbbing.

"Dimitri?" my princess called.

I kissed her shoulder and let go.

"Yes, my love?" I asked as I smiled and caressed her cheek.

"I'd like to go to the cafeteria," she said, making me furrow my eyebrows.

"Why, princess?" I asked. "You don't work there anymore. You never needed to work there. I allowed it because I couldn't tell you that I was your partner and that I would take care of you.
" "I know," she said. "I would still like to thank Molly for giving me a job."

She looked down at her lap and sighed.

"I need to talk to Seth too," she said quietly.

A wave of jealousy washed over me. I didn't want her around him. I didn't want her around any other man.

"About what, princess?" I asked, trying to keep the anger out of my voice.

She looked at me and sighed.

"He's my friend," she said. "He's been my friend since I got here. He thought that..."

She stopped talking and took a deep breath.

"That you were her mate," I finished, feeling the words burn my tongue and lips.

She nodded.

I swallowed and ran my fingers through my hair. I didn't want to be a dominant, possessive mate, but I really didn't want her to talk to any other male. Part of me wanted to lock her in a room and keep her to myself. Part of me wanted to be the only one who could look at her, talk to her, and touch her.

I knew how fucking crazy that was, but I couldn't lie to myself and tell myself it wasn't true. It was true. I wanted her all to myself. She was mine and I wanted it to be true in every fucking way possible.

Mine to look at. Mine to touch. Mine to do everything I wanted to.

Skol stirred and I knew she agreed with me completely. I was a werewolf and every emotion related to my mate was heightened. I loved her more than a normal werewolf loved their mate. I needed her more than normal werewolves needed their mates. He was more protective and possessive than they were.

But he was also a rational man who knew that locking her away and keeping her for myself wasn't an option. She was a Moon and a Queen. She was a wonderful woman who didn't deserve an irrational partner.

So I did something that went against all my animal instincts. I smiled and nodded at her with a small nod.

"Okay, Princess," I said softly. "Do you want me to come with you?"

She raised her eyebrows slightly and studied my face for a moment.

I smiled and caressed her cheek.

"Did you think I was going to forbid you from going to see him?" I asked and she nodded reluctantly.

I smiled again and gave her a soft kiss on the lips.

"I trust you, Princess," I said softly. "I know you won't do anything to hurt me. I also know that you'll let me know if he tries anything while I'm gone."

She'd also be able to sense it if he touched her. She'd know immediately and it would tear him apart.

No one touched what was mine. She was mine to touch. She was mine to kiss. She was mine to adore and love.

She nodded and I kissed her again. I tangled my fingers in her hair and kept my lips on hers until we were both out of breath.

I didn't mind dying like this though. Leaving this world with the taste of her in my mouth was the best way to die.

"Do you want me to go with you?" I asked again after I stopped kissing her.

She shook her head and gave me a small smile.

"Okay," she said. "I won't be long.

" "You better not," I said sternly. "An hour at most. I can't be without you any longer."

She smiled and nodded. I kissed the tip of her nose and stroked her back.

It was then that I remembered something.

"What's with the voices, princess?" I asked worriedly. "Are they back?"

She gulped and took a deep breath.

"Not while you're with me," she said. "But I'll be fine for an hour. I might even find a way to deal with them without you." I didn't like that, but I nodded and kissed her again. The kiss was short and sweet.

"Come back right away if it's too much, okay?" I said.

"Or put a mind link on me and I'll come find you."

She nodded and kissed me again. I wished she and I didn't have any obligations. I wished we could just stay in this room forever.

The cafeteria wasn't far away and that was one of the reasons I let her go without me.

The other reason was that I wanted to talk to Will alone. I needed to find someone who knew what those voices meant.

Someone had to know why he could read minds or whatever.

I was planning to start by talking to the doctor who helped me when Savannah told me she was pregnant with my pup.

I let go of Maddie and had to hold back a moan. I would stick her to me if it was possible.

"I love you," she said and gave me a small smile.

I rested my arms on the back of the couch. I clenched my muscles and smiled in satisfaction when I saw Maddie gulp.

"I love you too, Madeline," I told her, using the voice I knew would make her knees buckle. "I'll be back soon, okay?"

She nodded and turned around. She ran out of the room like her ass was on fire. "

Those muscles will be waiting for you when you get back, princess." I mentally connected with her.

I heard her moan and laughed.

I was so fucking happy that she was attracted to me. Seeing the lust and love in her eyes was all I ever wanted.

Chapter 71 Seth

Madeline's POV

"Luna!" Macy exclaimed excitedly when I walked into the diner. I flinched a little. I wasn't used to hearing that. It sounded weird. It sounded wrong. "

Stop it," Skye growled at me.

I ignored her and smiled at Macy.

"I'm Maddie," I said as I walked up to the counter. "Please don't call me Luna." Macy giggled and shook her head. I looked around. There were a few people eating breakfast, but it was mostly empty. People smiled at me and nodded. I smiled back before sitting down on one of the bar stools.

I could hear their thoughts. I didn't exactly understand what they were thinking, but I could hear them. I tried to ignore them. I tried to focus on Macy and shut out everything else.

I could hear their thoughts too, but I ignored them. I didn't want to know what they were thinking. I didn't want to intrude.

But it was hard. It was so hard to try to shut out those voices.

"What are you doing here, Maddie?" Macy asked. "You're not here to work, are you? Alpha will have my head if I let his Luna work."

I smiled and shook my head.

"I'm not here to work, though I wouldn't mind working," I said. "I came to talk to you and thank you for giving me a job."

Macy stopped cleaning and looked at me.

"You're welcome, sweetie," she said softly. "It's been a pleasure working with you."

She took my hand.

"You'll be an amazing Luna," she said. "Your mother would be so proud of you."

I felt tears well up in my eyes. Macy was the only one in the pack I talked to about my mother. She reminded me a little of my mother. They were both so kind and caring. They both made me feel safe when I needed it most.

"Thanks, Macy," I said, trying to swallow the lump in my throat.

The kitchen door opened and Seth stepped out. I looked at him and took a deep breath.

"Hey, Mads," he said softly.

I could hear the sadness in his voice and it made my heart clench painfully. I never meant to hurt him.

"Hey, Seth," I said, my voice quiet and raspy. "Can we talk for a moment?"

Macy let go of my hand and I stood up. Seth gave me a small nod and opened the kitchen door. I walked over to him, rubbing my palms together and trying to calm myself down a bit.

"Goddess, why didn't you just give her to me?"

The thought of Seth made me shudder a little. I gulped and turned to watch him close the kitchen door.

"Did she let you come in here alone?" Seth asked as he leaned against the door.

"If she were mine, I wouldn't let her walk around without me. She's too perfect for that."

The thought of her made me shudder. I clenched my jaw and forced my brain to shut everything off. I wanted to talk to Seth. I didn't want to hear her thoughts.

"She did," I said, giving him a small nod. "Trust me."

Seth nodded and took a deep breath.

"I'm sorry, Seth," I said quietly. "I didn't mean for this to happen. I didn't mean to hurt you."

Seth set his jaw and shook his head.

"You didn't hurt me, Maddie," he said quietly. "The Goddess did.

" "She doesn't have her mark yet. Did she reject him? Do I still have a chance? If she were mine, I'd sink my canines into her neck the moment I knew she was my mate. Did he just let her walk around unmarked? What the fuck is wrong with her?"

I shuddered and clenched my fists.

I pushed his thoughts away. I didn't want to hear these things. I didn't want to know what he was thinking.

My head started to throb and my stomach twisted. I was already exhausted and I hadn't been to the coffee shop long enough.

"Where's your mark, Maddie?" Seth asked as he started to approach me. "Did you reject him?"

The hope in his voice made my heart clench. He stopped in front of me and swallowed.

"I didn't," I said, shaking my head. "He'll mark me soon. "

An unfamiliar emotion flashed in Seth's eyes. He clenched his jaw and nodded. His eyes studied my face for a few moments.

I felt a little uncomfortable. He was too close.

"She's beautiful. Why isn't she mine? I'll never want anyone but her."

"Do you really want me to mark you, Maddie?" Seth asked as he reached up and caressed my cheek. "Do you really want him?"

I tensed and took a step back. His hand dropped from my cheek and a hurt look flashed in his eyes.

"I love him," I said quietly. "I love him. He's my mate."

Seth set his jaw and nodded.

"I'll be here if you change your mind," he said softly. "I'll always be here, Maddie."

"I'd take her even with his mark on her beautiful body. She'd be mine and nothing else would matter."

I shuddered and took another step back. Seth raised his eyebrows slightly.

"I have to go," I said, giving him a small smile.

"Dimitri's waiting for me."

Seth nodded and stepped aside so I could walk past him.

I walked over to the door and opened it. I looked back at him and smiled again.

"Call me if you ever need help in the cafeteria," I said.

"I'll miss working here."

Seth smiled and nodded. "I'll miss him too, Maddie."

"I'm going to miss seeing her beautiful face every day. I should have done something sooner. I should have kissed her sooner. I should have made her fall for me sooner. She would have rejected it then. She would have been mine if I'd done something sooner."

My stomach tightened. I needed to get out of there as soon as possible.

I forced another smile onto my face before leaving the kitchen.

"Are you hungry, Mads?" Macy asked and I shook my head.

"No, thanks," I said politely.

I didn't need food. I needed Dimitri. I needed him to hold me to feel safe. I needed him to make the voices stop. I needed him because I missed him already. I said goodbye to Macy before running out of the cafeteria. I couldn't wait to fall into Dimitri's arms.

Chapter 72 The Healer

Dimitri's POV

"You let her go alone?!" Will exclaimed. "Are you crazy?! He's in love with her!"

I looked at him and sighed. "I trust her, Will," I said. "I can't keep her locked up in here. Believe me, I'd be happier if I could just lock her up and keep her to myself, but that's not possible."

Will rolled his eyes and sat up.

"I don't trust him," he said. "He might try something." I shuddered and had to hold back a growl. I'd tear him apart if he tried anything.

"Why is that any of your business?" I asked, trying not to show how upset I was.

Will looked at me and rolled his eyes again.

"She's my Luna," he said like it was the most obvious thing in the world. "I swore to protect her from the moment I became your Beta. She's my priority and you know it."

He knew that. Protecting Maddie was the most important part of his job. If there was an attack and our lives were in danger, Will had sworn to save her, not me. He swore to protect her from everyone, even me.

"Seth won't hurt her," I said. "He's a good boy."

I was sure of that and it was one of the reasons I let her go alone. I knew I wouldn't hurt her. I knew she wouldn't do anything to hurt me and I knew she would tell me everything he did or said to her. I trusted her with every part of my body and soul.

"Will she be back soon?" Will asked.

"I told her to come back in an hour," I said, looking back down at the paper in my hand. "I can't be without her any longer."

"Is this a new contract for Dr. Jackson?" Will asked and I nodded.

"Yes," I said. "I'll offer her a job here in our pack."

" "When will she arrive?" Will asked and I glanced at the watch on my left wrist.

"In about four hours," I said. "He called as he was leaving his house.

" "Will you talk to him about Maddie?" Will asked, making me look up at him.

I took a deep breath and nodded. It made me nervous to talk to him about it, but I needed to. I needed someone to help me understand what was going on.

Will gulped and bit his bottom lip.

"I have to confess something to you," he said and I narrowed my eyes slightly.

"A confession?" I asked with confusion in my voice.

Will nodded and ran his fingers through his hair.

"I talked to Ellie about it," Will said, his voice heavy with guilt. "She said we should talk to a healer, not a doctor."

Will looked at me apologetically. I sighed and shook my head at him. I didn't like him sharing that secret with her, but Ellie was one of the people I trusted the most. She was smart, kind, and caring. She was an amazing wolf and a great asset to my pack. If she were older than Will, she'd probably be my Beta.

"I know I shouldn't have talked to her without your permission, but it's Ellie," Will said. "You know I can't keep anything from her."

I rolled my eyes. But he was right. I always told her everything.

"I know and it's annoying," I muttered, trying to keep from rolling my eyes again.

"She's excited to meet Maddie," Will said with a small smile on his face.

I smiled a little. I was excited for them to meet each other too. I knew they'd get along great. They looked a lot alike.

"When is she coming back?" I asked.

Ellie was at a training center just outside of our pack. Will often ran to the border to see and talk to her.

"In a few days," Will said excitedly. "She's almost done with the program."

She was in a training program for elite warriors. Mike was the one who started training our wolves, but word got around and other packs became interested in joining. Mike and I decided that it would be good for the Kingdom to have a few select elite warriors in each pack. Ellie was one of the ones who earned her spot in Mike's program and I was
incredibly proud of her.

"I was thinking of making her Maddie's personal guard," I said and Will nodded immediately. "I trust her completely and she's not a male so Skol won't feel too uncomfortable leaving Maddie with her.

" "I agree," Will said. "Ellie will do just fine. She's already so excited to meet Maddie and she's already so protective of her. She nearly went crazy when I told her what Savannah did."

Skol growled when Will said that bitch's name.

"I really want to exile her," I said angrily. "I just wish she'd tell me who the father is. I don't want that child to grow up without at least one parent."

Will sighed and shook his head.

"She'll never do that," Will said. "She knows that's the only thing keeping her here."

I knew it, and it was making me really angry. No one wanted to take that child away, and I wasn't cruel enough to take him from his mother and put him in an orphanage. I didn't want him to grow up a rogue, either.

"So, the healer?" I asked, changing the subject.

Will took a deep breath and nodded.

"Ellie said that healers might know more about that kind of magic than the doctor," Will said.

That made sense.

"We don't have a healer in our pack, though," I said. Will smiled. "Leave it to me. I'll find one."

I nodded. "We should talk to the doctor anyway."

"Of course," Will agreed. "Maybe he knows someone we can talk to about this."

I nodded again and took a deep breath. I glanced at the watch on my wrist. Maddie had been gone for about thirty minutes, but I already missed her terribly. I wished she would come back immediately. I wished I could hold her and kiss her. I didn't know if I could wait an hour for her.

Chapter 73 Who is Ellie?

Dimitri's POV

My wish came true just a few minutes later.

There was a knock on my door and I knew right away it was Maddie. I was a little confused because I was sure she would be gone for at least twenty more minutes.

"Come in," I said and stood up.

Why was she knocking on the door?

She opened the door and a wave of relief washed over me. I smiled brightly but my smile disappeared as soon as I saw her face.

"What happened, princess?" I asked as she walked around my desk.

She ran over to me and sighed in relief as soon as I grabbed her.

My heart was racing. Had someone done something to her? Had she hurt herself? Did Seth say something to upset her? Did she do something?

Did she try something?

"Mads?" Will called out to her worriedly. "What happened?"

I ran my fingers through her hair and kissed the top of her head,

"I'm okay," she murmured softly. "The voices were too much."

My heart wrenched painfully. I had to find a solution as soon as possible.

"Oh, princess," I murmured as I picked her up and walked back to my chair.

I sat down and placed her on my lap. I rubbed her back and she relaxed even more. I buried my nose in her hair and took a deep breath. Her scent calmed me and I was able to clear my mind a little.

I missed her so much and having her in my arms was amazing. I was dying to lay next to her tonight.

I couldn't wait to press my whole body against hers.

"Can you hear Dimitri's thoughts?" Will asked, causing her to tense up a little.

I looked at him and my eyes went wide. I never know, had that occurred to me.

Maddie looked at me and raised her eyebrows. I thought back to the first time I saw her. If she could read my mind, I'd want her to know what I felt the moment my eyes fell on her beautiful face.

"No," she muttered under her breath and looked at Will. "What does that mean?"

I was confused too. I could hear everyone's thoughts but my own.

"I don't know," Will shrugged. "I hope the healer has the answers."

" "The healer?" Maddie asked with confusion in her voice.

I leaned in close to her and placed a kiss on her jaw. I couldn't help myself. I needed to feel her soft skin against my lips.

"Ellie suggested we talk to a healer instead of a doctor," Will explained. "She said healers might know more about these types of magic."

Maddie raised her eyebrows.

"Who's Ellie?" she asked, making Will smile.

"She's my sister," Will said. "You'll meet her soon."

"She'll be your guardian, princess," I said, tucking a strand of hair behind her ear. "She's currently in an elite training program run by Mike. She'll be back in a couple of days ."

Maddie looked at me, her eyes widening slightly.

"Does Mike run a training program?" she asked.

"He does," I confirmed. "Your father is an amazing warrior and he came up with a course for elite warriors. Ellie is one of them. "

Maddie furrowed her eyebrows again.

"Why do I need a personal guard?" I asked, causing both Will and I to sigh at the same time.

"You're a Luna and a Queen," I explained. "I need to ensure your safety at all times."

I smiled and caressed his cheek.

"You'll love Ellie," I said. "You two look alike. She's kind and caring. She's one of my best friends and I trust her completely."

An unfamiliar emotion flashed in Maddie's eyes. I tried to catch her by focusing on our bond, but it was gone before I could realize it.

"She's so excited to meet you," Will said, making Maddie look at him. "She already likes you a lot, Mads."

I could see the confusion on Maddie's face.

"Will tells her everything," I said, trying to explain what Will meant. "Ellie already knows a lot about you, and she already likes you."

Maddie looked back at me and gave me a small nod. I stroked my cheek and used our bond to try and figure out what she was feeling. I got nothing, though. Will stood up, and I looked at him.

—I'm going to get everything ready for the doctor's arrival," Will said. "I'll be back later."

I nodded and watched as he left our office.

As soon as the door closed behind him, I pressed Maddie's cheeks together and kissed her softly. She put her hands on mine and moaned softly.

—Goddess, I've missed you," I murmured against her lips. —I don't like being separated from you. —

Maddie smiled a little. She kissed me again and I moaned.

—I don't like it either, she said softly.

I caressed her cheek and lifted my head to look at her better. Something didn't fit.

—What happened in the cafeteria? — I asked.

Something had to have happened there. Something upset her and it wasn't the voices. At least not completely. She sighed and bit her lower lip.

—Did Seth say something? — I asked as my heart raced.

—Did he try something? — Maddie shook her head immediately.

—No— she said. —I was a little worried. a little sad. She didn't do anything, but...— She stopped talking and took a deep breath.

"But?" I asked, trying to keep my voice from shaking.

I needed to contain the rage that was throbbing inside my body. What the hell had I done to her?

"Her thoughts were...," she said, but she stopped talking and took a deep breath.

I hugged her tightly. What was I going to say?

"The worst part is, I don't even know if those were her thoughts or if I'm making it all up," she muttered under her breath. "What if I'm crazy? What if I'm sick? What if—"

I cut her off by pressing my lips to hers.

"You're not crazy, princess," I said softly. "You're not sick.

You can hear other people's thoughts and we'll figure out what that means."

She took a deep breath and rested her head on my shoulder. I kissed her temple and wrapped my arms around her.

"What was I thinking, Maddie?" I asked. "I need you to tell me everything."

I needed to know if she was in danger. I needed to know if her thoughts were violent. I needed to protect her.

She was my entire world and I needed to make sure she was safe. I barely lived through those thirty-something minutes she was gone.

If something happened to her or if someone took her from me, I would die. I wouldn't survive that. I needed her to breathe. I needed her to live. I needed it to keep my heart beating.

Chapter 74 In his arms

Madeline's POV

"How are you, Princess?" Dimitri asked softly as I sat up in bed.

He wrapped his arms around me and all the aches in my body and soul vanished.

"Tired," I said. "And a little relieved maybe."

Doctor Jackson confirmed that I wasn't crazy. We did a little experiment. Dimitri left the room so I could hear the doctor's thoughts. It worked and I was relieved to know I wasn't crazy. Well, maybe I still was. Reading other people's minds wasn't exactly sane.

"We'll talk to a healer as soon as we find one, Princess," Dimitri said quietly.

I lifted my head and looked at him.

"I know one," I said, making his eyes widen.

"You know him?" he asked in surprise. "How?"

"There's a healer in my old pack," I said. "He helped my mother deal with her grief. We could ask him to come." I'm sure he'd be willing to help."

Dimitri smiled and leaned down to kiss my cheek.

"I'll bring him here tomorrow, princess," he said softly. "We'll figure it out. I promise."

He bent his head and gave my shoulder a small kiss. I shivered and pressed myself closer to him.

"Goddess, how much I love you," he murmured, making my heart skip a beat. "I love you with every part of my body and soul, Madeline."

I caressed his cheeks and kissed him. He moaned softly and wrapped his arms around my waist.

"I love you too," I said softly. "I never thought I'd love someone so much. I never thought I'd find my mate.

I'm so happy I did. I'm so happy it's you. I love you."

I could tell he was holding back tears. I leaned into him and kissed him softly. He tangled his fingers in my hair and held me close.

"You are my greatest treasure, princess," he said softly as he buried his nose in my neck. "I will love you even after my last breath. I will love you until the end of the world."

I ran my fingers through his hair and he kissed my neck. His words made me melt and my knees go weak. It was a good thing I was sitting down.

"Are you hungry?" he asked and I shook my head.

"Not really," I told him. "I want to take a shower."

Dimitri nodded and kissed my neck again.

"Would you mind if we took one together?" he asked softly, making me tense up a little. "I have no intentions other than to take a shower. I promise." He

lifted his head and smiled at me. I studied his face for a moment.

I was nervous. What if he didn't like what he saw? No one had ever seen me naked. What if he thought I was ugly? What if he rejected me after seeing me naked?

Dimitri leaned over and gave me a soft kiss on the jaw.

"Skye is the biggest gossip out of all of us," he said with amusement in his voice. "I think you're perfect and I'm not going to reject you after seeing you naked."

I groaned and rolled my eyes.

Skye! I whimpered but she ignored me.

"Are my thoughts ever going to be mine again?" I muttered angrily. "Why does she tell you everything?"

Dimitri lifted his head and huffed.

"You can read other people's minds," he said. "It's only fair that I get to read yours from time to time."

I rolled my eyes and Dimitri slapped my ass.

"Don't roll your eyes, Madeline," he said, lowering his voice making me flinch.

My breath hitched as he started to lift my shirt up. I held my hands up so he could take it off. My heart raced as I saw him staring at my breasts with a lustful gaze.

"Fuck, Maddie," he muttered as he ran his fingers along the seam of my bra.

I shuddered and gulped. He looked up at me and leaned down to kiss my lips softly.

"Can I take it off for you, princess?" he asked and I nodded.

He reached behind me and unclasped my bra. He looked down and moaned as it fell onto my lap. My nipples were hard and my chest was rising and falling rapidly.

"Oh fuck, fuck, fuck," Dimitri murmured as he reached up and gently caressed one of my breasts. "You're fucking perfect."

I shivered as he leaned into me and kissed the area between my breasts. His warm breath made me moan quietly.

I reached up and started to lift his shirt. My hands were shaking but I needed to see his perfect body. I needed to touch him. He helped me remove his shirt and I moaned as my eyes landed on his muscled chest. I reached up and ran my hand over his abs. He shuddered and groaned. He was breathing hard, and I could see his muscles tightening.

"Goddess, Maddie," he murmured. "I don't want you to stop touching me. This is yours. I'm all yours."

I leaned in and placed a soft kiss on his collarbone. He growled softly and wrapped his arms around my waist.

He picked me up and started walking to the bathroom. I continued to kiss his neck and his muscular shoulders softly. He was still shaking, moaning and squeezing every part of my body he could reach. I was in heaven and I never wanted to leave. I wanted to stay in his arms forever.

He laid me down on the floor and I wanted to moan so badly. He got behind me and turned on the shower. He caressed my cheeks and kissed my forehead.

"Can I take off your jeans?" he asked and I nodded, trying to swallow the lump in my throat.

I was sure the lump was actually my heart. My whole body was humming with tingles and need for him. He

unbuttoned my jeans and got on his knees. He started to pull down my jeans and underwear. He kept his eyes on me and I thought I would pass out. He leaned over and kissed me softly below my belly button. I couldn't help but cry out in pleasure.

The feel of his lips against my skin was incredible. He stood up without taking his eyes off mine. He took my hands in his and placed them on his hips. I hooked my thumbs under the waistband of his pants and began to pull them down.

"I can stay in my boxers if that's more comfortable for you," he said as he stopped me from taking off his pants.

I shook my head and continued to pull down his pants. He caressed my cheeks and kissed me hard. I moaned and let his pants fall to the floor. He

lifted me up and wrapped my legs around his waist. I felt everything and all I wanted to do was moan in pleasure.

I shuddered a little when my back hit the cold tiles of the shower wall, but everything was forgotten when I felt his hands grab and squeeze my ass.

His touch was like a drug and I knew I would never stop needing it.

Chapter 75 Savannah

Madeline's POV

"Are you sure you'll be okay alone, princess?"

Dimitri asked as he leaned down and kissed my neck. "I can stay. Will can handle it."

I looked at him and shook my head.

"It's okay," I said, giving him a small smile. "I'll be fine. You're an Alpha. You have to work."

He smiled and ran his fingers through my hair.

"I want to get started on this anyway," I said, gesturing to the books on his desk. "You're kind of distracting me."

He gasped, feigning pain. I tried to hold back a smirk.

"Me?" he asked, raising his eyebrows. "Distracting? Is it because I'm hot?"

I chuckled and felt.

"And because you can't keep your hands off me," I said, making him smile.

He leaned into me and gave me a soft kiss on the lips.

"Of course I can't," he said. "I can't keep my hands off something that's mine."

I smiled and he kissed me once more. I sighed in satisfaction, making him chuckle.

"We need to stop because I'm never leaving," he murmured and I nodded.

He let go of me and walked over to his desk. I watched as he grabbed some folders. My eyes fell on his muscles and I couldn't help but remember what it felt like to wrap me in his strong arms the night before when we showered together. He caressed every part of my body. He kissed and sucked on my skin until I felt like I was about to burst into flames. I ran my hands over his body and felt every part of him pressed against me. It was one of the best nights of my life and I couldn't wait to do it again.

"Stop it, Madeline, or I'll never leave," Dimitri growled and looked back at me.

I chuckled and looked back at the papers on my desk, trying to focus on something other than him. He leaned in close and kissed the top of my head.

"Put a mind link on me if you need me, princess," he said. "I'll be right back."

I looked at him and nodded. He wasn't far away. He and Will were just going to see if the preparations for the next Alpha meeting were going as planned. They were going to the training center and the throne room. The training center was 10 minutes away and the throne room was right here in the warehouse. I'd be close by at all times.

He caressed my cheek, smiled, and walked out of our office. I couldn't help but watch his muscles twitch as he walked. He smiled at me once more before closing the door behind him.

I took a deep breath and shook my head. I needed to focus. I looked back at the book in my hands. I was familiarizing myself with the laws of the pack and the Kingdom. Dimitri had told me that I didn't need to know them all, but I wanted to. I wanted to be a good Luna. I needed to prove to myself that I was worthy of sitting in this chair.

You're so annoying," Skye sighed.

I rolled my eyes and focused on the book in front of me. I ignored her completely. I was a little angry at her because she kept telling Dimitri everything.

"Of course I'll tell him everything," she said. "He's our mate. He deserves to know everything. He even deserves to know about Janet and—"

"No," I cut her off. "I'm not going to ruin his relationship with his mother."

"Stop it, Skye. You can't talk to him about that."

She sighed and fell silent. I focused on the book and took a deep breath.

Section 4: Conflict Resolution

4.1. Council:

A Council, comprised of respected members of the Kingdom, is to be established to deal with specific issues and concerns that the subjects have. The council will act as an advisory body to the

King and facilitate communication between the palace and the subjects.

" "I didn't like the council members," Skye muttered, making me nod slightly.

"Me neither," I said. "But we only met them once. We should give them a chance. We'll have to work with them."

Skye muttered something I didn't understand and I tried to focus back on the book. I had no idea how much time had passed. I was completely focused on the book and I flinched violently when a loud knock on the door interrupted me.

I lifted my head and opened my mouth to tell the caller to come in, but the door opened before I could.

My breath caught in my throat as I saw Janet and Savannah walking in.

Janet closed the door and growled at me.

"Aren't you ashamed to sit in the chair that was meant for me?" Savannah asked, making me look at her.

"Of course not," Janet answered before I could. "She came here to destroy everything, didn't you, Madeline? She came here to take Dimitri's mother, his mate, and his child away from him."

Hearing Janet call Savannah Dimitri's mate was like having a knife stuck in my chest. She wasn't his mate. It was me.

I clenched my fists and took a deep breath. I knew it would be useless to fight them. It was clear they were never going to give up on the idea of Savannah being Dimitri's mate and her child being his.

"Can I help you?" I asked, trying to keep my voice from shaking.

I needed them to tell me why they were here and for them to leave as soon as possible.

"You?" Janet giggled. "Orphan Luna? How could you help me?"

I clenched my jaw and swallowed. I couldn't let it get to me. I had to be strong. I was Luna and I wasn't going to let her insults get to me.

"Why are you here?" I asked, looking from Janet to Savannah.
"Are you here to talk or to insult me? If it's the latter, please leave."

Savannah's eyes widened. Janet growled.

"You can't kick me out," Savannah said. "I have more right to be here than you. I have a child with Dimitri. I'm his mate, aren't I."

I sighed and furrowed my eyebrows a little. I was truly delirious, wasn't I?

"I'd be scared if I were you, Madeline," Janet said, making me look back at her. "I told you I'd get rid of you, and I will. I won't let my son suffer next to a pathetic little girl like you.
" "You'll never be a Luna. I won't allow it."

I studied her face for a few seconds. The anger and hatred I saw made my entire body shudder.

She meant it, didn't she?

Chapter 76 Betrayals

Dimitri's POV

"Are you going to fight in the tournament?" I asked Will as we watched Mike explain something to one of the new apprentices.

"I don't think so," Will said, shaking his head. "There will be too much work. I'm sure Ellie will fight, though."

I chuckled and nodded, still staring at the newly changed boy. Mike didn't know what to do with him. He kept making the same mistakes over and over again and Mike was losing patience.

"It will be interesting to see," I said. "I wonder if any other packs will bring their warriors to compete."

It was tradition to hold a tournament during every Alpha meeting. The Three Kingdoms Tournament was held in the battle arena and in a large clearing in the middle of the forest. There were three different challenges that participants had to complete in order to win.

Moonlight Duels was a challenge where participants engaged in one-on-one combat in the clearing under a full moon. Pack Hunt was a challenge where participants formed alliances with werewolves from different packs. Together, they tracked and hunted an object or person of my choosing, demonstrating their hunting prowess and ability to work in harmony.

The final challenge was a Moonstone Gauntlet. It was an obstacle course created by Mike that combined physical endurance, mental agility, and determination.

At the end of the tournament, the werewolf who emerged victorious was awarded the coveted Crown of the Three Kingdoms. It was an emblem of honor and recognition throughout the realm, ensuring that their legacy would live on for generations.

Watching the tournament was a delight, and it got better every year. Each pack brought their best warriors, and the stakes were high in the tournament.

I had enjoyed it every year, but I knew this year would be different. The reason for the Alpha Gathering was different this year.

This year we weren't meeting to talk about light topics. We were meeting to discuss an impending threat to our Kingdom.

"What's Maddie doing?" Will asked and a small smile spread across my face.

I was so fucking proud of her. I was more in love than I ever thought possible. My heart and body were melting just thinking about her. That shower yesterday was something I'd never been able to fantasize about. I never knew there could be so much pleasure in just touching, caressing, and kissing. I didn't even have to make love to her to enjoy every part of her body. It was incredible and I was dying to do it again tonight.

"She's in our office," I said, trying to keep images of her naked body from appearing in my mind.

This was not the time for an erection.

"She's flipping through some books on the laws of our kingdom," I told him. "She's determined to learn them all."

Will smiled and shook his head.

"It's incredible, isn't it?" he said. "I'm so glad it's our Moon. You got a good one, Dimitri."

Heat spread through my body. My smile grew. It was so much more than good. It was fucking perfect.

"I did it," I said as I watched Mike slam the poor boy into the ground.

"God, Reece!" Mike exclaimed. "How many times are we going to go through this?!"

Will and I chuckled and I decided to give poor Reece a break.

"Mike!" I yelled, causing him to look up at me.

I motioned for him to come over and he looked at Reece with a pissed off look on his face. He said something to him before walking over to Will and me.

"Where's Maddie?" he asked with a hint of concern in his voice.

"In our office," I said. "She's working."

Mike smiled and visibly relaxed.

"I tried to talk to Janet about her but she refused to listen to me ," Mike said shaking his head. "I don't know what to do."

I clenched my jaw and balled my fists. I was so fucking mad at my mother and I knew I would explode if I had to deal with her.

"I can't understand why she's not pissed at Savannah," Will said. "She lied to us and she tried to with all of us. She lied to her too."

Mike sighed and raised his eyebrows.

"Your mother really wanted a grandchild," Mike said. "I think she's still holding on to that idea."

I took a deep breath and gritted my teeth.

"She's crazy," I said. "She knows Savannah lied. She knows Savannah's child isn't mine. I don't know why she likes that bitch so much, but I won't stand for it."

Mike gave me a disapproving look.

"I know you're angry, Dimitri, but don't talk about your mother like that," Mike said. "She'll come around. She needs time to get used to Maddie, that's all." I scoffed and rolled my eyes.

"She can get attached to her from afar," I said angrily. "I'm not letting her near Maddie again. Not after everything she said."

Mike sighed again, but I didn't give a shit. I wasn't going to let my mother insult my princess. I wasn't going to let her hurt my mate.

"We need to be careful," Will said, clenching his jaw. "We can't let her hurt Maddie."

"Oh come on," Mike said, shaking his head. "Janet would never do that. She would never hurt Maddie. She may be a little mean, yes, but she would never hurt her."

Will looked at him and narrowed his eyes a little.

"It's my job as a Beta to protect my Luna," Will said sternly. "I think we need to be careful when it comes to Janet and we will take all necessary precautions."

A small smile spread across my face. I was proud of Will and how seriously he was taking his oath to me.

"Dimitri!" Skol's panicked voice made me flinch.

My body froze and my heart stopped beating.

"What happened?" I asked, trying to stop it from taking over me. "Is Maddie okay?"

Skye told me that your mother and Savannah are in your office." Skol shouted. "Skye is panicking, Dimitri, you have to go there!"

He didn't have to tell me twice. I ran into the warehouse before he finished speaking.

I could hear Will following me and Mike yelling our names.

But I couldn't stop myself. I had to go to Maddie. I had to make sure she was okay. I would kill them both if they hurt her.

Chapter 77 Tell him!

Madeline's POV

I tried my hardest to ignore Janet and Savannah, but it was so hard. They refused to leave or stop insulting me.

I was close to exploding, but I didn't want to give them the satisfaction of knowing how much their words affected me.

"You sound pathetic, Madeline," Savannah growled. "This isn't your place. You don't belong at that desk. You don't belong in this office.

You—"

"Stop it!" I exclaimed, abruptly standing up.

My breathing was ragged, my fists still clenched.

"Stop it," I repeated, trying to calm myself down a bit. "I've been nothing but respectful to you two since I joined this pack.

I don't know why you two hate me so much, but I don't have to put up with this. Get out of my office now."

Janet growled and Savannah giggled.

"Respectful?" Savannah said mockingly. "You call stealing my partner respectful?"

I clenched my jaw and took a deep breath through my nose. I had to remain calm.

"Get out of my office," I repeated calmly. "Now,"

Janet walked over to my desk and narrowed her eyes at me.

"Who the fuck do you think you are, Madeline?" she asked. "Do you forget who you're talking to?"

Unfortunately, no. I could never forget who I was talking to. I could never forget the things they said and did to me.

"Don't worry, Maddie," Skye yelled. "Dimitri's on his way. They won't hurt you again.

" "What?" I asked, trying to hide my surprise. Why did you tell him, Skye? He's busy. I can take care of them."

"Stop it, Madeline," he growled at me. You're more important than work. We have to protect you.

A wave of anger washed over me. I clenched my fists and exhaled slowly.

She had the nerve to talk about protecting me. She was putting me in more danger by refusing to change. She was keeping things from me about her and me. She wasn't protecting me. She was putting me in more danger by forcing me to be without my wolf. I never expressed how angry I was about that. I pushed it aside because I had other things to worry about.

But I was angry at her. I was so angry and she had no right to talk about protecting me.

"Protect me?" I asked. "How are you doing by refusing to change?"

"Maddie..." she spoke, but I pushed her back.

I didn't want to deal with her. I was already angry enough and I didn't need to hear her excuses.

"I am Luna of this pack!" Janet continued, her voice growing louder with each word she spoke. "I am your father's mate! You can't talk to me like that, you spoiled brat."

She started to move closer to me and I knew what she was going to do. I recognized his gaze immediately. But I didn't back down. I wasn't going to give him the satisfaction of knowing how scared I really was. I stood up straighter and raised my head. I wasn't going to back down. Not again.

My stance infuriated her even more. She grabbed my arm and pulled me away from the desk. Her nails dug into my skin and her eyes narrowed. She started to raise her hand when the door slammed open.

Dimitri's gaze made me flinch. I knew he would never hurt me, but even I was afraid of him.

He looked at Janet's hand on my arm and a feral growl escaped him.

"Let her go," Dimitri said, his eyes changing color.

Janet held my arm tighter.

"We were just talking, Dimiti," Janet said. "Your precious little partner is safe."

Dimitri growled and grabbed Janet's hand, pulling her off my arm.

Someone grabbed me and pulled me back immediately.

I looked up to see a very angry Will.

"Dimitri..." Savannah spoke, but his loud growl cut her off.

Two warriors ran into the office and grabbed Savannah. She started screaming and thrashing around.

"Dimitri!" she screamed. "Help me."

She tried to get out of his arms, but they were too strong for her.

"Let me go!" she screamed. "Dimitri!"

Will pulled me behind him and held me tighter. He kept growling.

I could hear Savannah's screams until one of the warriors closed the door behind him. The only sound left was Will's growl.

"What were you going to do, Mother?" Dimitri spoke, his voice a mix of his and Skol's. "Were you about to hurt my mate?"

A sigh caught in my throat.

Janet's eyes widened. She looked at me, but Will stood up so she couldn't see me. I tilted my head so I could see her.

"Tell her, Madeline!" Skye screamed. Tell him what he was about to do. Tell him what he did.

I ignored her and pushed her back.

"Dimitri..." I called out, but his growl cut me off,

"I would never hurt her," Janet said, her voice shaking slightly. "We were just talking."

Will tightened his grip on me. He started to shake.

"Interesting," Dimitri said. "Why was your hand up when I came in, Mother? Why did it look like you were going to hit her?"

I froze. Had he seen that?

"I didn't," Janet exclaimed, shaking her head. "I would never hit her!"

She was a good liar. She seemed offended that he would even suggest that.

"Tell her, Madeline!" Janet yelled, looking back at me. "Tell her I've never hurt you!"

I gulped and tried to breathe a little. I didn't want to ruin his relationship with her. I didn't want him to have to choose between her and me.

I didn't want to hurt her.

"She would never..." I spoke, but Dimitri cut me off.

"I'm not talking to her, Mother," Dimitri growled. "I'm talking to you." She stared back at him, her eyes wide.

"Try not to lie, Mother," Dimitri said, claws reaching out. "I'll order you if I have to."

She gulped and shook her head.

"I'd never—" she spoke, but Dimitri's growl cut her off.

"I told you not to lie to me!" he yelled, making her flinch hard. "I know the truth, but I want to hear it from you!"

My heart skipped a beat.

Did he know? How could he—"

"I had to, Maddie," Skye whispered. "I had to."

My body went numb.

No.

No, no, no, no, no!

Chapter 78 Blinding Fury

Dimitri's POV

I wasn't angry.

No. Anger wasn't a word I would use to describe how I felt. I wasn't even sure that word existed.

No one had probably ever felt the way I felt the moment Skol told me I had already hurt my mate, so there was no need to make up a word.

The feeling was completely new and I didn't even try to name it. It was impossible anyway.

My own mother had hurt my mate. My own mother hurt the most precious part of my heart and soul. My own mother wanted to get rid of my mate. My fucking mother hurt me more than anyone else.

How was I supposed to feel?

I wanted to strangle her and watch the life drain out of her pathetic body.

"I never hurt her!" my mother screamed. "Whatever I told you is a lie!"

Anger blinded me for a second. I grabbed her by the neck and squeezed, making her eyes pop out. I growled at her and got in her face.

"Tell me what you did to her," I spat out as an order. "Tell me everything you said and did to my mate right now, dammit." I let go of her neck so she could speak.

"She didn't do anything, Dimitri," Maddie screamed, her voice shaking.

"It's okay.
" "She's lying," Skol told me, his voice shaking with anger. "Skye told me what that bitch did."

I knew Maddie was lying, but I didn't understand why. She should have told me. I would have protected her. She was my heart and I wouldn't have let anyone hurt her, not even my own mother.

Why didn't she tell me?

"Don't resist the order, Mother," I growled. "It'll only make it more painful

." My mother whimpered and tried to wriggle out of my grip. I took a few steps forward and pinned her against the wall.

"Tell me," I repeated my order, causing her body to jerk.

It was painful and I knew it. I didn't care. I had hurt my mate and I would pay for it.

The door slammed open and I heard a loud gasp. I knew it was Mike. He sensed my mother's pain and ran towards her.

"Dimitril," Mike yelled. "What the fuck are you doing? Let her go!

Grab him, Will." I mentally connected to my Beta. I don't want to hurt him.

I heard Will approach Mike.

"What the fuck?!" Mike yelled, "Let me go!"

Both Will and I ignored him. I focused back on my mother who was moaning in pain.

"Tell me," I growled in her face again.

"I hit her!" she screamed. "I called her names! I tried to get her to leave."

My heart broke. A small part of me still hoped she hadn't done it. A small part of me still hoped my mother cared about me.

"I didn't want her here because she looks too much like her mother," my mother continued. "I was afraid she would remind Mike of his fated mate and that he would start to question our relationship."

I removed my hand from her neck and took a step back. She was panting hard and I could tell she was still trying to fight the command.

Small beads of sweat formed on her forehead.

"I've been trying to get her to leave since the moment she got here," my mother continued. "I started with insults. I started hitting her when you refused to mate with Savannah." "

I didn't think my heart could break any more. My mother knew the baby wasn't mine all along.

" "I helped Savannah come up with that plan," my mother said. "I was angry when it didn't work. I could tell how much you liked Madeline even then and I wanted to make sure you couldn't end her no matter what."

The room was completely silent the entire time. I couldn't speak. I couldn't believe my own mother would do something like that.

"Savannah would call her names and hit her too," my mother said, making the rage inside me rise to a whole new level. "We threatened to kill her if she told anyone."

"Are you fucking serious?" Mike yelled. "Are you serious, Janet?"

My mother looked at Mike and sobbed.

"I'm sorry," she yelled. "I told you I didn't want her here. You should have never brought her here. You should have just left her in her pack." Mike growled loudly.

"That's my daughter!" Mike yelled. "I couldn't leave my daughter without a father!

" "You did it once!" my mother yelled at him. "You could have done it again!" "

Oh, you bitch!" Mike yelled again.

I could hear him trying to wriggle out of Will's arms.

"What else?" I asked, making my mother look back at me. "What else did you do to my mate?"

My mother gulped and shook her head.

"Nothing else," she said, her voice shaking. "I did it for you, Dimitri.

I wanted what was best for you. She's not good enough. She's not worthy of—"

I grabbed her by the neck again, stopping her from speaking.

"You're digging yourself a deep grave, Mother," I said, squeezing her neck again.

My skin burned and I just wanted to wash my hands away. I wanted to erase the feeling of my skin touching hers.

"You choose her over me?" my mother asked incredulously. "I'm your mother!"

Was I crazy?!

"Of course I choose her over you!" I exclaimed. "She's my heart and soul. She's my whole world. You're not my mother. You're nothing."

Her eyes widened and she tried to speak again, but I wouldn't let her.

"You're going to the cells until I decide what to do with you," I told him.

"You'll never be free again. Your life is over."

He sobbed loudly and started shaking his head.

"Take out the trash, Will," I said in disgust. "Put her in the cell next to Savannah. Then we'll decide what to do with them." I took one last look at the poor excuse for a mother before turning away. I immediately looked at my princess and my heart broke.

She was leaning against her desk, her head down. I saw her shaking and realized she was crying.

I didn't say a word. I walked over to her, picked her up, and started to walk out of the office. Having her in my arms kept me from killing my mother. Having her in my arms kept me from screaming in pain.

Chapter 79 Why, Maddie?

Dimitri's POV

I was sitting on the bed in our room, holding Maddie as close to me as possible. She was sitting on my lap, her whole body wrapped around me. But that wasn't enough for me.

I needed her closer.

I felt so fucking guilty. How the fuck did I not realize something was happening to my roommate? She was being abused right under my nose and I didn't realize it! I felt like the worst roommate in the fucking world and I wanted to rip my heart out.

We got back to our room almost ten minutes ago, but neither of us spoke. I couldn't speak because I had a huge lump in my throat. I could barely breathe.

I kept kissing every part of her body I could reach. I kept caressing her. I kept holding her tighter to me. I needed to make sure she was in my arms. I needed to make sure she was okay.

But I had to talk. I had to ask her why she hadn't told me. I needed to know why. I needed to know everything.

I kissed her head one more time and held her tight.

"Why, Maddie?" I asked quietly, pain in my voice. "Why didn't you tell me, Princess? Why didn't you tell Mike? Why didn't you ask for help?"

She stiffened a little and took a deep breath.

"I need the truth, Maddie," I told her. "I need to know the truth."

She tried to sit on my lap and I let her. But I didn't move my arms, I kept them over her, assuring us both that she was safe.

She took another deep breath and looked at me. Her cheeks were swollen and red. I reached up and wiped away her tears. My heart ached to see her like this, but I knew it was the last time, that I wouldn't let anything like this happen again. She would never hurt again.

"I was sure Mike knew," Maddie murmured, making me furrow my brows. "I was sure he approved. She hit me even when he was home and I was sure he knew it." I

seriously doubted it. Mike would never let her do something like that if he knew. Mike made mistakes, but he would never let anyone hurt Maddie.

"I don't think he knew, princess," I said softly. "He wouldn't let her do that."

She nodded and looked down at her lap again.

"I realized after a while," she said. "He would hit me when he was home because the whole house is soundproofed and he knew I wouldn't say anything."

She sighed and shook her head.

"I was sure he would leave this pack as soon as he turned 18," she said, making my heart clench. "I thought no one would care. I wasn't even part of this pack. I wasn't..." She

stopped talking and looked at me.

"I didn't think it was important because I thought I wouldn't see her again after my birthday," she said.

I clenched my jaw and nodded.

"And after you found out she was your mate?" I asked. "Why didn't you tell me then?"

Her eyes filled with tears and she swallowed.

"I didn't want you to lose your mother," she said. "I didn't want this to happen. I didn't want you to have to choose." I didn't want to come between you two."

My eyes widened. Was I crazy?! I would choose her over anyone else! I would choose her again and again. She was my heart and soul. No one came close.

I caressed her cheeks and looked at her sternly.

"Listen to me, Maddie," I said. "You are the most important thing in my world. You will always come first to me. You have my whole heart and I love you more than anything. I will choose you over anyone. I will choose you over myself. I will—"

She cut me off by leaning down and pressing her lips to mine. I groaned and kissed her back.

"I love you too," she murmured against my lips. "I love you so much."

I tangled my fingers in my hair and rested my forehead against hers. I wanted to keep kissing her but I needed to talk to her. I needed her to tell me everything and I knew if I kept kissing her I wouldn't be able to stop anytime soon.

My need to mark her only grew after finding out what my mother had done. I needed to tie her to me in every way possible. I needed everyone to know who she was to me. I needed to protect her and my mark on her was the first step.

"I need to know everything, princess," I said, panting hard. "I need to know everything she did."

Maddie shook her head and wrapped her arms around my neck.

"You know everything now, my love," she said softly. "She told you everything."

Hearing her call me her love made my entire body tingle.

I wanted to kiss her again, but she furrowed her brows and bit her bottom lip.

"What's wrong, princess?" I asked softly as I pulled her lip out from under her teeth.

I wanted to bite it.

"I almost left the pack one day," she murmured, and my heart stopped beating. "Seth caught me and kept me from leaving.

I couldn't feel my body. Did she almost leave? I almost lost her.

" "When?" I asked, a growl escaping me.

"When you found us in that cabin," she murmured under her breath.

"My lip was split, and I told you I fell."

My heart was pounding so hard it felt like it was going to jump out of my chest. I thought back to that day. I was so scared that she'd hurt herself that I didn't pay attention to anything else.

"Did my mother do that?" I asked, my voice tight.

Maddie nodded, and my vision went black. I held her tight and growled.

"You'll never leave me," I said. "You're mine, Madeline."

I had no idea what the fuck I would have done if she'd managed to leave that night. I just had Seth to thank for stopping her.

Did he know my mother had hurt him?

Maddie caressed my cheeks and gave me a small smile.

"I'm yours," she said. "I'll never leave. I promise, Dimitri. I can't leave. I love you too much to do that. I think I loved you even before I turned 18. I think a part of me knew who you were even then. I was so mad at Mike and I thought Savannah..."

I cut her off by kissing her hard. I didn't want to hear anything else. All I needed to hear was that she loved me. That was enough. That was all I wanted.

Chapter 80 I'm sorry

Madeline's POV

I finally managed to calm down a bit.

Dimitri was still kissing every part of my body he could reach. He kept telling me how much he loved me. In his arms I felt like I was floating on clouds and I never wanted to leave.

Dimitri lifted my head, caressed my cheek and pressed his warm lips to mine.

"Your father wants to see you, princess," he said when he stopped kissing me. "He's outside our bedroom."

I gulped and looked at the door.

"Please listen to him, love," Dimitri said as he tucked a strand of hair behind my ear. "He's really upset."

I looked back at Dimitri and nodded. He gave me another soft kiss on the lips and neck. I stood up and took a deep breath.

I watched as Dimitri walked to our bedroom door and opened it. Mike paced in front of our room. His hair was messy and he looked like he had been crying. He looked at me as soon as Dimitri pulled away.

"Oh, my baby," Mike exclaimed as he rushed in. He hugged me tightly and sobbed.

"I'm so sorry, my little girl," he murmured between sobs. "I'm so sorry about everything."

I hugged him back and looked over my shoulder at Dimitri. He was smiling at me and my heart skipped a beat.

"She'll get her punishment, sweetheart," Mike continued. "I promise. I'll punish her myself."

I patted his back.

"It's okay, Mike," I said, trying to comfort him a little. "She can't hurt me again."

Mike lifted his head and looked at me. He caressed my cheek and shook his head.

"It's not okay," he said, his voice breaking. "Nothing is okay, my baby. Nothing you've had to go through because of me is okay." I raised my eyebrows and Mike sobbed again.

"If I hadn't left you and your mother, she wouldn't have been able to hurt you," Mike said, stroking my cheek again. "I'm so sorry, baby. I'm so sorry. It's all my fault." He pulled me into his arms again and held me tight.

I looked at Dimitri and my heart tightened.

"I met Dimitri because of you," I said, still looking at my partner. "If I hadn't moved here, I would have never met him. I have only you to thank."

Mike looked back at me and shook his head.

"You would have found your way to him even without me," he said, his voice shaking. "You're so strong and so amazing and I had nothing to do with it. It was all you and your mother's doing."

He kissed my forehead and sobbed again.

"I can only be ashamed of the things I did," he said softly. "I can only be ashamed of my actions."

I sighed and stepped away from him. I took his hand in mine and pulled him over to the couch across the bedroom from Dimitri and me.

I made him sit down and sat next to him, keeping his hand in mine the entire time.

"You made mistakes, but what happened with Janet wasn't your fault," I told him and he looked at me. "It was just hers. She chose to do it, not you."

I took a deep breath and let it out slowly.

"It was meant for me to come to her pack," I continued. "Janet would probably do the same thing no matter who brought me here."

Mike gulped and caressed my cheek.

"She said she did it because you look like your mother, sweetheart," Mike murmured softly. "If I wasn't her mate, she would never..."

Mike stopped talking and shook his head.

I squeezed his hand tighter and gave him a small smile.

"It wasn't your fault, Mike," I told him. —I'm not blaming you for what she did. — Mike hugged me again. He rubbed my back and kissed my temple.

"I blame myself," he muttered. "I should have seen the signs. I should have realized something was up."

I looked at Dimitri and gulped. I didn't want him to hear those things. I was his mother, no matter what.

Dimitri came over to us and sat next to me. He put his arm around my waist and pulled me close to him. Mike let go of me and wiped his cheeks.

"We both should have seen the signs," Dimitri said. "I blame myself too, Mike. I should have realized my mate was being abused. I should have seen it sooner. I should have questioned hard."

"Dimitri..." I spoke, but he cut me off.

"We both screwed up, Mike," Dimitri continued, completely ignoring me. "But there's no use crying over it. We need to make sure no one hurts her again. We need to change for the better, not cry over what should have been." Mike smiled a little. You could tell he was very proud of Dimitri.

"You're right," Mike said, reaching out and taking Dimitri's hand in his. "We need to make sure no one hurts her again."

Dimitri nodded and squeezed Mike's hand tighter.

"I'm so fucking happy you're my daughter's mate," Mike continued. "You're an amazing man and I'm so proud of you." I smiled and rested my head on Dimitri's shoulder. I was so happy he was my mate too. I couldn't have asked for a better one.

"Please don't be as stupid as me, Dimitri," Mike said. "Don't hurt my little girl."

Dimitri's arm around me tightened.

"Never, Mike," he said. "I love her more than anything in this world. I'll never hurt her. I'd rather die."

My heart clenched painfully just thinking about him being gone. He was a part of me and I didn't want to exist without him.

Dimitri turned to me and kissed my forehead.

"I love you." I mentally linked.

"I love you too, my princess." He said softly and I couldn't help but smile.

I never wanted anything to change and I hoped it never would.

Chapter 81 His punishment

Dimitri's POV

I didn't want to leave Maddie, but Mike assured me she'd be okay. I let them talk even though I wanted to kick Mike out and drag Maddie to bed. I really wanted to be with her and make sure she was okay. But I had work to do. I had to think of a fitting punishment for my mom and Savannah.

I walked into my office and Will immediately looked at me.

"Where's Maddie?" he asked, looking behind me.

"With Mike," I said, closing the door and walking over to my desk. "Where are they?"

"Locked up," Will said, anger in his voice.

I sat up and nodded. I ran my fingers through my hair and took a deep breath.

"What are you going to do, Dimitri?" Will asked, walking over to my desk. "How are you going to punish them?"

I sighed and shook my head.

"I have no fucking idea," I said. "I want to kill them both, but..."

I clenched my jaw and balled my fists.

"But one of them is your mother," Will finished the sentence for me. I looked at him and nodded. Will sighed and sat down in the chair in front of my desk. He raised his eyebrows and crossed his arms over his chest.

"I never thought we'd have to deal with this," Will muttered under his breath.

I swallowed the lump in my throat and nodded. I still couldn't believe it. I couldn't believe my mother would do something like that. I didn't understand why. Just because Maddie looked like her mother?

What the fuck did my mother think was going to happen? Did she think Mike would leave her? Did she really think Mike would do that? I was sure he wouldn't. Mike loved my mother and he wouldn't leave him, even if Maddie's mother was alive.

There had to be another reason for my mother to hate Maddie so much. I couldn't believe I didn't realize something terrible was happening to my mate. I was a terrible mate. So fucking terrible.

I groaned and buried my face in my hands.

"It's not your fault, Dimitri," Will said, causing me to look up at him. "You didn't know."

I rested my arms on the armrest and clenched my fists.

"She's my mate," I said. "I should have known. I should have seen something was wrong with her. Goddess, I even saw that she was hurt once and I didn't do shit about it."

That realization was especially hard on me. I saw her split lip and I didn't do shit about it. I was so mad at her leaving without me and at the scoundrels on my borders. I was so focused on her turning 18 so I could finally have her that I didn't notice anything else going on around me. I should have asked her more. I should have known she wouldn't fall.

"What are you talking about?" Will asked, his brows furrowing.

I sighed and swallowed another lump.

"I saw her with a split lip one day," I muttered. "She told me she fell. She lied. My mother did that." Will growled and cursed under his breath.

"I should have known," I said, groaning softly.

Will sighed and ran his fingers through his hair.

"You couldn't have known, Dimitri," Will said. "They both hid it so well."

Knowing that didn't make me feel any better. Maddie was my mate. She was my heart and soul. I failed to protect her. I failed to protect my own heart. I clenched my jaw and forced the air into my lungs. I'd screwed up, but I couldn't change what had happened. All

I could do was make sure no one ever hurt her again. All I could do was make sure my mother and Savannah were severely punished for what they'd done.

"The law is clear," I said, clenching my fists again. "You both will be killed for what you did." My tongue burned as I said those words. My heart sank at the thought of killing my own mother. But the law was clear when it came to threatening and endangering Luna and Alpha's lives. It was a crime punishable by death.

My mother knew what would happen if I found out. She knew I wouldn't hesitate to kill her. My mate was my greatest treasure and I would choose her above all else. My father raised me to do it. I wanted to do it. Maddie was my everything and I wasn't going to let anyone hurt her.

"There might be a problem with your mother's punishment, Dimitri," Will said and I raised my eyebrows.

"What problem?" I asked. "The law is clear. She will be punished by death." Will sighed and gave me a small nod.

"I know what the law says, Dimitri," Will said. "I'm with you on that, but I'm not sure the Council is. She's the former Luna of this pack and a former Queen of the Realm. They might be against it."

I clenched my jaw. I hadn't thought about those bastards at all.

"You might need to consider another punishment for her," he said. Will.

"I'm a King," I said angrily. "The Council may advise me not to kill her, but my word is final."

" "It is," Will said, giving me a small nod.

"But you know the law, Dimitri. The Council has a say in these matters."

I clenched my jaw and stood up. I began pacing around my office, trying to calm myself down a bit. I was very pissed off. I wanted her punished for what she'd done.

"I'm not saying they'll be against it, Dimitri," Will said. "I'm just stating that it could happen and that you should prepare for it."

I looked at him and took a deep breath. I had to concentrate really hard to keep my temper under control.

"I'll have a workaround," I said. "But I'm not backing down. I'll do whatever I have to do to make sure she gets what she deserves. She's my mother, but that won't save her from being punished."

Will gave me a small smile.

"Fine," he said. "No one hurts Maddie."

I nodded and took another deep breath.

Will was right. No one would hurt what belonged to me. I had to show everyone what would happen if they did.

Chapter 82 Mark me

Dimitri's POV

"I think we should get this over with," I said as I glanced at my watch. "I need to get back to Maddie."

Will and I had spent the last two hours talking about the alpha meeting that was going to take place in my pack in just three days. I felt like I had completely neglected the event, but I had a good excuse for it. It wasn't every day that I found out about my mate being mistreated by my own mother.

"Sure," Will said, giving me a small smile. "You can tell you miss her already."

I didn't miss her. I was burning up without her and I needed to get back. This was the longest we'd been apart in days and it felt like my lungs were shutting down. I needed her to breathe.

"Yeah," I said as I closed the folder in front of me. "

We can continue tomorrow."

"I'll stay and finish," Will said. "Go be with your mate."

My fingertips felt like they were burning. I already knew the only thing that would help was Maddie's skin. I needed to touch her. I needed to kiss her. I needed to fill my lungs with her sweet scent.

"See you tomorrow," I said as I stood up and ran to the door.

I heard Will chuckle and a small smile spread across my face. I was dying for him to meet his mate and be able to experience how wonderful it felt to finally have her.

I barely noticed anyone or anything as I hurried back to my room. I passed a few of my warriors so I forced a small smile on my face as they bowed to me.

I was dying to get back to my room.

My heart raced as I approached the door. I was so excited I was dying to hug her. I was barely breathing as I finally grabbed the doorknob.

"Princess," I let out a sigh of relief as I entered the room.

My heart stopped beating. She wasn't there.

My breath caught in my throat. I wanted to scream, but I couldn't. I could feel my heart beating in my eyes. I could hear the blood rushing through my veins.

A thousand different scenarios ran through my mind.

Someone took her. My mother and Savannah ran away and took her. Someone broke into our room and took her. She was gone. She couldn't handle what my mother had done to her and she left.

"Madeline!" I cried out, my voice quiet and raspy.

I tried to scream. I tried to scream. But I couldn't. Fear choked me. I'd never been so scared in my entire life.

If something happened to her...

A noise behind me made me spin around so fucking fast I almost lost my balance.

It was her.

She was my princess.

I screamed in relief as I closed the distance between us and pulled her into my arms. My whole body calmed down and I could finally think clearly. I was okay. I was in the bathroom.

"Dimitri?" she called out worriedly as she wrapped her arms around me.

But I still couldn't speak. There was still a huge lump in my throat. "

Give me a second, Princess," I said through the mind link as I buried my nose in her neck.

She didn't respond, but she ran her fingers through my hair and kissed my temple. I relaxed even more and was finally able to breathe deeply. It was okay.

I held her tighter and pulled her even closer to me.

"I'm sorry, Princess," I murmured into her neck. "I didn't see you in the room when I came in and I thought something had happened to you. I thought someone had taken you. I thought you were gone."

Just saying those words hurt like hell. I had no idea what I would do if she really wasn't here. I would probably go crazy.

"I'll never leave, Dimitri," she said softly as she kissed my temple again. "I'm yours and I will never leave you."

I smiled a little. Hearing her say that cured all the aches in my body. I placed a soft kiss on her neck and ran my hand down her back. It was then that I realized she was only wearing a towel and her skin was still a little damp.

A growl escaped me as my fingers reached the back of her neck. I kissed her neck again and she moaned softly.

"You're killing me, princess," I said softly. "You should have waited for me. I really wanted to shower with you again."

Maddie giggled a little and I lifted my head to look at her beautiful face. I couldn't resist kissing her so I did. I captured her lips with mine, gently squeezing the back of her neck and holding her in place.

"I've missed you," she said softly as I lowered my lips to her jaw.

I smiled and lifted my head to look at her.

"I've missed you too, princess," I said. —I missed you so much, damn it.

—She smiled back and caressed my cheek.

"Can I ask you something?" she asked and I nodded immediately.

"Always, Maddie," I told her. "You can always come to me and ask me anything."

She smiled and pulled me in for a kiss. I groaned and kissed her back, enjoying the feeling of her lips pressed against mine. I really wanted the kiss to last longer but I also wanted to know what she wanted to ask me.

"Ask me, princess," I told her as I pulled back and tucked a strand of hair behind her ear.

She looked perfect like this. She was wet, wearing a towel, her hair up in a messy bun and her cheeks flushed. It was a dream. It was my fucking dream.

"Will you mark me?" she asked and my heart stopped beating.

I couldn't do anything but stare at her.

Had I heard her right?

Skol stirred and groaned in excitement.

Had she really just asked me that?

Maddie smiled a little and pulled me in for another kiss. I could barely kiss him back.

"Do you want to mark me, Dimitri?" he asked again and I almost fainted from the excitement.

Chapter 83 Mine

Dimitri's POV

I couldn't hold back the loud, lust-filled growl that escaped me. Maddie squealed in surprise as I picked her up and walked over to the bed.

"Are you sure?" I asked as I gently laid her down on the bed.

I didn't know what the fuck I was going to do if she told me she changed her mind. I was already salivating and my canines were ready to pierce her soft skin. My cock was painfully hard and I really needed to get it inside her.

"I'm sure," Maddie said as she reached up and caressed my cheek.

I looked down at her body and groaned, my heart racing as I reached between us and slowly began to unwrap the towel.

It was like opening a present. The best fucking present I'd ever received. My breath caught in my throat as I finally caught sight of one of her already hard nipples. It wasn't the first time I'd seen her breasts. I'd seen them when we were showering together, but I wanted to be respectful and never touched them. Knowing that I was finally going to be able to touch them, lick them, and suck them was driving me crazy with lust.

"Oh fuck, Maddie," I cried out as I hurriedly pulled the rest of the towel off.

I really wanted to take it slow, but my resolve to do so went downhill when I saw how perfect she looked lying beneath me.

She was panting hard and I could feel her nervousness.

I forced myself to stop what I was doing. It was so fucking hard, but she was my priority, not my desire to get inside her.

"You're in control, Maddie," I said softly as I leaned down and placed a soft kiss on her lips. "Tell me to stop and I will."

It would be so fucking hard, but I would stop.

She shook her head and wrapped her arms around my neck, holding me close to her.

"I don't want you to stop," she said. "I want this. I want to be yours."

I smiled and caressed her cheek.

"You're mine already, Maddie," I said and looked down at her neck.

A growl escaped me as I imagined my mark there. It would be a beautiful sight and I was dying to see it.

I leaned into her and placed a soft kiss on her neck. I pulled the rest of her towel off and she was now completely naked beneath me.

"Oh, Dimitri," she murmured softly as she reached up and tangled her fingers in my hair.

My entire body vibrated. Her caresses continued to send jolts of lust to my cock. I wanted to growl and moan every time she moved, but I had to keep kissing her. I had to keep tasting her.

She reached down with her other hand and began to lift my shirt. I stood up, knelt between her legs, and pulled my shirt over my head. I heard her moan softly and a shiver ran through me.

I didn't take my eyes off her as she began to unbutton my dress pants. She gulped and looked down at my hands. I went slowly on purpose. I wanted her lust to take over. I wanted her to want me to go faster.

My wish came true when she sat up and began to help me remove my pants. She didn't take her eyes off me and I was sure I would pass out.

I had to hold back a groan as my boxers brushed the tip of my cock. I was already very turned on.

Maddie looked down at my hard cock and another small moan escaped her.

She reached out and made to grab it but I stopped her. She looked at me with confusion written all over her beautiful face.

"I'll explode if you touch me, Maddie," I said, my voice low and raspy. "Besides, tonight is about you, not me. You'll have plenty of time to touch me and suck me off."

Just imagining it made me close to cumming.

Maddie's eyes widened as I pushed her onto the bed. I looked down at her beautiful body and moaned. She was mine. She was mine to worship and pleasure.

I lay on top of her, not wanting to waste any more time. I had to start kissing her immediately.

I started with her lips and jaw. She wrapped her arms around my neck and pulled me close to her. I felt her nipples press into my skin and I nearly went crazy.

Fuck. She was fucking perfect.

"I need to taste every part of you," I told her as I started kissing her neck.

She moaned and moved her head so I could have better access.

I smiled as I started sucking on her sweet spot. She shuddered and pressed herself even tighter against me.

I was breathing hard and had a hard time going slow. But I would do it for her. It would tear me apart if I hurt her or did anything wrong. This was about her, not me.

I kissed her collarbone and started slowly moving down. I stopped when I reached her chest. She was panting hard and her cheeks were completely red.

I kept my eyes on her as I gently caressed her breast. She shuddered and gulped. I touched her nipple with my thumb and her eyes went wide. I could feel my heart pounding in my throat.

I slowly lowered my head and kissed her breast. I didn't take my eyes off her. I wanted to see if she was uncomfortable. I wanted to know if she needed me to stop. Luckily, I only saw lust in her eyes.

I continued kissing down her breast until I reached her nipple. I licked it slowly, making her gasp and arch her back a little. I smiled as I closed my mouth around her nipple and sucked.

"She cried out and tangled her fingers in my hair, trying to keep me in place.

But I didn't need to. Nothing would make me move. I was in heaven and I wasn't leaving anytime soon.

I grabbed her other breast and began to gently caress her other nipple. We had barely started and she was already moaning.

Chapter 84 Your

Madeline's POV

I was completely lost in his touch. I was completely his. He was right. I belonged to him even without his mark on my body.

It was amazing. Everything he did or said was incredible. Every grunt and moan that left his lips only made my body more sensitive.

I had never wanted anything like I wanted him.

I couldn't believe I was almost gone. I couldn't believe there was a time when I wanted to push him away. I was an idiot and I was lucky he didn't let me. I had so much to be thankful for.

I had so much to make up for. Luckily, I would have my whole life to show him how sorry I was. I would have my whole life to show him how much I loved him.

I was completely lost in ecstasy and I didn't even notice that Dimitri was now lying between my legs, kissing and sucking softly on my thigh. A wave of shame washed over me and I tried to cover my pussy.

I didn't know why I was doing it. I wanted him. I wanted to continue. It was more of an instinctive reaction than anything else.

"Don't do that, princess," Dimitri said softly as he pushed my hand away. "Don't cover up what belongs to me."

My lower belly tingled with arousal as he growled and leaned closer.

"This is mine, Madeline," he said and I could feel his breath on my pussy. "This is mine alone. You can never keep that from me."

I gulped and nodded. He winked at me and smiled.

He kept his eyes on mine as he leaned into me and gently licked my clit. My eyes
rolled back in my head and I moaned loudly.

"Fuck," he said, his voice husky and deep. "You taste so fucking good."

He continued to lick me gently and I couldn't help but arch my back and pull myself closer to him. He grabbed my waist and pinned me to the bed.

"Don't move," he said sternly, his voice sending shivers of pleasure through my body.

I couldn't help but obey him.

I looked back at him and swallowed. He kept his eyes on mine as he continued to lick me gently. I thought I would completely break down when the licking turned into sucking.

"Oh my..." I moaned loudly, throwing my head back.

"Look at me, Madeline," Dimitri said sternly. "I really like it when you look at me." I

nearly exploded from his words alone.

I looked back at him and he smirked at me. He started sucking on my clit again and it took a lot of effort to keep my eyes open and focused on him.

"You taste amazing, my love," he murmured as he stopped sucking me and just stroked my clit with his thumb. "I thought about what you would taste like, but I never would have imagined it would be this good."

He moved his hand and suddenly I felt his fingers at my opening. I gasped quietly and shuddered a little. Dimitri looked at me with so much love that I felt like sobbing.

"I won't hurt you, princess," he said softly. "But I won't continue if you don't want me to either."

I shook my head immediately.

"Please continue," I said, my voice shaking slightly. "I've never done this before, so I'm a little nervous."

Dimitri smiled and leaned down to kiss my thigh.

"I know, princess," he said softly. "It makes me so happy that you've done this before. That means only I can do it."

He started sucking on my clit again and I cried out in pleasure. I felt his finger at my entrance and the desire to have him inside me overwhelmed me.

Dimitri gently pushed his finger inside me.

My gasp was followed by a loud moan. The sensation was strange, but so pleasurable. I wanted more.

"You're so fucking tight," Dimitri growled.

His growl sent vibrations to my clit and I almost screamed in pleasure. I felt a strange, new sensation in my lower belly. My insides began to throb. My toes curled and I couldn't help but grab Dimitri by the hair and pull him even closer to me.

"Watch me while you cum," he said, growling again.

I shuddered and tried not to take my eyes off of him. I was panting hard and so focused on the thousand tiny explosions in my body that I hadn't even realized Dimitri had a finger inside me. He started pressing down on a spot deep inside me that sent me flying through the air.

"Fuck yes!" Dimitri exclaimed as I arched my back.

His movements quickened. He gripped me tightly, preventing me from moving. He was growling softly and I could feel his entire body vibrating.

I felt an explosion in my clit. There were no other words to describe what happened. It was an explosion of pleasure that left my entire body shaking and melting with pleasure.

I didn't even realize I had gotten my legs around Dimitri's neck. My fingers were completely tangled in his hair and I was holding him so tight I wasn't even sure I was breathing.

As soon as the shaking in my body subsided, I pulled my legs away from his neck and let go.

"I'm so sorry," I murmured, my voice shaking. "..."

Dimitri cut me off by grabbing my legs and wrapping them around his neck again.

"Fuck, Madeline, don't ever say you're sorry," he growled as he licked my pussy from the entrance to my clit. "This was the hottest fucking thing that's ever happened to me.

If I could spend the rest of my life with your legs around my neck and my entire face buried in your delicious pussy, I would."

I felt the blood rush to my cheeks and a shaky giggle escaped me.

"You're so fucking wet and ready for me,"

Dimitri murmured as he placed a soft kiss on my clit, making me shudder and moan.

He looked up at me and smiled.

"Do you even know how fucking perfect you are?" he asked me and my eyes widened slightly.

I didn't answer. I wasn't perfect.

Dimitri stood up and slowly moved towards me. He kissed me softly and I could taste myself on his lips and tongue.

"I fucking love you," he murmured as he lowered his lips to my jaw.

"I fucking love you too," I told him, making him laugh a little. He moved closer to me and I was dying to feel him inside me.

Chapter 85 Marked

Dimitri's POV

My heart was beating so fucking fast that I felt like it was going to jump out of my body. If it did, it would probably jump out of my mouth. I could feel my heart drumming in my neck.

I had never experienced anything like this. I never thought having sex with her could be so fucking perfect. I imagined it a million times, but it was never this good. I never felt so fucking amazing. I was never more in love than I was right then. I completely lost my mind when I tasted her. It was the best thing I had ever tasted and I wasn't about to stop. When she wrapped her legs around my neck and pulled me even tighter against her delicious pussy, I thought I was going to explode and cum all over the fucking bed.

I was floating on a cloud and I had no fucking idea how I was going to get off. How the fuck was I going to leave this bed?

I was so infatuated with her and I hadn't even fucked her yet. What would happen when I finally entered her? What would happen when I finally experienced what it felt like to be inside her?

Maybe I would go crazy with lust. Maybe I would lose my Kingdom because I wouldn't be able to leave the bed and stop fucking my mate. Maybe they would start calling me crazy and insane. Maybe I would lose everything.

But that was okay with me. I would be a happy man if all I had to keep was her. I would give it all up for her. I didn't need anything if I didn't have her.

"Please, Dimitri," she murmured softly as she kissed my neck.

A shiver ran down my spine. Hearing her say my name in that needy tone made my entire body shake with arousal. I knew what she needed, but I was going to make her say it.

I wanted to hear her say it.

"Please what, princess?" I asked as I began to suck on her earlobe.

She moaned and dug her nails into my shoulders.

"I need you," she cried out.

I smiled a little and continued kissing her neck softly and slowly.

"You need me to do what?" I asked, knowing full well what the answer was.

She needed me to fuck her and I wanted to hear her say it in that perfect, needy voice of hers.

She moaned and gasped loudly but didn't say anything.

I lifted my head to look at her. She was fucking gorgeous, her hair tousled and her cheeks flushed.

"You need me to do what, princess?" I asked again.

She gulped and licked her bottom lip. I growled and ground my cock against her. I had to say it. I had to say it immediately.

"I need you inside me," she said, her voice shaking slightly.

It wasn't exactly what I was expecting her to say, but I would take it.

It was her first time and I didn't want to push her and make her uncomfortable.

"Your wish is my command, my queen," I said as I grabbed my cock and gently placed the tip at her entrance.

Her eyes widened slightly and she moaned softly.

I clenched my jaw, trying hard not to cum before I entered her. I already knew how tight she was and I knew I wouldn't last long. I kissed her softly as I began to thrust into her.

She arched her back and I grabbed her hips.

"Don't move," I murmured against her lips.

I would explode if she moved. I would see fucking stars if she moved.

I kept thrusting, feeling her tight pussy grip my cock. She was wet and warm and slick. It was heaven.

I stopped completely when she shuddered. I saw pain in her eyes and my heart clenched painfully.

"It's okay, princess," I told her as I gently kissed her cheek. "It'll just hurt for a second."

I hated that it had to hurt. I wished it wouldn't.

"It's okay," she said softly as she kissed me. "I'm okay."

I kissed her softly and reached between us to gently rub her clit. I wanted to distract her from the pain. She moaned against my lips.

I kept thrusting and rubbing her clit at the same time. Her eyebrows raised slightly, but she moaned. Her pain was mixed with pleasure and rubbing her clit was the best thing I could do at the moment.

I was fully inside her now and I waited for her to tell me I could move. I reveled in the feeling of being inside her. I enjoyed feeling her pussy wrapped around my cock tightly. I enjoyed feeling her wetness on my thighs. I enjoyed every fucking second of being with her. She wiggled her hips a little and I took that as a sign to start moving. I pulled out a little before shoving it back in. My eyes rolled back in my head. Maddie moaned loudly.

I groaned and moaned as I continued to slide in and out of her slowly.

"Oh, Dimitri," she cried out, and I almost came as I heard her say my name in ecstasy.

I started rubbing her clit again. I wanted her to cum again. I wanted to feel her cum on my cock.

"I need you to cum all over me, princess," I told her, lowering my voice because I knew how much she loved it. "I need to feel you squeeze my cock hard."

I was so fucking close to exploding inside her. She moaned loudly and I felt her pussy squeezing me. I was close. My canines lengthened. I lowered my head and licked her mark spot.

That put her over the edge and I felt her pussy throbbing and gripping my cock hard. I couldn't hold back any longer. I sank my canines into her neck and exploded inside her pussy.

I felt her canines pierce through my skin and my vision went black. My whole body shuddered and I buried myself as deep inside her as I could. I calmed down completely and growled in pleasure.

I took a deep breath as I licked my mark on her neck, stopping it from bleeding.

"I love you, princess," I told her softly.

"I love you too," she said, wrapping her arms around my neck and pulling me closer.

I was in complete ecstasy and I didn't want to stop feeling this way. She was finally completely mine. She was marked, mated, and she was mine.

Only fucking mine.

Chapter 86 The boy she liked

Dimitri's POV

My heart rate finally slowed a little. I lifted my head and looked at my beautiful partner.

I smiled at her and she sighed contently. She ran her fingers through my hair and an overwhelming wave of love washed over me. I recognized her emotions and my heart skipped a beat.

"I can feel your love for me," I murmured as I leaned into her and kissed her softly on the cheek. "I love you too, Maddie. I love you with all my heart.

" "I know," she said as she tangled her fingers in my hair and kissed me softly on the lips.

I kissed her back and pulled out of her. I could feel the base of my cock starting to swell and I didn't want to tie a knot in it. Not yet.

She moaned quietly and closed her eyes. She was still sensitive.

I laid down beside her and pulled her to me immediately. She rested her chin on my chest and looked up at me. I ran my hand down her bare back and smiled at her.

"I love you," I told her again.

I couldn't stop saying it. It felt amazing and the spark I saw in her eyes every time she said those words made my heart flutter.

"I love you too," she said softly as she gave me a kiss on the chest.

I tangled my fingers in her hair and lifted her head slightly so I could kiss her forehead.

"Are you okay, princess?" I asked. "Did it hurt much?"

She immediately shook her head.

"No," she said, giving me a small smile. "It's been amazing. Thank you for being so patient and kind with me."

I caressed her cheek and leaned in to kiss her.

"Always," I told her. "I will always be patient and kind, princess."

Well, the tricky part was going to have to be discussed a little later. I would make love to her, but I would also fuck her, and I wasn't about to be gentle then.

She smiled and laid her head on my chest.

I ran my fingers through her hair and took a deep breath. I slowly let go and smiled. This was all I had ever wanted.

"I can't believe you're finally mine," I murmured, causing her to look back at me.

"I was always yours," she said. "Even before I knew it."

I smiled and nodded. A thought came to my mind and I instinctively frowned.

"What's wrong?" she asked worriedly.

I swallowed and caressed her cheek. I wanted to ask her something, but I wasn't sure I wanted to know the answer.

"Dimitri?" she called worriedly.

I leaned towards her and kissed her forehead. I took a deep breath and held her tight.

"Was there someone before me?" I asked. "Did you like someone before me?" I mean, I know you never slept with anyone before me, but did you do anything with anyone else?—.

The jealousy was clear in my voice and I knew how hypocritical that was of me. I slept with someone else. She knew it. She had to listen to lies about her child being mine.

"Oh," he said, laughing a little. "No. There was no one else before you. I grew up pretty much alone because Mike abandoned my mother and me.

When I got a little older I had to take care of my mother. Boys were never even on my mind."

He smiled and I breathed a sigh of relief.

"But I once foolishly fell in love with a boy," he said, laughing again. "I didn't even know his name, but he saved me and I liked him."

Great. Now he was jealous of someone neither she nor I knew.

"Saved you from who, princess?" I asked, trying to keep the jealousy out of my voice.

Maddie sighed and raised her eyebrows slightly.

"Kids were sometimes mean to me at school," she said, making my protective instincts kick in. "They made fun of me because I didn't have a father. One day I was leaving school when one of my classmates tripped me, pulled my hair, and started making fun of me." She sighed and smiled a little.

"A tall boy with blue eyes and dark hair came to my rescue," she continued. "He chased the bullies away, wiped the tears from my cheeks, and told me everything would be okay."

My heart skipped a beat.

"I never saw him again," she added with a sigh. "I never got to tell him how grateful I was."

I stared at her with wide eyes, not even breathing. She stopped smiling when she saw the shocked look on my face.

"What's wrong?" she asked, a little scared. She was actually always mine.

She was mine before I knew she was my partner. She was mine before I knew she was my mate.

She was mine since I was twelve.

A smile started to spread across my face. Maddie's confusion only grew.

"Blue eyes and dark hair?" I asked quietly. She nodded and began to study my face closely. Her eyebrows furrowed slightly and I saw the exact moment she realized why I had asked her that question.

"I was on a business trip with my father because I was going to be taking over the pack soon," I began to tell her the story of how she had always been mine. "We were visiting the Red Moon pack and we were just passing by a school when I saw a very naughty boy trip over a little girl with the cutest pigtails. I got really mad at him and immediately ran to help her."

I swallowed and saw a tear fall down Maddie's cheek.

"I chased the boy away and helped the girl," I continued, my voice shaking. "She looked so sad and helpless and my heart broke for her." I told her everything would be okay. I told her she would grow into a strong woman and that no one would ever bully her again. Maddie sobbed quietly.

"It was you," she murmured. "It was always you."

I pulled her to me and kissed her hard.

"It was always me and it will always be me," I murmured against her lips.

She wrapped her arms around my neck and kissed me hard. I held her close and let myself enjoy the feel of her body completely wrapped around mine.

I was always hers. I was the boy she liked.

Chapter 87 Torture

Madeline's POV

I woke up when I felt Dimitri place a soft kiss on my collarbone. I smiled and reached up to run my fingers through his hair.

"Good morning," I murmured softly.

"Goddess, I can't believe this is real," Dimitri said, making me furrow my eyebrows a little.

I opened my eyes and turned to him.

I was staring at his mark on my neck with a small smile on my face. He was so handsome and my heart skipped a beat when he looked at me.

"I can't believe you're finally mine," he said to me. "I've dreamed of this day for months. I can't believe it's finally happened."

"I was always yours," I told him, making him smile widely.

I smiled back and leaned in to kiss him. He moaned softly and pulled me closer to him. I took a deep breath, letting his scent fill my lungs. He smelled a little different now. Our scents had mixed together and he smelled even better than before. It was because he was completely mine now. Dimitri stopped kissing me. He caressed my cheek and rested his forehead on mine.

"Goddess, I don't want to get up," he murmured. "I want to stay in this bed forever."

I wanted that too, but I knew how much work we had to do.

"But we have so much to do," Dimitri moaned as he buried his face in my neck.

I chuckled and kissed his head.

"We'll be back soon," I said, trying to convince him and myself.

Dimitri looked at me and sighed.

"I'll close my eyes while you go to the bathroom," he said as he placed a soft kiss on my lips. "Get dressed inside."

I furrowed my eyebrows. What? Why?

Dimitri sighed at my confused expression. He kissed the tip of my nose and caressed my cheek.

"I'm not getting out of this bed if I see you naked," he said and my eyes widened. "I'm going to have to drag you over here and fuck you. As much as I want to, we don't have time. We have work to do."

I studied his face for a second. He was serious, wasn't he?

"Are you serious?" I muttered.

"Deadly," he said, smirking a little. "I'm suffering here as I try so fucking hard not to pull the blanket off and just touch and kiss every part of you. I can barely keep my hands on your back. I want to caress your chest and rub your clit so badly."

I gasped quietly and my body burst into flames.

"And you're not helping with those sounds," he said, growling under his breath. "Get up and get dressed before I cancel every fucking thing we have to do today."

I bit my bottom lip to hold back my laughter. Dimitri closed his eyes and waved his hands. I stood up and walked over to the closet.

"Fuck," Dimitri moaned and I glanced over my shoulder at him.

He threw his arm over his head, covering his eyes.

"Did you climax?" I asked laughing and shaking my head.

"Of course I did," he said sighing quietly. "Apparently I love torturing myself."

I chuckled and headed to the bathroom. I heard Dimitri get up from the bed as soon as I closed the bathroom door. I had the urge to open the door and look at him but I knew that would just end up with us back in that bed and we really didn't have time for that.

I got dressed and brushed my teeth as quickly as I could. I wanted to get back to him as soon as possible. My attraction to him was greater than ever and I needed to be by his side.

I opened the bathroom door just in time to see him put on a t-shirt. I could see his muscled back and I swear I drooled a little. It was really dark in the room last night so I didn't get a good look at his body. I bit my bottom lip as I looked down at his muscled arms. I remembered how tightly he held me and I couldn't help but picture it again.

"I can practically hear you moaning," Dimitri said as he turned around. "That's enough."

I sighed and gave him a small smile.

"Stop being so handsome," I said, making him smirk.

"No way," he said as he slowly approached me. "I like having you drooling behind me."

He closed the distance between us and caressed my cheeks and kissed me softly. My knees almost gave out.

Dimitri groaned and stopped kissing me. He rolled his eyes and grabbed my hand.

"What's wrong?" I asked worriedly.

"Will is annoying," Dimitri said as he started to pull me towards the door. "Ellie's here and she keeps bugging me to go see her.

" "Oh," I said, laughing a little.

"Don't laugh," Dimitri said, staring back at me. "I just dialed you. I should be inside you right now and not on my way to work."

I pulled him over and placed a kiss on his upper arm.

"I know," I said softly. "I wish you were inside me right now."

Dimitri groaned and ran his fingers through his hair.

"Goddess, Maddie, you're going to kill me," he muttered and I had to bite the inside of my cheek to keep from laughing.

Dimitri opened the door to our office and my eyes immediately fell on a gorgeous girl sitting on the couch talking to Will. I could tell she was tall even when she was sitting. She had long blonde hair and blue eyes. She was young, but I couldn't tell how old she was. She looked a lot like Will. She looked

up as soon as we walked in. He smirked and stood up.

"Dimitri!" he exclaimed as he walked over to us and hugged my partner tightly.

My body froze and I could feel the anger boiling in my veins. I couldn't help but let out a silent growl.

Chapter 88 I'm sorry

Dimitri's POV

I didn't even get a chance to tell Ellie not to hug me.

Maddie and I had just tagged each other so our protective and possessive instincts were even higher than normal. I knew how Maddie would react because I would have done the same if a guy had hugged her. To be honest, I wasn't even comfortable with her being in the same room as Will. I would explode if he touched her.

Ellie immediately let go of me. She looked at my neck and her eyes widened.

"Oh Goddess, I'm so sorry!" she exclaimed as she looked at Maddie. "I didn't realize you two tagged each other!"

"You did?!" Will gasped as he stood up and looked at us.

He had a huge grin on his face but he knew better than to get any closer. His eyes didn't even linger on Maddie for too long. I was so grateful for that and it confirmed to me what a good friend he was. She knew I would be very possessive of Maddie for a few days after the mark and she didn't want to make me feel threatened in any way.

"Oh no, I'm sorry!" Maddie said, making me look at her. "I don't know what came over me. I didn't mean to do that."

Maddie looked at Ellie with a horrified face.

"Oh, Mads, it's normal," Ellie said, smiling widely. "

You'll be a little obsessed with Dimitri for a few days after the mark. You don't have to apologize. I should have been more careful."

I put an arm around Maddie's shoulders and pulled her close to me.

"He's right, princess," I said as I placed a kiss on the top of her head. "Our instincts will be heightened for a few days."

You did well, my love. I added through our mental link. "

I'm proud of how you've stood up for me."

She looked at me and giggled. I winked at her and placed a kiss on her forehead.

"Oh my god, you're so cute," Ellie sighed, drawing our attention back to her.

I smiled and held Maddie tighter. I wanted her even closer to me. I wished I could rip her clothes off and feel her naked body against mine. That was the only thing that would help with this burning desire I had for her.

"I'm so glad to finally meet you, Maddie," Ellie said. "I've heard so much about you."

Maddie smiled and held out her hand to shake it. I tensed a little but managed to control myself.

"Nice to meet you too, Ellie," Maddie said softly.

Ellie smiled widely and looked at me.

"She's perfect," Ellie said. "She's exactly what I always wanted for you."

Will and I both laughed. Maddie giggled.

"You talk like you're my mother," I said, shaking my head at her. Ellie sighed and rolled her eyes.

"Well, considering how many times I've stopped you and Will from doing something stupid, I might as well be your mother," Ellie said as she walked back to the couch and sat down.

"Oh, I can't wait to hear about it," Maddie said, making me frown at her.

"No way," I said as I looked back at Ellie. "You can't tell him anything.

" "I would never!" Ellie said, faking a gasp.

She looked at Maddie and winked. I groaned and Maddie laughed.

"Stop making fun of him, Ellie," Will said, sighing quietly.
"We have work to do."

Ellie rolled her eyes. "You always knew how to kill the fun."

Will looked at her and groaned a little. I shook my head, smiled, and started to guide Maddie towards my desk. I sat down and pulled her onto my lap.

I kissed his shoulder and looked at Will.

There was something very important I wanted to talk to him about. I should have dealt with it already, but with all the shit going on, I pushed it aside.

"Did you manage to get in touch with Maddie's pack healer?" I asked, placing another kiss on Maddie's shoulder.

I couldn't go too long without kissing her. My body craved her more than anything.

"I did," Will said, looking at Maddie. "He's waiting for further instructions. I didn't send anyone to get him yesterday because of everything that happened. "

My jaw clenched, a silent growl escaping me.

"Him?" I muttered as I felt possessiveness boil through my blood.

"A 70-year-old him," Maddie said softly as she turned her head and placed a small kiss on my cheek.

I gritted my teeth. The rational part of me knew I was making a fool of myself. Her age didn't matter. Nothing would happen. She was my mate and no one was taking her from me.

But that irrational, possessive, animalistic part of me was fuming.

That part of me saw everyone as a threat. Even a 70-year-old man. Even Ellie, who was looking at Maddie with a smile on her face. Everyone was a threat.

"Should I call him?" Will asked, caution in his voice. "Maybe we can find someone else. A healer."

I tightened my arms around Maddie and shook my head.

Finding another healer would take too long. This wasn't about my irrational jealousy. This was about Maddie's health. She'd be fine and I wouldn't be so jealous in a few days. This was all because the mark was new.

"No," I said. "We don't have time to waste. Call him and tell him to come as soon as he can."

I was hoping there was something we could do before the Alpha meeting in four days. I was worried about Maddie and her abilities. There were going to be a lot of people and it might overwhelm her.

"Okay," Will said, giving me a small nod. "I'll call and see if she can come over tomorrow."

I nodded and turned my head to kiss Maddie's temple. She was in my arms, but I missed her. I wanted to be alone with her so I could kiss her and touch every part of her.

"Will told me a little bit about your mom and that bitch Savannah
," Ellie said, making me look back at her. "What are you going to do?"

I clenched my jaw so hard it hurt. I hadn't met with the council members yet. I hadn't discussed the punishment with anyone yet except Will. I'd been living in my happy bubble since last night and I really didn't want it to burst.

"The law is clear," Will said. "But we think the council is going to give us a hard time with Janet about the punishment."

Maddie shifted in my lap.

"What's the punishment?" she asked quietly.

Will looked at me and raised an eyebrow. I gave him a small nod. I was too angry to speak and explain.

Will looked back at Maddie. He took a deep breath and let it out slowly.

"Death," he said quietly. "The punishment for endangering the Moon is death."

Chapter 89 Death

Madeline's POV

Death? The punishment was death?

No! I couldn't let that happen! I couldn't let Dimitri kill his mother because of me.

An overwhelming wave of guilt washed over me, but before I could do or say anything, Dimitri cupped my cheeks and forced me to look at him.

"This isn't your fault, Maddie," he said sternly. "You don't have to feel guilty. It's not your fault."

I felt tears burning the corners of my eyes. Of course it was my fault. She was going to be punished because of me. She was going to lose her mother because of me.

"You shouldn't have said anything, Skye," I told my wolf. "You should have just kept quiet."

He sighed, but didn't respond.

I focused back on Dimitri and shook my head.

"Of course it's my fault," I said, my voice quiet and raspy. "She's going to be punished because of me."

"No, Mads," Will spoke up before Dimitri could. "

She's going to be punished because she chose to hurt an innocent person. She's going to be punished because she chose to hurt a future Luna."

I looked at Will and swallowed a lump in my throat. Will smiled at me.

"This can't possibly be your fault, Mads," Will said quietly. "She made a terrible decision and the law is clear on what must be done."

Dimitri caressed my cheek and made me look back at him.

"It's not your fault, Princess," Dimitri said as he leaned towards me and kissed the tip of my nose. "Janet and Savannah are the only ones to blame here."

The intensity of the guilt lessened, but it didn't go away.

I understood what they were saying, but if it weren't for me, Dimitri's mother wouldn't be in this situation. What if one day Dimitri looks at me and sees the person who took his mother from him? What if she starts blaming me for it? What if she starts hating me?

Dimitri's eyes narrowed and I knew Skye had given me away.

'Skye,' I moaned just as Dimitri mentally linked me.

'Stop it, Madeline,' Dimitri said sternly. 'It's not your fault and I will never blame you for it. My heart would break if I tried to hate you. It will never happen. It can never happen. Stop thinking it will happen, princess.'

I swallowed and took a deep breath. Dimitri leaned in and kissed me softly. I kissed him back, feeling a tingle all over my body.

'It might not even happen, so there's nothing to worry about,' Will said, and I could hear the annoyance in his voice.

I looked at him and raised my eyebrows.

'Oh, it will,' Dimitri said angrily. 'The council can go to hell. I'll make sure you both get punished for what you did.'

"The council?" I asked, looking back at Dimitri.

"Unfortunately, they have a say as well," Dimitri said as he tucked a strand of hair behind my ear. "Will and I are worried that they'd be reluctant to punish a former Luna◇.

" "But the law is clear," Ellie said, her brows furrowing. "No one is above the law, not even you, Dimitri. They can't let her get away with what she did."

Dimitri looked at Ellie and sighed. "They won't let her get away with it.

They'll probably suggest a lighter punishment."

My heart raced. I agreed. I didn't want her dead. I didn't want Dimitri to have to go through that.

"That's unacceptable," Ellie said angrily. "She's not a Luna anymore. She screwed up. She needs to be punished."

I looked at Ellie and gulped. Her eyes met mine and she took a deep breath.

"I know you feel guilty, Mads," Ellie said softly. "I know you don't want it to happen, but it has to happen. She hurt you...

She hurt Dimitri when she hurt you. She hurt all of us when she hurt you. She almost left an entire pack without a Luna and an entire Kingdom without a Queen. She hurt a lot of people by hurting you, and she needs to be punished for it."

Dimitri leaned over to me and kissed my temple.

"Ellie's right, Princess," Dimitri said softly. "She needs to be punished."

I agreed, but was death really the right punishment? Maybe there was something else we could do.

"Okay," I said softly. "But does she really need such a severe punishment? Maybe there's another punishment we can consider ◇."

Dimitri gave me a small smile and kissed me softly again.

"I'm so in love with your kind heart," he murmured softly. "You're an amazing Luna, Princess."

I smiled back and caressed her cheek.

"No, Maddie," Will said, making me look at him. "The law is clear.

The only thing that could stand between us and the law is the council. They could protest and ask for a lighter punishment.

" "I have a feeling they will," Ellie muttered angrily.

"Kendrick is a piece of work and he was always cozying up to Janet."

Dimitri and Will nodded. Ellie took a deep breath and smiled at me.

"Well, at least we can be sure that Maddie won't get hurt again now that she has such an awesome bodyguard," Ellie said, her smile turning into a grimace.

"Oh, you can bet on that," Will added, laughing. "Ellie is a true warrior and everyone should be afraid."

I chuckled and Dimitri smiled.

"Do you know how to fight, Mads?" Ellie asked me.

I shook my head. "Not really." I'd say I know the basics that we were taught in my old pack, but I'm a little clumsy so I'd probably end up hurting myself more than the other person ."

Ellie laughed and shook her head.

"Well, that's about to change," Ellie said. "You need to know how to defend yourself and I'll teach you."

I smiled and nodded. She was right. I needed to learn how to defend myself. If I knew how to do that, Janet wouldn't be able to hurt me. I wouldn't have to punish her and Dimitri wouldn't have to make such a difficult decision.

I needed to get stronger. Not just for myself, but for my mate as well.

Chapter 90 Getting out of the bubble

Dimitri's POV

As hard as it was, I had to get out of this blissful bubble I was in. I really wanted to spend all my time with Maddie. I wanted to make love to her. I wanted to lay naked next to her. I wanted to touch and kiss every part of her. I wanted to talk about our future. I wanted to know more about her. I wanted to hear the sound of her voice and let it lull me to sleep.

But I couldn't do that. There was so much to do and I had to force myself to focus on work.

"I don't want any male wolves sleeping on our floor," I said as I looked at our guest lists. "Maddie is mated, but some of them don't care."

I felt anger rising inside me. I knew some Alphas who cheated on their mates. Their mates knew, of course.

We could sense if our mates were unfaithful. It was unbearable pain and I couldn't understand how those bastards could hurt their mates like that. It would tear me apart if I ever did anything to hurt Maddie.

"I would never do anything, Dimitri," Maddie said quietly.

I could hear the pain in her voice and my heart stopped. She misunderstood me in the worst way possible.

"Maddie, princess, no," I said, clenching my fists. "I didn't mean it like that. I know you wouldn't do anything, but some do. Some cheat on their partners and I'm afraid they might try to do something inappropriate."

Maddie's eyes widened.

"You're going to rip the paper, Dimitri," Will muttered as he continued to write something down.

I looked down at the paper in my hands and placed it back on the desk.

"Are they cheating?" Maddie asked quietly. "Why?"

"Because they're pigs," Ellie muttered angrily.

I sighed and nodded. Maddie furrowed her eyebrows and bit her bottom lip. "There are no males sleeping on our floor," Will said, making me look back at him. "I've arranged for everyone to stay on the lower floors. Entry to our floor will be off-limits."

I nodded and looked at the paper. An unfamiliar name caught my eye.

"Who's Alpha Rhys?" I asked, furrowing my eyebrows.

"Alpha Ryker's son," Will said, looking at me. "He recently took over his father's pack."

I raised my eyebrows. "Is he eighteen already?" I swore Ryker's son was still a child the last time I visited his pack.

"They grow up fast," Will muttered as he looked back down at the papers in his hands. I heard footsteps approaching my office and immediately knew who it was. I tensed and had to hold back a growl.

Skol shifted and I could feel his tension rising.

"Come here, Maddie," I said, causing him to look up at me.

I was sitting on the couch and talking to Ellie. I didn't want her so far away from me when I came in. Her eyebrows rose and I reached out for her just as we heard a quiet knock. Maddie looked at the door and I felt a wave of panic wash over me.

"Come in," Will said calmly.

"Maddie!" I exclaimed and she immediately stood up.

I was only a few steps away when the door opened and Kendrick walked in.

He glanced around the room and smiled when he saw Maddie. I wanted to jump up and tear his eyes out.

"Morning," Kendrick said as he closed the door. " Can I talk to you, Alpha?"

Maddie was finally close enough for me to grab. I pulled her onto my lap and immediately relaxed. I wrapped my arms around her waist and took a deep breath, trying to calm myself down a bit. I knew why she was here.

"Of course," I said, gesturing to the chair next to Will. "Sit down, Kendrick, please."

Kendrick walked over to the chair and sat down. He looked at Ellie and smiled,

"Hi, Ellie," he said. "It's good to have you back."

Ellie smiled gently. "I'm glad I'm back."

Kendrick looked back at Maddie and his smile widened.

"It's nice to see you again, Luna," Kendrick said. "I wish we could have talked more at the celebration the other day."

"What do you need to talk to me about, Kendrick?" I asked before Maddie could answer.

I didn't want her to talk to him any more than necessary. She didn't want him to look at her. I could see the lust in his eyes and it was driving me crazy.

I wanted to kill him.

Kendrick looked at me and took a deep breath.

"The council was informed that our former Luna was imprisoned yesterday," Kendrick said. "Can you explain why we didn't hear about it from you, Alpha?"

I clenched my jaw and focused on Maddie's scent. I knew it was the only thing that would keep me calm.

"It's a delicate matter, Kendrick," I said calmly. "I wanted to set up the meeting with the council in the next few days so we could discuss it. I haven't had time to do it until now because the Alphas' meeting is in a few days and there's still a lot to do."

Kendrick nodded and leaned back in his chair.

"I understand, Alpha," Kendrick said. "But imprisoning a former Luna is something that needs to be discussed urgently. The council would like to meet with you today."

I tightened my arm around Maddie's waist. I needed her to be even closer to me. Her condescending tone was pissing me off to no end.

"I agree, Kendrick," I said, trying to remain calm. "It's an urgent matter and we'll meet to discuss it tomorrow morning."

"Alpha..." Kendrick spoke up, but I cut him off.

"Tomorrow morning, Kendrick," I said sternly. "Be here at eight in the morning."

Kendrick's jaw tightened and I could tell my stern tone was pissing him off. I didn't give a shit. I was the Alpha. I was the King. I had to respect them and I had to listen to them, but they were the ones who bowed to me, not the other way around.

"Yes, Alpha," Kendrick said as he stood up. "I'll see you tomorrow morning at eight." Kendrick looked at Maddie and smiled.

"Bye, Luna," he said. "See you tomorrow ."

"Bye, Kendrick," Maddie said politely.

Kendrick smiled at Ellie and Will and left my office.

I buried my nose in Maddie's hair and took a deep breath. Her scent calmed me a little, but just thinking about tomorrow's meeting made my anger burn.

Chapter 91 My queen

Dimitri's POV

I started kissing Maddie's neck as soon as I closed our bedroom door.

I couldn't wait for the day to be over and for us to finally have some alone time. I missed her even though she was right next to me. I missed kissing her. I missed touching her.

I missed hearing those sweet moans come out of her mouth.

"I wanted to..." she murmured but stopped when I started sucking my mark on her neck.

She moaned and pressed herself closer to me. I took a few steps back and pressed her against the wall. I brought my lips to her jaw and she tilted her head to give me better access.

"What, princess?" I murmured against her delicious skin.

She was panting hard and I knew I wouldn't get a response unless I stopped kissing her. I didn't want to but I needed to know what she wanted. Her needs were my priority. Mine were second.

So I reluctantly stopped. I caressed her cheeks and forced her to look at me. Her eyes were wide and her lips were slightly parted. I wanted to kiss her so badly.

"What did you want, princess?" I asked softly.

She gulped and took a deep breath. I smiled and caressed her soft cheek.

Knowing she was this nervous because of me made me proud. I was the only one who could do it.

"I wanted to ask you about tomorrow," she murmured after trying to calm her breathing. "About the council meeting."

My anger returned and my jaw instinctively clenched. Knowing I would have to be in the same room as that asshole Kendrick made my blood boil. He looked at her like he wanted her and that pissed me off to no end. I would be pissed even if she wasn't my mate. The guy was a piece of shit and I felt sorry for any woman he wanted to touch.

But now he wanted to touch mine and that made me want to tear this place apart.

"Dimitri?" Maddie called out worriedly.

She placed a hand on my cheek and I relaxed instantly. I took a deep breath and gave her a small kiss on the lips.

"You don't have to worry about that, princess," I said softly. "I'll take care of it."

Her eyebrows rose slightly and she bit her bottom lip.

My cock twitched. I was dying to be the one to do it.

I was dying to bite and suck on every part of her perfect body.

"But they'll ask me questions," Maddie said, snapping me out of my lustful thoughts. "I'm sure they'll want to talk to me."

Anger washed over me again. She wasn't wrong. Kendrick would want to talk to her even if it wasn't about her. But I wouldn't allow it.

"I'll answer everything, Maddie," I said. "Don't worry about that part, okay? You'll sit next to me, hold my hand and listen. I'll take care of it."

Maddie studied my face for a few moments.

"What if they insist?" he asked quietly.

I sighed and stroked his cheek with my thumb.

"You'll talk if they insist," I said, trying to hide my anger. "But you'll be brief and only answer their questions, nothing more."

I didn't want her to talk to them any longer than necessary. I didn't want Kendrick to look at her and I didn't want to see that stupid smile on his face. Plus, I knew she was against the punishment I wanted and I was afraid she'd slip up. They'd probably use it to convince me not to kill my mother and I wasn't going to let that happen. She was going to pay for what she'd done.

"Will they release her?" Maddie asked quietly.

"No," I answered immediately. "They can't do that, Maddie. I'm the King. I'm the Alpha. I'm the one who decides whether or not they release her. They can only argue about the punishment I choose."

I was sure they were going to do that. Kendrick loved my mother because she always did what he told her. She convinced my father to make decisions based on what Kendrick had said. One of the reasons Kendrick didn't like me was because I refused to listen to him and my mother after I took over the Kingdom. My mother tried to persuade me to make the changes Kendrick suggested, but I shut her up right away. Kendrick didn't like it. He lost a lot of power after I became King.

"Okay," Maddie said softly.

I gave her a small smile and kissed her again.

"Don't worry about a thing, princess," I said softly. "I'll take care of it. I'll make sure he pays for what he's done."

I lowered my lips to her neck and began to kiss and suck on it gently. I wanted to end this conversation and get back to enjoying my mate's body.

Maddie moaned quietly and I could feel her relaxing. I smiled a little as I ran my hand down her back. I grabbed the hem of her shirt and began to pull it up. She raised her arms so I could take her shirt off. I moaned at the sight of her breasts. They were perfect and I was dying to suck on her nipples.

"Fuck, Maddie," I murmured as I unclasped her bra. "You are so fucking perfect."

She tangled her fingers in my hair and pulled me in for a kiss. I pulled her bra off and cupped her breasts, flicking my thumbs over her already hard nipples. She moaned and the sound sent a pleasurable jolt through my cock. I really needed to get it inside her.

"Is my Queen ready for me?" I murmured as I moved my mouth to her neck.

"Yes, my King," she said, breathing heavily.

I nearly came in my pants. The sound of her voice, her words, and her body were all perfect. Everything was so fucking perfect and I was dying to bury myself inside her and forget about everything else.

Chapter 92 The meeting

Madeline's POV

I was worried. I wasn't sure if staying quiet was the right thing to do. I was sure the council would expect me to say something. I was sure they would want me to say something. She was here because of me. I was sure they wouldn't want me to stay quiet.

I was also worried that Dimitri wouldn't let me help him. Did he not trust me? Did he not think I would be a good queen? Did he think I would embarrass him or do something bad?

I had so many questions in my head, but I was afraid to look for answers. What would I do if I found out Dimitri didn't trust me? What would I do if I found out he thought I would be a bad queen?

A knock on my bedroom door made me look away from the window.

"Come in," I said, and watched as the door opened.

Ellie walked in and smiled at me.

"Are you ready?" she asked, looking around the room. " Where's Dimitri?"

"In the shower," I muttered as I turned around and leaned against the windowsill. "He'll be here in a minute."

Ellie closed the door and looked me over.

"What's wrong?" she asked. "You seem worried."

I gulped and took a deep breath.

"There's nothing to worry about, Mads," Ellie said softly. " Dimitri will take care of it."

I shook my head and looked down at my feet.

"That's exactly what I'm worried about," I muttered.

Ellie was silent for a moment.

"Why?" she asked, her voice filled with confusion. "He can handle them, Maddie. You don't have to worry about him."

I looked at her and sighed.

"I'm not," I said, shaking my head a little. "I know he can handle them. I believe in him. I just..."

I trailed off and bit my bottom lip. I wasn't sure I could share this with Ellie. She seemed cool, but I barely knew her.

"Just what?" Ellie asked, furrowing her eyebrows.

I took a deep breath and let it out slowly. There was nothing to lose by telling her. At least, I hoped not.

"I wish she'd let me help her," I said. "I don't want her to deal with that stuff alone. This is all about me anyway. I'm the reason she's being punished."

"No, Maddie," Ellie said immediately. "She's the reason she's being punished. She chose to be a bitch and hurt you. She chose to do those things and you're not the reason she's in that cell. "

I looked back down at my feet and took a deep breath.

"And I'm sure Dimitri wants to take care of this himself because of Kendrick," Ellie finished with a sigh.

I looked back at her and raised my eyebrows.

"That guy is disgusting, Maddie," Ellie said, rolling her eyes. "Didn't you see the way he looked at you? Didn't you read his mind?"

I furrowed my eyebrows, trying to remember if I'd ever read his mind. I couldn't remember though.

And then I remembered why.

"He was always with Dimitri," I said. "I couldn't read his mind because he was always with Dimitri."

I didn't know why, but I never heard other people's thoughts when I was around him. I didn't even think about that whole thing the last few days. Something more important always came up. Plus, I was with him all the time lately, so I couldn't read anyone's mind."

"Well, that explains it then," Ellie muttered. "I wonder if you could read his mind if you were alone with him?

" "Alone with who?" Dimitri's voice made both Ellie and I shudder.

I looked at him, my heart racing. He looked amazing in the suit he was wearing. I bit my bottom lip and imagined taking it off of him.

"Madeline. He's mind-linked me." "Don't go on."

Her eyes narrowed and I gulped.

"Alone with Kendrick," Ellie said, interrupting our silent conversation.

Dimitri growled loudly. "That's never going to happen! She's never going to be alone with that pathetic excuse for a man."

Ellie held her hands up in surrender.

"I didn't say I would, Dimitri," Ellie said calmly. "I was just wondering if I'd be able to read his mind if I was alone with him."

Ellie looked at me and raised her eyebrows.

"Well, not alone," she added. "If I was with him without you being there."

Dimitri growled again. He stepped closer to me and pulled me against his chest.

"We'll never know the answer to that question," he said angrily.

"I'll never let him be around her without me being there. I don't need Maddie to read his mind to know what he's thinking."

Ellie raised her eyebrows and nodded.

"I agree," he murmured. "It's easy enough to tell what the bastard is thinking."

Dimitri was shaking a little. I rubbed his back and he looked up at me.

"It's okay," I said softly. "I'll never be alone with him. You'll always be there."

I smiled at him and he leaned in to kiss me softly.

"Mine," he murmured softly.

"I'm yours." I mentally linked it. "I'm only yours and no one will take me away from you."

He caressed my cheek and took a deep breath.

"I love you," I told him through our mental link.

"I love you too," he replied. *More than anything in this world, Maddie.*

I smiled at him and he placed another kiss on my lips.

"Okay, that's enough," Ellie interrupted, sighing heavily. "You have to go. You'll be late."

Dimitri took my hand in his and brought it to his lips. He kissed my knuckles and smiled at me.

"Everything is going to be okay, princess," he said softly. "Let's get this over with."

I nodded and he began to lead me out of our bedroom.

My stomach was churning painfully. I had a bad feeling about the meeting.

Chapter 93 It happened before

Madeline's POV

My heart was racing. My palms were sweating. I was having trouble breathing. I kept gulping, even though my mouth was completely dry.

I didn't know why I was so nervous.

"Maddie, princess, everything's going to be okay," Dimitri said again. "Don't worry, my love. I'll take care of everything." He pulled

me into his chest and I relaxed a little.

"I love you, princess," Dimitri said softly as he ran his hand down my back. "Everything's going to be okay. I promise."

I looked up at him and forced a small smile on my face.

He leaned in and kissed me softly. I relaxed even more and was able to breathe a little easier.

"My love," Dimitri murmured as he caressed my cheek. "My whole world."

My heart skipped a beat and I felt tears welling up in the corners of my eyes. He loved me so much and I couldn't believe how lucky I was. I loved him too. I loved him with everything I had. My heart was pounding for him.

A knock on the door made me tense again. Dimitri placed a soft kiss on my forehead and I sat up straighter, smoothing out the wrinkles in my dress.

"Come in," Dimitri said calmly.

The door opened and the three council members walked in. I looked at Kendrick immediately. He had a smile on his face, but it turned into a grimace when his eyes caught mine.

What I would do to her. I would fuck her until she screamed and cried. I wouldn't stop until she was a bloody, sobbing mess. I would use her like the pretty doll she is.

My heart stopped beating.

I could hear her thoughts. They were her thoughts, weren't they?

But how was that possible? Dimitri was beside me. He was holding my hand.

I looked at Landon and Rayan, but I couldn't hear what they were thinking. I looked back at Kendrick and was met with another one of his thoughts.

I bet she's a great fuck. I bet she has a perfect little pussy. I bet she'd fuck me really good.

My stomach turned and I almost threw up. His smile made it all worse.

"Please, have a seat," I heard Dimitri's voice. "My Queen and I, unfortunately, don't have much time. We're preparing for the Alpha meeting."

"Understandable, my King," Landon said as he sat down in one of the chairs in front of Dimitri's desk. "We won't take up much of your time. We'd just like to know why our former Luna is locked away in a cell."

Her skin looks so soft. That bastard Dimitri is so lucky.

How the fuck did he manage to get a mate like her? Why couldn't she be mine? Will I ever get the chance to touch her? Will I ever get the chance to hear her scream while I fuck her?

My heart was about to jump out of my body. The bile kept rising and I kept swallowing it down.

Dimitri started to explain what happened, but I couldn't focus on him. I wasn't listening. I couldn't look away from Kendrick.

Why could I hear his thoughts and not Landon's or Rayan's? Why his? That had never happened to me. I could never hear anyone's thoughts when Dimitri was near me.

And then I remembered.

It wasn't true. Something like this had happened before. It happened with Janet.

I could hear her thoughts when I tried to talk to her. Dimitri was there, but I could still hear her thoughts.

So much happened after that and I completely forgot about it. But it happened before.

Kendrick was looking at my mate now and the hatred in his eyes made my whole body shudder.

This fucker doesn't deserve anything he has. He doesn't deserve to be a King. He doesn't deserve a mate like her. He doesn't deserve to fuck her every night. He should never have become King.

I clenched my jaw. I felt anger rise through me. I was thinking badly of my mate and my protective side came out.

I had to hold back a growl. I wanted to punch him. I wanted to show him what happened when you messed with me. I wanted to—

"Was it that bad, Luna?" a voice interrupted my thoughts.

I flinched and looked at Rayan. My eyebrows furrowed slightly.

"The abuse, Luna," Rayan explained as he saw my confused face. "

Was the abuse that bad?" "

Say yes." Dimitri mentally bound me severely.

"Yes," I said immediately.

"Look at those lips. They would look perfect wrapped around my cock. I would make her suck me off until I saw tears running down her pretty face. Maybe I would even make Dimitri watch. I would make his mate my little whore and make him watch while I fucked her.

I felt my heart stop. I felt my blood run cold.

"Are you okay, Luna?" someone asked. "You look a little pale."

The disgust and fear he felt must have been very evident.

"Maddie?" Dimitri called out to me worriedly.

He caressed my cheeks and forced me to look at him.

"What's wrong, princess?" he asked as he studied my face.

"Maybe I could take her to the pack hospital while you three finish up the meeting," Kendrick said. "She doesn't look well." "

No!" I yelled through the mind link. "Don't let her take me."

Dimitri furrowed his eyebrows and I saw anger in his eyes.

I would never let her take you anywhere, Maddie. She said before looking at him.

"Thank you, Kendrick, but I will be the one to take care of my mate," Dimitri said politely, but I could hear the anger in his voice.

What a pity. I was hoping to have a moment alone with her. Maybe I could touch her soft skin.

I started to shake. Dimitri looked at me and I saw fear in his eyes.

What's wrong, Madeline? he asked. Talk to me, princess, please.

I swallowed and tried to take a deep breath.

I can hear his thoughts. I told him. I'm terrified and I can't listen anymore. I can't.

Dimitri's eyes widened. I could tell he was holding back his anger.

"Can we take a little break, please?" Dimitri asked as he looked at the three of them. "My Luna isn't feeling well."

"Of course," I heard Landon say. "We'll be waiting in front of the office." I

heard them stand up, but I didn't want to look at them. I was trying hard to push my thoughts away from Kendrick. I was afraid that all of my efforts would be useless if I looked at him. I didn't know if I was more scared or more disgusted, but I knew that I didn't want to see him again.

Chapter 94 Exceptions

Dimitri's POV

My whole body was shaking with rage. I saw the fucking red and wished I could wrap my hands around that bastard's neck and squeeze.

Why the fuck was Maddie so scared? What was the bastard thinking?

Can you and Ellie come to my office? I mentally linked up with Will as I watched those three bastards leave.

"Is everything okay?" Will asked worriedly. Is the meeting over yet?

No. Come here.

I cut our mental link and focused on Maddie. I pulled her onto my lap and held her tight.

"Princess..." I spoke but she cut me off.

"I'm so sorry," she murmured. "I couldn't take it anymore. I couldn't listen to that anymore. I didn't want to ruin the meeting. I didn't want to..."

I cut her off by lifting her head up and placing a soft kiss on her lips.

"You didn't ruin anything, Princess," I said. "You should have told me sooner. You should have told me as soon as it happened."
"I would have ended the meeting immediately."

I caressed her cheek and kissed the tip of her nose.

"You come first, Madeline," I added. "You always come first, my love."

I didn't give a shit about that meeting. Maddie was scared and I would do absolutely anything to take that fear away from her.

The door to my office opened and Will and Ellie walked in. They both had worried expressions on their faces.

"What happened?" Will asked, looking from me to Maddie.

"Are you in front of my office?" I asked Will through our mind link.

"Yes," he said.

"Close the door and sit down," I told him.

He did as I told him and walked over to my desk. Ellie was already sitting in an armchair, looking at Maddie worriedly.

"What the hell happened?" Will asked as he sat down.

I kissed Maddie's temple and took a deep breath.

"Maddie could hear Kendrick's thoughts," I said quietly.

My office was soundproof, but I still didn't want to take any chances.

Ellie's eyes widened. Will gasped quietly.

"What?" Will muttered. "How? I thought I couldn't hear them when I was with you.

" "What was I thinking?" Ellie asked at the same time.

I looked at Maddie and saw her close her eyes and swallow. What the fuck was I thinking? Was I thinking about hurting him? If the answer to that question was yes, I was going to kill the bastard.

Skol growled and I felt his anger pulsing inside me.

"Ask Skye," I told him. Maddie probably won't tell me. She'll want to protect me.

"I'm on it," Skol muttered.

"How is that possible, Maddie?" Will asked. "Is this the first time something like this has happened?"

Maddie sighed and shook her head. My whole body froze.

"What?" I muttered. "Has it happened before? Could you hear her thoughts before?"

Maddie looked at me and shook her head.

"No," she said quietly. "This was the first time I could hear her thoughts."

I furrowed my eyebrows in confusion.

"But you could hear someone else's while you were with Dimitri?" Ellie asked, causing Maddie to look at her.

Maddie nodded and my blood began to boil. Why hadn't she told me? Whose thoughts could she hear while she was with me?

"Whose?" Will asked her.

I was too angry to speak. Maddie looked at me and took a deep breath.

"Janet's," she said quietly.

My mother's?! When?! Why didn't she tell me?

I'm so sorry, Dimitri. She mentally linked me and I could hear the fear in her voice. Please don't be angry. Please don't be angry.

My heart clenched painfully and I pulled her into my chest.

I wasn't angry at her. I was angry at the whole fucked up situation we were in. She was shaking and I instantly wanted to rip my heart out. I'd scared her.

"I'm sorry, princess," I told her. "I'm not mad at you, okay? Please don't be afraid of me."

She wrapped her arms around me and I felt her relax a little. "I'm not afraid of you," she said. "I just hate it when you get mad."

I kissed her temple and ran my hand down her back.

"When did that happen, Mads?" Will asked, interrupting our moment.

Maddie lifted her head and looked at him.

"When Dimitri and I went to talk to our parents," she said. "I wanted to talk to Mike and Janet. I wanted to start over."

She started screaming and then Skol took over Dimitri and we left. "

I thought back to that day. Skol was so fucking pissed off. I clenched my jaw and made her look at me.

"Why didn't you tell me?" I asked, trying to remain calm.

She shrugged and raised her eyebrows.

"I don't know," she said. "A lot has happened since then and I had completely forgotten about it. I didn't even remember it until I heard Kendrick's thoughts and thought it was the first time something like this had happened."

"So Kendrick and Janet are exceptions to the rule," Will muttered, making her look at him. "I wonder why that is."

"Did their thoughts have anything in common, Maddie?" Ellie asked.

Maddie shuddered a little. She clenched her fists and swallowed.

"Skol?" "I called my wolf. Has he told you?"

Skol fell silent. I hadn't even realized I couldn't feel it that well.

"Skol?" "I called him again when he didn't respond. '

Give me a moment to calm down,' he muttered. 'I'm going to kill that bastard.'

He must have moved away to stop him from taking me over.

Yeah," Skol muttered. I need a moment.

What the fuck was I thinking?

Skol growled and I took a deep breath. I really needed to let him cool off a bit because I would kill him if I took control. I was impressed by his ability to restrain himself and think rationally. I

knew killing Kendrick would cause chaos. I was impressed that he could pull away to calm himself down and control himself like that. He was an animal, after all.

'You are an animal,' he growled at me. 'I may be a wolf, but I'm also an alpha. I have more control than you think.

I'm sorry,' I said, 'can you please tell me what Skye said to you?'

Skol growled and started to speak. The anger I felt towards him grew with every word Skol spoke. It pulsed inside me and threatened to explode. Rage blinded me.

Chapter 95 Nothing to do but wait

Madeline's POV

Dimitri was shaking with rage after Skol told him everything.

Skye talked to me before she told Skol. She told me she was going to do it. I was very grateful for that. I wasn't surprised by the three of them, for a change.

'I only did those things to protect you, Maddie,' Skye sighed. 'I couldn't let that woman keep harassing you. I had to punish her.'

"I know, Skye," I said as I ran my fingers through Dimitri's hair. "But it's nice to be informed, for a change. '

I'll try to do that in the future,' Skye said, laughing a little.

I hoped it wouldn't be necessary for me to inform Skol of anything anymore, but I appreciated that he wasn't keeping anything from me anymore. Well, at least I hoped so.

'I'm going to fucking kill him,' Dimitri said, his eyes darkening. '

He's a fucking dead man.'

Will raised his eyebrows and looked at me.

"Skye told Skol what Kendrick was thinking," I explained.

Will raised his eyebrows and looked back at Dimitri, who was shaking and growling under his breath. His arms were around my waist and they felt like steel bars. I couldn't get away from him even if I wanted to.

"He'll never be able to do those things," I said as I leaned in and kissed his temple. "I'm yours."

Dimitri looked at me and held me even tighter. But he didn't calm down.

"I'm going to take what the bastard said," Will muttered angrily.

Dimitri growled and closed his eyes. I ran my fingers through his hair again.

I hated seeing him so upset. I didn't want him to know because I didn't want to hurt him. I didn't want him to feel that way.

But Skye would have told him whether I agreed or not.

"Of course I would," she said. "You can't keep things like that from him, Madeline.

He needs to know so he can protect you."

I sighed and kissed his temple again, "I wanted to protect him too. I needed to protect him too."

"We don't need to waste time on that," Ellie said, making him look at her. "He'll never get a chance to touch her.

I'll kill him if I have to. We need to focus on the fact that she could hear him while standing next to you. That's more important."

Dimitri growled and narrowed his eyes at Ellie.

"Don't look at me like that, Dimitri," Ellie said, crossing her arms over her chest. "You know I'm right. Do you really think any of us are going to let him get close to her?"

Ellie snorted and shook her head.

"Will's the first one who would rip his head off his shoulders," Ellie continued. "He may not have made his oath to her yet, but he's already living up to it."

I looked at Will and saw him smiling a little.

"He's not going to get close to her, Dimitri," Ellie added quietly. "Don't let his words get to you. They're just words.

They'll never come true."

I felt tears well up in the corners of my eyes. I never thought they'd be so dedicated to protecting me.

"The things I was thinking about were vile," Dimitri said, his voice raspy and deep. "Are you seriously telling me to just let it go?"

I looked at him, my heart clenching painfully. He looked like he was in pain. I tangled my fingers in his hair and placed a kiss on his lips. I rested my forehead on his head and took a deep breath. His pain hurt me more than the things Kendrick was planning to do to me.

Dimitri pulled me closer to him. He held me tighter.

It was starting to get awkward, but I would never tell him that. He needed it.

He needed to know he was here and he was okay.

"He is and he's right, Dimitri," Will said. "Was he forming some kind of plan to take her away or was he just thinking about the things he wanted to do to her?"

He could hear the anger in Will's voice.

"If he was forming a plan he'd be dead already," Dimitri said, growling under his breath.

Will sighed. "I thought as much. You know you can't kill him, Dimitri. He hasn't done anything. You can't punish him for his thoughts.

" "And not to mention you'd be putting Maddie in danger if you did," Ellie added. "No one needs to know what she can do. Not until we figure out what all this means."

Dimitri clenched his jaw and swallowed.

"We're right, Dimitri," Will said after a few moments of silence. "You're going with your gut, but I'm here to be the voice of reason. I wouldn't be a good Beta if I didn't talk some sense into you from time to time."

I looked at Will and smiled. He was an amazing Beta and an even better friend. I was glad Dimitri had him in his life.

Dimitri took a deep breath and let it out slowly. I kissed his temple again. He ran his hand up my back and tangled his fingers in my hair, holding me close to him.

"Mine," he murmured softly.

"Yours," I said as I smiled and caressed his cheek.

"When is the healer coming?" Ellie asked, making me look at her.

"Tomorrow morning," Will said. "I hope we know more when he gets here."

I hoped so too. Oscar was an amazing healer and had helped my mother so much. I knew I could talk to him about what I was going through. I knew he would listen to me and keep an open mind. I knew he would try to help me even if he didn't know anything about what was wrong with me.

"Well, I guess there's no choice but to wait," Ellie murmured softly.

I sighed and looked back at Dimitri. He seemed a little calmer, but I could still see he was upset.

I love you. I connected it mentally.

He looked at me and hugged me.

I love you too, Maddie. He said. No one will hurt you as long as I live and breathe. I promise.

I took a deep breath and relaxed in his arms. I believed him. I knew he would never let anyone hurt me, and I knew I was safe with him. I would always be safe with him.

Chapter 96 Keep calm

Dimitri's POV

"Are you going to be able to finish the meeting?" Will asked as they started walking toward the door.

I kept my gaze fixed on Maddie, trying to keep my composure. We decided that she would go with Ellie and Will while I finished the meeting. I didn't want her in the same room as him.

I didn't want her near him.

But it was so hard. I wanted to keep her by my side. I wanted to make sure she was safe. I wished I could just tell the council members to fuck off and kill them like I would kill my mother, but I couldn't do that.

"I won't kill him if that's what you ask me to," I muttered, making Will raise an eyebrow at me.

I sighed and clenched my jaw.

"Just keep Maddie safe, okay?" I said, clenching my fists. "I'll finish as soon as I can and we'll meet at the training center."

We agreed that Ellie and Will would take Maddie to the training center. Mike was there and I knew she would be safe with him.

If I had to let her out of my sight, I'd make sure she was as protected as possible.

Don't worry. She mentally linked me. Nothing will happen to her as long as I'm around.

Ellie took Maddie's hand in hers and pulled her closer. My heart clenched painfully. I really didn't want to let her go.

I love you, princess. I mentally linked her. I'll be there soon, okay? Stay with Will and your dad the whole time.

That's it. She said, giving me a small smile. Don't worry, I'll be okay. I'll be okay.

I clenched my jaw and forced a small smile. I would always worry. I carried my whole heart and soul with her. If anything happened to her, I would be a dead man.

I watched as Will opened the door. The three of them started to leave my office and I thought my heart was going to jump out of my body. I could hear Will talking to the council members. I could hear them responding. But I couldn't make out what they were saying. I couldn't see Maddie anymore and I started to panic.

Kendrick was the first to enter my office. My vision blurred and I wanted to jump him. I could already picture ripping his throat out with my canines. I could already picture the bastard bleeding out on my polished floor. I could already hear him panting as I growled above him.

Rayan closed my office door, the sound bringing me back to reality.

"Is our Luna okay?" Landon asked. "She was a little pale."

I clenched my fists and forced a small smile.

"She is," I said. "She's a little overwhelmed by everything that happened with my mother and Savannah. Talking about it upsets her."

Landon nodded. "Understandable. But I wish we could talk about it with her. Her testimony is of great value, my King."

"I'm here to answer all of your questions," I said, trying to remain calm. "She shared everything that happened with me. I'm more than capable of speaking for her."

Landon and Rayan gave me a small nod. I could tell they weren't happy, but there was nothing they could do.

I tried not to look away from them. I didn't want to look at Kendrick. I was barely able to keep my composure.

"We are concerned about the consequences for the Kingdom, my King," Landon said. "What will your subjects say when they find out their King killed his own mother? It could lead to anarchy, my King."

I clenched my jaw and tried to take a deep breath.

"My subjects know the law, Lord Chancellor," I said. "They know what happens if one threatens their King or Queen. I fear more the consequences if I don't punish my mother properly. My subjects might see it as favoritism."

"Have you ever truly endangered the Queen's life, my King?" Rayan asked. "Was the abuse that severe?"

Anger flared within me.

"Are you really asking me that, Rayan?" I asked, gritting my teeth. "Does it matter how hard he hit her? He abused her for months. He put her in danger more than once. He admitted to threatening to kill her. What else do you need to hear to agree with my decision?"

"We would agree immediately if it were anyone else," Kendrick said and I had no choice but to look at him. "We agree on Savannah's punishment. But we're talking about our former Luna here. She's not just anyone, my King."

I had to force myself to breathe. I wanted to tear his eyes out.

"The law is the law, Kendrick," I said, trying to sound calm. "Titles don't matter. The law doesn't exclude anyone, not even you and me. We'd be sentenced to death if we acted against her, just like my mother is going to be sentenced to death. "

Kendrick narrowed his eyes slightly.

"I think it's important that we present a united front to your subjects, my King," Rayan said and I was finally able to look away from Kendrick. "I don't think we'll come to an agreement today. Shall we meet again after the Alphas' meeting?"

"My decision will remain the same," I said sternly. "If you need time to come to an agreement, I'd be happy to meet with you again after the Alpha meeting. I wasn't going to execute her before then anyway."

Rayan sighed and looked at Landon.

"Think about it, my King," Landon said. "She is your mother, after all." I clenched my jaw and shook my head.

"She is not my mother," I said angrily. "She is someone who hurt my mate. She is someone who tried to take my mate from me.

Reminding myself that she is the woman who gave birth to me will not make me reconsider my decision. I will kill anyone who tries to take my mate from me."

I looked at Kendrick and narrowed my eyes slightly. I hoped the bastard had gotten the message.

"If there are no more questions, I would like to end this meeting," I said, looking back at Landon. "I have work to do."

"Of course, my King," Landon said as he stood up. "

We will speak again after the Alpha meeting."

I nodded and watched the three of them leave my office.

They were fucking crazy if they thought that would change my mind. I would kill my mother and watch her die with a smile on my face.

No one would hurt my partner. No one.

Chapter 97 My father

Madeline's point of view

I missed Dimitri the moment I left our office.

I worried about him, too. Would he be okay? Would he be able to finish the meeting? Maybe I should have stayed with him.

"He'll be okay, Mads," Will said softly as he put an arm around my shoulders. "He'll be back with you soon."

I looked up at him and he smiled.

"I just hope he doesn't let Skol kill Kendrick," Will added with amusement in his voice. "That would just create more work for me."

I chuckled and shook my head at him.

"He won't kill him," Ellie said. "But I wouldn't be surprised if he did."

I took a deep breath and let it out slowly. I wasn't going to kill him. I knew it would be wrong to do so.

We walked into the training center and Mike immediately looked at us.

"Honey!" he exclaimed and ran over to me. "What are you doing here?"

He hugged me and I patted his back.

"Dimitri's in a meeting," Ellie said. "We wanted to show Maddie the training center. We'll be coming here daily, so she needs to get familiar with the place."

Mike smiled widely.

"Oh, I can't wait, honey," he said. "It'll be nice to spend more time with you.

I can't wait. Maybe spending more time with her will be good for us. I'll finally be able to show her how fucking sorry I am for what I've done. Maybe she'll finally see how much I love her."

Thoughts of Mike made my heart race.

Mike smiled and hugged me again.

My little girl. I love you so much. I'm terrified that you'll never know how sorry I am. I'm terrified that you'll never know how much I've missed you all these years. I'm terrified that I'll never be able to show you how important you are to me. I wish you knew how much I love you.

My heart clenched painfully and I did something I never thought I would do. I wrapped my arms around Mike and hugged him tightly.

I closed my eyes and rested my head on his chest.

I could tell he was a little surprised. Every time he hugged me I would stand still like a statue. I would gently stroke his back and pull away a second later. I never hugged him back like that.

"Oh, my girl," he murmured as he put a hand on my head and held me close to him.

"It'll be nice spending more time with you too, Mike," I said softly.

Something between a sob and a laugh escaped Mike's lips. He kissed my head and rubbed my back.

"I can't wait, sweetie," he said softly.

"Maddie?" I heard Seth's voice.

I let go of Mike and looked to my left. Seth was standing a few feet away. He was smiling and seemed so happy to see me.

"Seth," I said as I started to approach him. He held out his hand but Will pushed me away.

"Don't touch," Will said. "Dimitri will go crazy if he smells it on you." He just marked you, Maddie."

Oh, right. I completely forgot about that.

" "Did he mark you?" Seth muttered and looked at my neck.

My heart tightened. He looked so sad and I wished I could do something.

"He did," Will said sternly. "You need to stay away, Seth. Especially now that the mark is fresh."

Seth gulped and looked at Will. Will gave him a small nod.

"How are you, Seth?" I asked, giving him a small smile. "I feel like I haven't seen you in years."

A lot had happened in the past few days and I couldn't say for sure how long it had been since I last saw Seth. It really did feel like years.

We saw each other every day leading up to my birthday and this was kind of weird, going a few days without seeing him.

"I feel that way too, Mads," he said and I could hear the sadness in his voice. "We missed you at the diner."

I smiled and took a deep breath.

"I miss you guys too," I said. "I miss working there."

"You can always come back," Seth said with a hint of amusement in his voice. "I'm sure we'll have a lot more guests if word gets out that our Luna is working there again."

I laughed and nodded.

"I'm available if you need me," I said, making Seth smile.

"That's not going to happen, Madeline," Will said sternly. "You're a Luna. You're not going to be working there again."

I looked at Will with a confused look on my face. Seth and I were joking.

Will was looking at Seth with an angry expression.

We're just joking, Will. I mentally linked it. *What's so bad about that?*

Will looked at me and clenched his jaw.

He wants you, Madeline. He said. *I need to let him know, you're not available.*

"How about I show you this, Mads?" Ellie said, taking my hand in hers. "We didn't come here to talk."

Ellie started to pull me away, and I looked at Seth.

"See you later," I said.

"See you later, Mads," he said, giving me a small smile.

Goddess, will I ever stop being in love with her? I don't even care that she's marked. I still want her. Will this feeling ever go away?

I looked away from Seth and did everything I could think of to silence his thoughts. I didn't want to hear that. I didn't want to know.

"Why is Will so mad at Seth?" I asked Ellie, trying to distract myself. "Seth's just being nice."

I obviously knew how Seth felt about me, but he never did anything inappropriate. He did kiss me, but that was before we knew Dimitri was my mate.

Ellie looked at me and raised an eyebrow.

"You're not blind and you can read his mind, Maddie," Ellie said. "I know you know Seth has a crush on you."

I sighed and gave her a small nod.

"But it was never inappropriate," I said quietly. "He was always a good friend to me."

"Well, Will is being a good friend to Dimitri," Ellie said.

"He won't let anyone near you, Maddie. Especially not someone who has a crush on you."

I sighed again and looked back at Seth. He was talking to Will and Mike. All three of them seemed a little tense.

I wished I could somehow explain to them that Seth wasn't a threat. He was my friend and he wouldn't do anything inappropriate. I was sure he would get over his feelings and I knew he would never act on them. I wished they knew that too.

Chapter 98 Your king

Dimitri's POV

I practically ran to the training center. I couldn't wait to have Maddie in my arms. I needed to spend time with her before I got back to work. I was too pissed off to be productive. I needed to relax. I needed to bury myself in my partner and forget every fucking thing that man wanted to do to her.

I was the only one who could do it. I was the only one who could fuck her. I was the only one who would ever know how amazing her pussy felt wrapped around my cock. I was the only one who would know how amazing she sounded when she orgasmed.

Only me. Only me.

Both Skol and I were on the edge. We both needed to hold her. He kept trying to convince me to let him out, but I wasn't going to. I wasn't going to stand by and let him get to her first.

Fuck no. I was the one who was going to fuck her before him.

'You're being a dick,' Skol growled at me. 'I can't fuck Skye. You could at least let me fuck Maddie.'

"I will," I replied. "But you'll have to wait your fucking turn."

I was in no mood to argue with him. I was close to exploding and his attitude was only making things worse.

I yanked the door open and walked in.

I nearly moved on the spot when I saw Seth talking to Mike and Will.

What the fuck was he doing here? Talking to her? Touching her? I'd go crazy if I found any traces of his scent on her.

Calm down. Will mentally linked me. He didn't do anything. They just talked. I handled it.

I growled. I didn't want him talking to her. I didn't want him anywhere near her.

I looked around and saw my roommate talking to Ellie across the hall. I started walking towards her immediately. I could feel my canines lengthening. I was so fucking angry.

Ellie saw me first. She sighed at the state I was in. I could feel hair starting to grow on my arms.

I was having a hard time holding Skol back. Maddie had her back to me and didn't see me coming. She should have heard me, but she was focused on Ellie. She was talking to her about something, but I didn't care what.

Dimitri... Ellie tried to mentally link me, but I blocked her immediately.

I didn't want to talk to her. I just wanted Maddie. I needed to get her home and I needed to get inside her. I needed her like I needed air to breathe.

I grabbed Maddie as soon as I was close enough. She yelped in surprise as I spun her around and slung her over my shoulder.

"Dimitri..." she spoke, but I cut her off with a growl.

I turned around and started walking backwards.

What happened? She mentally linked me. Can you put me down?

Fuck no.

No. I replied. I'm going to take you to our room. I need to fuck you.

Maddie wiggled in my arms and a second later I could smell her arousal. It wasn't helping matters one bit.

"Dimitri..." Mike started to speak but I cut him off with a growl as well.

I couldn't understand why they insisted on talking to me. I wasn't in the mood to talk.

I kept my eyes fixed on the door. I knew I would go crazy if I looked at Seth. I knew he was looking at my mate and I didn't need confirmation. I didn't need to add fuel to the fire already burning inside me.

I started running as soon as I was outside. I grabbed Maddie tightly and turned my head to bury my nose in her perfect ass. She squealed in surprise but I only held her tighter to keep her from moving. I took a deep breath, letting the scent of her arousal calm my anger.

"Fuck," I muttered. "You're going to let your King fuck that wet pussy?"

Maddie moaned and I could hear her gasp. I reached under her dress and dragged my hand up her thigh until I reached her perfect little ass. I squeezed it and she moaned again.

I looked around, making sure no one saw what I was doing or heard her moans. Only I could see her perfect body. Her moans were mine alone to hear.

Luckily, we were already in front of the warehouse and I wouldn't have to wait long until I was inside her. I walked in and ran upstairs, ignoring everything and everyone around me.

I burst through our bedroom door and slammed it shut.

I threw Maddie onto the bed and she started pulling up her dress and removing her panties immediately. I knew what I needed and I was going to give it to me.

Normally I would spend a little more time making sure she was ready for me, but I really didn't want to do that now.

I was already wet enough and I needed to get inside her.

I took off my belt and practically ripped my pants off my body. Maddie spread her legs and I lay on top of her, placing my painfully hard cock at her entrance. I pushed into her and we both groaned at the same time.

"Mine," I growled as I began to thrust in and out.

I wrapped my arms around her and buried my nose in her neck.

"Mine, mine, mine, mine," I repeated after each thrust.

Maddie moaned and bucked her hips in time with my thrusts.

My whole body hummed with a mix of rage and pleasure. I continued to lick and suck at Maddie's neck, trying to get as much of her taste into my mouth as possible. "Dimitri," she screamed as she came all over my cock.

I saw fucking stars as she began to clench around me and I couldn't hold back any longer.

I groaned loudly as I came. I exploded and my vision went black.

I couldn't stop grunting and fucking her. My cock was already painfully sensitive but I kept going. I couldn't stop. I didn't want to stop.

"Mia," I growled as I tangled my fingers in her hair and pulled her against me.

"Yours," he said softly, wrapping his arms and legs around me. "Only yours."

He pushed me deeper and my eyes rolled back in my head.

She was mine. Only mine.

Chapter 99 So you don't know?

Madeline's POV

Dimitri was a little calmer after we spent the night together. We didn't get much sleep, but I wasn't complaining. We both needed to be with each other.

"He'll be here in a few minutes," Will said as he sat down on the couch.

Dimitri nodded and put his arm around my waist. He refused to let go. He was nervous and looked at everyone like they were a threat to me. I wished I could do something to calm him down, but nothing seemed to work. No matter what I did or said, Dimitri just kept staring and growling at everyone.

Will told me to give him time, but I hated seeing him so upset. I wanted to help him right away.

"What's his name?" Ellie asked.

"Oscar," I said. "He's great. You'll like him."

Ellie smiled and gave me a small nod.

"So you fuckers want another meeting after the Alphas leave?" Will asked angrily.

Dimitri nodded. "They hinted at giving me time to change my mind. That's never going to happen and I told them so. Nothing will ever change my mind about wanting that bitch dead."

A shiver ran down my spine. I wished things were different. I wished Dimitri didn't have to go through that.

I wished he didn't have to talk about his mother like that.

"Did you go see her?" Ellie asked.

"No," Dimitri said, shaking his head. "I don't want to see that bitch. She asked about me but I told them to fuck off."

" "What about Savannah and her son?" Ellie asked.

Dimitri sighed and ran his fingers through his hair.

"The boy's with a couple Will and I found," Dimitri said. "They always wanted puppies but they can't have their own. They were more than happy to take him in."

Ellie nodded and raised her eyebrows.

"I wonder who the father is," she said. "Why didn't he take the pup in?"

Dimitri shrugged. "I don't know. She refused to tell me who he is and he never introduced himself."

"I think the boy is better off without them," Will muttered. "His father can't be a good man."

I took a deep breath and let it out slowly. I felt bad for that boy. He didn't deserve parents like that.

Dimitri kissed my cheek and hugged me tightly. I gave him a small smile.

I didn't think it was possible, but I love you more every day. He mentally linked me.

My smile grew. I wrapped my arms around his neck and hugged him tightly.

"I love you more every day too," I replied. *My heart keeps getting bigger. Soon it won't fit in my chest.*

Dimitri chuckled and rubbed my back gently.

"Okay, that's enough you two," Will said as he stood up and walked over to the door. "Oscar's here."

I let go of Dimitri and tried to get up.

"Fuck no," Dimitri said, pulling me onto his lap. "You're staying here, Maddie."

I gave him a small nod and turned to face Will. He opened the door and smiled.

"Beta Will," I heard Oscar's voice. "Nice to meet you."

"Likewise, Oscar," Will said as he stepped aside so Oscar could enter.

Oscar walked in and I smiled brightly.

"Maddie!" Oscar exclaimed as he approached Dimitri's desk. "So nice to see you. You look radiant, kiddo."

My smile only grew. However, Dimitri growled at him.

I looked at him and furrowed my eyebrows. What had happened?

"That's enough, Oscar," Dimitri said sternly.

My eyes widened and I looked at Oscar. I was going to apologize to him, but he smiled and nodded.

"You're newly marked, aren't you?" he asked as he sat down in one of the armchairs in front of the desk. "I'm so happy for you. Congratulations."

"Thank you, Oscar," I said, giving him a small smile.

He smiled back and looked at Dimitri.

"Why am I here, my King?" he asked. "I hope no one is sick."

Dimitri clenched his jaw and shook his head.

"You're not here because no one is sick," Dimitri said. "You're here for Maddie."

Oscar looked at him worriedly. "Is everything okay?"

I gulped and took a deep breath. What if he told me I was crazy?

"I'm not sure," I said. "Something weird happened after I became part of this pack. I thought it was a mental link, but..."

I stopped talking because I got so nervous. How was I going to explain to him what was going on? Should I tell him that I could read other people's minds?

Oscar narrowed his eyes slightly.

"But?" he asked after a few moments of silence.

I felt small beads of sweat rolling down the back of my neck. My stomach tightened. A huge lump formed in my throat and I wasn't sure if I would be able to say it.

"Maddie?" Dimitri called softly. "Do you want me to?"

We talked beforehand and I asked him to let me tell Oscar.

I wasn't sure if I could though. So I looked at Dimitri and gave him a small nod. He kissed my shoulder and looked at Oscar.

"He can read minds," Dimitri said and I felt my heart stop. "He knows what other people think."

I stopped breathing. I stared at Oscar, expecting him to look at me like I was crazy. But instead he looked at me and gasped.

"Is your wolf completely black?" he asked, making me furrow my brows.

Why did it matter what color my wolf's fur was?

"I don't know," I said, trying to swallow the lump in my throat. "He refused to change. He said he was protecting me. But I don't know from what."

Oscar's eyes widened. He looked from me to Dimitri.

"So you don't know?" he muttered under his breath.

I felt Dimitri tense. His grip tightened. Will growled softly. My heart raced, and I felt my stomach tighten.

"Know what?" I asked after a few moments of silence.

Oliver looked at me and gave me a small smile.

"That you're a werewolf, Maddie."

Chapter 100 Throne

Unknown's POV

The room made me sick. It always disgusted me. No matter how many times I'd been there, I'd never gotten used to the smell.

It was a small, lightless room. The only light came from the candles scattered haphazardly on the table in front of me.

The walls were covered in mold and the musty smell was suffocating. It always made my stomach turn. An occasional drip of water from an unknown source made me nervous. I wanted to find it and make it stop. It was annoying.

We were sitting around the table. There were six chairs, but there were only five of us. They didn't like that one bit.

"We're missing a limb," he said, looking around the table. "What happened?"

I sighed and resisted the urge to roll my eyes.

"I'm working on it," I said, clenching my jaw. "It won't be easy."

He laughed and shook his head. The others were still staring at me with angry expressions on their ugly faces.

"Nothing is easy when you take over a throne," he said. "You know that. You should have expected it."

I felt a wave of anger wash over me. How the fuck could I have expected this? She'd gone completely crazy. She screwed up and they were blaming me for it?! Did they mean it?

"How the fuck could I have seen this coming?" I asked, clenching my fists.

She did it all by herself. I had nothing to do with it. If I'd known, I would have stopped her."

He snorted and shook his head. The others were still completely silent. Their silence was getting on my fucking nerves. They were hiding behind him. Like always.

"There had to be signs," he said. "You should have known."

I took a deep breath through my nose to try and calm myself down a bit.

"He still wouldn't react," I said. "I had no idea she was his partner. It changed everything.

" "You suck at your job, huh?" he asked, chuckling

darkly. "How did you not see that coming? My sources tell me he'd been pining for her for months. They say it was fucking obvious."

I resisted the urge to roll my eyes again.

"I wasn't following him," I muttered. "I was as close as I could be." He laughed again. "I obviously wasn't close enough

," I growled. I couldn't stop.

"Okay, that's enough," I said angrily. "It fucking happened, and there's nothing we can do about it. We can go over everything I did or didn't do, but it won't change shit. We need to figure out what to do now, not what we should have done before."

He raised his eyebrows. "Do you have any suggestions?"

I took a deep breath and let it out slowly.

"We'll all be at the Alpha Gathering," I said. "I'm sure we'll be able to get a lot done while we're there. "

He looked at the rest of the members and sighed.

"I was hoping to avoid that," he said. "We're risking a lot."

I snorted and shook my head. He looked back at me and narrowed his eyes.

"We've been risking a lot since we started meeting here," I said. "We'll be executed if we're caught here or there. It doesn't make much of a difference."

He set his jaw and smiled. It was forced, though.

"You're not wrong about that, my friend," he said, and my stomach twisted.

We weren't friends. We were just two men who wanted to achieve the same goal. We were just two men who wanted to take his throne from him.

"His mate is the key," I said. "He'd give his throne for her. I'm sure of it."

He nodded. "What should we know about her?"

"Nothing," I said. "She's a regular wolf with a pretty face." She's not worth much to us, but she's worth everything to him.

" He smirked. "Pretty face, huh?"

I laughed and nodded.

"A very pretty face," I said. "I'm sure you'll enjoy spending time with her."

I looked around the room and smiled.

"We'll all enjoy spending time with her," I said, causing the others to smile a little.

I was dying to have her under me. I had been dreaming about it ever since I first laid eyes on her. I thought about all the different ways I would fuck her. I thought about all the ways she would scream out my name. Hell, I didn't even have to scream my name. Just hearing her scream as I buried my cock in her would be enough.

"I'm looking forward to it," he said. "Will it be easy to take her?"

I looked back at him and sighed.

"No," I said, shaking my head. "He's very protective. It won't be easy to take her." He

took a deep breath and clenched his fists. He didn't like that one bit.

"Nothing comes easy when you take a throne," I reminded him, trying not to smirk.

He growled and narrowed his eyes.

"Don't use my words against me, rat," he said. "Remember who will sit on that throne. If I were you, I'd be careful what I say."

I bit the inside of my cheek to keep from laughing. He was going to be a terrible king, but that was exactly what I wanted. I wanted a king I could control, and he was stupid and arrogant enough to let me use him as a puppet.

"I apologize," I said, bowing my head slightly.

He rolled his eyes and leaned back in his chair.

"So taking his mate is our main objective," he said. "We need her to convince him to give us his throne."

I nodded. "I'm sure it won't take much convincing. He'll give it to us in no time."

He smiled. He seemed satisfied.

"That's wonderful to hear," he said. —I can't wait to get back what belongs to me—.

Chapter 101 She is a werewolf

Dimitri's POV

She was a Lycan.

She was a black werewolf.

I was in shock. I could tell Oscar had asked us a question, but I couldn't hear him. I could only see his lips moving. I could only hear my blood pumping through my veins and my heart hammering against my chest.

If it was true, she was the rightful heir to the throne. If it was true, she was the most powerful wolf in existence.

If it was true, then I was in more danger than ever.

"Alpha Dimitri?" Oscar's voice finally reached me.

I flinched and looked up at him. I tried to get my body to calm down a bit so I could hear what he was saying.

"Who else knows about her ability?" Oscar asked.

I cleared my throat and shook my head.

"The four of us and the pack doctor," I muttered.

I looked at Will and Ellie. They were both staring at Oscar in shock.

"Let it stay that way," Oscar said sternly. "No one else needs to know and no one else can know now." If I'm right then she's..."

Oscar stopped talking and looked at Maddie.

"She's the heir to the throne," I said, making her look back at me.

She nodded slowly.

I finally looked at my mate. She was pale and I didn't even know if she was breathing. She was staring at Oscar with wide eyes.

"Princess," I called out to her as I caressed her cheek and turned her head towards me. "Breathe, my love. Everything's going to be okay."

I didn't know if she heard me.

I pressed my lips against hers and pulled her even closer to me.
"Breathe, Maddie," I murmured as I rubbed her back. "Come on, my love."

She gulped and shook her head a little. I could tell how confused and scared she was.

I looked at Oscar, Will, and Ellie.

"Could you give us a moment please?" I asked them.

I knew Maddie needed space. I could tell she was overwhelmed. I had to help her. I needed to calm her down a bit.

"Sure," Will murmured as he stood up. "We'll wait outside."

I nodded and watched as the three of them left my office. Will glanced at Maddie one more time before closing the door.

I glanced back at her as soon as they were gone. Her eyes were fixed on me, but I could tell she was completely lost in thought. Her eyes were fixed on me, but she wasn't looking at me. She was somewhere else.

"Princess," I called softly as I leaned down and kissed her cheeks. "I need you to focus on my lips on your skin, okay? I need you to come back to me."

I began placing soft kisses all over her cheek and jaw. I kept my eyes on hers the entire time.

I finally reached her lips and kissed her as softly and delicately as I could.

She grabbed onto the back of my shirt and buried her head in my neck.

"Oh, princess," I murmured as I kissed her temple. "It's okay. I'm already here." Nothing bad will happen, I promise. I won't let anything or anyone hurt you."

I rubbed her back gently and took a deep breath, letting her scent calm me.

"I'm not a threat," she murmured. "I promise. I won't..."

Her voice cracked and she stopped talking.

I raised my eyebrows. A threat? What the hell was she talking about?

I made her lift her head and look at me.

"A threat?" I asked. "What do you mean, Maddie?"

Her eyes widened and she shook her head.

"I'm not a threat," she said, her voice shaking. "I won't do anything, Dimitri. I promise. I don't care. I never have to change. No one has to know."

She sounded more and more terrified with each word she said. I could feel her shaking.

I was so fucking confused. What the hell was she talking about?

"A threat to who, Maddie?" I asked, caressing her cheek.

Her eyebrows raised slightly.

"For you," she murmured, making my heart stop. "I won't take your throne from you, I promise. I'm not a threat. I don't need it. I don't want it. I want you. I only want you. Please, please don't be mad at me. I didn't know. I really didn't know."

She was sobbing and shaking when she finished speaking.

I was in shock.

What the fuck was she talking about?

She buried her face in her hands. I was too shocked to move.

Did she really think I saw her as a threat? Did she really think I was mad at her?! Did she really think anything between us was going to change?!

The only thing that would change would be the number of guards she would have now. The main one would be me. I was going to glue her to my side and never let her out of my sight.

I didn't give a damn about the throne. She could have it all. All I cared about was having her.

I forced myself to move. I had to tell her all of this. I couldn't keep it to myself. I had to know.

"Princess," I said as I pulled her hands away from her face. "I'm not mad. I don't care if you're the heir. I don't care if you have a bigger claim to the throne than me."

She gulped and I wiped the tears from her beautiful face.

"All I need is you," I said softly as I leaned down and kissed the tip of her nose. "I don't see you as a threat, Maddie. I don't care about any of that. All I want is you. All I need is to keep you safe ." I hugged her and kissed her temple. She wrapped her arms around me tightly.

"I love you, Madeleine," I added as I tangled my fingers in her hair and held her close to me. "Nothing will change that. Nothing is more important to me than you ."

She sobbed and tightened her arms around me.

"I was so scared," she cried. "I thought…"

Her voice cracked and another sob escaped.

"I know, princess," I murmured as I kissed her temple again. "But there's nothing to fear. I would never choose that throne over you. I would never choose anything or anyone over you."

I rested my head on hers and took a deep breath.

"You are my heart and soul, Maddie," I added softly. "

You are my everything, and I need nothing else in this world."

Chapter 102 She was still his

Madeline's POV

My whole body was shaking. I was in shock. I was scared.

I was in complete disbelief.

I was shocked when Oscar said I was a werewolf, but hearing Dimitri say I was the heir...

It was too much. The first thought that came to mind was that Dimitri would see me as a threat. He was the King. This was his Kingdom. This was his throne. He deserved to be the leader. He deserved to sit on that throne, not me.

All I wanted was my mate. I didn't want the throne. I didn't want to be the leader. I didn't want to be a Lycan. I wanted Dimitri.

When he said he didn't see me as a threat, a huge weight was lifted off my shoulders. I felt like I could finally breathe again. I couldn't stop sobbing. I was relieved.

But I was also scared. What did it all mean? Was this the reason Skye refused to change? Was she protecting me from finding out she was a werewolf?

Was she real? Maybe Oscar was wrong. Maybe it wasn't true.

"Oscar could be wrong," I murmured under my breath. "Maybe it's not true."

Dimitri kissed my temple and ran his fingers through my hair.

"Maybe," he said. "But I doubt it, princess. You being a werewolf explains a lot."

I lifted my head and Dimitri gave me a small smile. He wiped the tears from my cheeks and gave me a soft kiss on the lips.

"Like what?" I asked quietly.

Dimitri raised an eyebrow.

"Me being a werewolf explains what?" I asked.

Dimitri tucked a strand of hair behind my ear and sighed.

"That Skye refused to change to protect you," he said. "That you have powers."

I nodded and took a deep breath. Dimitri caressed my cheek and smiled.

"Don't worry, Maddie, okay?" he said softly. "I won't let anything happen to you." "I'll protect you from everything and everyone."

I wrapped my arms around his neck and kissed him.

"I really want to be alone with you," I murmured against his lips. "I'm so scared of losing you. I need to feel you inside me. I need to feel your skin against mine. I need you."

Dimitri growled, pulling me tighter against him. He lifted his hips and I noticed how hard he was. An intense feeling of need washed over me.

"Fuck, Maddie," Dimitri murmured as he lowered his head and kissed my mark. "You're driving me crazy."

I moaned and moved my head to give him better access to my neck. He meant every word he said. I wanted him. I needed him. I needed him so bad. I was so scared. I really thought I would lose him. I really thought he wouldn't want me anymore. I needed to feel him everywhere to make sure he was still mine.

His mouth and tongue were driving me crazy. He kept biting, sucking, and licking my neck and I felt like I was going to burst. I kept touching him and grinding myself against him, feeling him shudder every time I ran my hand down his perfect back.

"Dimitri," I cried out softly as the need I felt was starting to become painful.

"Fuck, Madeline," he growled softly. "I can't fuck you when there are three people waiting outside."

I didn't care about them. I needed him.

"But I can do this," he muttered as he unzipped my jeans and slowly snaked his hand into my underwear.

I gasped as his fingers touched my clit.

"Oh fuck," he cried out. "You're so fucking wet."

I was. I could tell. My underwear was completely soaked.

He rubbed my clit and my eyes rolled back in my head. Dimitri grabbed the back of my neck with his other hand and kissed me hard.

"You're going to cum on my fingers," he told me in a deep, lust-filled voice. "You're going to keep your eyes on mine while you cum." You're not going to scream or make any noise."

I dug my nails into his shoulder as he pushed two fingers into me.

"If you do as I say, I'm going to fuck you so hard tonight that you'll never think about me leaving you or choosing someone or something over you again," he continued, making me shudder. "Is that clear?" I just nodded. I couldn't speak.

"Good girl," he growled as he kissed me again.

He began to thrust his fingers in and out of me. I gasped quietly and grabbed the back of his shirt.

"Rub yourself against me," he ordered as he lowered his head and began kissing my neck again.

He didn't have to tell me twice. I began to move my hips, my clit beginning to rub against the palm of his hand. I had to bite the inside of my cheek to keep from crying out. I closed my eyes and began to move my hips faster.

"Very well, my Queen," Dimitri said as he lifted his head and caressed my cheek.

He turned my head and kissed me hard.

"Look at me," he said, and I opened my eyes immediately.

The love and desire I saw in his eyes made my whole body tremble. He was so close. A few more thrusts and I would explode.

I bit my tongue to keep from crying out as he pushed his fingers deeper. He hit that amazing spot inside me and I exploded around his fingers.

"Fuck yes, Madeline," he said as he kissed me hard.

I continued to grind against him, trying to prolong my orgasm. My movements slowed after a few moments. I was spent. He smirked as I looked down at his hand in my underwear.

"So fucking wet," he murmured as he gently pulled his fingers out of me.

He looked back up at me and took the fingers inside him into his mouth.

He moaned and closed his eyes.

"Fuck," he murmured. "You taste so fucking good."

I nearly came again.

I was staring at him and not even breathing.

He opened his eyes when he finished cleaning his fingers. He smirked and pulled me in for a kiss.

"I can't wait to be inside you tonight, my queen," he murmured, making me moan softly. "You were so good."

You deserve to be fucked and pleasured as soon as we get back to our room."

I smiled and kissed him again.

I love you. He mentally linked me. You're mine.

He was right. I was his. I was still his.

Chapter 103 What now?

Dimitri's POV

Every word of hers was true.

She was so scared of losing me. She really needed me. I felt everything through our bond and my heart almost gave out.

Like I would ever choose something or someone over her.

Like I would leave her. Like I was so stupid that I would give up on the best thing that ever happened to me.

No. I was a lot of things, but I wasn't crazy.

I knew I had to give her what she needed. I felt her desperation. I felt her need for security. I felt her burning desire and passion. I felt her need to have me.

But I knew I couldn't fuck her here. Not because of the people waiting outside our office, but because I knew I wouldn't be able to stop myself. I already knew we would have to close the office and spend an entire day here if I stuck the tip of my cock in her.

I was as desperate to reassure her as she was to be reassured.

I knew I had to stay in control, so I found another way to give myself to her. I was still horny as fuck and I still wanted to close those doors, bend her over the table and fuck her. But I definitely had more control than I would have had if my cock had tasted that wetness and that pussy.

I kissed her temple and ran my fingers through her hair.

"Feeling a little better, princess?" I asked after a few minutes of holding and caressing each other.

"Yes," she murmured softly. "Thank you, Dimitri. I needed that."

She looked up at me and smiled.

"And I can't wait to have every bit of you tonight," she added softly and a quiet moan escaped me.

"I can't wait either, my love," I murmured as I kissed her softly.

I reached between us and buttoned her jeans. I looked back at her and smiled.

"Can we call them back?" I asked. "The sooner we finish with them, the sooner we can get back to our room." She smiled and nodded.

"Come back, Will." I mentally linked it immediately.

I gave him another soft kiss on the lips just as the door opened. Will walked in followed by Oscar and Ellie.

"Are you okay, Maddie?" Ellie asked worriedly.

Maddie looked at her and nodded. "I feel a little better. I feel a little better." She was a little shaken up.

"No need to apologize, Mads," Will said as he sat down. "It's understandable."

Maddie looked at Oscar and took a deep breath.

"Could you be wrong?" she asked.

Oscar sighed and raised his eyebrows.

"I don't think I am, Maddie," he said. "The kind of power you have could only be explained by you being a werewolf and a direct descendant of the Kingdom of the Goldfangs."

Maddie raised her eyebrows slightly.

"The Kingdom of the Goldfangs?" she muttered.

Oscar nodded. "Legends say that the royalty of the Kingdom of the Goldfangs had powers." They ranged from controlling other people's behavior to being able to see into the future.

"Wow," Will muttered under his breath.

"But I can't do that," Maddie murmured.

Oliver gave her a small smile. "You have your own power, Maddie."

She sighed and bit her bottom lip.

"Have you talked to Skye?" Oscar asked her.

She looked at him and shook her head.

"Talk to her, Maddie," Oscar said. "Try to get her to change shifts. We need to confirm."

'Skol... I called my wolf, but he interrupted me.

"I'm talking to her, Dimitri," he said. Maddie's shutting her out. I think she's afraid to know the truth."

I swallowed and tried to take a deep breath.

"So is it true?" I asked, "Is she a werewolf?"

Skol was silent for a moment.

"Yes," he said, making my heart race. "That's why Skye refused to change. He was protecting her from anyone else knowing."

She's in a lot of danger, Dimitri. If anyone finds out who she is...

Skol stopped talking as a wave of panic washed over him.

"I know," I told him. "I'll protect her, Skol. We'll protect her."

"What do we do now?" Will muttered, interrupting my conversation with my wolf.

I tightened my grip on Maddie.

"No one can know," I said, using my Alpha order. "You're not allowed to tell anyone who she is and what she can do."

All three of them bowed their heads immediately.

"Yes, Alpha," they said at the same time.

Oscar wasn't part of my pack, but I was his King and my Alpha order worked on him too. I barely knew him and I had to make sure he wouldn't betray his King and Queen.

I trusted Will and Ellie with my life, but I needed to be sure they wouldn't tell. Being tied to the Alpha order was the best way to do that.

The pack medic wasn't going to tell anyone. He was already under my Alpha's order not to tell anyone about his power. He didn't know who she was and it was going to stay that way.

No one could know.

"I have to tell Mike," Maddie murmured, making me look at her.

She gulped and took a deep breath. She looked at me and I saw fear in her eyes.

"You don't have to tell him, Maddie," I said as I caressed her cheek. "He doesn't have to know."

I didn't want him to know. Becoming a werewolf was his obsession for many years. He abandoned his family for it. I wasn't sure how he would react knowing that Maddie was a Lycan and he wasn't.

"I have to, Dimitri," Maddie said, shaking her head.

"He can't find out from someone else. I have to tell him."

"He won't find out, Mads," Will said and she looked at him. "We're all under Alpha order. We can't tell anyone." Maddie shook her head.

"It will eventually come out," she said. "We'll have to tell the pack at some point. I don't want them to find out like this."

She was right. Eventually, everyone would find out who she was.

Not before I made sure she was safe, though. Not before I knew what it all meant.

She looked at me and gulped.

"I want to tell them now," she added.

I took a deep breath and let it out slowly.

"Okay, princess," I said and caressed her cheek. "We'll tell them now."

Chapter 104 How will he react?

Dimitri's POV

Maddie was shaking all over and I was beginning to doubt my decision to let him tell her.

"We don't have to, Maddie," I told her as I rubbed her back gently. "He doesn't have to know yet."

She looked at me and shook her head.

"He needs to know, Dimitri," she said. "He deserves to know. I can't keep it from him."

I sighed and looked at Will. He was looking at Maddie with a mix of worry and anger on his face. I could tell he wasn't too happy with her decision. I wasn't either, but I didn't want to be a jerk. Mike was her father and if she wanted him to know, I wasn't going to do anything to stop him.

But I wasn't sure how he would react. How would he react once he found out she was a Lycan?

I was sure Mike would never hurt her. I would never let him tell her even if there was a small part of me that thought he was a danger to her. Mike was a lot of things and made a lot of mistakes, but he would never hurt his daughter. I was damn sure of that.

But would he get mad? Would he get depressed? I had no fucking idea.

I heard him approach the office. Maddie started to move her leg up and down. I put my hand on her and raised an eyebrow at her.

"It's not too late yet," I said.

She shook her head and looked at the door. Mike walked in with a smile that disappeared as soon as he looked at Maddie.

"What happened?" he asked worriedly. "Why are you so pale?"

He closed the door and started to approach her.

"Hey, Michael," Oliver said, making Mike stop and look at him. His eyes widened.

"Oscar?" he murmured softly.

Oscar smiled and stood up. He walked over to Mike and pulled him in for a hug.

"Nice to see you, Mike," Oliver said, rubbing Mike's back. "I'm so sorry about Leah." "I did everything I could."

I could feel Maddie tense up. I took her hand in mine and squeezed it tightly.

Mike swallowed and let go of Oscar.

"Thanks for being there for Leah and my little girl," Mike said. "

Thanks for making it easier for Leah."

Oscar nodded and gave him a small smile.

"I wish I could have done more," Oscar said. "I wish she was here with us today."

A wave of sadness washed over Maddie. I put my arm around her shoulders and pulled her close. "

Your mother is always with you, my love." I mentally connected with her. She's watching over you. Maddie put her arms around my waist and I kissed the top of her head.

Mike nodded and looked back at Maddie.

"Maddie, honey, what's wrong?" he asked worriedly as he continued walking towards us.

"Sit down, Mike, please," I said calmly.

He looked at me and raised his eyebrows.

"I'll explain everything in a minute," I said, giving him a small smile. "Sit down, please."

Mike looked at Maddie and sat down next to Will.

"Are you okay, Maddie?" Mike asked. "Is something wrong? Please say something. I'm going crazy."

"She's okay, Mike," I said. "There's something we need to—"

"I'm a werewolf!" Maddie exclaimed, cutting me off.

I looked at her in surprise. We agreed to take it slow, explaining everything we knew so far. She was staring at Mike with wide eyes and wasn't breathing. She also seemed shocked at what he had done.

"Wow, subtle, Maddie," Will muttered, shaking his head at her.

I heard Ellie snort quietly.

I looked at Mike and saw him staring at Maddie with a confused expression on his face.

"What?" he asked quietly.

Maddie was silent now. I sighed and ran my fingers through my hair.

"She's a werewolf, Mike," I said, causing him to look at me. "She's not a normal wolf."

His eyes widened.

"I knew there was something different about her when her wolf refused to change on the night of her eighteenth birthday," I began to explain. "Skye said he refused to do it to protect Maddie. We didn't know what he was protecting her from then."

Mike looked at Maddie and took a deep breath.

"Maddie started hearing voices the day I made her a member of our pack," I continued, deciding to be as direct as possible. "She thought our pack members were mind-linking her, but she was wrong. I could hear their thoughts. I could read their minds."

Mike visibly paled. He looked at her and let out a loud gasp.

"She's the heiress," he murmured, shock written all over his face.

I raised my eyebrows.

How did he know?

Maddie tensed again.

"I'm so sorry," she murmured, her voice cracking. "I didn't know. I didn't want this, Mike, I promise."

Mike's shocked face turned to one of confusion.

"What are you talking about, Maddie?" he asked quietly.

Maddie took a deep breath, but it caught in her throat. She knew she wouldn't be able to explain it to him.

"I was worried about how you would react," I said, making Mike look back at me. "We were all kind of worried."

Mike's eyes widened, and I saw flashes of pain in them.

"Did you think I would hurt her?" he asked quietly,

his voice filled with pain and sadness.

"No, Mike," I said sternly. "Never. I know you and I know you would never hurt her."

He gave me a small nod and took a deep breath.

"I was worried you would be mad," I said. "Maybe a little sad."

I wasn't sure how to explain it.

Mike nodded and looked at Maddie. He took another deep breath and stood up. I watched him walk over to Maddie. She tensed a little and I rubbed her back, trying to relax her.

Mike knelt in front of her and took her hands in his.

"I love you, Maddie," he said. "I love you with all my heart and I would never do anything to hurt you. I did once and I hate what it did to you and me and our relationship. I will never make that mistake again."

Maddie let out a quiet sob and Mike pulled her into his arms. She hugged him tightly and I couldn't help but smile a little.

I was glad she had him in her life. Mike made a huge fucking mistake, but he was a different person now. He was the father she needed.

Chapter 105 Explain it to me

Madeline's POV

I felt so relieved. I was so scared that Mike hated me. I was terrified that he would leave me again. I was terrified that he would be angry or resentful towards me.

I didn't want that to happen. We started to mend our relationship. I felt ready to let him back into my life. I didn't want to lose him before I even got him back.

"Oh, my baby," Mike murmured as he kissed the top of my head and rubbed my back. "It's okay.

Everything's going to be okay."

I took a deep breath and let go. He gave me a small smile and wiped my cheeks.

"My precious baby girl," he said softly as he leaned in and kissed my forehead.

It felt weird to hear him call me that, but I'd be lying if I said it didn't feel good.

I was so mad at him, but I missed him too. I missed having a father. I missed, like, playing with him. I missed laughing with him. My mother used to tell me stories about him and she always said he was a great father. She would tell me stories about how he would play with me, read me fairy tales before bed, and make me my favorite breakfast in the morning. She would tell me stories about the three of us having a wonderful time together and I always missed him.

I missed my father.

I didn't want him back in my life because I was too angry.

I didn't want him back because I was afraid he would leave me again. That fear exploded inside me when Oscar told me he was a werewolf. I was sure Mike would be angry. I was sure he would leave me again.

"Thank you," I murmured, my voice low and raspy.

Mike smiled and stroked my cheek again.

"Why, honey?" he asked.

I swallowed and tried to take a deep breath.

"For not making you angry," I said. "For not blaming me."

Mike's eyes widened. He cupped my cheeks and shook his head.

"Never, Maddie," he said. "I would never blame you. There's nothing to blame you for. If anything, I'm incredibly proud of you."

He sighed and let go of me. He looked at Dimitri and ran his fingers through his hair.

"I understand why you thought I'd be angry," he muttered. "

I was an idiot and made the biggest mistake of my life when I left you and your mother."

Mike took my hands in his and squeezed them.

"But I was a different person then, Maddie," he continued. "I was twenty when you were born. I was young and delusional.

I believed in stories I shouldn't have even heard. I'm not the same person anymore."

He pulled me closer to him and wrapped me in a tight hug.

"I'm more than ready to be the father you need, Maddie," he said as he gently rubbed my back. "I love you so much, my little girl, and nothing will ever change that."

I felt a tear fall down my cheek.

Mike let go of me and wiped the tears from my cheeks.

"You could be turning into a cat and I'd still love you," he said, smiling a little.

Will and Dimitri snorted. A quiet chuckle escaped me.

Oscar and Ellie smiled. Mike smiled widely before his smile faded and he became serious again.

"I mean it, Mads," he said, running his fingers through my hair. "I'm here. I'll never leave again or choose anything or anyone over you. I promise."

I smiled and wrapped my arms around his neck again. Mike kissed my temple and hugged me back.

"I love you, baby," he said softly.

I loved him too, I really did. I loved him even when I was so mad at him. I loved him even when I didn't know where he was. I wanted to tell him that I loved him too, but the words refused to leave my lips.

Mike kissed my temple again and let go. He took a deep breath and looked at Dimitri.

"I want you to explain everything to me," Mike said as he took my hand in his. "How did you find out she can hear other people's thoughts?"

Dimitri sighed and looked at me.

"She was complaining about everyone trying to mentally connect to her at the same time," Dimitri said, giving me a small smile. "She said her head hurt and she needed to get used to it. I immediately knew something wasn't right."

Mike took another deep breath and let it out slowly.

"Can you hear my thoughts now?" he asked.

I shook my head. "I can't hear anyone's thoughts when Dimitri's with me."

I furrowed my eyebrows and bit my bottom lip.

"Well, except Janet and Kendrick's," I muttered.

I could feel Dimitri tense up.

"What do you mean, Maddie?" Oscar asked.

I looked at him and took a deep breath.

"I can't read minds when Dimitri's with me," I began to explain. "The only exceptions are Janet and Kendrick. I could hear their thoughts when Dimitri was with me.

" "What were they thinking?" Oliver asked, furrowing his eyebrows.

I gulped. Dimitri growled.

"They were thinking about hurting me," I said quietly.

Mike squeezed my hand tighter, and I could feel the anger rolling off of him in waves.

"What does that mean?" Mike asked angrily. "Why could I hear his thoughts but not everyone else's?"

"I wish I knew the answer to that question. "

"Well, one thing occurs to me," Oscar said, sighing loudly.

I looked at him, and I could feel my heart racing.

"What?" Dimitri asked angrily.

Oscar took a deep breath and raised his eyebrows.

"They were a real threat," Oscar said. "Their thoughts were so vile that they posed a real threat to you.

Their thoughts were stronger than your protector."

My heart began to drum against my ribcage.

"What the fuck were they thinking, Maddie?" Mike asked, his voice thick with anger.

I kept my gaze fixed on Oscar, fear twisting in my stomach.

They were a real threat.

Chapter 106 Overwhelmed

Dimitri's POV

I closed our bedroom door and looked at Maddie. My heart ached. She looked so tired and so overwhelmed.

"Princess," I called softly as I walked over to her.

She looked up at me and took a deep breath. I finally reached her and hugged her.

"I'm done with it all," she murmured as she hugged me back. "I'm tired."

I ran my fingers through her hair and kissed her temple.

"I know, my love," I said softly. "I realize that."

I had to find a way to relax her. I had to find a way to show her that she wasn't alone in this. I needed to find a way to show her how much I loved her.

"What day is it today?" she asked after a few moments of silence.

"When does the Alpha Meeting start?"

I ran my fingers through her hair again. I honestly didn't know the answer to that question. I'd completely lost track of time. Maybe in a day or two? Or even longer?

Three or four days? I had no fucking idea.

But I knew I wasn't going to talk about it with her. She needed to relax. She needed to forget about everything. She needed a night of peace and quiet.

"We're not going to talk about it, princess," I told her as I gently rubbed her back. "You're going to let me take care of you. You're going to let your partner do everything he can to help you relax."

She sighed and leaned into me more.

"Sounds good," she murmured under her breath.

I smiled and an idea occurred to me.

I picked her up and she yelped in surprise.

"What are you doing?" she asked with wide eyes.

"Helping you relax," I said, giving her a small smile.

I opened the bathroom door and walked over to the vanity. I placed her on top of it and kissed her forehead. She raised her eyebrows and I winked at her.

I let go of her and started running our bath. Maddie giggled , making me look at her.

"That already looks amazing," she said.

I smiled and turned to her. I had a minute or two before the tub filled up and I really wanted to hug her.

I smiled and caressed her cheek.

"I love you, princess," I said as I started to take off her shirt.

She lifted her arms so I could take it off. I started to softly kiss her neck and tossed the shirt to the floor behind me.

Maddie sighed contently and wrapped her arms and legs around me.

"I love you too," she murmured. "I love you so much it hurts. I can't imagine my life without you. I don't want to imagine my life without you."

I gave her a soft kiss on the jaw and looked at her.

"Good thing you don't have to," I said smiling a little. "You're kind of stuck with me. "

She laughed and caressed my cheek.

"Really?" she asked raising an eyebrow.

"Oh yes," I said as I walked up behind her and unclasped her bra. "I'm yours and I expect you to treat me as such, my Queen."

She laughed and softly kissed my neck.

"Well then I must order you to take off your clothes and let me worship what's mine," she said, making my entire body shiver.

She didn't have to ask me twice. A few seconds later I was standing naked in front of her. She smiled and ran her hands down my chest.

"I think the bath's done," Maddie laughed, making me look over my shoulders.

"Fuck," I muttered and hurried to turn off the water.

Maddie hopped off the counter and walked over to me. I turned around and saw that she had taken off the rest of her clothes. My heart skipped a beat.

I had seen her naked so many times since her birthday, but I would never get used to how beautiful she was. It always took my breath away. It always made my heart skip a beat.

I helped her into the tub.

"Is the water okay?" I asked and she nodded.

"Get in," she said as she held out her hand to me.

I smiled and climbed into the tub. I sat behind her and pulled her close to my chest. She sighed contently as I wrapped my arms around her. I kissed her temple and she rested her head on my shoulder.

"Thank you," she murmured softly.

"Why?" I asked as I ran my hands down her body.

I gently squeezed and caressed every part of her body. She continued to sigh and moan softly.

"For doing this," she said. "I needed it."

I smiled and turned my head so I could kiss her cheek.

"Of course, princess," I said softly. "You're not alone in this. I'm with you. I'm here for you in every way possible."

She looked at me and smiled.

"How did I get so lucky?" she asked as she caressed my cheek.

I shrugged and smiled.

"I'm a catch, aren't I?" I said, wiggling my eyebrows.

Maddie giggled and nodded. "Oh, you are."

I leaned in and kissed her softly. I ran my hand down her body until I reached her shoulders. I started massaging her firmly, but gently. I moved my lips down to her jaw and neck. She moaned softly and it made me smile. I could feel her relaxing and that was all that mattered to me.

I started kissing her collarbone and shoulder and massaging her upper arms.

"Dimitri," she sighed softly.

I enjoyed the taste of her skin on my lips and tongue. I wanted more and I couldn't stop kissing her.

She laid her head on my shoulder and sighed again. I smiled and gave her another kiss on the neck.

"I love you," she murmured. "You're the best thing that's ever happened to me."

My heart skipped a beat. I didn't respond. I reached my mark on her neck and kissed her softly. She moaned and put her hands on my thighs. She started to move her hands up, making me shudder and moan. She

turned around and straddled me. I felt the

pressure of her warm, wet pussy against my hard cock and I groaned loudly. She kissed me softly and I knew we wouldn't be getting out of the tub for a long time.

Chapter 107 She asked to see you

Dimitri's POV

I opened the door and walked into my office. I finally managed to compose myself and realized that the Alpha Meeting wasn't in three or four days.

It was tomorrow.

"Where's Maddie?" Will asked as he closed the door.

"Sleeping," I said as I walked to my desk. "I didn't want to wake her up."

I was reluctant to leave her, but Ellie assured me that she would keep her safe. I only left because she was close and I could go see her immediately if she needed me.

"How is she?" Will asked worriedly. "She seemed a little overwhelmed yesterday."

I sat down and sighed.

"I was," I said. "But I totally understand her. She's been through so much in such a short time. I'm overwhelmed and I can't even imagine what she's going through."

Well, I felt her emotions, so I knew a little. But knowing how someone feels and actually having to go through something like that were two completely different things.

Will nodded. "I agree. I was stunned yesterday and didn't know how to react." I can't imagine how he must be feeling."

I nodded and ran my fingers through my hair.

"She'll be okay," I murmured. "I'll make sure of it."

I wasn't going to let anything or anyone hurt her. I wasn't going to let anyone use her. I was going to make sure she was safe.

"Did you talk to Skye?" Will asked me. "When will she change?"

I sighed and furrowed my eyebrows. He was so focused on

Maddie yesterday that I didn't even remember to ask him about Skye.

"I'm not sure," I said. "I talked to Skol yesterday and he told me that Maddie was pushing Skye away."

Will sighed and shook his head a little.

"She needs time," he said.

"She does," I nodded. "I won't pressure her into it.

You'll talk to her when she's ready."

Will nodded again.

I looked down at the papers on my desk and took a deep breath. I had work to do and my focus was terrible. I wanted to get back to my mate. I didn't want to be away from her for too long.

"Dimitri," Will called my name.

I looked at him and raised my eyebrows. I could immediately tell something was wrong. Will looked apologetic and I didn't like it one bit.

"What?" I asked, narrowing my eyes.

He took a deep breath and let it out slowly.

"Tim came to talk to me this morning," Will said and I immediately tensed.

Tim was one of the guards watching my mother and Savannah.

"What did he want?" I asked even though I already knew what Will was going to say.

He sighed and clenched his jaw.

"Your mother asked to see you," Will said, and I could feel the anger pulsing through my body.

I didn't want to see her. I would see her at her execution. I hadn't seen her since she was dragged out of my office, and I wasn't about to speak to her again. I hated her with all my body and soul.

"Well, she's asked to see Maddie, too," Will added quietly.

My eyes went wide, and I could feel the anger exploding inside me. Every muscle in my body contracted.

I felt like I was being electrocuted.

Fuck no. Over my fucking dead body.

"No," I growled, trying to stop my canines from lengthening.

"She'll never breathe the same air as my partner. She'll never lay eyes on her again."

Will nodded. "I completely agree. I nearly went crazy when Tim told me that."

I gritted my teeth.

"You shouldn't have even asked me," I growled. "

I should have known the answer would be no."

Will sighed and rolled his eyes.

"Come on," Will said with a hint of annoyance in his voice. "It's not Tim's fault. He's just a guard, Dimitri."

I knew that, but I was angry and I wasn't really choosing who to be angry at. I was angry at everyone.

I couldn't even believe my mother had the nerve to ask to see Maddie. I couldn't believe she thought I would agree. I'd have to be a fucking idiot to let something like that happen. My mother and Savannah would never see my mate again. They would never hurt her again.

"Maybe you should go talk to her," Will said quietly.

I looked at him with wide eyes. Was I crazy?! I never wanted to see that bitch again.

Will sighed and ran his fingers through his hair.

"I know you don't want to see her, Dimitri, but I want to know what she has to say," Will said.

I clenched my fists and narrowed my eyes.

"Then you're free to go see her," I said angrily. "I'm not joining you. I don't give a shit what she has to say. "

Will sighed again.

"Aren't you just a little curious?" he asked. "I want to know why she did it. I don't believe all that crap about Maddie's mother."

"I don't give a shit," I said. "She did it and she's going to be punished. It's over."

Will furrowed his eyebrows and crossed his arms over his chest.

"But what if she knows something?" he asked. "She chose to torture Maddie for a reason. What if she knows something about Maddie?"

My heart raced.

"Like what?" I muttered, gritting my teeth.

"I don't know," Will shrugged. "I just don't think she did it just because Maddie looks like her mother. What did she think Mike was going to go after Maddie? She's her daughter, for fuck's sake." It's a stupid excuse and I think there has to be another reason he went after Maddie."

I clenched my fists.

Fuck.

He was right.

"Just talking, Dimitri," Will added after a few moments of silence. "It can't hurt."

I gritted my teeth again.

Fuck, fuck, fuck. I really didn't want to do this.

But Will was right. There could be another reason and I had to find out what it was. I had to find out if she knew something. I had to do everything I could to protect my mate.

Chapter 108 I will change

DIMITRI

The dungeon where I kept my prisoners was a dark underground place. The silence was only occasionally broken by the sound of water dripping from places I couldn't see. The air smelled old and damp, and it was much colder than outside. The smell burned my nostrils and I couldn't wait to get out of the place.

Upon entering the dungeon, I immediately felt a chill run down my spine. The walls were made of rough stone blocks, with moss and lichen growing on them. The torches on the walls were the only source of light. If I weren't a werewolf, I would have a hard time moving.

The floor was uneven, with rocks and weeds in the way. Old chains and shackles of rusty iron hung from the walls, reminding me of some good times I had down here with some of my prisoners.

The ceiling was low and from time to time I felt drops of water fall on my neck. It gave me the creeps. I hated damp places.

As I walked deeper into the dungeon, I couldn't help but feel more and more furious. I wondered what the fuck my mother would have to say.

"God, I hate this place," Will muttered, breaking the silence.

I glanced at him. He was walking behind me because the hallways were too narrow for us to walk side by side.

"I have some good memories here," I said, looking back ahead. "I wouldn't mind it being a little drier, though."

Another drop of water fell on my neck and I growled softly.

Will chuckled.

"Good enough memories to torture your enemies with?" he asked, already knowing the answer to that question.

"Of course," I said just as we approached the door. "I am ruthless when it comes to my prized possessions.

Up until nine months ago, my only prized possession was my Kingdom. Then Maddie came into my life and everything changed. I still valued my Kingdom, but not as much as I valued her. She was everything."

"Alpha," the guard said, tilting his head.

He grabbed the key from his belt and unlocked the door.

"Thanks, Jeff," I said as I grabbed the knob and pulled the door open.

He led me into another hallway. This one was wider, with cells on either side. My mother and Savannah were in the last two. I specifically asked to be put there. Those two cells were in the worst condition of all.

As I approached the cells, I heard sniffling and my anger grew. Did they think I was going to take pity on them?

"Did he want to see me?" I said as I approached the first cell.

They were silent for a moment, but then they both jumped to their feet and ran to the bars separating us.

I barely recognized my mother. She was always an elegant woman, but now she looked like a sewer rat. It made me smile a little. She deserved it.

"Dimitri," Savannah called out. "Get us out of here, please. "

I looked at her and raised my eyebrows.

"Are you serious?" I asked, looking from Savannah to my mother. "Is that why you called?"

My mother gulped and held her hand out through the bars. I looked at her hands with disgust written all over my face.

"Dimitri," my mother called, her voice shaking. "I'm your mother. Please help me.

" "I have a son, Dimitri!" Savannah blurted out before I could speak. "You can't take him away from me! My son needs me! He needs both of his parents!"

I rolled my eyes. Her delusions were starting to get on my nerves.

"Your son is in good hands," I said, looking back at my mother. "He's with people who will truly love and care for him."

" "You gave up our son?!" Savannah yelled.

I looked at her and clenched my jaw.

"I gave up your son, yes," I said, trying to remain calm. "The father never showed up, so the boy was left alone. I couldn't let that happen, so I found him a family."

Savannah's eyes widened. She sobbed loudly. I looked back at my mother and squinted.

"Why am I here, Mother?" I asked. "What do you want? " "I'm sorry

," she said. "I'll change, Dimitri. I promise, son."

I chuckled and shook my head.

"Do you really think I'm that stupid, Mother?" I asked as I took a step closer to her. "Do you really expect me to believe that?"

My mother looked at Will.

"Please, Dimitri," she yelled. "It's the truth. I'm willing to change. I'm willing to accept Mad—"

"Don't say her name!" I exclaimed, a loud growl escaping me. "You're not allowed to say her name ever again."

I could feel the anger pulsing through my veins. I didn't want my mother or the bitch in the other cell to ever say her beautiful name again. I didn't want her name sullied.

"That goes for you too, Savannah," I said, still looking at my mother. "You're not allowed to say her name again."

My mother gulped and looked back at Will. She growled softly.

"They won't forgive you for what you've done," I said, clenching my fists and setting my jaw. "You'll never make it out of this cell alive."

My mother sobbed loudly. Savannah screamed.

"What did you think was going to happen?" I asked, narrowing my eyes at my mother. "Did you really think I'd forgive you for torturing my mate?"

"We thought you might want a strong mate," Savannah replied instead of my mother. "We thought you might want someone more suitable than that little—"

"Careful," I interrupted. "You're already sentenced to death, but I get to choose how painful that death will be. Don't piss me off."

Savannah's eyes widened.

I looked back at my mother and sighed.

"Well, my visit was pointless, just like I thought it would be," I said.

"I was hoping that you might want to share some new information with me, but I was wrong."

I looked at Will and narrowed my eyes slightly.

"Well, Will was wrong," I said, making him raise an eyebrow.

I looked back at my mother and clapped my hands theatrically.

"Well, I'd say it's been a pleasure seeing you ladies, but I'd be lying," I said. "I'll see you again on your execution date."

I turned to my right and started walking away, ignoring his cries and pleas.

Do you think we made an impact? I thought of Will as we walked out of there.

We'll see. he replied. *All we can do is wait.*

I clenched my jaw and took a deep breath. My lungs were burning and I couldn't wait to get out of there and breathe fresh air.

Chapter 109 Tree House

Madeline

"Why did you go to see them?" I asked, my brows furrowing.

I felt nervousness creeping up on me. I knew they couldn't hurt Dimitri, but my fear wasn't rational. I was afraid they'd get to him somehow. I was afraid they'd say something that would hurt him.

Ellie sighed and looked at me.

"I'm not sure," she said. "Will mentally connected me to explain it to him, but he did a terrible job."

Ellie looked back down at her book. I took a deep breath and let it out slowly. I was nervous and I wanted Dimitri back. I wasn't going to calm down until I saw that he was okay.

Even if they hadn't done or said anything to hurt him, seeing his mother and ex-girlfriend locked in that place was going to be hard on him.

Skye growled.

"She's not his girlfriend," Skye said angrily.

I ignored her. I had been doing that ever since I found out why she refused to change shifts. I wasn't ready to talk to her.

I wasn't ready to let her out. I wasn't ready to see if Oscar was right.

"Why don't you just mentally link it to him if you're worried?" Ellie asked.

"I don't want to bother him or distract him," I muttered as I looked out the window.

Ellie snorted quietly.

"As if you could bother him," she muttered.

I took another deep breath and let it out slowly. I really wanted her to come back.

"Sit down, Mads," Ellie said. "You're making me nervous."

I turned around to look at her. She was sitting on the couch reading a book. She didn't seem nervous at all. I heard her anyway. Looking out that window was going to drive me crazy.

I sat up and glanced around her room. It wasn't very decorated. I could still see her suitcase in front of the closet.

"Why haven't you unpacked yet?" I asked.

"I haven't had time," she muttered, not taking her eyes off the book.

I sighed and forced myself not to roll my eyes.

"Do you want to put that book down and talk to me?" I said, trying to hide the annoyance in my voice. "I'm going crazy."

Ellie looked at me and snorted, "Yes, my Queen," she said as she closed the book and placed it on the small table between us. "What do you want to talk about?"

I shrugged. "I don't know."

Ellie raised her eyebrows and smirked.

"Well, you're certainly more interesting than my book," she said, making me sigh and roll my eyes.

"Okay, fine," I muttered. "Tell me something about yourself. How old are you?
" "I'm 20," she smiled at me.

My eyes widened.

"And you're already one of the best warriors in our pack?!" I exclaimed. "That's amazing, Ellie."

She smiled and shook her head.

"I had no choice," she said. "I had to grow up with Will and Dimitri.

I had to learn how to fight as a child to outlast those two. "
I laughed a little.

"How old is Will?" I asked.

"23," Ellie said, giving me a small smile. "Same as Dimitri."
I nodded and smiled.

"So you've known Dimitri forever?" I asked and she nodded.

"Oh, yes," she said. "I have so many embarrassing stories to tell him. But don't let him find out I've told you anything because he'll order me to stop."

I laughed and shook my head at her.

"I'm waiting," I said, raising an eyebrow at her.

Ellie laughed and looked towards the door.

"Dimitri and Will tried to build a treehouse once," Ellie said. "They were eleven or twelve. I told them they wouldn't be able to do it. They were fucking clumsy back then."

Ellie smirked and shook her head. I chuckled

"I was right, though," she sighed. "I watched as Will dropped a plank on Dimitri's head. He knocked him unconscious. Dimitri's father almost started a war because he thought his son had been attacked in the woods."

I laughed just as the door to Ellie's room opened.

"Well, that's the most beautiful sound I've ever heard,"

Dimitri said, making my heart skip a beat.

I jumped up and ran over to him. I sighed in relief when he finally hugged me.

"Hello, princess," he whispered as he lowered his head and kissed my jaw. "Maybe I should leave you alone more often if I'm going to get a hug like this every time I come back.

" "No," I said immediately. "You can't just leave me ever again."

Dimitri chuckled and kissed my head.

"Oh, you don't have to worry about that," he said softly.

"It'll be hard for me to leave you again. Being without you is torture."

He was absolutely right. I couldn't breathe normally without him. I needed him by my side.

"What were you laughing at, princess?" Dimitri asked as he let go of me.

I bit the inside of my cheek and shook my head.

"You're welcome," I said, trying not to smile.

Dimitri narrowed his eyes and looked at Ellie.

"What story did you tell him?" he asked, and I couldn't hold back my smile any longer.

"I have no idea what you're talking about," Ellie said, shaking her head.

Dimitri looked back at me and raised an eyebrow.

"Let's just say if we ever decide to build a treehouse for our kids, I'll be the one doing all the work," I said as I put my arm around his waist and smiled at him.

"Ellie," he growled as he looked at her.

Both Ellie and Will were holding back their laughter.

"Stop laughing," he said as he pulled me over to the couch. "It's not funny." I was twelve.

Dimitri and I sat down on the couch. I pulled him close and kissed his cheek.

"It's kind of funny," I said, making him sigh and roll his eyes.

"Okay, enough about the treehouse," Ellie said, smiling at Dimitri. "Did you talk to Janet? What did she want?"

My smile immediately disappeared and worry hit me like a train. I looked him up and down and sighed in relief. He wasn't hurt. Well, physically at least.

What did she ask him? What did she say? Had I hurt him?

I moved closer to him, wishing I could absorb his pain.

Chapter 110 Just a few hours away

Dimitri

Being with Maddie was healing my body and soul in ways I never thought possible. I felt more at peace as she wrapped her arm around my waist and rested her head on my chest.

I smiled at her and gave her a soft kiss on the forehead. I missed her so much.

I never would have imagined I would feel this way. I knew the mating bond was a powerful thing, but I never imagined I would have a hard time being away from her for more than an hour.

"She wanted out," Will answered Ellie's question. "She said she would change."

I could feel the anger starting to throb inside me, but it never even developed as Maddie turned her head and placed a soft kiss on my chest. I ran my fingers through her hair and inhaled deeply of her scent. I smiled and sighed in satisfaction.

"Oh, what a load of crap," Ellie said angrily. "She's clearly lying."

I looked at Ellie and smiled.

"Obviously," I said calmly.

Ellie raised her eyebrows and looked me up and down.

"Why aren't you mad?" she asked. "Or upset? Or anything other than happy?"

I ran my fingers through Maddie's hair and sighed.

"It's hard to be mad when I'm with my mate," I said.

It was so hard. I wanted to be mad. Just thinking about my mother made me furious, but it was like something was stopping me from feeling anything other than pure happiness.

Ellie raised her eyebrows and shook her head.

"Anyway," she sighed. "Why did you agree to go see her?"

We all knew what she was going to say.

"I just can't get her reasoning for hurting Maddie out of my head," Will began to explain. "I'm sure there had to be another reason other than what she told us."

Maddie tensed a little. I ran my hand down her back, trying to relax her.

"And you thought she would tell you?" Ellie asked, huffing. "Let me guess, she didn't."

Will looked at me and smirked.

"We didn't ask him," Will said.

Ellie raised her eyebrows and looked at Maddie.

"Do you have any idea what they're talking about?" Ellie asked.

" I'm completely lost."

Maddie shook her head and looked at me.

"I knew she wouldn't tell if I asked," I said as I caressed Maddie's cheek. "I knew she wouldn't tell even if I told her to. She didn't tell me last time.

" "And what did you do?" Maddie asked quietly.

"I told her what her punishment would be," I said as I looked at Ellie. "Will and I thought she might need some encouragement to talk."

Ellie smirked.

"How did she react?" Ellie asked.

"But what if he told you the whole truth?" Maddie asked before Will or I could answer Ellie's question. "

I was under your orders. I had to tell you everything."

I looked at her and sighed.

"There are ways to lie or not share everything even under Alpha's order, Maddie," I said softly. "It's painful, but it can be done. "

Maddie furrowed her eyebrows.

"You wouldn't know if he did?" Maddie asked. "You would have noticed, wouldn't you?"

I took a deep breath and let it out slowly.

"I don't remember, Princess," I said. "I was so angry and so focused on protecting you that everything from that day is a blur."

I frowned and tried to remember the conversation with my mother.

All I remembered was rage and an overwhelming need to grab Maddie and take her away.

"Why don't you order her to tell you now?" Maddie asked, fiddling with her fingers. "Maybe it's not necessary to scare her with punishment."

I sighed and caressed her cheeks.

"She deserves it, Princess," I said softly. "She hurt you. She hurt my greatest treasure."

I leaned toward her and gave her a soft kiss on the lips,

"Please don't feel sorry for her," I added. "She's hurt you. She wanted to break us up. She helped Savannah come up with the plan to lie to me about her pregnancy."

I caressed Maddie's cheek and took a deep breath.

"She's not a good person, princess," I told her. "She doesn't deserve your pity."

"Dimitri's right, Mads," Will added, causing Maddie to look at him. "She doesn't deserve it. She deserves to pay for what she's done."

Maddie took a deep breath and looked down at her lap.

"Besides, we're just hours away from having nine Alphas in our territory," she added. "I'm not dealing with my mother right now."

Maddie looked up at me and gave me a small nod.

I smiled and pulled her into my chest.

"Thanks for being so kind, princess," I said as I wrapped my arms around her.

She hugged me back and I could feel her relax in my arms. My smile grew wider. Knowing she felt relaxed around me made me so fucking happy. I wanted to be her safe place, just like she was mine.

"Is Maddie staying with me tonight?" Ellie asked, making me furrow my eyebrows.

Why...?

Oh shit.

I groaned and ran my fingers through my hair.

"Why?" Maddie asked as she looked at Ellie.

"You'll need it, princess," I muttered, trying to keep the annoyance out of my voice. "I have to go to the border and greet the Alphas."

Maddie looked at me and raised her eyebrows.

"It's tradition," I explained as I kissed her forehead. "The King has to welcome his Alphas at the border, grant them entry into our pack, and lead them to the throne room."

"There's usually a short meeting right after," Will added.

"Dimitri will probably be staying late."

I wanted to grunt and moan. I didn't want to leave her. I'd completely forgotten about meeting them at the border.

"Can I go?" Maddie asked and I wanted to say yes.

"Only men can go," I said and let out a loud sigh.

"Oh," Maddie murmured and my heart broke.

I wanted to take her with me. I didn't even want her to fall asleep without me by her side.

"We'll keep it short," Will said, smiling at Maddie. "Dimitri will be back soon, I promise."

Maddie smiled back and I pulled her against my chest.

I hated leaving her. I just hated it.

I kissed the top of her head and buried my nose in her hair.

I hadn't left her yet and I was already dying to get back with her.

Chapter 111 Come back to me

Dimitri

Letting go of Maddie was the hardest thing I had to do. I knew I wasn't going to see her for the next few hours and I already missed her so much.

I didn't want to leave. I really didn't.

It would be the first night since her birthday that she would go to sleep without me. It would be the first night since her birthday that I couldn't wrap my arms around her and listen to her heartbeat as I fell asleep. I hated it so much. Falling asleep in her arms was the highlight of my day. I wasn't going to be able to do that tonight and it pissed me off.

"Come back to me," she said softly.

I held her tight and buried my nose in her hair.

"Always, princess," I said, breathing in her scent deeply. "You're my home. I'll always come back to you."

I wished I didn't have to leave her.

"I miss you already," she said, tightening her arms around my waist.

I smiled a little and rubbed her back.

"I miss you too," I said. "I wish I could, stay here with you." I can't believe you're going to fall asleep without my arms around you.

She looked at me and shook her head.

"I doubt that will happen," she said. "I'll stay up waiting for you. I can't sleep without you."

I smiled and caressed her cheek.

"Try it, princess," I said softly. "We have a big day tomorrow."

"Okay, that's enough," Ellie sighed heavily. "You'll be back in a few hours. It looks like you won't be seeing each other for days."

I looked at Ellie and frowned.

"God forbid," I said, shaking my head. "A few hours is all I can take."

Maddie giggled and placed a soft kiss on my chest. I turned to her, cupping her cheeks, and captured her lips with mine.

I had to stop myself from moaning. She tasted amazing and it made me want to stay even more.

"I love you," I whispered as I reluctantly stopped kissing her.

I had to because I was never leaving .

"I love you too," she said, giving me a small smile.

"Come on, Dimitri," Will said impatiently. "We're going to be late."

I sighed and rolled my eyes. Maddie laughed again.

"Go," she said. "I'll wait for you.

" My heart skipped a beat. I gave her another soft kiss on the lips before forcing myself to let go.

I can't wait to get back. I mentally linked her. I can't wait to have you in my arms.

I can't wait either. She handed me the mental link back and smiled.

"Go before Will's eyebrows stay in that position," Maddie said, smiling a little.

Ellie snorted loudly. I glanced over at Will and saw him frowning.

I smiled and shook my head.

"This isn't funny, Madeline," Will said as he opened the door. "We can't be late."

"We won't be late," I said as I started to walk out of Ellie's room. "Relax a little, Will."

She rolled her eyes and looked at the girls.

"We'll be back in a few hours," he said. "Stay here."

I glanced at Maddie one more time before Will pushed me out of the room. He smiled, and my knees buckled.

"Goddess, you'll be back in a few hours," Will murmured with a hint of annoyance in his voice. "What's wrong with you?

" "You'll understand when you find your mate," I said, frowning at him. "It's hard to leave her. I worry when she's not with me."

Will looked at me and sighed. His frown disappeared and his eyes softened a little.

"She'll be okay, Dimitri," he said. "Ellie won't let anything happen to her.

I knew that. I still didn't feel comfortable leaving her alone. I still wanted to run back to her.

Will and I walked out of the warehouse and I looked around. The workers were making sure everything was ready for our guests. The Alphas' families and pack members would be the first to arrive. My warriors would greet them at the border and escort them to the stable. Will and I would remain at the border to greet the Alphas and their Betas, leading them into the throne room and starting the meeting with a short speech.

As soon as Will and I approached the edge of the woods, I took off my shirt and pants. I tied them to my leg with a rope I always carried. I let Skol take over, and the first thing he did was whimper and look toward Ellie's room. "

We can't go back, Skol," I told him.

I know, he said quietly. I miss her.

I know, I said quietly. I miss her, too.

She turned and started running toward the border. Lowell, Will's werewolf, was running beside us.

"Will you let me be with Maddie when we get home?"

Skol asked. "It's been so long since I held her. I need you to let me be with her for a little while.

Of course," I said. "You'll be able to see Skye soon, too."

Skol sighed. "I'm not so sure about that. Maddie keeps ignoring her.

"I'll talk to her, Skol," I said. I promise.

I focused on the forest, and Skol started running faster.

The border was an hour away, but Skol and Lowell were both fast runners, and I knew we'd get there first.

Skol groaned softly and I resisted the urge to roll my eyes at him. I kept thinking about Maddie and it was distracting us both. "

Stop it, Skol," I growled at him. "We need to focus. We'll be back with her soon.

I know," he muttered. "I just miss her so much."

I sighed but decided to ignore him. I had to focus on the meeting. I had to focus on the Alphas that were coming.

I would be back with my love soon. I would be holding her soon.

Nothing would stop me from getting back to her as soon as I could.

Chapter 112 Nine Alphas

Dimitri

I took a deep breath as I approached the border. All nine Alphas were already there.

"Welcome, Alphas," I said, giving them a small smile. "I am honored and grateful to be here before you. Thank you for coming. I look forward to spending some quality time with you all."

They all knelt down.

"Thank you, my King," they said at the same time.

I was silent for a moment.

"Stand up and approach my territory, please," I said, watching as everyone followed my command.

The first to approach me was the oldest Alpha in the group. He was the alpha of the Blue Moon pack.

Alpha Alistair was a charismatic leader. He was known for his strategic thinking and determination. His Beta, Benjamin, was intelligent and very resourceful. If I ever needed a war strategist I would turn to both Alistair and Benjamin.

"My King," Alistair said, bowing his head slightly.

"Welcome, Alistair," I said politely, pointing to the spot I had assigned him behind me.

He smiled and entered my territory.

Next to approach was the Alpha of Maddie's old pack, Red Moon.

"My King," Alpha Jack said, tilting his head. "I'm happy to be here."

"It's good to have you, Alpha Jack," I said, giving him a small smile.

"I can't wait to see Madeline," he said, smiling back. "Is she still here? Is she okay?"

My heart skipped a beat when he mentioned her name.

"He's here," I said, nodding. "I'm sure he'll be glad to see you."

Alpha Jack smiled brightly as he and his Beta Samuel walked away.

"My King," Alpha Xavier said as he and his Beta Maximus approached me. "Thank you for having us."

Alpha Xavier, Alpha of the Midnight Pack, was a brooding, enigmatic Alpha with a mysterious aura. I could never figure him out, no matter how hard I tried. Beta Maximus was a brilliant tactician and the perfect foil for Alpha Xavier.

"Thank you for coming, Xavier," I said, giving him a small smile.

I watched as he and Maximus walked away before looking back at the next Alpha in line. Alpha Theodore approached me with a small smile on his face. It was the Alpha of the Dark Moon Pack.

"Alpha Theodore," I said as he and his Beta James approached. "Nice to see you."

Alpha Theodore was a fierce and fearless Alpha with a fiery personality. He was known for his exceptional combat skills and determination. His Beta James was his Alpha's shadow.

"Thank you for having us, my King," Alpha Theodore said politely.

I smiled and glanced over his shoulder at the Alpha of the Silver Moon Pack.

"Alpha Lincoln," I said politely.

"My King," he smiled, bowing his head.

Alpha Lincoln was a refined and elegant Alpha. He used his humor and charm to mask his strategic brilliance. People thought he was naive, but he was actually brilliant. His Beta Aron was fiercely protective of him.

"It's lovely having you here," I said, smiling.

They walked away.

"It's lovely being here," he replied as he and his Beta

"You haven't changed a bit, my King!" Alpha Ezekiel of the Crescent Moon Pack said.

I smiled and shook my head at him.

"I'm still as young as I was a year ago," I said, laughing a little.

I visited his pack a year ago and could see how determined and unwavering Alpha Ezekiel was. His Beta Gregory was the same way and they complemented each other perfectly.

"It's good to see you again, my King," Ezekiel said.

"I'm glad to see you too, Alpha Ezekiel," I said smiling at him.

My cheek started to hurt from smiling so much. I had to hold the smile just a little longer.

"My King," Alpha Lucius of the Shadow Moon Pack said as he approached me.

He was a very kind and charismatic Alpha. His people loved him and so did his Beta, Blake. He never left their side and was very loyal to his Alpha.

"Alpha Lucius," I said politely. "Thank you for coming."

"Thank you for having us, my King," he said as he and his Beta walked away from me.

Alpha Marcus and his Beta Killian of the Rising Moon Pack were next in line.

"My King," Alpha Marcus said, bowing to me. "Thank you for organizing this meeting. I believe it will be very useful and instrumental in our fight against the rogues."

Alpha Marcus's pack was the one that suffered the most damage at the hands of the rogues.

"I hope so, Alpha Marcus," I said, giving him a small nod.

He smiled and walked away, his Beta following close behind.

The last and youngest of all the Alphas was Alpha Rhys, Alpha of the Blood Moon Pack. He'd recently taken over his pack and was already doing a very good job. His Beta Aiden was a bit older than

Rhys and I thought he offered incredible support and guidance to his young Alpha.

"Alpha Rhys," I said, smiling at him. "Welcome, and congratulations on taking over your father's pack."

"Thank you, my King," Alpha Rhys said, bowing his head. "

My father sends his regards."

"Thank you, Alpha Rhys," I said. "Your father is an amazing man.

Is he okay?"

"Oh, he's doing great now that he's retired," Alpha

Rhys said, making me laugh.

"I'm glad to hear that," I said, smiling at Rhys.

Rhys bowed again before heading to his

assigned spot.

I turned around and looked at all the Alphas and Betas. I smiled and looked at Will. He was standing next to me and hadn't moved an inch since we arrived.

"Thank you all for coming," I said. "It's my hope that this meeting will help us fight off the rogues and

make sure that our territories and people are safe

." I paused for a moment and smiled again.

"My Beta Will and I will now lead you to the throne room so that we can officially begin this Alpha Meeting," I said, making all the Alphas nod.

I took a deep breath and let it out slowly.

Here we go.

Chapter 113 She is asleep

Dimitri

I couldn't wait for the meeting to end.

It had been five hours since I last saw Maddie and it was driving me crazy. She was so close, yet so far away. The Alphas kept asking questions, wanting to talk about everything at once.

Not only was it impossible to cover everything in one meeting, but I didn't feel like it at all. I wanted to get back to my partner. I looked at the clock and had to suppress a groan. It was 3:20 am Maddie was probably already asleep.

"We have to fight back," someone said. "We can't let them keep attacking us."

I couldn't focus enough to figure out who had said it. I didn't care anymore.

I was still thinking about Maddie. Her soft skin against mine. Her soft, wet lips. Her amazing scent. Her sweet moans.

The way she pressed herself against me the moment I laid down next to her. The taste of her skin. The way her—

"My King," someone called, interrupting my thoughts.

I looked up to see all the alphas staring at me with questioning looks.

I cleared my throat and straightened my tie.

"I'm sorry," I said, giving them a small smile. "What was the question?"

"We asked if we should continue this tomorrow," Alpha Alistair said and I nearly jumped out of my chair. "Some of us are a little tired after the trip here."

I had to bite my cheeks to keep from smiling. In a few moments I would be with my princess.

"Of course, Alpha Alistair," I said. "We'll continue this tomorrow.

" "I heard you found our Queen," Alpha Rhys said, making me look at him.

I wanted to growl at him. Everyone was about to get up and leave, but now they were all looking at me and smiling.

Fuck, Rhys.

I forced a small smile on my face.

"I did," I said, feeling my nervousness growing. "

You'll get a chance to meet her tomorrow at the opening ceremony."

The Alphas nodded and smiled.

"I hear she's a real beauty, my King," Alpha Lucius said.

Jealousy flared up inside me. I almost growled at him.

Dimitri. Will mentally linked to me, a hint of warning in his tone.

I set my jaw and smiled wider, trying to hide my anger.

"She is," I said. "She's not just pretty. She's also very kind. She'll make an amazing queen."

Alpha Lucius nodded.

"I look forward to meeting her," he said, making me clench my fists. "

We'll keep her away from him tomorrow. I made a mental link to Will.

She sighed quietly.

"I'm so happy for you, my king," Marco Alpha said. "

What's your name?"

I forced some air into my lungs. I wished I could keep her away from all of them. I wished they didn't know about her. I wished it was my little secret. She'd be safer that way. No one could hurt her or take her away from me if no one knew she existed.

But it was impossible. She was a queen. People would find out everything about her.

"Madeline," I said, trying to hide my displeasure with a small smile.

"Madeline?" Jack asked, surprised. "My Maddie?"

I flinched a little. She wasn't his Maddie. She was mine. Just mine.

"Mine," Skol growled under his breath.

"Your Maddie?" Alpha Theodore asked, furrowing his eyebrows at Alpha Jack.

"She was a member of my pack," Alpha Jack explained. "She came here about nine months ago to live with her father."

Alpha Jack smiled.

"Is that her?" he asked. "Is that the same Madeline?"

I nodded and smiled. I still couldn't speak. I was still pissed that he called her his Maddie.

"Mine," Skol growled again.

"Oh, my goodness!" Alpha Jack exclaimed. "I can't wait to see her tomorrow.

Fuck, I couldn't wait to see her tonight. I needed the meeting to be over. Right fucking now."

I forced a smile on my face and stood up.

"Well, I'll see you all in the morning," I said. "My Beta will show you to your rooms."

Will stood up and pointed to the door.

"Please follow me," she said and everyone started to get up.

I was going crazy watching them. They were so fucking slow. I wanted them to hurry up and leave so I could run to Maddie.

My entire body was shaking as the last alpha left the room. I exhaled in relief as I ran out the other door and started running up the stairs.

Ellie. I mentally linked her. I'll be back.

Okay. She replied immediately. Maddie fell asleep.

You can let her sleep in my room tonight.

Fuck no. As if I could sleep without her. As if I could go another minute without her.

No, I said sternly. I'll go get her.

Okay, Ellie replied. Should I wake her up?

No. Let her sleep.

I was just a few steps away from Ellie's room. My hands were shaking and I swore I was sweating profusely. I needed Maddie so badly.

I opened the door and nearly sobbed in relief.

There she was.

"Princess," I murmured as I practically launched myself at her. "Oh, my love."

I finally reached her. Finally, I caressed her cheeks and pressed my lips to hers. My body immediately relaxed. It was like my entire body had been in a knot since I left her.

Maddie sighed quietly and opened her eyes a little.

"Shh, princess," I whispered. "Go back to sleep."

She smiled a little and I nearly melted into a puddle. I picked her up and she pressed herself against me.

"I've missed you," she murmured sleepily.

"I've missed you too," I said as I gave her a kiss on the forehead. "Sleep, my love."

I looked at Ellie for the first time since I walked into the room. She was smiling and shaking her head.

"It's been five hours," she said softly.

I rolled my eyes. I didn't have time to argue. I wanted to take Maddie back to our room and feel her next to me.

"Goodnight, Ellie," I said as I walked out of her room.

"Goodnight," she said, giggling a little.

Maddie wrapped her arms around my neck and took a deep breath.

I felt her body relax and smiled. I started kissing her all over.

"I love you," I said when we finally entered our room.

Chapter 114 Mark you

Madeline

I woke up when I felt Dimitri's lips on my neck.

I moaned softly. It was the most amazing feeling in the world.

His lips on my neck, his arms wrapped tightly around me, his scent enveloping me like a warm blanket. Everything was perfect and I never wanted it to end.

"Good morning, princess," he said, his voice deep and filled with lust.

I felt a familiar tickle between my legs and my heart raced.

I opened my eyes and turned my head to him. I didn't even have the chance to say anything before he captured my lips with his.

I rolled onto my side and wrapped one leg around his waist. We were both naked.

"Did you take my clothes off?" I asked, laughing a little.

"Of course I do," he said as he began placing soft kisses along my neck and jaw. "I've been without you for five hours.

I've been dying to feel every part of your body against mine."

I ran my fingers through his hair and moaned quietly as he kissed his mark on my neck.

"I'm sorry I fell asleep," I said, pressing myself closer to him. "I tried to stay awake but I was too tired as I was trying so hard to push my thoughts of Ellie away. I didn't want to—"

Dimitri cut me off as he ground his hard cock against my pussy.

"Later, Madeline," he said sternly, making my entire body shudder.

I obeyed. Of course I obeyed. I would do absolutely anything he told me to.

His hand ran down my body until his fingers gently caressed my clit. I cried out in pleasure.

"I'm going to fuck you, my queen," Dimitri said as he lowered his head and gently sucked on my nipple. —You're not getting out of this bed until you cum on my cock.

I gulped and moved my hips a little, grinding against him. He growled and grabbed my waist.

"Not like that," he said looking down at me. "Like that."

He kept his eyes on mine as he slowly pushed his cock inside me.

I cried out in pleasure as I tried to move my hips. I needed him more inside me. He grabbed my waist and stopped me.

"No," he told me firmly. "We'll do this at my pace. You'll cum when I tell you to."

My breathing quickened.

I'll cum immediately if you keep talking like that. I mentally connected it.

I couldn't speak. I was completely out of breath and all I could do was moan and grunt.

Dimitri laughed and shook his head.

"Does my queen like me giving her orders?" he asked as he began to slowly thrust in and out of me.

I dug my nails into his arm and moaned.

"Do you like it?" he asked when I didn't respond.

He picked up the pace and began to thrust deeper into me.

I kept moaning.

"Yes," I managed to say.

Dimitri leaned in and kissed me. He began sucking on my bottom lip and I cried out in pleasure again. His movements quickened and I could feel my orgasm building in my lower belly.

I tried to move my hips again but he was still holding my waist tightly.

"Someone's a little impatient," Dimitri said as he lowered his lips to my neck.

He began to suck on the mark and I gasped. A small explosion from my clit made me cry out again.

"That's it, my queen," he said in a deep voice. "Cum on your King's cock."

It was an order he didn't have to repeat twice. I collapsed around him, moaning and shaking slightly. His grip on me tightened as he continued to thrust in and out of me, prolonging my orgasm until I had to squeeze him harder and make him stop.

"Fuck yes," he murmured as he entered me one last time.

I was a moaning mess. My whole body was shaking and I couldn't focus on anything but him.

"You tightened around me so good," he said as he kissed me softly. "I've felt it all, princess, and it was amazing."

I tangled my fingers in his hair and kissed him back. I felt him smile a little before he pulled away from me and flipped me onto my stomach.

I didn't even have time to gasp before he was back inside me.

"My turn now," he told me as he grabbed my hips and pulled them up.

My moans were muffled by the pillow.

"Fuck," Dimitri moaned. "You feel so fucking good like this."

He grabbed my hair and pulled my head back.

"Do you like it when I fuck you like this?" he asked as he began to trust me quickly and deeply.

I could barely speak.

"Yes, Alpha," I said between moans.

"Fuck," Dimitri growled loudly.

His movements became erratic. He started panting hard. He gripped me tighter and I cried out in pleasure. My whole body was shaking. I was in a sweet mix of pleasure and pain, and I wished he would never stop. I wished he would grip me tighter. I wished he would pull my hair harder.

I wished he would shove his cock even deeper inside me.

He moaned loudly and pulled his cock out of me. I felt his hot seed on my back and ass a second later. I turned my head slightly so I could look at him. The sight almost made me cum again.

He was panting hard. His chest and abs were glistening with sweat. His eyebrows were furrowed and he was growling quietly as he stroked his cock. It was perfect.

"Fuck, yes," he muttered as a few last drops of his seed landed on my ass.

He took a deep breath and swallowed. I watched as he bit his bottom lip and smiled a little. I felt his soft fingers rubbing his seed into my skin.

"What are you doing?" I asked, making him
look at me.

"Marking you," he said as he reached down and rubbed his seed all over my pussy. "If I have to spend a whole fucking day watching those fuckers drool over what's mine, I'm going to do it knowing my cum is all over this perfect little pussy that belongs to me and only me."

I had to hold back a giggle.

"Yes, Alpha," I said, making him grunt and smack my ass hard.

I couldn't hold back the giggle this time.

Chapter 115 Did you do it?

Dimitri

"You look gorgeous, Luna," I heard Jessica say as I approached our room.

I was in my office discussing some last minute things with Will while Jessica helped Maddie with her hair and makeup.

"Thanks, Jessica," I heard Maddie say softly.

I opened the door and had to hold back a gasp.

She wasn't pretty. She was so much more than that.

She was just wearing a little makeup and her hair was up in a low bun. Her dress was long and covered everything I wanted it to cover. The dress hugged her breasts and waist and the rest of it fell freely down her body. It showed everything off perfectly, but at the same time, it was modest. She looked amazing.

I just wanted to bend her over something and fuck her until I passed out from exhaustion.

"Alpha," Jessica said politely.

I tried my hardest to look at her and say hello, but her eyes were glued to my roommate.

Maddie raised an eyebrow and smiled a little.

"You like it?" she asked as she turned around, giving me a clear view of her entire dress.

She wanted Jessica out of the room.

"Yes I do," I somehow managed to say. "

Are you ready?

" My voice was shaking. I needed a few minutes alone with her.

I couldn't let her leave the room without touching and kissing her first.

"I am," she said, smiling at me.

I forced myself to look at Jessica. I smiled, trying to hide how impatient I was.

"Thank you, Jessica," I said as I walked away from the door. "Can you give us a moment please?"

Jessica smiled and nodded.

"Of course, Alpha," she said and looked at Maddie. "It's been my pleasure, Luna. You look amazing."

Maddie smiled at her.

"Thank you, Jessica," Maddie said softly. "You made it all happen."

I totally disagreed. Maddie was just gorgeous. She could have worn a sack of potatoes and she would still have looked amazing.

Jessica bowed to the two of us before she left the room. I was wrapping my arms around Maddie's waist before Jessica even closed the bedroom door.

"Fuck, princess," I murmured as I buried my nose in her neck. "You look gorgeous."

She chuckled and wrapped her arms around my neck.

"Thank you," she said. "You look stunning too. This outfit fits you perfectly."

She ran her hands up my back, making me sigh.

I lifted my head and looked at her.

"Are you wearing your underwear?" I asked, raising an eyebrow.

She shook her head and smiled.

"You told me not to," she said softly.

I smirked. I told her not to. It would just get in the way of me slamming my cock into her when the ceremony was over.

"Fine," I said as I leaned down and pressed my lips to hers. "I can't wait to rip this dress off of you tonight."

She frowned a little.

"I like this dress," she murmured. "You don't have to rip it off of me."

Oh yes I did have to rip it off. I was looking forward to watching her breasts fall out.

"I'll buy you a new one," I murmured as I started kissing her neck. "I'll buy you a hundred new ones and rip each and every one off this perfect body of yours."

Maddie moaned as I placed a soft kiss over my mark on her neck.

Fuck.

I needed to stop. Unfortunately we didn't have time for sex.

I took a deep breath as I lifted my head and looked at her. She was slightly flushed and her eyes were filled with lust. She was gorgeous.

"I love you," I told her softly as I placed a kiss on her lips.

"I love you too," she said and caressed my cheek.

I remembered something she sold me this morning before we went to bed.

"You said you tried to block out thoughts of Ellie last night," I said as I stopped kissing her. "Did you?

Did you manage to stop them?"

Maddie sighed and gave me a small nod.

"I did," she said. "It was hard though. I was exhausted afterwards. That's why I fell asleep."

My eyes opened a little.

"How did you do it?" I asked and she shook her head.

"I don't know," she said. "I tried to imagine there was a wall around my brain. It didn't work at first, but after a while I got it right."

I nodded and caressed her cheek.

"I'm proud of you, princess," I said softly. "

We'll talk about it with Oscar.

We couldn't do it today, but I would call Oscar first thing tomorrow. We had to find a way to make it easier for my princess."

Maddie kissed me softly and I smiled.

"Stay by my side the whole time, okay?" I said as I moved my lips to her jaw.

"Of course," she said. "There's no other place I'd rather be."

My heart skipped a beat. I stopped kissing her jaw and looked at her. I was smiling and my whole body tingled.

"You're killing me," I murmured as I placed a soft kiss on his lips. "I just want to stay here with you."

Maddie giggled and ran her fingers through my hair.

"I know," she said. "But we have work to do. We'll be back here tonight."

I deepened our kiss just as our bedroom door opened.

"We're late," I heard Will's voice.

I was so enthralled with Maddie that I didn't even hear him arrive.

I turned around and saw him watching us with a frown.

I really needed to relax a little. His eyes landed on Maddie and he smiled a little.

"You look amazing Mads," Will said. "I didn't know Dimitri had such good taste."

Maddie giggled and I rolled my eyes at her. I took Maddie's hand in mine and began to lead her out of the bedroom.

"We're late," I said as we walked past Will.

I heard Will and Maddie laughing quietly.

I tried to ignore them. I took a deep breath and let it out slowly. I couldn't wait for the ceremony to be over.

Chapter 116 Our Queen

Madeline

I was a little nervous as Dimitri and I walked into the throne room.

Meeting the nine Alphas and their Betas was the first thing we had to do today. After the meeting, we had to go to the celebration dinner where I would meet all the Lunas and the rest of the Alphas' families and staff that came with them.

I was nervous and excited at the same time. This event was my first official act as Luna and Queen, I didn't want to disappoint Dimitri. "

You won't let him down," Skye said softly. "You were born for this. He's already incredibly proud of you."

I ignored her. I didn't want to talk to her. Not yet.

You'll have to talk to me sometime, Maddie,"

Skye sighed. "You can't ignore me forever!

I can ignore you tonight," I told her as I pushed her back.

I took a deep breath as I finally got a clear view of the table where eighteen men were waiting for me, Dimitri, and Will. They all stood up and bowed.

I tried to get a good look at each and every one of them, but I was a little nervous and had a hard time concentrating. I knew their names, but it was the first time I had seen them in person, so I couldn't connect names and faces.

My eyes landed on the only Alpha I knew. Alpha Jack.

He was smiling brightly, and I couldn't help but smile back.

Dimitri led me to my seat and pulled out the chair for me.

"Thank you," I said quietly.

"Anything for my Queen," he said with a wink.

He sat down next to me and took my hand. Will sat down on the other side of me. "

Don't leave my side for a moment," Will said sternly.

I looked at him and raised my eyebrows slightly.

"Dimitri told you that some of these alphas don't care about their mates," Will explained, clenching his jaw. "I'm sure you didn't notice the looks they gave you the moment you walked into the room."

My eyes widened slightly and I shifted a little in my seat, feeling a little uncomfortable.

"Are you sure?" I asked Will.

"Yes, Maddie." He said, clenching his fists. "Stay with us, okay? Don't walk away from me or Dimitri.

Okay." I said, forcing a small smile on my face.

I didn't want the Alphas to know I was uncomfortable.

Why would they want me? I was just a normal girl. Nothing special about me.

"Nice to see you all again," Dimitri said, his hand tightening on mine. "I hope you're all rested and ready."

"We are, my King," one of the Alphas said. "We're looking forward to continuing our conversation from yesterday."

"We're also very excited to meet our Queen," another Alpha said. "We're so glad you finally found her, my King."

Dimitri looked at me and smiled.

"I'm very excited to introduce her," he said, looking back at our guests. "This is Madeline Clark, your Queen."

Each of our guests bowed to me. I felt a little awkward, but I kept the smile on my face the entire time.

"It's an honor to meet you, my Queen," one of the Alphas said.
"
I'm excited to work with you and get to know you better. "

That's Alpha Theodore. Dimitri mentally linked to me.

"Thank you, Alpha Theodore," I said politely. "I'm just as excited."

"You're even more beautiful than we've been told," another Alpha said, causing both Dimitri and Will to tense.

I smiled pleasantly. I wanted to thank him, but I didn't know his name.

I looked at Dimitri and squeezed his hand. I needed to know who this was.

Lucius. He mentally linked me and I could hear the anger in his voice.

"Thank you, Alpha Lucius," I said politely.

"Oh, you don't need to thank me," she said, smiling brightly. "Our King is a very lucky man."

Dimitri let go of my hand and gripped my thigh tightly. I put my hand over his and forced myself to keep smiling. "

I'm yours, Dimitri." I mentally linked it. No one can take me from you.

Dimitri clenched his jaw. He took a deep breath and let it out slowly.

"You're right, Alpha Lucius," he said, trying to sound polite. " I am a very, very lucky man. "

I gently rubbed his hand.

"Yours." I said softly. "Breathe, my love. I am yours."

Dimitri looked at me and I could see him relax a little.

"It's so lovely to see you again, Maddie,"

Alpha Jack said brightly, causing me to look back at him. "I'm so happy for you."

I smiled at him.

"Thanks, Alpha," I said. "I love seeing you again too."

"Ali's here," Alpha Jack said, making my heart race. "She asked to come so she could see you. We weren't sure if you were still in this pack though. You said you'd be leaving as soon as you turned 18. I'm glad you're not."

Dimitri shuddered a little. "

I'm not leaving you. I mentally linked it. I'll never leave you.

I know that, princess." He returned the mental link to me.

I focused back on Alpha Jack.

"Is Ali here?" I asked and he nodded.

"She's really excited to see you," he said, making me smile brightly.

I was excited to see her too. I missed her so much.

"I'm excited to see her too," I said, making Alpha Jack's smile widen.

"She has no idea you're a Queen," Alpha Jack said.

—I can't wait to see his face when he realizes.

I chuckled and shook my head a little. Ali was always very expressive. I could already picture her gasping and screaming.

I would have to calm her down so she wouldn't draw too much attention.

"It'll be fun," I said, making Alpha Jack laugh and nod.

I looked at Dimitri and he smiled at me. He lifted my hand and kissed my knuckles.

"Shall we continue the conversation from last night?" he asked as he turned to our guests.

I took a deep breath and let it out slowly.

It was time to get to work.

Chapter 117 What do they want?

Dimitri

I was so fucking pissed off.

Every fucking man in the room was staring at my partner.

I wanted to reach out my claws and rip their eyes out one by one.

I hated the way they looked at her. I hated the way they smiled at her. I hated the fact that I knew exactly what they were thinking. I hated the fact that I knew exactly what they wanted.

I didn't like the idea of Ali spending time with my partner either. I didn't know her. I didn't know what she wanted. I didn't know if Maddie would be safe with her.

I was angry and I wanted to get Maddie out of there. I wanted to hide her from their prying eyes. I wanted her all to myself.

I knew how irrational and selfish I was, but I didn't care.

Are you okay? It connected to my mind.

No. I said angrily. I want to get you out of here. I don't like the way they look at you. I know what they want and it makes me mad.

Maddie reached out and placed her hand on my thigh. She squeezed lightly, and my whole body shivered.

None of that matters, Dimitri. She said softly. I'm yours. Every part of me belongs to you. They can look at me and think whatever they want.

It's you sleeping in my arms tonight, not them.

My whole body tingled. My heart raced. The need to be alone with her and show her how much I loved her exploded inside me.

I love you. Maddie added. Just you, Dimitri. No one else.

I put my hand on hers and squeezed. It was a good thing we were linking minds and not talking, because I had a huge lump in my throat and I wouldn't have been able to speak.

Fuck, Maddie, I love you too. I replied. I can't wait to fall asleep in your arms tonight.

She looked at me and smiled. I was lucky I was sitting up because my knees buckled.

"We have to join forces and protect our borders," someone exclaimed and I turned my attention to the discussion. "We can't let them destroy our herds and our lands!"

I took a deep breath and let it out slowly.

I needed to focus on the meeting. I needed to stop imagining all the ways I would end the Alphas' lives.

"Have you managed to capture any rogues?" I asked, causing the Alphas to look at me. "Did any of them speak?"

"No, my King," Alpha Theodore said. "All the rogues we captured refused to talk. Some died during torture."

Maddie flinched a little. I squeezed her hand tighter.

"I'm sorry, princess." I mentally linked it. "I know it's not something you want to hear, but it's the truth. Rogues and enemies are being tortured for information."

Maddie sighed quietly.

"I know that," she said quietly. "But I wish there was another way."

I lifted her hand and kissed her knuckles. I almost smiled when I saw the jealousy in Alpha Lucius' eyes.

"We need to find out who's behind the attacks," I said. "The rogues aren't organized enough to pull off something like this. Someone is behind it. Someone sent them to

do this.

" "What do they want?" Alpha Rhys asked. "What is their ultimate goal?"

He looked around the room, but everyone was silent.

"The throne," I said. "Someone wants my throne.

" There was really no other explanation.

"But who, my King?" Alpha Alastair asked. "Who would want to go against you? Who would want to go against the Kingdom?"

"We are finally at peace after years of endless wars and battles," Alpha Jack added. "Is there really anyone out there who would want to go through that again?"

I sighed and shook my head.

"I don't know," I said. "People would do so much to gain power. They would sacrifice anything and everything."

Alpha Alastair raised his eyebrows and looked at Maddie.

"When did you find your mate, my King?" he asked and my entire body tensed.

I resisted the urge to growl at him.

"Why?" I asked, trying to remain calm.

Alpha Alastair looked at me and took a deep breath.

"I'm just wondering if the attacks started before or after you found her," he said. "There's a chance it's her. Maybe they don't want your throne. Maybe they want your mate."

I saw the damn red. My grip on Maddie's hand tightened. My heart was trying to break through my ribcage.

No. Fuck no.

"It's not about me," Maddie said, causing everyone to look at her. "Rogues were attacking our borders before I turned eighteen."

I could feel my heartbeat in my eyes and ears.

I could feel my blood coursing through my veins.

Alpha Alastair nodded.

"They could still use you as a conduit to the throne, my Queen," he said. "We have to protect you."

I forced myself to breathe. I needed to focus. I had to stop thinking about someone taking Maddie from me.

If they knew who she was...

"She's safe, Alpha Alastair," I said, trying to sound calm. "She's protected. Nothing and no one can get to her. Nothing and no one can hurt her."

Alpha Alastair looked at me. An unfamiliar emotion flashed in his eyes. He gave me a small smile and nodded.

"I'm sure you're taking very good care of your mate, my King," he said. "I'm just offering you my support and my knowledge. I wouldn't want anything to happen to our queen."

My stomach twisted. Nothing would happen to her. She was safe and protected. They'd have to kill me to get to her and that would never fucking happen.

"Thank you, Alpha Alastair," Maddie said. "We'd love to hear your opinion on the matter. Your knowledge and experience are sure to be of great help."

Alpha Alastair looked at her and smiled.

"It's a privilege, my Queen," he said, bowing his head slightly.

Maddie stroked her thumb along my thigh and I immediately relaxed

. Her touch was like a cure. It took away the pain and the fear.

She was everything to me and I would go to hell and back to keep her safe.

No one was going to hurt her. No one was going to take her away. I

wasn't going to let that happen.

Chapter 118 Ali

Madeline

"Maddie!" I heard Ali yell, lunging at me a second later.

I stumbled back a little, but Dimitri caught me. I could feel the anger exploding inside him. He growled and started to pull me away from Ali. I could feel his fear. I could feel his need to protect me.

It's okay. I connected it mentally. I'm okay. He didn't hurt me.

"Oh, Maddie, I've missed you so much!" Ali said excitedly, tightening her arms around me. She

didn't even notice Dimitri standing behind me. She didn't even notice me trying to push me away from her. She didn't even hear him growl.

Her fear and nervousness were growing by the second.

It's okay, my love. I told him mentally, trying to sound as calm as possible. She's my friend. She means well. She's not a threat.

His hands on my waist tightened.

"I've missed you too, Ali," I said as I hugged him back tightly. "I'm so glad you're here."

She released me and smiled widely. Her eyes fell on my dress and she let out a gasp.

"Fuck, Mads, you look amazing," she said. "That's an amazing dress.

What are you-"

She stopped talking when her eyes fell on what I assumed was a very angry Dimitri. I smiled even wider, trying to make her feel a little more comfortable.

"My King," she muttered, her eyes wide. "I'm sorry, I don't-"

She looked at me and gulped.

"It's okay, Ali," I said, reaching out and taking her hand in mine. "This is-"

She gasped and I realized she was staring at Dimitri's hands on my waist. She looked back at me with wide eyes.

"Are you-" she spoke but couldn't finish her question.

"My mate?" Dimitri said angrily. "Your queen? Yes, she is."

I nudged her in the ribs with my elbow. He didn't have to be so rude. He just growled under his breath and gripped me tighter.

"Oh, I'm so sorry!" Ali exclaimed, looking back at me. "

I was just so excited to see you and I didn't—"

"It's okay, Ali," I said, pulling her into another hug. "I'm really excited to see you, too. "

She hugged me back, but I could tell she was being extra careful this time. I chuckled and looked at her.

"I'm still the same Maddie," I said. "You don't have to treat me like a queen, you know? We ate dirt together. "

Ali snorted softly and shook her head at me.

"What?" Dimitri asked, and I looked at him.

"It was a dare," I said, shrugging a little. "I don't like losing, so I did it. Ali was kind enough to do it with me."

Dimitri sighed and shook his head.

"Let's not spread that story," he said. "It's not very royal.

Neither is building a tree house and having a board knock you over." I put a mind link on him and smiled a little.

He looked at me with narrowed eyes. "

You just earned yourself a punishment, my Queen." He replied, my lower belly immediately starting to tingle. "You shouldn't be teasing your King.

I'm dying, Alpha," I said, trying to sound seductive. "I'm not wearing any underwear, you know that? I'm completely naked under this dress and I'm ready to be—"

He stopped me from finishing what I wanted to say by growling. "

Don't finish that sentence," he said sternly. "I'll rip that fucking dress off your body and fuck you right now."

I bit the inside of my cheek to hold back my laughter. I wasn't going to do that. I'd never let anyone see. But I wasn't going to finish my sentence. He wouldn't fuck me here, but he could drag me somewhere else and we really didn't have time for that.

"Maddie?" Ali called out to me, making me look at her.

She was looking at me with a confused expression on her face.

"I'm sorry, Ali," I said, giving him a small smile. "What did you ask me?

" "I asked if we could catch up while I'm here." "I know you'll be busy tonight, but maybe tomorrow?"

"Yes, Ali, of course," I said, smiling brightly. "I'd love to."

Ali smiled and opened her mouth to speak, but was interrupted by Alpha Alastair. He walked over to her with a small smile. He looked at Ali, then back at me.

"I'm sorry to interrupt, my Queen, but I was wondering if you could lend me our King for just a minute," Alpha Alastair asked, tilting his head at me.

"I'm not leaving my Queen," Dimitri said sternly.

Alpha Alastair looked at him and smiled a little.

"It'll just be a minute, my King, I promise," he said.

I looked at Dimitri and nodded.

"Okay," I said quietly. "I'll be here with Ali."

No. He mentally linked me. Will isn't here yet and I'm not leaving you alone.

I'm not alone. I replied. I'll be fine. Go talk to him.

Dimitri set his jaw.

"We don't even have to leave the room, my King," Alpha Alastair said. "Let's just get away so we can exchange a few important words."

Dimitri looked around and pointed to the rather empty spot

by the door. He could still see me from there.

"I'll be right back, Princess," he said quietly as he kissed my head.

I gave him a small smile. He reluctantly let go of me and walked away a little to talk to Alpha Alastair.

"Wow, Mads," Ali said as soon as they were away. "You're a queen?! I'm so proud of you."

I looked at her and smiled.

"It's kind of crazy," I said quietly. "I feel like I don't belong here."

Ali opened her eyes and shook her head.

"You do belong, Mads!" he exclaimed. "You should see yourself!

You look amazing and so confident. I'm so proud of you."

I smiled and shook my head.

"Enough about me," I said. "What about you? Have you found your mate?"

Ali sighed and shook her head. "Not yet. I hope to find one soon. I'd love to have someone who looked at me the way Alpha Dimitri looks at you.

" "With a frown?" I asked teasingly.

Ali laughed and shook her head.

"Like you're her whole world," she said, and I felt a tingle all over my body.

I looked at him, and my heart skipped a beat. She was talking to Alpha Alastair, but he kept staring at me.

"I'm her whole world," I said. "Just like he is mine."

Ali was silent for a moment, but then asked something I hadn't expected her to.

"What's that smell?"

Chapter 119 Among us

Dimitri

I didn't like being away from her.

I could see her. I deliberately chose this spot because there weren't as many people around and I could still see her. But she was still too far away from me. She wasn't within my reach and it was driving me crazy. I wanted her by my side. I wanted to be able to touch her and hold her.

"I won't take up too much of your time, my King," Alpha Alistair said.

"I see you don't like being away from your Queen."

I looked at him and nodded.

"I don't like being away from her, Alpha," I said. "We're newly mated."

Alpha Alistair nodded and gave me a small smile.

"That's understandable, my King," he said. "It's been almost 40 years since I met my amazing mate and I still get nervous when I have to leave her alone even for a few minutes."

He laughed and shook his head.

"Sometimes I still can't believe how much I love that woman," he added quietly. "The mating bond is truly incredible."

I looked at my princess and my heart skipped a beat. She was smiling and I couldn't believe how beautiful she was. Every second that passed I wanted her more. Being away from her was torture. I wanted to feel her. Seeing her wasn't enough.

"I asked to speak with you alone because I didn't want your mate to worry," Alpha Alistair said, causing me to look back at him.

My whole body tensed. I had to hold back a growl.

"Worry about what?" I asked, clenching my fists.

Did she know something? Was my princess in danger? I nearly ran back to her. Why would she ask me to leave her alone if there was something to worry about?

Alpha Alistair took a step closer to me and looked around.

He took a deep breath and looked back at me.

"I think there's a traitor among your alphas, my king," Alpha Alistair said quietly.

My eyes widened.

"You shouldn't trust them, my King," he continued. "You have to protect your Queen."

My heart raced and I immediately looked out at the crowd. Alpha Theodore was the closest to my princess. He was just a few steps away from her. I glanced at Alpha Lucius, he was a little further away, but still within reach of her. Alpha Rhys was...

"My King," Alpha Alistair called out to me, drawing my attention back to him. "She's safe here. Whoever it is, they're not crazy enough to try and hurt her in a room full of witnesses."

I gulped and clenched my fists. I felt fear burning inside me.

I looked towards the entrance to the throne room and saw that Will had just entered. "

I'm talking to Alpha Alistair. I mentally connected him. I need you here. It's very important."

I looked back at Alpha Alistair and took a deep breath.

"Why would one of my Alphas betray me?" I asked. "

They all want peace."

Alpha Alistair sighed.

"No, my King," he said. "They all want power. They all want what you have."

He looked to his left and took a deep breath.

"They want your throne," he continued. "They want your mate. They don't want peace."

I gritted my teeth.

"They'll never take her from me," I said angrily. "They'll have to kill me to get to her and I'll never let that happen. I live and breathe for her and that will never change."

Alpha Alistair looked at me.

"I know, my King," he said. "But that doesn't mean they won't try. Your mate is the most direct path to your throne and that means she's in grave danger."

My stomach twisted. I knew that even before he said it, but knowing the threat was even closer than I expected terrified me.

"Alpha Theodore and Alpha Lucius are most likely on her side, my King," Alpha Alistair continued. "I spoke to them and they both agree the traitor is among us."

I narrowed my eyes slightly.

"Alpha Lucius?" I asked, my voice thick with anger.

I didn't like the way he looked at Maddie. I wanted him as far away from her as possible.

Alpha Alistair laughed and shook his head.

"He wanders a lot, but he would never do anything, my king," Alpha Alistair said, shooting me a knowing look. "He's harmless."

I seriously doubted it.

I set my jaw and looked around the room.

Where the fuck was Will? I needed him here. We needed to start discussing the possibility of a traitor being one of the Alphas immediately.

Where the fuck are you? I mentally linked him. *We have important things...*

I stopped mentally linking him when I saw him standing next to

Maddie and her friend. He was staring at Ali with wide eyes and I wasn't even sure if he was breathing.

But what...

They're mates! Maddie mentally linked with me excitedly. *Will and Ali are mates!*

My eyes widened. Mates?

"Oh, wonderful!" Alpha Alistair exclaimed. "I'm so happy for your Beta."

I watched as Will cupped Ali's cheeks and kissed her.

I was both surprised and happy for him.

"Go enjoy the evening with your friends and mate, my King," Alpha Alistair said and I forced myself to look at him. "We can continue this tomorrow."

Well, I didn't want to do that. I wanted to continue immediately.

"Your mate is safe," Alpha Alistair assured me and gave me a small smile. "We'll talk tomorrow."

Alpha Alistair walked away before I could protest. I clenched my jaw and tried to take a deep breath. I didn't like this. I wanted to investigate right away. I wanted to know who the bastard was immediately. If something happened to Maddie...

"Dimitri!" My partner's excited voice interrupted my thoughts.

I turned to my right and saw her approaching me.

"Will and Ali are partners!" she repeated excitedly.

I forced a smile on my face and grabbed her as soon as she was close enough. I buried my nose in her hair and took a deep breath.

"I can't believe this," she exclaimed. "I'm so excited for them!"

I swallowed and tried to force myself to feel the emotion she felt.

But it was so fucking hard. Someone wanted to hurt her and I only felt blinding rage and paralyzing fear.

I ran my hands over her body, letting myself feel. I needed to make sure she was really here. I needed to remind myself that she was okay. I needed to know that my princess was in my arms.

Nothing and no one was going to take her from me.

I would kill them before they tried.

Chapter 120 Happy for you

Dimitri

Maddie dragged me back to Will and Ali.

"What's your name, gorgeous?" Will asked quietly as he caressed her cheek.

He was completely enthralled with her and didn't even look at Maddie and me.

Ali was quiet. She was staring at Will with a mix of wonder and excitement on her face.

I pulled Maddie to my chest and wrapped my arms around her. I looked around, trying to see if anyone looked like a threat.

I could only see the excitement on people's faces. Some of the ones closest to us realized my Beta had found her mate. They looked at them and smiled happily.

Some looked at Maddie and me. But their gazes weren't threatening. They looked at us with admiration in their eyes. I could see both men and women looking at Maddie and smiling.

I noticed a hint of jealousy in some of them, but nothing that worried me.

"Her name is Alison," I heard Maddie say, giggling a little.

"Alison," Will said, his voice thick with so much love and adoration. "I'm William and I adore you already, gorgeous."

I looked away at the Alphas. None of them were looking at us.

None of them were looking at Maddie. They were talking, eating, and having fun with their pack members. None of them looked threatening and it was driving me crazy. I wanted her to prove to me that she was a threat. I wanted her to show herself immediately so I could kill the bastard.

"Dimitri?" My mate's soft voice made me look back at her. "Is everything okay?"

She looked at me with a mix of confusion and concern on her beautiful face.

I reached up and caressed her soft cheek. Goddess, I loved her with every bit of my body and soul.

"Of course, my love," I said softly.

I leaned down and gave her a kiss on the forehead. I grabbed her hips and pulled her tighter against me.

She was here. She was okay.

"Oh my god!" I heard Ellie's excited voice.

I looked behind me and saw her approaching us with a wide smile on her face. She looked so excited and I wished I could feel the same as her.

I was so happy for Will but the anger and fear I felt clouded every other emotion. I wanted to be excited but I couldn't stay in that emotion. It flared up inside me for a second but it disappeared when I remembered what Alastair had said.

Maddie turned around in my arms and wrapped hers around me. I relaxed immediately. I put a hand on her head and held her close to my chest. "

I feel like something's not right my love." She mentally linked me.

I gulped and buried my nose in her hair. With each passing second I felt more relaxed. Her touch once again took all the fear and anger out of me. "

I'll tell you everything later princess," I replied. "I promise."

She turned her head slightly and gave me a soft kiss on the chest.

My whole body trembled.

"Hi!" Ellie's excited voice drew my

attention back to Will and Ali.

I felt that spark of excitement again, and this time it lasted longer.

I even managed a small smile.

"My name is Ellie, and I'm so glad to meet you two!" Ellie exclaimed as she hugged Ali.

Will groaned quietly.

"Oh, relax," Ellie said as she let go of Ali. "I need to say a proper hello to my sister-in-law."

Ali's eyes widened slightly, but she managed a smile.

"Hi," she said quietly. "Nice to meet you. I'm Ali."

Will pulled Ali into his arms again. He buried his nose in her hair and took a deep breath. He smiled, and I could see his body relax.

Congratulations. I mentally linked it. I'm so happy for you.

He looked at me and smiled.

Thank you. He replied. I can't believe it. I'm in shock. I found her.

I saw him wrapping his arms around her and smiled,

"I'm so happy for you, Will!" "Will!" Ellie exclaimed, giving her a sideways hug.

Will smiled and placed a kiss on her temple.

"Thanks, Ellie," he said softly.

Maddie turned around and took Ali's hand in hers.

"I'm so happy for you," Maddie said softly. "Will is an amazing man, Ali. You deserve someone like him. He'll love and cherish you with everything he has. I'm sure of it.

" "He'll annoy you with everything he has, too," Ellie added mockingly.

I snorted and Maddie giggled. Ali bit her bottom lip to keep from smiling.

Will groaned and narrowed his eyes at Ellie.

"Oh, don't worry, Ellie," he said. "I save that part for annoying little sisters."

Ellie raised her eyebrows. "Little sisters? You have more than one?

How did I not know? I'm hurt, William."

Will rolled his eyes and looked at me.

"Would it be okay if I took Ali...?" he spoke, but I cut him off before he could finish his question.

"Go," I said, giving him a small smile.

He looked at Maddie, a hint of worry flashing in his eyes.

"Do you need me here?" he asked. "I can stay..."

Go." I interrupted him again. "I'm here. Maddie's going to be okay." He

gave me a small nod and leaned down to whisper something in Ali's ear. She looked at him and nodded. He smiled and kissed her forehead. I watch him take her by the hand and lead her out of the throne room.

"Oh, I'm so excited for him," Ellie said softly.

"Me too," Maddie said. "Ali's an amazing girl."

Our guests started to approach us now that Will and Ali were gone. They wanted to talk to Maddie and me.

The fear I felt earlier came back, and I squeezed Maddie as close to me as possible. I could feel my muscles tightening and my alpha aura creating a protective circle around Maddie and me. I didn't want anyone to get too close. I didn't want anyone to touch her.

Ellie raised her eyebrows slightly.

Is everything okay, Dimitri? She mentally connected with me.

I gulped and shook my head slightly.

No. We have a problem.

Ellie opened her eyes and I saw her posture change from carefree and relaxed to careful and protective.

What's wrong? she asked. Is Maddie in danger?

My heart raced.

Not right now, I said, trying to remain calm. "But we have to see each other tomorrow morning. We have important work to do."